Effex Series:
Book Two

RESILIENCE

L.R. Burkard

Lilliput Press

Cover by Design Xpressions, Dayton, OH
Contact TheDesignXpressions@gmail.com

RESILIENCE
Copyright © 2016 by Linore Rose Burkard
Published by Lilliput Press, Ohio

Library of Congress Cataloging-in-Publication Data
Burkard, L.R.

ISBN 978-0-9792154-5-2 (print)
ISBN 978-0-9792154-9-0 (ebook)
1.Apocalyptic—Fiction   2. Post-Apocalyptic—Fiction   3.YA Futuristic—Fiction 4. Christian—Fiction

All Scripture quotations are from THE HOLY BIBLE, NEW INTERNATIONAL VERSION®, NIV® Copyright © 1973, 1978, 1984, 2011 by Biblica, Inc.® Used by permission. All rights reserved worldwide.

This is a sequel.

Don't miss the gripping start to **The Pulse Effex Series:** *PULSE*

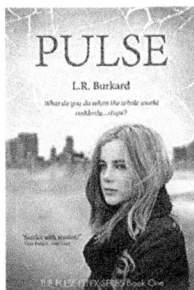

No one forgets the day the world stopped.

Andrea, Lexie and Sarah are just ordinary teens until a mysterious event shuts down all technology. In this suspenseful Christian tale, most of the population doesn't survive. Pitting faith and grit against a world without power, the girls and their families must beat the odds. But can they survive when society collapses and technology fails?

Told through the eyes of three 16 year old girls, PULSE takes readers into a chilling future for America, while affirming the power of faith in the darkest of times.

"CHILLING DYSTOPIAN NOVEL"
Stories like this one get me very excited for today's young adult reader.
DEENA PETERSON, Blogger, Reviewer

"COMPELLING"
I had trouble putting it down. I kept reading, wanting to know what happened next. This is a must-read for people of all ages!
DOUG ERLANDSON, Top 50 Reviewer, Amazon

"GRABBED MY HEART AND NEVER LET GO"
Had me spellbound! You won't want to miss this gritty and powerful series.
NORA ST. LAURENT, CEO, Book Club Network

WHAT READERS ARE SAYING ABOUT
RESILIENCE

It's a great time to be a fan of YA novels! L.R. Burkard is back with the next tale in her dystopian series, and the bar of excellence is raised to new heights with this top quality literary offering!
DEENA PETERSON, Blogger, Book Reviewer

I'm not a fan of first person narratives. However, L.R. Burkard changed my opinion with ***RESILIENCE***. She plucked me out of my safe and sane world and set me squarely in the lives of three teenage girls coping with our nation's potential worst nightmare!   **LINDA F. HARRIS**, Author, Reviewer

I really love this series of books. They are suspenseful, emotional, spiritual, and fun! You can't find a better example of this type of disaster and survival story.   **LEE BROOM**, Blogger, Book Reviewer

Linore Burkard has a tremendous ability to draw the reader into the world of these young teen women. Her words paint a real-life that is very believable and that tantalize all the senses!   **GINA BURGESS**, *Vine Voice*

Rip-Roaring Read! This book was just as riveting as the first one. While I'm usually a historical romance reader, I'm finding dystopian novels to be a fun read too, especially these two books by L. R. Burkard. She does an exceptional job at portraying a world gone awry and what happens. Pick up a copy. You won't regret it!   **JODIE A. WOLFE**, Author, Reviewer

This second book in the *Pulse Series* is even more exciting and thought provoking than the first!   **D.E. TAYLOR,** Amazon Reviewer

This series is a must read for all ages. PULSE EFFEX has become my favorite YA trilogy. I can't wait for the third book in a series I will read again and again!   **JUDITH B.**, Amazon Reviewer

A long-awaited sequel and Burkard does not disappoint! Excellent writing, pure and simple! A must read! Warning: do not begin this series if you have urgent things to attend to, because you WILL have difficulty putting it down!
R. KAYE, Amazon Reviewer

(L.R.Burkard) did it again…got me caught up in such a fantastic story and then BAM left me wanting more! These three girls and their families have stolen a piece of my heart.   **D.MITCHELL**, Blogger, Amazon Reviewer

Oh My Goodness! ***RESILIENCE*** was another page turner. I was up all night finishing it. I can't wait for the conclusion!   **J.REAVIS**, Amazon Reviewer

(***RESILIENCE***) moves at an even faster pace than book one! Just know that you will be on the edge of your seat all the way through this book.
                        DIANE ARCHIBALD, Amazon Reviewer

I agreed to read this book and post a review. I didn't know what I was getting myself in for. I LOVED THIS BOOK!!! I couldn't put it down. I was sneaking it at work and am so very sad now that it is done. I can't wait for the next one.
                        HEATHER, Amazon Reviewer

A fast-paced, enthralling read! Each chapter is just brief enough you find yourself deciding over and over again that you can fit in 'just one more'; and the action is so non-stop that your 'one more' quickly becomes 12-15!! Can't wait for Book 3!   **NICOLE**, Amazon Reviewer

This author was somehow able to come up with action on almost every page! Like ***PULSE***, (the first book in this series) ***RESILIENCE*** continues to grab the reader and make you feel as though you are in the story with the other characters! A "page-turner" for sure!   **LISA BOGAN**, Amazon Reviewer

Once I began reading this book, I couldn't put it down, so I highly recommend it.   **GERALD E. GREENE**, Amazon Reviewer

I was torn between wanting to read fast to see how it would turn out, and wanting to read slowly to enjoy the story!   **T. GLAZE,** Amazon Reviewer

Burkard ratchets up the tension. The much anticipated sequel to ***PULSE*** did not disappoint. I loved this story!   **TERESA SLACK**, AUTHOR

Like the first book in the series, ***RESILIENCE*** is a gripping work. I found myself thoroughly engrossed, so much so that I could hardly believe how quickly I arrived at the last page. And, of course, I eagerly await the sequel to this volume!   **DOUG ERLANDSON**, Top 100 Amazon Reviewer

Dedication

To **Joe Perri** my brother-in-law, recently graduated from this life. *I'll see you on the other side.*

And to **Dana McNeely**, who has been with me since Chapter One, faithfully reading and critiquing. You're a smart, funny friend and invaluable critic and cheerleader. *I couldn't have done it without you!*

The fifth angel poured out his bowl on the throne of the beast, and its kingdom was plunged into darkness.

Revelation 16:10

It is worth being in the darkness to see the stars.

Harriet Beecher Stowe

CHAPTER ONE

SARAH

MAY 11
Four months after the pulse

I knew before we left that something was wrong but Richard never listens to me.

It was dusk, time to get moving. Most people stay in after dark, which is why we travel at night. It's safer this way. People are the primary threat. Not regular, normal people like your grandmother or neighbors, or kindergarten teacher; those people are mostly gone. All the nice ones, gone! The ones left? They're the reason we move at night.

"We don't have time, Sarah." I looked up at my brother, my only family in the world I know for sure is still alive now that the EMP has sent our country into the dark ages.

"Almost done."

He frowned as I hurried to scribble a few more lines in this journal, one of the meager belongings I've held onto from the time life was normal. Since before the EMP—the electromagnetic pulse that took down the power grid of the nation.

We were in an abandoned barn, where we'd slept on old, musty hay. It was far cleaner than other places we'd spent the night recently. Richard brushed hay out of his hair, and pulled a comb from his back pocket. I have to hand it to him—he's grown a beard, but still manages to stay neat and groomed. His hair is short—he shaved his off not long after I shaved mine and for the same reason—*lice*. But unlike me, he looks good with the crew cut, like a military guy off duty. Except

Richard is on duty. He's always on duty. Life is too dangerous to ever relax, ever let down our guard.

"C'mon, time's up." My eyes met Richard's and I sighed, shutting my book and letting him pull me to my feet. He was right. I could hardly see what I was writing in the fading light. I shoved my journal and pen into my purse, strung it around my neck and tied it across my torso, close to my body. I shook hay off and pulled on my coat and zippered it, hiding the purse. Richard had already replaced his knife into its ankle holster, checked the pistol in his pocket, and was ready to move on. He slung the military-issue daypack over his back, then his rifle, and nodded at me.

Sometimes it was hard to remember this was Richard, my brother who had gone off to college and come home thinking guns should be banned. Or that building a strong military was foolish. Now he looks for firearms *all the time*. Sometimes we find them on fallen bodies... that's all I can say right now about that.

"Ready?" He peered outside at the gathering darkness. "There'll be little moonlight. We might be able to stay on the road."

My heart rose. I was sick to death of traveling across fields and brush and woods. I never disliked nature particularly, but I never dreamed I'd be stuck out in it in all kinds of wind and weather, trudging through woods and fields at night where no one was really meant to walk. Following a trail would have been easier, but we didn't dare. We had to forge our way, relying heavily on a topographical map Richard picked up once at a much-looted hardware store. The map helped immeasurably, but it couldn't help us avoid the myriad little brooks and streams that dot Ohio, making our progress towards Aunt Susan's house in Indiana slow and cumbersome. We might have been there by now if we didn't have to follow waterways until we found a good crossing. Roads were so much easier. Civilized—as long as you didn't run into other people. Starvation was a constant threat, but people were the scariest one.

Aside from other human beings, nothing creeps me out the way it used to. We'd come across wild dogs, coyotes, deer, foxes, raccoons, corn snakes, and the occasional skunk numerous times—but the sight of a wild critter was welcome. It might mean dinner. I try to keep my distance from snakes, sure, but ever since Richard caught and cooked a few, I lost my horror of them.

I am definitely no longer a normal American girl. How can I be? There is no longer a normal America.

This is my life every night: A long, hard hike with few breaks and precious little to eat or drink.

Richard helped me get my large daypack on my back. I adjusted the straps until they weren't digging into my shoulders, and we moved to the door of the barn. I waited while Richard peered out. He looked in all directions, then stepped out and looked around again. He turned to me and nodded.

I took a deep breath, and walked out of the barn. We'd been safe and relatively comfortable there. Would we find another refuge by morning?

I'd only gone a few feet when I started feeling it. Something wasn't right. I couldn't put my finger on it.

"Richard--I don't want to go tonight."

"Why not?"

I looked at the scrubby field of grey stubble around us. Normally by this time in May, the fields would be rich brown, plowed and ready for the new year's crops. Soon the scene before us would be a rolling swell of greenery. Instead, it was barren, dotted only with weeds. Most farm machinery had died with the EMP, so there was little large-scale planting. Bare farms like this were common. But it wasn't the desolate field that had my attention, giving me pause. It was the sky. Dusk was usually yellowish-brown, sometimes blue-brown, but tonight it had an eerie greenish glow.

"I think weather's coming in."

Richard surveyed the sky. "I think it's from that." He pointed to my right. A plume of smoke was visible, rising above the tree line. We'd seen it the day before when it was much stronger. We'd seen lots of houses burning since we hit the road. Dark plumes were depressingly common. It seemed to be one of the new dangers since the EMP; out of control fires. Anyway, I didn't think the greenish sky had anything to do with that fire.

"No; it's the whole sky, especially that way." I pointed west. But as I said, Richard never listens to me. He took an impatient breath.

"I've told you, Sarah, time is everything. If we don't reach Aunt Susan's before summer there won't be time to grow food. If we don't grow food, we don't survive next winter. We have no choice. C'mon."

I knew he was right, but I felt sure we were in for some kind of storm. "Just one night! I'm tired."

"Look, if we don't move, we starve. And I don't mean next winter. We've got enough provisions for two more days. The fact we've not already starved is a small miracle. I'm not going to push our luck. We have to keep going while we can, while we've got something to nourish us. If we run out of food before we get there we're dead. You understand? Dead."

Sometimes Richard's laser focus on getting us to Indiana was helpful. Having Aunt Susan's farm as a goal, a place to look forward to—even if we were living in fantasy land—helped my spirits when the weariness set in. And it did, making me want to give up, collapse, die on the spot. Why not? Mom and Jesse had died, my father was probably dead, my previous life was a faint memory, like a childhood book I'd read and enjoyed, but which was never real—but Richard's quiet talk about how our lives would improve when we reached Aunt Susan—it gave me hope.

Hope is a powerful thing. Like food, it could get me moving.

Tonight I wasn't thinking about hope, or the future, or anything other than that ominous looking sky. The last storm we'd been caught in left me miserable for three days because that's how long it took for my shoes to dry. I didn't want that to happen again.

But I followed my brother. We usually went to the edge of fields just inside the brush line, out of sight, staying west as much as possible. We did that tonight. Richard said we had to wait for thicker darkness before hazarding a road. After awhile I thought maybe I'd been wrong about bad weather coming in. Maybe the sky just looked greenish sometimes and I'd never noticed it before.

Then, little by little, a breeze picked up. By the time we'd gone maybe three miles, it was strong. I tried to ignore it. I didn't want to say, "See? I told you so," because Richard is such a good brother. Except for not listening to me, he is a much better brother now, than before the EMP.

But as the wind increased, dark clouds—visible even in the night sky—scudded with increasing speed across it. A jagged bolt of lightning revealed the greenish glow I'd seen earlier. Sudden, heavy rain pelted us, and I got cold—fast. I'd lost my hat the week before and was sorrier at that moment than ever; my head, with only two inches of stubby hair, was unprotected. And the wind was gaining force. The trees to our right were bending low, and sounds of snapping branches surrounded us.

"C'mon," Richard called. He motioned me away from the edge of the brush-line, deeper into the stand of woods. The brush and trees we came to for shelter were now alive with energy, snapping, twisting and hitting us in the face and arms and legs. I covered my head with my hands, trying to protect my face.

"I'm looking for shelter!" Richard called, much to my relief. He was no more than a foot away but I almost hadn't heard him above the wind. Walking felt more and more difficult, like fighting an ocean tide. This was no thunder storm like any I'd ever experienced!

Then, we heard it. At first, it was a low rumble like a distant train. Soon it sounded like a roaring crowd at a packed stadium. We stopped, squinting into the wind and dust and stood there, gasping, gaping at the incredible scene before us. The sky was alive, reeling and churning. Branches and other objects too dark to recognize were swirling eerily aloft as if being played with by some giant, invisible hand. We were looking at the growling belly of the storm, approaching like a snarling dog.

"What's happening?" I screamed.

"It's a tornado!" Richard yelled. His words terrified me. I felt paralyzed, leaning hard into a wall of wind, fighting to keep myself from flying backwards like a dandelion scattering in the breath of a child. Even my weighty backpack offered no extra resistance against this force.

Richard grabbed my hand and pulled me. "C'mon!"

"We'll never outrun it!" I panted, feeling heavy and defeated. Panic was sapping my strength. I tried to unstrap my pack, I wanted to be lighter, but he cried, "No!" and yanked me along.

"This way!" He dragged me after him behind a huge old tree, and shoved me unceremoniously to the ground, against the trunk.

"Put your head down! Maybe the tree will shelter us!"

"Trees aren't safe in a storm!" I yelled. "They're lightning magnets!"

"It's not lightning we have to worry about!"

As we huddled behind the tree, I looked past Richard's head and up into the green sky. The top of our tree swayed above me like a dancer taking a bow. My eyes widened. Richard couldn't see it. His head was over me, facing down. I stared, horrified but unable to look away. How far would it bend?

Around us the woods were alive, dancing like demons, the very trees possessed of a passionate dark tune that threatened to engulf us forever. We'd be killed at any moment, I just knew it! Amidst the awful swaying was a continual ripping and cracking of trees and limbs and branches—a symphony of terror. Then, *thud!* Something landed beside my head. *How long could we survive?*

Above us, outlined against the green sky, the treetop bent lower like a witch hunched over her cauldron. Lower, lower, she stooped.

"It's going to break!" I gasped. Richard didn't hear me.

The roar was louder still. The tree held, but something inside *me* snapped. My sense of peril was unbearable. I felt a spurt of energy, pure adrenaline I'm sure. I jumped up and ran.

"Sarah!" There was no time for me to reason with Richard, and I couldn't stop anyway. In seconds I could feel him behind me, glad he was there, and kept going, not knowing how long we'd be able to run before the snarling twisting mass in the sky would bowl us down like ants on a sidewalk. I hardly noticed the branches whipping my face or arms now. I didn't care. That living, moving, howling force behind us was what frightened me.

I usually struggled to keep up with Richard during the nightly hikes, but now I ran like wildfire. We'd been living on fumes, dreams of food, for so long I guess my body was used to functioning on practically nothing. We came to a sharp drop, a ravine which held a narrow brook and I froze at the precipice.

"C'mon!" Richard jumped. I didn't want to move but he grabbed my hand. As I flew over the edge after him helplessly, a sudden flash of lightning revealed every line on his face. His eyes were wild. We were in the air for only a second, but it felt like slow motion. I heard a cry as I went and knew faintly that it was me.

Richard had forced us off the edge where the ground sheared away into darkness. I hit the dirt—hard, falling against the bank, landing on rocks, roots, mud and whatever else was there. The roar was deafening. My heart pounded painfully through my whole being but all I heard was that ferocious roar.

"Keep your head against the bank!" My brother's muffled yell was unnecessary because I was already huddled against the earthen wall as small as I could make myself while terror coursed through my body. Holding my eyes shut fiercely, I stifled a scream. Just when I thought I might pass out, Richard threw himself over me. His weight felt crushing.

I knew he was trying to protect me.

CHAPTER TWO

LEXIE

MAY 12
Four months after the pulse

The sound of a shot, piercing the silence and my lovely dream, woke me. I blinked awake while an uneasy feeling saturated my being. Something was wrong. Then I realized: *A shot!* I came fully awake and went into autopilot, grabbing my rifle from its high perch on my dresser and rushing to the window. Carefully, so as not to give someone a target, I stayed to one side, peering out from behind the curtain.

Dawn had just broken. The landscape surrounding our farmhouse was a sultry, foggy cloud, leftover moisture from last night's storm. Anyone could be hiding out there. What I needed to know was who had fired that shot? *Was it us, or them?*

I saw nothing. Taking a quick peek at the top bunk to see if Andrea had heard it, I saw she was up already, her bunk empty. For a moment I wavered between throwing on clothes or keeping my lookout. Since I hadn't heard more fire, I hurried to slip on jeans and a light sweat top. It would be chilly until the sun got higher in the sky.

Just last night at the council meeting we'd been warned: Every day as the weather warmed more people were on the move, people who would come our way. They were not to be trusted. Some, it's true, were harmless; others, possible allies, maybe even future members of our compound. But we couldn't assume anything. And if they'd fired first, that told us all we needed to know. They were "number fours"—threats.

An even greater threat than number fours was the possibility of foreign military. Rumor on the AR (amateur radio—my dad's a ham operator) had it that enemies of the US were using the EMP to try and take over our country.

There'd been sightings of guerrilla outfits on our soil. So far we hadn't seen any, but how long would it be until we did? Even worse, how would we ever fight them off? Our little compound of thirty or so people could hardly put up a resistance to trained soldiers. Most had no experience with firearms. The very idea terrified me. I tried not to think about it.

Number fours were bad enough, marauders who roamed the land and stole food and supplies from people, often killing those they'd just robbed. Our compound had successfully fought off more than a few bands of such people. (Have I mentioned the compound before? Probably not. I stopped journaling because I had no energy at the end of the day. Chores are all-consuming. And time with night-lights is rationed—oil and batteries run out and we never know if we'll get more—and most nights I'd rather read than write. It seems like a lifetime ago that we had electricity, though it was only four months.)

Anyways, the compound started out as a small community of Christian preppers, but we'd grown, taking in others who brought skills or knowledge we needed. They in turn got food and shelter. My science teacher would say it was a symbiotic living arrangement, a way for all of us to survive in a world gone dark and dangerous.

At first it was just us and the Pattersons. They hadn't done any prepping but we took them in, mostly because Andrea is my best friend and I knew her family needed us. Plus, we felt led in prayer to help them. Then the Buchanans joined us, whom I'll talk about later; and slowly, other people. Many of them had only survived since the EMP by the skin of their teeth, barely keeping starvation at bay. But we all knew we're vulnerable individually, even those of us who stored food and supplies. There's safety in numbers. Banding together was really the only solution.

Some people didn't want to leave their land or home to join us. There were arguments about where to build, whose property was the best for defense, for farming, and for water. But we had the best land assets of anyone else—a high hill (which is a natural vantage point for lookouts), a well with a manual pump, a running stream, flat farmland plus some woods, not to mention chickens, rabbits, a cow and horses—so in the end our farm was chosen.

I was glad it was chosen because it meant we didn't have to leave everything and start new somewhere else. And there's something comforting about the sounds of work going on around us. The pounding of hammers, the steady rhythm of saws making logs and beams from downed trees; even the shouts of men as they talk and work together. It means we're not under attack. But privacy, and our old way of life is gone. It was gone anyway due to the EMP—and it's a blessing to have other people in our lives, people we can trust and form close relationships with. But Mom sometimes looks out at the work sites, the clearing of brush and trees, and looks wistful. I miss having our house and land to ourselves, too.

Except for the Buchanans! Blake's family started building a cabin behind our barn shortly after we brought Andrea's family here. Their livestock was raided so often they got critically low. When their last rooster got stolen they decided to join forces with us. (We have a few roosters. You don't need a rooster for eggs, but if you want to keep getting eggs for years and years, then you do. A hen only lays well for a couple of years and then you need a younger one.)

Anyways, with the birds disappearing and the increasing foot traffic on their road, the kids weren't able to play outside anymore. Their house was on a main road. So they will have more cover here, more protection. And so will we.

I feel bad they had to leave their home but it gives me a happy feeling to know Blake will be close by now. Everyone knows Blake and I will get married one day—*as long as we can stay alive that long.* (He hasn't formally proposed, but I know it's coming.)

Andrea entered the room, nonchalant, not acting like we were under attack. She saw me with my rifle and said, "Oh. It's okay! It was a warning shot and they've gone."

I peered out at the misty fog hanging over the land, giving even the detached garage, adjacent to the house, a ghostly demeanor. "How can they be sure? We can't see anything out there."

Andrea smiled. "Jared's on duty and says so." Andrea likes Jared. He's new to the compound, ex-Army, and came with a lot of surveillance tips and defense practices and other know-how. His word is sort of law. If he said it was all clear, then it was all clear.

I put my rifle down and considered returning to bed. I didn't have to be up so early as morning barn chores were Andrea's today. If I could sleep in, I liked to. But I thought of the coffee that was probably hot in the percolator (which had a permanent spot on the woodstove these days) and my mouth watered. I didn't used to drink coffee. Now I'll drink anything that's available. Nothing edible or potable is ever taken for granted.

By the specks of straw clinging to her jeans, I could see Andrea had already been to the barn so I asked, "How's Rhema?" She met my eyes. Andrea's a pretty brunette. Since coming to live with us, she'd changed. The new Andrea hardly wears make up, doesn't complain about clothes that haven't been washed properly in months, doesn't do her nails or hair, and has basically become a lot like me. Actually, I don't miss the old Andrea. I always liked Andrea, but I guess I did think she worried about all that girly stuff too much.

"She's good. Wanna ride today?" We both loved riding. I was teaching Andrea but I usually managed to get in some time with my horse, Rhema, too. We need riders because none of our vehicles work (except one small diesel tractor, which we'll use until we run out of fuel. That was dad's least favorite piece of farm equipment—until the pulse!) Anyways, sometimes we have to search out new supplies. So Mom designated "Horseback Riding" as a new school subject. And she appointed me, the best horsewoman in the family, to teach Andrea.

"I'll ask Dad." We both knew it wasn't on our schedule. Everyone in the compound had to follow a schedule, even we teenagers. And, while homeschooling was important, running the compound had to come first. Without electricity, almost every single thing we do takes more work, more time, more planning.

The door opened. Aiden, one of Andrea's little brothers, came bouncing into the room, followed swiftly by Quentin, his twin.

"Don't come in without knocking!" Andrea scolded. "How many times have I told you that?"

Aiden's face fell but Quentin was unfazed. "I heard a shot before," he said. Gleefully he added, "Did we kill anyone? Did we kill anyone?" His eagerness was eerie and, not too long ago, would have been unthinkable.

Andrea frowned. "You should be happy because no, we didn't have to kill anyone."

"Oh." They'd spoken, in unison, the way twins sometimes do. They were disappointed.

"C'mon, you guys," I said. "Your sister's right. It's GREAT, we didn't have to kill anyone!"

They looked at each other. Quentin looked back at us. "We just want there to be less bad guys," he said, his eyes big and earnest. "If there's no bad guys, we can play outside like we used to."

Andrea and I exchanged glances. She got on one knee in front of the boys. "You still get to play outside," she said, softly.

"Only a little. Not as much as we used to."

"It's summertime," added Aiden. "We used to play outside a lot more in summertime." He dragged out the last syllable, tiiiime.

"It's only spring," Andrea said. "And nobody gets to play as much as we used to."

The boys nodded. Aiden sniffed. "Are you gonna take us outside today?" he asked.

I spoke up. "I am." It was part of our rotation on the schedule. Besides two hours we were supposed to spend on lessons, we shifted between childcare, nursery, kitchen chores, and livestock chores. Kitchen chores could be lots of things, but the other stuff was fairly routine. I liked doing childcare, whether playing with the kids or leaving them to their own devices. When they were happily entertained among themselves, I could read. They were never happily entertained without me for long, but it was something.

When the boys didn't even crack a smile, I added, "Well, I'M glad I'll get to play with *you*!"

When they remained silent, Andrea turned to me with a sheepish grin. "They like it when it's my turn because I raid food storage for treats we haven't had in a long time."

I gasped. "Andrea!"

The boys giggled.

Andrea put a finger to her lips. "Shhhhh!"

"We know," said Quentin. "It's a secret."

"My folks would kill you if they knew you were doing that!" In truth, I felt angry. I liked the treats from food storage as much as anyone. There hadn't been any shopping since the EMP. That meant the only chips or chocolate bars or packaged cookies we ever got to eat came from storage. And there wasn't a great amount of that stuff. My mom had concentrated on nourishing food when she did the storing. I made a mental note to get down to the main storage area and check the buckets labeled "GOODIES." The only way Andrea could be scavenging for treats was from those buckets. I was surprised she'd discovered how to open them, but they were like gold, now. I'd reseal the ones she got into and hide the bucket opener.

Suddenly we heard a barrage of fire. It sounded close.

"Get down!" Andrea pushed her brothers to the ground. Aiden started whimpering.

"Get under the bed now!" I ordered.

Quentin said, "It's okay, Aiden. We'll get the bad guys. Maybe we'll get them all!"

Aiden quieted. Andrea grabbed her rifle and the two of us crouched beside the windows. We peeked furtively outside. The fog was lifting. I gasped as I saw a figure holding a handgun dart out of the brush on one side of the house, heading towards the back.

"We've got company, all right! Number fours!"

"Company?" called Quentin. "Who's here?"

I raised the window enough to take a shot if I got one, frowning as I did so. I had no idea who was there, actually, but it wasn't military so that left four possibilities and three of them had just been eliminated. A non-threatening person didn't go darting about one's property, holding a firearm. Jared had obviously messed up. He'd said all was clear; but all wasn't clear. Someone was out there, and probably lots of someones—looters rarely came alone—and they were after our animals, at the least. At worst, they were after us.

"Who's out there, Lexie?" Quentin asked, again.

"Bad guys."

I heard our dogs barking from behind the house. *Someone, please, get the dogs inside!* Pets, we'd learned the hard way, were fair game for hungry looters. We'd lost our beautiful, harmless golden retriever, Kasha, last month during a raid. How anyone could eat someone's pet—my thoughts were cut off by another volley of fire ringing out, also coming from the back.

"They're at the barn or the coop!" Andrea said, turning to rush from the room.

"No, stay here!" She looked at me, questioning. "My dad and the others will be back there. We need to be here so if they retreat back this way, we can give them grief."

Giving them grief was really not an accurate way to put it. We were supposed to shoot anyone who had used violence while trying to steal our animals or supplies because these people, if not stopped, were dangerous and would always come back. So far, I'd never had to shoot someone for stealing or for trying to. I prayed I never would.

Andrea returned to her window. We heard more shots, still from

13

behind the house. And then just as I leaned my rifle down for a moment to put my hair up with a stretchy band, a sudden ping at my window, right near my head, had me scrambling to get back in position to fire.

"They're back out front!" I gasped. Andrea already had her rifle at the window, leaning it on the sill as she took aim at something. In her slow, calm voice—Andrea was almost mystically calm during dire moments like this—she said, "No. They're not. There's just more of them." She glanced at me. "We've got to hold them back."

Worriedly, I looked out at the front. A line of ghostly figures, just visible through the lifting fog, were emerging from the brush that faced the street side of our property. Andrea was right! There were a lot of them and they were armed. One had a raised shotgun. And with a skirmish already going on in the back, I feared she and I were alone to contain this second wave of marauders.

I wasn't sure I was up to it.

CHAPTER THREE

SARAH

The earth shook. I sobbed, numb with terror, and begged God to protect us. Richard's arms tightened around me as I felt us both being lifted. I had unknowingly grabbed hold of something which I now clung to for dear life. Richard's hold on me increased while I felt the terrible pulling trying to sweep us away. Then, without warning, he let go! He lifted off me and was gone!

I screamed but didn't let go of my hold, fighting the pull that had whisked him away like words on the wind. With every bit of strength I possessed I dragged my body into a crevice where my head had somehow found its way. I hadn't even realized the crevice was there; either that, or it had just been created when the embankment shifted from the force of the storm. Clinging to what felt like a large tree root, I huddled in the fetal position while the world around me screamed in protest, cracking and lashing and pounding.

The crevice shuddered as the embankment felt the power of nature's fury, taking the pummeling. I tasted dirt, wondering if it would cave in around me, on top of me, leaving me buried. And then, as quickly and surprisingly as it had come, the force suddenly lessened. A few seconds later it was gone! It was like the air had been let out of a giant balloon. The roar moved on.

Blinking away soil, I lifted my head, withdrawing it from the crevice. The sky flashed. I saw I was next to a jutting root system, part of which had formed my crevice. If the trees to that system had been uprooted I'd have gone right along with them. But the air felt charged, electric. I heard the rumbling again, the warning sound we'd heard right before the tornado hit. The sky flashed and I saw another wall of sky, twisting and alive, coming my way! Was it a second funnel? Or had I been in the eye of the storm?

The roar increased quickly and I dove back into my crevice, this time clawing at the wall of dirt, trying to get deeper. I felt the embankment jump, heard the same awful snapping and tearing of trees and branches struck by the swirling madness. I covered my head with my arms and prayed. An indescribable sound filled my ears as the wind wreaked havoc on the brook and the opposite bank, and then its awful scream grew more distant. The train wreck of nature had passed, this time for sure. The only pounding left was my heart, echoing in sharp thuds throughout my being.

------◆------

I crawled backwards from the crevice and sat on my haunches, taking deep breaths and getting my bearings. Our tree, that stooping witch during the storm, had unbent itself. The creaking and groaning and rain had ceased, leaving a silence so deep it was eerie.

Distant lightning blinked, and I saw the crevice again. It was the sort of hole which normally you couldn't pay me *ten thousand dollars* to stick my hand into! The thought that I'd crawled into it without even thinking about it, folding myself up like a dinner napkin, seemed unreal. Yet it had saved my life. But Richard! How would I find him?

Darkness was deep, broken only by occasional flashes from the sky revealing a greenish-brown atmosphere, more brown than green, now. But only one thought filled my shaking, weak-kneed body: Where was Richard? And, when I found him, would he be alive?

------◆------

When I felt strong enough to rise, I took a few tentative steps and called Richard. My voice was weak but, desperate to find him, I kept calling. I hoped, by some miracle, he was close by.

I climbed up the opposite embankment. When I reached the top and made my way through a flattened thicket, I saw the path the storm had taken through the trees. Then lightning jagged the sky about a half mile away and I saw the next grove of trees bowing like meek subjects before the furious gale. More lightning. And there! The plume! Before we'd been too close to see it clearly but now I did, a gigantic, rotating black thing, wider at the top, writhing along at its condensed bottom like an enraged, twisted demon, clearing all in its path.

I fell back down. All I wanted to do was sit and cry. I did not want to be alive if Richard was not. He was all I had left in the world. I reflected how he'd lifted off me like a moth in a fan's breeze. Would it be possible for him to be alive? I remembered reading about people who had survived tornadoes after being caught up in the air, sometimes traveling for miles before landing somehow, somewhere. These accounts were from people who had survived. Richard might have, too.

I couldn't tell if my hope was reasonable or born of desperation— maybe even starvation. Maybe I wasn't thinking straight. But the thought that other people had survived such storms gave me hope and I got up. I slung off my pack and dug inside for the flashlight. We considered it almost sacred, this flashlight. We didn't use it for convenience. If we had, it would have died long ago. We saved it for only the direst circumstances. To my mind, finding Richard fit the bill. As I groped inside, my fingers came across the last piece of a granola bar I'd been saving. I grabbed it and ate it quickly, trying not to think about the fact that Richard had been carrying the rest of our food, meager as it was.

The one good thing about not having light most of the time was that now using the flashlight felt magical. It raised my spirits, and I began calling out to my brother, moving in the path of the storm, working my way around debris and brush.

The wake of the storm was obvious, for trees in its path were mostly stumps, some as high as my waist; but following it was another thing. Limbs, broken branches, and trunks littered the path. Trees half-pulled from the ground leaned at odd angles. I had to watch my step to keep from walking into them or getting tangled or falling.

Seeing the wide swath of destruction, I realized that the force which had snatched Richard from me probably wouldn't have deposited him anywhere close. But just in case, I moved slowly, calling Richard and searching trees that were intact for his body. I half expected to find him hanging lifeless from a tree limb, high in the air. But I fought against such thoughts and trudged on. I resolved to search as long as it took. There was nothing else for me to do.

I couldn't go on without Richard.

CHAPTER FOUR

LEXIE

The band of marauders crept closer, and I panicked. "Andrea, let's pray!" She was zeroing in on one of the intruders, getting ready to shoot, and didn't answer.

"What if they're friendly?"

"Lex, they just put a bullet in your window! That could have been your head!" She let out her breath and I saw her finger squeeze the trigger. The shot made me jump though I knew it was coming. I turned and ran to my dresser. I threw a pair of protective ear muffs at her and put down my rifle to position my own pair. I'd been in skirmishes before which had left my ears ringing for hours and I hated that sensation.

Outside, Andrea's shot must have reached its mark because the intruders scattered to all sides (some, back the way they'd come! Hoorah!). Andrea kept shooting while there I was, taking stock of the situation like a bystander, not a soldier. But I am supposed to be a soldier. We all are. We have to be.

I returned to my position, crouched, and aimed. I took a single shot and then suddenly Blake knelt beside me.

"How's it going?" he asked, his gaze quickly scanning the view out front. More of our people entered the room to get to our windows, which gave a good vantage point for the front. Jared dropped down beside Andrea, falling into position to shoot. It seemed to be as natural for him as breathing.

I felt better having the guys with us. But then I heard the sound of a window crashing in below us.

"They're getting in the house!" I cried. Jared and Blake's eyes met. They jumped up.

"We got it," Jared said.

"Be careful!" I whispered to Blake. I grabbed his hand and he gave mine a squeeze.

Before taking off with Jared he stopped to say, "Lock the door

18

behind us."

As I did, I said, keeping my voice low, "I wish we'd gotten the kids to the safe room."

"This is more fun!" Quentin's muffled voice came out from below the bed. I had hoped the boys wouldn't hear me. Andrea and I shook our heads. What kind of boys would the twins grow up to be if they thought armed encounters were fun?

"He doesn't understand," Andrea said. "To them, we're playing cops and robbers." We heard a shot from downstairs, then another, then another. My heart was in my throat.

"I see movement!" Andrea cried. I spun back to my post in time to see two people who had just emerged into view from the porch beneath us. A second later she took a shot and one fell. Andrea is an amazing shot—it's a natural skill for her, like horseback riding is for me. I have trouble staying calm and focused when it comes to hurting other people—even when we are under attack. Andrea seems immune to misgivings about it. Like she's trained not to see marauders as people. I have to sternly remind myself they mean us harm, that they're the enemy, or I can't handle fighting.

While I mused and tried to get the other guy out there in my scope, Andrea took the shot and felled him. Downstairs we'd heard a few more shots but it was quiet now. We stayed at the windows watching. Minutes ticked by and all was still. Andrea turned to me. I hurriedly lifted my ear protection. "What?"

"Why didn't you shoot one?" Her voice was calm, but in her eyes I saw something lurking. I just stared at her a moment. I hadn't meant NOT to shoot.

I shrugged. "I don't know. You got it done."

"Yeah. Thanks," she said, heavily. Turning back to the window, she added, "You're not a bad shot, Lexie. You could have taken one of them, too."

I bit my lip, staring at the front. So maybe it did bother her, having to kill people. I had let her do the dirty work. I'd let my dislike of shooting at human targets stop me. I loved shooting as a sport—but it wasn't fun, anymore. It was deadly serious.

I gave her my feeble defense. "They were leaving," I said. "I can't shoot anyone in the back."

Andrea's eyes widened. "They came to kill us and to steal! You

19

know we can't let them get away after they shoot at us! You know the rules, Lex! They'll come back! You can't pick and choose who to fight when they start it. If you do that again, I'm gonna tell your dad!"

"I'm sorry. I'll do better next time." I could hardly stand to look into Andrea's large, reproving eyes at that moment.

Quentin and Aiden crawled out from under the bed. "We can come out now, right?" Quentin asked.

"No!" Andrea's sharp cry startled them. I saw Aiden's lip quiver, but his brother said, "C'mon, Aiden. It's okay." They backed under and were out of sight. I was still feeling guilty and looked at Andrea, trying to come up with an explanation. To my surprise I saw her cheeks were wet! Andrea was rarely emotional after a skirmish. I felt helpless. I didn't know how to comfort her.

"I'm sorry," I said again. She ignored me. But then we heard two shots from outside. It wasn't over!

Coming to attention at her window, she said, "C'mon! There's more of them. Help me this time!"

I did. I bit my lip so hard I could taste blood. I saw people out there grow blurry and realized I was crying. I wiped away the tears quickly so I could focus, but I couldn't deny I hated having to live on the defensive with rifles practically attached to our bodies. We went nowhere unarmed. I wanted to be a normal teenager again. Not a soldier in this civil war where survivors fought survivors.

If there really were foreign troops on the ground, wouldn't it be better for everyone if all Americans came together to resist them? But instead we had to constantly be on the alert for the ruthless "number fours" whose existence meant we were never safe. And there seemed to be a lot of them today.

I could hear shots hitting the house but fortunately our people downstairs and at other strategic places on the grounds were giving return fire. Shots rang out for the next fifteen minutes, on and off, and at least two more men out there fell within our view. The "bad guys" were hurting. I heard my mom, evidently from the room beside us at her window, cry out, "Take that, you rascally varmint!"

Andrea and I giggled through our tears. When my mom got emotional she reverted to southernisms from her youth. No doubt "rascally varmint" was a favorite saying of her grandma's or grandpappy's. We'd tease her about it later. We laughed too much—I think we were slightly unhinged. It was taking an emotional toll on us, living this way.

There was sporadic cross-fire for a few more minutes—then silence. *Thank God, silence.*

Andrea and I had no choice though, but to stay as lookouts for as long as it took until we heard an official "all clear." We saw no more intruders, and after about half an hour, sounds of normalcy, children's voices, came from below. During a skirmish, children are hurried to the safe room and kept there until it was safe to come out. I was sure we could hear my little sisters and other kids below—which meant the threat had to be over.

My dad finally popped his head in to give the all clear. Andrea and I sighed with relief.

"Next time, Dad, could you send someone up here sooner?"

"Sorry, honey. There was a lot going on."

We woke the boys who had fallen asleep—lulled by having to keep still.

Downstairs, I hugged our German shepherd, Bach, while Mozart, our Great Dane, enjoyed Andrea's attention. We learned that Jared had taken two guys with handcuffs, the ones who broke the window, I supposed. (Handcuffs: One of many "interesting" accessories Jared brought with him to the compound.) Their capture was supposed to be good news because it meant we could get information from them. When the attackers were organized in a group, we wanted to know who was in charge, how they'd organized, what their targets and plans were. Were they just passing through or did they plan on scavenging the area completely?

Andrea and I were just starting to tease my mom, calling her a "rascally varmint" when we saw Jared marching the prisoners towards an out-building. The smiles vanished from our faces. We knew what awaited those men.

CHAPTER FIVE

SARAH

I found Richard face down on the grass. I thought my heart would stop. I was sure he must be dead. I approached him feeling like I was a foot off the ground, like walking without feet. I couldn't feel them. I've had lots of scary things happen since the pulse, and I'd been searching for Richard for hours—I don't have a watch so I can't say exactly how long—but this felt like the scariest yet. Because if anything happens to Richard, I'll never make it on my own. I wouldn't even want to.

Dawn was rising. I fell to the ground beside my brother and shook his shoulder. Amazingly, his backpack was still there. I unlatched the strap circling his waist and gently drew it off him. Again I tried nudging him awake. When he didn't answer, I started crying. I was too dehydrated to shed tears but my body shook with sobs. I pounded on his back.

"Don't be dead, Richard!" Stupidly I didn't think of checking for a pulse; I just assumed the worst. But an amazing thing happened after I pounded him: Richard moaned!

I gasped and tried to turn him over. He is as skinny as can be but I still had trouble turning him. He was like dead weight. I finally got him turned over. He blinked at me. I removed my pack and found the only water we had—a plastic bottle we'd been refilling from any source we could find. This water was from a little trickling spring, so we'd already treated it with an iodide pill—a miraculous concoction we picked up from a military guy (I'll explain later about that). I didn't want to waste a single drop of this precious water, so crouching down next to him, I raised his head and carefully placed the bottle by his mouth. He managed to take a sip, then another.

"Are you okay?" His voice was croaky.

"I'm fine. Don't talk." I gave him another sip and then let his head rest on the ground. I took a shirt from my pack and folded it up and put it beneath his head.

"I gotta get up," he said. "Gimme a hand."

"Don't you think you should rest?"

"No. Help me up."

But he hadn't moved. A new fear washed over me. What if Richard had broken his back? What if he couldn't walk?

"Can you feel your legs?"

He blinked at me again. In a second I saw his feet rise, first one, then the other.

"Thank God!"

"C'mon, help me up." He lifted an arm towards me, so I got to my feet and braced myself to help pull him up. We got him to a sitting position.

"I can't believe it—the storm took you, and you're okay!"

He nodded, pulling in a deep breath. "I know." He started to rise, so I hurried to help him. He plopped back down heavily, saying, "Wait. Sit down."

I sat beside him. "Are you dizzy? Is your head hurt?" A slew of worries were coming at me. Richard could have a concussion or hidden internal bleeding. He might collapse on me. He might have something like major whiplash from his tornadic ride. I have a long habit of cataloging things to worry about, and right now it was in full force.

"I'm okay." He grabbed his pack and rummaged in it, and then pulled out two MREs—"Meals, Ready to Eat," issued by the military, originally for the armed forces. These are the best food we've found anywhere since we hit the road. I don't mean they taste the best—but they're dense in calories. We need all the calories we can get. Like our single flashlight, we treated MREs like gold. We'd eaten a few before, but resisted these last two since we'd gotten them. I didn't like to think about how we got them. (How we got a lot of Richard's gear, and even a couple of things for me. I'll write about it one day…but not today.)

Afterwards we each took a few sips of water. That was more nutrition and liquid than we'd allowed ourselves in days. Richard suddenly popped up, literally jumping to his feet. He winced in pain, though.

"What is it?"

"Just sore. I think I hit a tree before landing here."

"I knew it! That's what I'm afraid of! What if you have a concussion?" I stared at him but he only shrugged. "Did you? Did you hit a tree?" We looked around. There was no tree close to where we were, and my fear went down a notch. "What was it like? Being swept away by a tornado?"

He looked at me a moment, thinking. "You know, I remember letting go of you. I was afraid we'd both get taken. I felt this tremendous wind against me…and then…nothing. Like I was floating on air. And then…" he lapsed into silence, searching his memory. "I don't remember how I got down. I feel like I hit something. I must have hit something, I feel sort of like a train wreck…sore all over. But otherwise I'm okay."

"You realize, God spared your life."

He looked away, moving his jaw as though stretching his jaw muscles. But he didn't answer.

Suddenly, I felt the long night's ordeal catching up to me. I was exhausted. I lay back, closing my eyes.

"Sarah, c'mon, we've eaten. We should get moving."

"I'm tired."

"We're always tired. But we have to go."

"I can't." We were in the middle of a field, adjacent to the swath of disorder left by the tornado.

"We can't stay here. We have to at least find somewhere with cover."

I let Richard pull me to my feet. Minutes ago I'd had to help him. Right then I felt like it was impossible to move. The sudden rise in blood sugar had the opposite effect on me as it had on Richard. He'd gotten instant energy whereas I only wanted to sleep. I mean, I *longed* to rest. I felt drunk with the need. My body wasn't used to getting quality nutrition, and I'd been up all night in dread of finding him dead. "I am really…tired."

"I know," he said. "C'mon, we'll find a shelter."

CHAPTER SIX

LEXIE

Two shots from the outbuilding were enough for us to gather what happened. I was peeling the last of the potatoes from last year's harvest for dinner that night, and stopped, taking in the sound.

"Mom, can I go upstairs for a few minutes?"

She was at the sink which was half-filled with hauled in water, doing dishes. She took one look at me and understood.

"Sure, honey, you go ahead."

Knowing two more had died on our compound, even though they were "bad guys," made me want to be alone. I needed daily prayer time, anyways. Sometimes I prayed about what a pain life is these days. Everything takes so much work! Work, work, work. Today, when I got upstairs I just sat on my bed and cried.

I told God that none of this is right. Teenagers should be going to school, studying, making friends, having fun. We shouldn't have to live like soldiers! I've told this to the Lord before. *You have made your people see hard things; you have given us wine to drink that made us stagger.* That's Psalm 60, verse 3. It helps to tell God how I feel. But I came away with the same conclusion I always get. The United States is apparently under judgment, and judgment is bleak. In Zechariah 1, it says, *The Lord All Powerful did as he said he would do, he punished us for the way we lived and for what we did.* I know our country deserved this. But I don't feel like we did, personally.

My hope is for our nation to be restored—but I don't see it happening. I think we need to repent, first. How do you get a whole nation to repent? Only God can. But it takes time. And in the meantime, people are still desperate and violent. And what if some marauders catch us off-guard one day? What if we run out of ammunition?

Jared brought thousands of rounds, as well as an impressive collection of firearms. (My dad wanted to know how he got it all but Jared would only say, "It was waiting for someone to take it. Better us than them.") And even my dad stockpiled thousands of rounds over time, building his stores. He made bullets ("casting bullets" he calls it) as well as buying them. It was a hobby. I often found him outside his workshop with a messy set-up of folding tables holding all kinds of strange equipment, melting lead, and with scads of used bullet casings which he cleaned in some kind of solution. He actually found this relaxing. (Proof that guys are a mystery. But I guess it's no different than how Mom would hum away in the kitchen while she baked or cooked.)

Anyways, he can't make bullets indefinitely. He can re-use the cases and melt lead for bullets—but he can't make his own primer or propellant. So even though we have a good amount of ammunition, it won't last forever.

And what if the government gets its act together and sends out troops and confiscates our weapons? They did that after Hurricane Katrina in New Orleans. Dad says it was totally unconstitutional but they did it anyways. They took legally owned firearms from people— just when they might need them most! And get this—they don't confiscate firearms from the bad guys—they can't. There's no purchase record if you don't buy a weapon legally, and the bad guys don't. It makes me so mad! We've had to defend ourselves numerous times since the pulse. I don't think we'd still be alive or have any supplies left if we didn't have means to defend ourselves.

I was talking about this to Andrea once in the kitchen when Jared came in after his lookout shift ended, seeking coffee. He overheard me talking and came over.

"What are you worrying about?"

Andrea smiled. All he has to do is come near us and she's smiling. Personally, I find Jared on the creepy side. He always looks grim. Anyways, we told him.

"If your weapons are from local gun dealers, don't worry."

"Why not?" I did not subscribe to the "what Jared says is law" belief system Andrea lived by. I wanted a reason to take his word for it.

"There's no gun shop records to lead them here," he said. "We can only be traced through their files. And there's no files."

"What happened to the files?" I asked. For the first time since I've met Jared, a smile curled his lips. He leaned his head back, thinking. He seemed to be considering whether to tell us or not; but evidently the answer to my question amused him.

He looked back at us. "Shops got burned down. Apparently, some people don't like the government overstepping their bounds." He paused. "That's where I got a lot of my gear."

"From a burning gun shop?" My question made him level a stare at me. I didn't like what I saw in Jared's eyes. Challenge? Defiance? Had my question angered him?

"Why not?" He asked. "Someone had to take the stuff."

"So there's no federal file with those records?"

"S'not supposed to be. No paper trail, no electronic trail—not that anything electronic is working. Including most of the government, by the way. But they're not the only ones who might want gun records. Did you see "Red Dawn"?" Andrea and I shook our heads, no.

"In the movie, the Russians try to take over the western United States and the first thing they did was go for gun owners and guns, using those records to trace them." I felt a chill go down my spine.

"How do you know for sure those records got destroyed?" This time the question came from Andrea. I did not see the same suspicion on Jared's face as he answered her.

"The shops burned to the ground. Nothing left." He tipped an imaginary hat at us, and went to fill his empty coffee cup. Andrea smiled at me. "He's great, isn't he?"

"He's an arsonist and a thief!" I hissed, whispering so he wouldn't hear me.

Her face dropped. "You don't know he was the one who burned those places down."

"So he just happened to be there when they did, and was able to help himself to the goods?" I gave her a sardonic look. "Really?"

She wavered a moment, but then her face hardened. "Lighten up, Lex! He did it to protect us! I'm glad he got rid of those records." She paused, staring at me. "Aren't you?"

"I guess."

"He did us a favor. We need all the favors we can get."

This afternoon Andrea and I got a rare break from chores. Seems the adults were talking about how we kept our posts at the bedroom windows during that skirmish yesterday and thought we should be rewarded. I grabbed Butler the cat and we headed upstairs to lie down and read or do nothing. Doing nothing is a luxury. I climbed up my bunk with my Bible and journal. Andrea was resting on the bottom bunk.

"You like Jared, don't you?" I asked.

"Can you tell?"

I could hear a smile in her voice. I tried not to laugh. "Um. Yeah! You break out in a big smile every time he's around."

"He's cute, isn't he? Like in a cowboy kinda way?" Jared was tall and lanky, wore camo clothing, combat boots, and, often, an army issue cap. He didn't look anything like a cowboy. But I didn't want to hurt Andrea's feelings, so I just said, "Well…maybe if he didn't always look so sinister; like he's angry at the world."

"Everyone's angry at the world, Lex."

"But Jared looks extra angry."

"I don't think he looks angry. Just intense. He thinks a lot."

"Did he tell you that?"

"No. He doesn't have to. I can tell." I turned over, hanging my head down to get a glimpse of her beneath me.

"Blake thinks a lot, too. But he doesn't give me the creeps when he's doing it."

"Jared gives you the creeps?" She stared up at me, wide-eyed. I nodded.

"What do we know about him, anyway? When he got here he had stuff normal people don't have."

"Like what!"

"Like a new front door for the house."

"I can't believe you're complaining about that! Your door was all smashed up by Roy's gang. You said yourself; it was a constant reminder of that whole horrible episode."

"It was, but still. Where'd he get a beautiful new front door?"

Andrea shrugged. "Maybe he salvaged it from one of those burning houses. It would've been destroyed anyway, so it's good if he did."

"IF he did. And how do you know he didn't burn that house just like the gun shops?" I had to pull my head back up because it was heavy from being upside down.

"You're letting your imagination run away with you! How do you

28

know he didn't take it from his mother's house? Lots of our people dismantled things from their own houses to use for building."

"Only expendable things. Not their front doors! And his mother's house was old; she did NOT have that beautiful new door. It's an expensive door." And it was. It was made of reinforced steel but painted a deep blue-grey. It complemented the farmhouse look of our home. It also strengthened it, being made of steel. I guess I should have appreciated that Jared brought it. But at the moment, all I could think of was reasons to distrust him.

Before the pulse, Jared was mostly away, as he lived in Hawaii. His mother was a neighbor down the road with a little old house much like Mrs. Preston's, only smaller, and in need of more upkeep. If Jared was so wonderful, why hadn't he kept up his mother's house better? Mrs. Preston's son had hired help for his mother before he'd gone off to Europe on a business venture. Why hadn't Jared done that for his mother?

Andrea was silent, thinking. "You want me to ask him where he found the door?" Her voice was doubtful. Like she was hoping I'd say not to.

"My dad already did. He says he just finds these things. That he's not taking them from anyone who needs them. Like the windows, and mirrors, remember?" He'd even offered to replace our shattered hutch with a new one—but my dad told him severely that going around to gather furniture was foolhardy. Leaving the compound was always risky. No one was to do it just for the sake of getting STUFF. Only food, fuel, and necessary housing materials were worth venturing off the property for.

"You never know, Lex. So many people are gone…" I knew what she meant. Gone, as in dead. "Jared is probably taking stuff from abandoned houses."

"No kidding. That's what I mean." I couldn't see Andrea but I swear I could feel her glaring at me. Her next words confirmed it.

"Even YOU took stuff from Mrs. Preston's!"

Blake and I had gone to Mrs. Preston's to scavenge anything useful, but I did it knowing she would want us to.

"That is so totally different! She would be GLAD we took it. And we labeled her things. If her son ever returns he'll get it all back! That is nothing like looting the homes of strangers!"

I heard her let out a breath of frustration. "I'm taking a nap," she announced, in a voice that said, "conversation over." But suddenly she added, "EVERYONE else is doing it! If Jared didn't take it, someone else would have!"

"That doesn't make it right."

But she'd reminded me of Mrs. Preston, and now I felt sad. I missed the old lady. We'd buried her on the hill (which, sadly, I now think of as Burial Hill) but I've always wondered if she'd prefer to be on her own land. My dad says it's too late: he's not about to go dig her up when she didn't have a coffin, and besides, the extra work is about the last thing he needs right now. Life is work. Speaking of which, when we got to Mrs. Preston's house, we could tell other people had been there—and trashed the place. Her nice little house. I could understand hungry people looking for food; but what I don't get is why they have to destroy every place they loot. The mess really bothered me. Blake reminded me that lots of homes got burned down after being looted so leaving a mess wasn't really too bad.

But I couldn't leave it. So Blake and I cleaned it up, spending hours. We threw broken furniture on dad's cart, canning equipment, pots and pans, and some gardening tools from the shed. There was no food left, not even a ketchup packet from a fast food joint. She'd been thoroughly cleaned out. I blinked back tears once, passing the empty tray in the hallway where she used to keep chocolates. I miss Mrs. Preston. But I'm glad she's in peace.

I still treasure Butler for her sake, since he was her cat. I pet him as much as he'll let me, though he isn't the most affectionate of cats. Moppet is far more of a people-cat, but the girls like to claim her as theirs. I don't begrudge her pets their food allowances, either, which reminds me of the last reason I don't trust Jared. He said feeding the pets is only worthwhile in case we need to eat them one day!

I hope Andrea will be cautious about Jared. I don't feel any better about him.

CHAPTER SEVEN

SARAH

Old, weathered barns seem to be our lot in life. We were fortunate the one we found had hay to sleep in. Sometimes with no animals in residence, hay would be cleaned out too. But we never slept in a barn that had animals—they were usually guarded, for one thing; and we didn't know what kind of people might discover us there if we overslept and they found us. It could mean our lives.

I woke up long before dusk, but as usual Richard wanted to wait for nightfall to get moving so we stayed put, resting, and conserving our energy. I marveled as I stared out the opening at the surrounding countryside. You would never know a tornado went through yesterday. The sky was blue and cloudless, sunny and warm. The countryside looked so peaceful! If only... If it was, we wouldn't have to do our moving at night.

It used to be hard for me to rest when I didn't want to—but I fell back asleep easily until it was finally growing dark, and Richard woke me.

———————————◆———————————

We were making good time, using Richard's compass and heading steadily towards the Indiana border. Well, steadily as much as was in our power. I've learned when you're walking in woods, it's not much different than having to take roads somewhere. Meaning, as Richard says, we can't walk as the crow flies. But instead of following a winding road, we had to wind around ravines, impassable brush, and houses and fields. All while trying to stay westward. We'd learned, if Richard didn't check the compass every so often we could get surprisingly off kilter. Tonight he thought we were getting near the state border.

Fortunately, the population was sparse over here. Small towns were surrounded by hundred-acre farms—now defunct and weedy, but unpopulated. So we could avoid the towns, sticking to the edges of farmland and woods, skirting pastures as usual. Even through darkness, we saw those ever-present plumes of smoke in the distance. A large, dark plume was due west, in our path. It looked like a giant inferno as we drew closer.

When we finally reached the area, we saw an entire row of houses was burning. All these fires! Why are there so many? I could understand in winter when everyone was doing anything to stay warm, including building indoor fires which got out of control. But I don't understand why there are so many now when the weather is much warmer. Granted, it still isn't hot at night. But it's hard to believe so many fires could be started from carelessness.

It seems like there's always smoke in the sky rising from somewhere just out of view. Always plumes of smoke. Sometimes they remind me of the tornado—except they are fainter as they rise.

We walked through the night, eating one half of our rations. But we'd run out of water. Seeing a lone farmhouse with a pond in front, Richard stopped to study it. The place looked absolutely forsaken. Like so many other homes, it was probably abandoned. And yet we never knew for sure because most houses looked rundown even if they were still occupied. The lack of power mowers and other power equipment, combined with the struggle for just plain survival, meant no one kept up their property any longer.

Worse, even if it was abandoned, it could be home to opportunistic looters (I never thought of Richard and myself as such) and they could be dangerous. Or, the homeowners might be jumpy and take a shot at you just for being on their property.

Richard came to a decision. "We can fill the water bottle here."

He looked around warily, then told me to lay low while he went to the pond. I stayed behind a large bush and tried to watch but Richard's outline faded into the dark night quickly. I heard a sound and saw a man carrying a lantern emerge from the front door of the house.

"Richard!" I didn't know if he'd heard me or not. "Watch out!" In his other hand the man held something I couldn't identify but I was sure it was a weapon. And then I saw Richard coming into view carrying the bottle, trying to cap it as he hurried towards me.

Behind us the man yelled. "Get out of here! We got nothing here!"

"We were just getting water!" Richard yelled back. When he reached me we turned to leave, automatically taking the road though we usually avoided them because it was clear and easier to manage. We'd gone maybe five feet when the man was there, on top of us. He'd come out through an opening in a hedge. He had a rifle in his hands and a ferocious look on a weathered, wizened face.

We froze. Richard grasped my arm painfully, shoving me behind him. The man, only a foot away now, held up the lantern, searching Richard's face. Then he stretched around Richard to get a good look at me. I held my breath, thinking he was surely going to do us harm.

Richard held up our water bottle. "I was just filling this. That's all we wanted."

Again the piercing, suspicious look was fastened on my brother. Then he spoke. His words were gruff and ominous. "You can't drink that water."

Richard and I were mute. Was he saying he wouldn't let us keep the measly bottle of water?

"You'll get sick," he added.

Richard replied, "We can treat it."

"How?"

"Purification pills. I've got a few left, hopefully enough to get us to Indiana."

"Why? What's in Indiana?"

"Our aunt. She has a farm. We have nothing left here."

He eyed Richard again, thinking, as if trying to decide whether to speak. Finally he said, "How d'ya know your aunt's still there?"

"We don't."

Now he shook his head, muttering something to himself.

"I'm Richard Weaver and this is my sister Sarah—"

"Don't tell me your names! I don't-want-to-know-your-names!" In a strident tone.

He looked regretful after saying that, shook his head some more and then said, "If you need water, I have some. It's about all I have, but I can give you some before you go."

Richard and I looked at each other. This was the first time anyone had shown us kindness since we'd been homeless. From the time we left our town, no one had given us anything, not even spoken nicely to us!

We followed him towards the house but Richard whispered in my ear behind the man's back, "Stay alert." I noticed he'd taken his pistol and put it in his front coat pocket. As we walked, the old man stopped every few feet to study the ground, holding out his lamp with a look of deep perplexity. Often he'd move us to one side or the other before continuing on. He gave no explanation but we followed his lead, especially after he said, "Follow my footsteps EXACTLY—or you'll live to regret it."

As we walked, Richard asked, "Where do you get your water?"

"Stop! This way!" he barked suddenly, pulling Richard's arm hard, moving him sharply to the right, and then watching for me to follow. As we moved on, he said heavily, answering my brother, "From a well. I have a hand pump. It's old-fashioned." He actually turned and smiled at those last words. "We old-timers have a good amount of information you young people have no clue about. We know how to survive."

As we entered the house, he stopped to face us. "That is, if we're left to do it. People keep trying to kill us, though. Don't they, Martha?"

"They do," said a voice, to our left. And there, on her feet in a little side room stood "Martha," the littlest old lady you can imagine. She had on a nightgown and robe, and an old-fashioned sleeping cap from which white curls stuck out on the sides. She would have been cute, like anyone's grandma—except she glowered in our direction and held a shotgun—pointed right at us.

Chapter Eight

LEXIE

This morning we woke to a brand new dark plume in the sky, to our south. A big one. I tried to ignore it and headed to the barn to tend the animals. While I was there, Jared and another of our newer residents, a young black father by name of Mr. Washington, came in to get Molly the mule. Molly came to us with Mr. Washington and his eleven year old daughter. I felt queasy as soon as I saw them saddling her because I knew why they were doing it.

"How's your horse?" Mr. Washington asked, pulling me from my musings. I'd been shoveling hay into her stall, not realizing I'd stopped working to watch them. "What's 'er name again?"

"Rhema."

"That's an unusual name."

"It means Word of God." I watched for his reaction. He nodded, but I figured he was being noncommittal, not wanting to show he thought it was a weird name. I guessed he was trying to distract me from their grisly business. See, there is so much work to be done on the compound without any power tools that we can't bury the dead marauders—the fours. There is simply too much sheer manpower necessary. So I knew they were gonna put the bodies on Molly's back, take her for a long walk, and dump them in a ditch somewhere off our property. They'd throw brush and leaves over them, and then return. I understood—it needed to be done. I just hated thinking about it.

While Jared readied the mule, Mr. Washington came over to pet Rhema. I took a good look at him—smooth, light mocha skin, short black hair—he was younger than my folks, and wore jeans and cowboy boots. He and Andrea's mom are good friends. Andrea resents him; she says her mother flirts with him. He's a widower, and Andrea's mom is a widow, so they have that in common. But Andrea's dad's only been gone a few months, so their friendship upsets her. She really loses it when she sees them near each other. Anyways, it's great having a mule, and Washington's daughter, Evangeline, plays very patiently with both sets of twins. They are a good addition to our community.

Jared finished saddling up Molly and nodded darkly at me as they left.

After they'd gone I thought about the four kinds of people in the world now. I never got to explain about this in my journal, so here goes: The first type, the number ones, are people like us. Survivors who have made it this far by living off their ingenuity and stored supplies. Most are homestead preppers like we are; or urban preppers—meaning they didn't have land or livestock, but they stored a lot of provisions and it's kept them alive. Urban preppers are valuable to a compound because they usually know how to garden—even if they've only done it on a balcony—and how to purify water; many of them are trained to protect themselves with a firearm, too.

Most of the people in our compound are number ones who were running low on resources and needed a place to live where they could work and eke out a living—but the main thing about number ones is that we mean no harm to others and only fight to defend ourselves. That is important! We deplore the violence of our attackers and we deplore having to be violent in return! I never told my folks this (not even Andrea. Blake alone knows about it), but I got sick after we fought off Roy and his gang. I still feel sick about shooting at people. I worry that I'm weaker than the others, but really, there is something very wrong about teenagers having to fight for our lives.

Anyways, number ones can be self-reliant with the proper tools. But if we lost our home and property, we'd be about as helpless as the unprepared. Some number ones are true survivalists—they're like preppers on steroids!—and can live off the land without a home or property of their own. But that isn't us. They're often loners and keep to themselves, which is good because Dad says if they're not friendly, they could be as dangerous as number fours—maybe worse, because they're often well-trained in combat.

So anyways, then there are the number twos. These are folks who have survived the first wave of death, but just barely. (Blake once called it "mass extinction," but I asked him not to say that, because it sounds so horrible.) Number twos had enough supplies or managed to find enough to survive but are at the end of themselves. They can't make it through another winter without help. Unlike number ones, they are clueless about methods of survival; they don't know gardening or food preservation, and they have no necessary skills for the compound.

There aren't a lot of number twos, simply because most people without food storage or survival skills didn't make it through the winter. The ones that survived are not usually a threat, but they can lead number threes or fours to us. But mostly they're just regular people who are scared. They roam in pairs or small groups, wearing backpacks and looking like hikers who've been on the trail too long. They come in all kinds of weather, morning or night. They see the flickering light of our oil lamps, or smell our grill fire, or see someone heading from the barn to the house and they come.

We sometimes give small amounts of food or water to such people, but we can't take them in. I hate to be around when my dad or someone else turns them away. It's heartbreaking! But I know the reason, I know it's necessary. Because if we let them join us, we'd deplete our stores and soon we would be in no better shape than they are. Our only option for long-term survival is to follow FARMSEC (farmstead security) rules, which says we can't open our doors to these people.

Everyone in the compound gets instruction in FARMSEC, from the youngest to the oldest. (It's a play on words from OPSEC, a military term meaning Operational Security. Survivalists and preppers took the term for themselves, so that OPSEC means any type of security measure taken to protect one's home or compound, or farm—you get the idea.) Anyways, FARMSEC means border security so we can keep operating; keep milking, keep growing chicks and kits (baby rabbits), and keep up a survival garden. We have to be our own little army. We are the military inside our compound and any stranger—no matter how innocuous they may look—is a civilian. And civilians are automatically suspect. I hate to see people this way—as immediate needs for threat assessment. But that's what many people are—a threat.

Most number twos would starve before killing another human being, no matter how desperate and destitute they are. I wish we could help every single one of those people. I have to accept that we can't.

If a number two approaches the farm, a single warning shot from a lookout will turn them away. Sometimes that isn't enough. Then we know they aren't a number two at all. They're either a number three or four.

Number threes are a bigger threat than number twos, a more insidious threat, because like Roy the bus driver, they look normal.

They act innocent, like they're a number two, a miraculous survivor who just happened to make it this far. They approach us with their hands up (so we can't shoot; they count on us not being heartless, and we're not); but when we turn them away, they retreat only far enough to be out of sight. We've learned they'll wait for an opportunity to take something, to sneak up on us. Sometimes they creep up behind the brush line and then charge the chicken coop or make a dash for the barn.

Number threes aren't necessarily willing to kill us for what we've got, but they're more than willing to relieve us of some of it. Sometimes they will open fire. Most of them don't want it to come to that. They aren't well organized, and they don't want a full-scale battle; they're looking for the easy targets, and often when they realize we're not one, they go away.

But then, there are the number fours. These are the most dangerous, because they're reckless, ruthless, and vicious. They don't come alone. Like Roy and his gang, they're organized. They've got leaders and followers and they're armed and ready for battle. Other than the foreign troops we hear about, I fear them the most. They have no moral compass, and the only life they respect is their own. They are the ones who stole Kasha, our dog—probably for food. They are the main reason we maintain FARMSEC. Why we continue to have target practice, and security drills, and other things; the reason Dad painstakingly removes lead casings from old wiring and pipes and melts it into new bullets.

I still feel bad for people who need help. But it's hard to feel bad when some of them just want you dead.

I was almost done with my chores. When I'd emptied the chicken manure into the garden, glad for the spring air, I remembered Dad's warning that all types of people would keep coming until next winter set in. The tricky thing was every so often we might get someone (or a family) who would be an asset to have with us. For instance, take our infirmary. It's a tent, nothing like a true infirmary as far as supplies go, but we have a D.O., Mr. Clepps, who came looking for handouts. A D.O. is just like an M.D., so he stays. (The other day we picked up an obstetrical nurse and her husband. But I'll write about that later.)

All our families brought valuable supplies or skills. Andrea's didn't, but it turned out she is a sure-shot; she even saved my dad's life. We have a woodworker, an ex-timber guy who is invaluable when it comes

38

to downing trees for timber, and Mrs. Schuman, who can sew clothing by hand. She brought fabrics—lots of them. All the skilled people we get are Godsends.

Even Blake's family, though they are probably the closest friends my parents have (and have known each other for ages) brought their own homesteading skills and tools and animals and know-how. Being fellow Christians didn't hurt, either. We have Bible studies every week again now, and on many mornings we meet for devotions and praise while breakfast is being prepared.

I really appreciate Bible Study even though I'm not always in the mood for it. Questions arise for me when I'm reading my Bible and, while commentaries help, study is the perfect place to air my questions. And I do. I'm not taking anything for granted. I'm not a Christian just because my parents are. I'm a Christian because I've felt the presence of God, and I've heard his voice, and I know he's real. In some ways, I think I'm closer to God now than I used to be. Devotions and group prayer used to be sporadic in my family. Not anymore.

Some people think Christians shouldn't defend themselves; that we should just give up our stuff to those who want it. But there is a time for everything—"a time for war and a time for peace." Like it or not, it is a time for war. (Even Jesus told his disciples once, "If you don't have a sword, sell your cloak and buy one." That's Luke 22:36. There is a place for self-defense in the Christian's life.)

Anyways, as I thought about this stuff, I realized we have nothing less than a new class system in America right now. It's a threat assessment system, but it works pretty much like a class system if you ask me. The fours are the lowest class—the ones we don't bury.

———————————————◆———————————————

After my chores were done, I ran into Blake in the kitchen as I took out school supplies. Andrea would be bringing the children in soon, and I had to get their snack ready, too.

"Council meeting, tonight."

I met his gaze. "Okay. Are you going?" We teens didn't always attend the council meetings; sometimes it was all about administrative stuff that we didn't need to be in on. Other times we would be ordered to attend, as when FARMSEC rules would be gone over.

"Yeah. Did you hear?"

"About what?"

"A radio contact from Indiana reported seeing soldiers. A military unit that wasn't American. I guess we'll hear more about it tonight."

"Okay." I waited, hoping he would say something more personal. Blake and I have an understanding—we are boyfriend and girlfriend, see, but his idea of a relationship isn't my idea of one. He thinks we can get by with eyes meeting, holding hands now and then, and sitting together at events like the Council meetings. I dunno, maybe it's because I'm a girl, but I want a little more than that from him. Even though his family is now living on our property, we don't spend a lot of time together. Like everyone else on the compound, Blake and I both have schedules we have to follow.

Blake is one of our lookouts, too, which means he is away, up on the hill or at another post on one of our borders, keeping watch most days, on twelve-hour shifts. When he's up there on duty, I sometimes manage to finagle my dad's walkie-talkie from him and I call Blake. But we both know during those conversations that every other lookout can hear us, as well as people at the house. We have a lot of connected walkie-talkies. We can't say anything that means anything.

What I really want to do is accompany Blake on lookout duty. My dad never lets me. He thinks we'll talk or start giving each other moonie eyes or something and totally forget about keeping watch. But that's not it at all! I just want to be near Blake. We're gonna be married one day, so we ought to learn to work together. Why can't my dad trust me to do the job if I'm with Blake? It isn't fair.

CHAPTER NINE

ANDREA

"Hey." I was approaching Jared from behind while he worked on the side of the small cabin he was building for himself and his mother. Jared hadn't wanted to build; he'd asked if he and his mother could stay at the farmhouse like me and my family. But Mr. Martin wouldn't let him. I didn't know why, except the Martins have already taken in one extra family—us! And I'm sure glad they did. If they had already formed the compound before we got here, I don't think we would ever have been allowed to stay. We didn't bring any useful skills that we knew of.

It turned out I'm a good shooter—one of the best we've got—but even I didn't know I would be. I'd never shot a real gun before I got here, so I was just as surprised as anyone when it turned out I was good at it.

So anyway, it seemed for awhile that I wouldn't have anyone special. I mean, other than my family. Lexie had Blake—I was jealous, but I was trying to accept it. At least we were alive and well fed. Then other families started to arrive. But it was uncanny how none of them had teenagers, particularly of the male persuasion. Very disappointing. We had a few older couples, two more young families, and then…Jared arrived. He's older than me—I think he's upper twenties, though I haven't worked up the nerve to ask him yet.

Today I brought him lunch. We send out a call on the walkie-talkies when lunch is ready. Everyone is supposed to come to the house if they want to eat. Except the lookouts; they're supposed to stay put and wait for someone to bring them their meals. But Jared hadn't come in like everyone else. I took a look outside and saw him at work so I grabbed a plate of grub and headed out. I figured it was a good time to get his attention.

He glanced over at me, saw I was holding food, and nodded.
"Thanks."
"No problem. You even have milk today." I smiled. Most people

41

were happy to get milk. The Martins' one cow only gives about four gallons of milk a day and it goes fast. Some days no one gets milk except the toddlers, because Mrs. Martin uses it for cheese or butter. Today I'd had to hustle to get a cup of it for Jared. He didn't seem to care.

"You can just leave it there." He nodded towards a workbench. "I'll bring in the dishes when I'm through."

"That's okay. I'll wait." He glanced over at me again, I think he was surprised. I gave him a big smile. I wanted to make it very clear to Jared that I was interested in him. His gaze lingered on mine for a moment.

I think he got the idea.

CHAPTER TEN

SARAH

"They're not after anything! They just wanted water," the old man cried, as we looked down the barrel of Martha's formidable gun.

I took a deep breath, trying to steady my hammering heart. One thing after another! We can never relax or rest! When will it end! What particularly bothered me at that moment was how disparate the situation was—these two old folks looked like the safe, kindly types. I felt so distressed at finding ourselves in front of a gun at their hands instead, that without knowing I was going to, I burst into tears.

Oddly, it turned out to be the best thing I could do. Martha hurriedly put down her weapon and came towards me, utterly transformed, with a look of sheer maternal concern.

"You poor thing!" she cried, giving my brother a quelling look as though he were to blame for my condition. Putting her arm around me, she led me forward down a hallway that led to a kitchen.

I felt something jarring loose inside me, ripping at the hardness I'd erected around myself in order to survive—in order to live the way we did, as scavengers and homeless outcasts. There was something about having an older woman caring for me that went straight to my heart of hearts. I felt a wave of longing for my mother and fresh sobs came out of me, wracking my body like a dry cough. This is it, I thought. I'm finally losing my mind!

I was ashamed, and wouldn't meet Richard's gaze even after Martha shooed me to the table, saying, "You sit right here while I get you some tea!" She glanced at Richard, who had followed us, along with the man, who I figured was her husband. "Oh, you too, sit down! Both of you take your coats off. We've a good hot stove going in here, as you can see."

And they did. It was an amazing sight, too! The stove looked like a relic from an earlier century. In fact, as Martha went around lighting oil lamps, I saw the whole kitchen looked like a scene from another era. I dried my eyes (not very wet, after all. I was always somewhat dehydrated) sniffed, and finally got hold of myself.

We were in a large, old-fashioned room, not a granite counter-top or tiled floor in sight. The black stove was antique and immense, wider than tall, and with a gigantic hood above it which was almost as large as the stove itself. A black kettle graced the broad stove-top, roomy enough to hold numerous pots. The front had two oven doors with ornate steel handles, some lower compartments (which I realized afterwards were for loading fuel) and an additional black shelf over it, holding pottery, utensils and baking implements.

As if that wasn't enough, to the right of our table against a wall was a smaller stove, with a second kettle upon it, and a lidded black enamel pot. The ironwork—or maybe it was steel--was more ornate than on the large stove. It was really pretty; with clawed steel feet, and two oven doors, both of which had ornate metalwork décor on them and a long, metal handle for opening.

Past the stove was a worktable; and then, against an adjacent wall, a long, steel double sink filled with soaking clothes. Between the sink and the stove stood a wooden drying rack, upon which hung some wet towels. Copper pans and metal pots of all sizes hung from pegged shelves on the walls. Pitchers and canisters and such lined the shelves. I found myself staring. When I finally looked back at Martha, she smiled at me, enjoying my amazement.

Richard let out a low whistle. "This is…really something," he said. I met his eyes and smiled.

The old man pulled out a chair and sat across from us. "That it is," he said, glancing around the room with pride in his eyes. "Martha and I used to own an antique shop. We collected lots of things over the years. Our plan was to open a museum shop, with a working old-fashioned kitchen. But we liked the older things so much we started designing our own kitchen to use them. Only the Man upstairs," he said, chuckling, and looking at his wife, "could have known we'd need this stuff to survive!"

I found it amazing that this warm, sweet old man was the same person who had surveyed us with such hostility and suspicion only minutes earlier.

"The good Lord takes care of his own," added Martha, confidently.

I noticed Richard blanch; if I knew my brother, he wanted to disagree with Martha just then, but didn't dare insult our hosts. I was glad he didn't. I wanted to stay on their good side. Richard shook his head, and I silently pleaded with him with my eyes, afraid he'd aggravate them. But all he said was, "How do you manage to keep looters away? I know you have firearms, but there's just the two of you..."

"We have a son with a wife and children," said Martha. "When they get here, they'll help us protect the place."

The man nodded.

"But you've survived this long without them; how?"

Martha and her husband exchanged a look. "Oh, may as well tell them," she gushed, while taking a steaming kettle and beginning to fill the tea cups sitting before us. She used a potholder to manage the hot handle. I watched, almost mesmerized. It was such an ordinary action— pouring tea. But I felt suddenly outside of myself, like this couldn't be real. It was too ordinary. It felt incredible, like a picture in a storybook. But the hot steam caressed my cold face, and I smelled the tea. You may think tea has no aroma when it's poured—it does. To a starving girl, it smells just about like heaven.

The old man sat forward, clasping his hands together on the table. A bit sheepishly he admitted, "The yard is dotted with mines. They're homemade, mind you—a trick I learned in the war. But they work."

"Boy, howdy, do they work!" chimed in Martha, nodding. She now had a tray with cream and sugar on it—and cookies—which she set down before us. Looking at the tray, I had the same sense of unreality. It threw our recent existence into such stark relief—the desperation, the dirt, the anguish—and now this ordinary tea tray! For a few moments I could only stare, doing my utmost not to burst into tears again.

Richard had no such compunction and grabbed two cookies. I could tell he wanted to wolf them down but forced himself to be polite.

I looked up to see Martha watching my face, and quickly tried to gain control of my features. She reached out an arm and softly patted my hand. "It's okay," she said, softly. "You eat all you want."

"Martha, they don't want cookies," the old man said, although Richard's hand was already out for seconds. "Whip us all up some breakfast! Some good eggs and bacon!"

Richard and I stared at each other. I think we both felt we'd died and gone to heaven. My only worry was, how long would they let us stay?

CHAPTER ELEVEN

LEXIE

So about that council meeting. Tonight's wasn't mandatory for us teens, but I knew Blake was going. Something about seeing that ominous dark plume in the sky made me want to be with everyone else anyways, and I wanted the scoop about that sighting of soldiers.

I felt cozy sitting next to Blake. Sometimes I have to put Bach out of the room because he likes to jump up beside me on the sofa and doesn't take kindly to Blake taking his spot. Tonight the dogs were outside. Anyways, Blake usually takes my hand right away but tonight he didn't. I waited and waited for him to do it. When he finally did, I gave him a look that said, what took you so long? It was after that first time we kissed (right in the chicken yard, I love that memory) that I've known we'll get married someday. But I do wonder at times if Blake has the same idea.

I'll be seventeen in two months. I can handle being married. We can't go to college. We can't even finish high school. I love him. (I think.) We may as well get married. Except Blake is still shy at times and doesn't seem to be in a hurry. If we ever talk about it I'll point out that our lives are dangerous—we don't have all the time in the world. We ought to get married while we can. But it may be, by the time he gets around to asking me I'll be thinking the same thing I did tonight: What took you so long!

Anyways, back to the council. All the adults are council members but if there's a disagreement only the leadership team can vote. My mom and dad, the Buchanans, the Wassermans and an ex-cop by name of Mr. Simmons are the leadership team. Tonight, they did most of the talking.

First they discussed the most recent sightings of foreign troops and the possibility of our facing an attack. It was agreed that tomorrow all building will cease so the men can block the driveway that leads to the road. We'll put fallen tree trunks and brush and garbage across the whole front of the property, hoping to make it look abandoned. Since we're a quarter mile off the road, you can see the house through the trees only in winter, when leaves are bare. The spring growth has started, but it isn't enough cover yet. They went on to emphasize the importance of drills and practice and protocol to follow during an attack. I felt my hands grow clammy and had to pull one from Blake's to wipe it off. I dread such an attack.

Next up was about creating a firebreak inside the compound, a dead zone perimeter with nothing flammable. Almost every day we see plumes of smoke rising from somewhere on the horizon across the fields, or over the trees in the distance. Sometimes, like the new one today, they're close, within five miles. A few of our men have ridden out to investigate them in the past and found it's nearly always houses burning. What's causing the fires? It doesn't seem likely that so many homes would burn by accident.

We fear it's only a matter of time until whoever is causing these fires reaches us. Our farm has a large perimeter—126 acres—but even if we just tried to protect the compound area, it would be fairly impossible. And anyways, the only way to have a good dead zone would be to start our own controlled burn. My dad was afraid we'd burn the house and cabins down if we tried.

"It's too risky," he said. "We've only got manpower and a well for water to put out any wandering flames."

I wish people didn't have to be so destructive! Isn't it bad enough they're looting and oftentimes killing? But it seems like they're not happy unless they burn things, too.

So there were three theories about the cause of the fires, and I didn't like any of them. The first is, people were still trying to heat their homes using wrong methods. That theory was least popular because if anyone was going to burn their house down by heating, it should have happened during the winter. The second was, marauders are torching homes after they loot them; either to destroy evidence, or just because they're "mean and loathsome," in my mother's words. That was the most popular opinion. The third was, those foreign troops are doing it—the ones we keep hearing about.

Mr. Simmons says it's guerrilla warfare, and they'll do whatever they can to lower our morale, to make us cower. My hatred for these foreign soldiers grows by leaps and bounds though I've not laid eyes on one of them yet. Are they burning people right out of their homes? Are they killing these people? The looters could be doing that, too. All three theories made me nervous.

Simmons insisted that to be safe, we shouldn't allow any strangers on the compound under any circumstances. "We could put warning signs out front, so they know," he said.

"Warning signs are welcome signs to looters or military," said Jared. "We need to keep a low profile and try to go unnoticed." He paused. "If anyone comes through all that brush and debris, they're looking for trouble. We shoot on sight."

My mom had been knitting while she listened to the talk, but she looked up and added, "Not everyone who has survived this long is dangerous. We can't just shoot anyone who approaches us."

Jared gazed at her, unconvinced. "Only ruthless people are still alive."

"You don't know that," my mother insisted, in her soft, southern twang. "We're still alive. We have not lost our humanity or compassion. If you can't live with that, Jared, you'd best pack up and go." Those were awesome words coming from my mother! Jared said nothing, but I don't doubt he would shoot on sight.

The conversation turned to talk about those survivors. How many were there? My dad said roughly three million households in the U.S. were like us, prepared for a disaster, and some even ready to face life comfortably without electricity. I thought three million prepared households sounded like a lot—until Blake added that 3 million prepared meant 350 million weren't.

Blake perked up at this point because he's a numbers guy. He said that of the 350 million who weren't prepared, 71% were already casualties. (I don't know how Blake arrives at his figures. I mean, why not 75%, right? But he said 71%, which means he used a calculation to reach that figure. So we believed him.)

"That means roughly 270 million people have died," he said. I started blinking hard to get rid of tears that surprised me by wanting to surface just then. 270 million! Could it be true? God forbid! I can hardly wrap my mind around that.

"That makes the EMP the deadliest thing to hit mankind since Noah's flood," Blake continued. "Unless people have received help we don't know about, in all of history, no plague, pestilence, war, or natural disaster has killed as many people, except the Flood—because it was global."

Jared actually snorted. "I'm sure there were less people alive at the time of the Flood."

That was precisely the wrong thing to say to Blake. I happen to know he's studied that very thing, the world population at the time of the Flood. Sure enough, Blake said, "That's a common myth. Based on numerical values in Genesis, including lifespan, lengths of generations, and childbearing ages, (remember, people lived up to 900 years before the Flood), the numbers are closer to a world population of anywhere from 7-10 billion." Jared didn't reply, just stared blankly, so Blake went on, "Anyway, this means about 80 million people who are alive right now are struggling to survive. Some of them are number twos or threes, but some of them are going to be number fours."

"80 million people!" My mom cried, softly. "Thank the Lord for survivors! But now you need to tell us how many of them are gonna come by our neck of the woods."

Blake answered with a sad smile. "That would be impossible to know. Although I could—"

"Never mind, son," my dad said.

"Some of them will go into government camps," a newer member of our compound, Mr. Philpot, said. He was grey-haired and probably around my dad's age.

"I haven't heard of any sightings of such camps," said dad. "Some speculation, but that's it."

"We saw one." An immediate hush fell over the room. Mr. Philpot and his wife had come to us on bicycles carrying heavy packs, both on the bikes and their backs. Mrs. Philpot is the nurse I mentioned earlier. (As soon as we learned her profession, she and her husband were shoe-ins to the compound.) They proceeded to describe a camp surrounded by barbed wire fencing. They'd witnessed a military open-backed truck bringing in a load of people. Mr. Philpot said it looked like they'd been herded up like cattle.

"Did you see a sign? Did it say it was a FEMA camp?"

They looked at each other, thinking. "Not sure," said Mr. Philpot.

"If it's not FEMA, who would it be?" asked young Mrs. Wasserman. "A relief organization?"

"Relief organizations don't get military trucks and soldiers," said Jared.

"So it could be terrorists, or any enemy of our country," said my dad.

"Meaning, it's either a refugee camp—" said Jared, and then he smirked. "Or a prison camp. Maybe it's both." I think we all felt a chill at his words.

I piped up. "Yeah; otherwise what's with the barbed wire? Are they worried about people trying to get in—or out?"

Blake nodded at me. "Yeah."

"Hopefully, they'll round up the loose cannons—the number fours," Jared interjected. "Every four they round up is one less we'll have to deal with."

"But you don't know they forced those people to go, right?" Mrs. Buchanan asked the Philpots.

"We don't know for sure," Mrs. Philpot said, while her husband nodded his agreement. "But they didn't look happy. We stayed out of sight until they closed the gate."

"Did you see the people driving the truck?" asked Mr. Buchanan. "Did they look like U.S. soldiers?"

Mrs. Philpot frowned. "They were military; wore green fatigues. We couldn't tell what country."

———————◆———————

Later I thought about those camps. Many people wouldn't survive another winter without them, so I guess they have their place.

I told that to my dad and he said, "Sure they have a place, for people who need them. Our fear is that they won't be as tolerant of us as we are of them. No one knows if our freedom to live on our own has been lost."

The idea of losing our freedom makes me angry. I think back to when everything still worked: Why didn't the government warn people to prepare? They even called people like us (preppers and Conservatives) a threat to society! And yet those who didn't prepare are now the threat—or an excuse for the government to force us into camps! My dad says bad governments purposely make people helpless and dependent. It gives them justification to run their lives and control everything.

50

CHAPTER TWELVE

ANDREA

Horrible day. Every time I saw my mom near that man, Mr. Washington, I tried to work my way over to them so I could hear what they were talking about. I am INSANELY upset about the way she flirts with him. I just know she wants a relationship with this guy and I am determined to be a monkey wrench.

My dad was not Mr. Wonderful, I'll be the first to admit that; but she has no right to get serious with another man, no matter how bad my father was! He's only been gone a few months! I once read that in the old days they used to have set periods for how long a widow should grieve and wear black. I wish we had a set period for grieving. You would hardly know my mother has lost her husband, judging by how she acts. It makes me sick!

The other day she got really mad at me and told me to lay off. I had sidled over to where they were even though I was supposed to be with the children at the play area. (I could still see them.) Mr. Washington was leveling a place for a small cabin for him and Evangeline. So, I saw my mother talking and laughing with him, and my blood started to boil. I couldn't stand it. So I went over and just stood there. I was letting my mother know, I AM SEEING THIS. I AM NOT OBLIVIOUS TO WHAT YOU'RE DOING.

Later I saw her in the kitchen. "Stop spying on me," she said.

"I'm not spying."

"I'm not blind, Andrea! What are you trying to do, anyway? Mr. Washington jokes that you're my mother, instead of the other way around."

"Oh, he would!" I said, bitterly.

"What does that mean?"

I stared at her. "It means I don't like him, and you're too friendly with him."

"Too friendly? How can someone be too friendly?"

I heard Lexie calling me then; it was time for our riding lesson. "I think you know what I mean!" I glared at my mom and left. Just being friendly, really! Friendly enough to make him my step-father, I bet!

———————◆———————

So I was in the kitchen this afternoon, and Washington came in for a cup of water. Everyone's allowed two cups a day from the filter here at the house if they're helping with the building; after that, they have to boil their own water or use their own filters. I felt like telling him he'd already used up his quota, though I really had no idea. He smiled at me—a big smile. (Now that he knows I'm Tiffany's daughter, he is extra friendly to me.) Happily, I had just picked up baby Lily so I showed her off to him, emphasizing how young she is. The message, in case he's an idiot, is that my mom has just had ANOTHER MAN'S BABY.

I want to say, "Wake up! She's not really available like she pretends to be. Can't you see you're wasting your time?" That's what I want to scream at him, but sadly I don't think he is wasting his time. I just wish he was. I wish my mom could at least pretend she loved my father. I used to think my dad was pretty awful, but when I see how violent people are now because they're hungry—well, my dad might have considered selling me to that creepy Mr. Herman, but at least I know he wouldn't have killed anyone to feed us. He got desperate, but it didn't make him a murderer. So I wish my mother could act like we had a real family. I'm embarrassed by her behavior. She may as well announce that our family was a sham.

Tonight every time I looked at her, we exchanged angry looks. If she's really only friends with Washington, why is she angry? I'm not stupid! It's easy to see she's guilty and she knows it.

Tomorrow I have kitchen duty and I bet I'll have to bring water out to the workmen. That includes Washington. I'm not going to fill his water bottle all the way. It sounds petty but I really resent that man. He'll probably give me one of his stupid, big smiles, too. I will not smile in return. Lexie says I have a wicked "evil eye" at times. That is what Washington will get from me.

Lexie will have childcare tomorrow and Jared, I believe, is going out on a reconnaissance mission with Blake and a few other men. They want to find out what's burning and, as always, hunt out more fuel. Just once I would like to go with them. I am so tired of this compound! If I close my eyes, I can pretend to be at a mall shopping, having fun. Sometimes I picture myself at school, with friends in the cafeteria—even sitting at a desk during math class—which I used to hate. I'd give anything to have one normal day of school again. My old life. Our house and my own bedroom! Even my dad. I think I'd be kinder to Dad now than I used to be. He was grumpy and preoccupied a lot, but he wasn't a bad man, not at heart. I wish I could have seen that.

Got to stop here. If I go on like this, I'll be an emotional wreck. Mrs. Martin says we should use our imaginations to picture a bright future—I don't seem able to do that.

———◆———

When I went to give out water, my mom was actually working with Washington—she was helping lift logs, of all things, when I came around. She saw I refused to smile back at him and asked me about it later. That's how it started. That's all it was. And now it's turned into one of the worst days of my life.

"Why can't you be civil to Mr. Washington?" she asked, finding me in the kitchen doing cleanup after the children's snack time. I didn't even look up.

"Because I don't like him."

"Why not?" She waited for an answer, but there was nothing I wanted to say.

"Why not, Andrea? Because he's my friend? Is it so terrible if I have a friend?"

I looked at her. I have to say, my mom looked good. She was never big on makeup so not wearing any didn't detract from her fine-featured prettiness. And the extra work seems to have agreed with her. She looked healthy and yes, easily able to attract a man.

"Is he really just a friend, Mom?" I knew my voice was laced with bitterness.

She stared at me a moment, the color rising in her face. "First of all, he is just a friend. Secondly, if he wasn't, it's none of your business. Thirdly--"

"None of my business? You're my mother! Of course it's my

business!"

"Don't raise your voice to me, young lady!"

"Then don't talk to me about Mr. Washington. It seems to me if you had any respect for Dad you wouldn't be so friendly with him. Or any man."

She put her hands on her hips. "This has nothing to do with your father!"

I turned on her. "Yeah, Mom—that's just it! Why doesn't it have anything to do with him? Why don't you have the decency to wait longer before getting cozy with some guy?" I felt bad as soon as the words left my mouth but I'd said them and I couldn't take them back. My mother was glowering at me.

In a way, I was glad I'd said them. It was the truth. She ought to have been—she ought to have been MOURNING.

She took a deep breath. "You know your father and I were not on good terms, not for a long time."

"You were on good enough terms to wait longer before starting a new relationship! You were married!"

"Our marriage was struggling for a long time, you know that," she said, anger causing her voice to shake.

"Yeah—but you were still married. And you got along good enough to have Lily!" That, I felt, was my trump card. My baby sister. She was evidence the marriage hadn't gone totally to the dogs, that there had been recent intimacy, enough to have a child. I planned on showing Lily to Mr. Washington whenever possible, making sure I'd emphasize she was only six and a half months old. She was indisputable proof that my parents had loved each other, at least some of the time.

What my mother said next devastated me. I never saw it coming, never had the least suspicion.

"I'm glad you brought that up," my mom said, not sounding glad in the least. Tears brimmed in her eyes. "Lily is not your father's child." She opened her mouth to say more but shut it, waiting. I stared at her in shock.

She nodded. "She's your half-sister."

"I don't believe you."

"Andrea! Why would I make that up? Think about it! She's the only person in the family with blonde hair and blue eyes! Your father and I were not on good terms since the twins were born!"

54

I stared at her, feeling such rage it scared me. For a minute I didn't know what to do or say, but inside I was reeling. I guess it wasn't that big a deal, I don't know, but it felt like a big deal. I felt like something inside me died.

"Who's the father?" My voice was low, controlled, but inside I wanted to scream and lose my temper. And I hated my mother at that moment.

"Lars."

I gripped the edge of the sink. "Your trainer? That is pathetic!" I wanted to say, YOU are pathetic!

"No wonder you weren't on good terms! You were an awful wife!" I stormed off. I was so mad I could hardly see where I was going but I headed upstairs, hoping I might find the bedroom empty. Lexie and I both sometimes brought the kids up there because children need diversity. Going outside is risky, so we try to move around the house with them. Lexie was just leading the kids out of our room and she nearly bumped into me. She carried Lily, and had the other kids in tow. She looked like a day care teacher.

"Hey," she said.

I couldn't talk yet but I stared at Lily. She wasn't my father's child! She was only my half-sister! Suddenly the miracle of her amazingly blond hair wasn't a miracle—it was a sad travesty. It was blond because of LARS!

"You okay?" Lexie could always read my face. Neither of us was much good at hiding our emotions.

"No. I'll tell you later." But I wasn't sure if I would ever talk about it. I was ashamed of my mother.

"Okay." She hesitated, studying me. "You sure?"

I nodded. Lily reached out her little arms for me, whimpering, so Lexie handed her over. As I took her, a couple of tears escaped and ran down my face.

"What happened?" Lexie's whispered question sounded so caring, it weakened my resolve not to talk. I wished I could tell her what I'd just learned but with both sets of twins there, I didn't dare. Both our family and the Martins have twins, which is actually how Lexie and I became friends—at a Twins' Club meeting that our moms had dragged us to. When we recognized each other from school, even though we never talked at school, we became friends at that meeting. It was a God-thing, as Mr. Martin would say.

Aiden held up a Lego car he'd built. "Look, Andi! Like my car?" His little face beamed with pride, but seeing my expression, his eyes widened. "Whats'a matter, Andi?"

I brushed away tears. "Nothing. I'm okay."

"Is it your turn to watch us?" asked Laura, looking up at me wide-eyed.

Lexie said, "If you want to switch, I'll take over kitchen and you can sit with the kids."

Babysitting seemed more appealing to me than doing anything near my mother, who was also assigned to kitchen, so I nodded.

Laura exclaimed, "Yay! Lexie wouldn't play with us today, because she was holding the baby. Will you play with us?"

"Sure." This elicited cheers from all the kids. Lainie patted my arm. "It's okay," she said, her little eyes filled with compassion. "We'll play whatever game you want, and you'll get happier." She smiled up at me, revealing a missing front tooth. For the girls, getting to choose the game of the moment was the ultimate honor. I smiled and thanked her.

It actually amazes me how little the children are suffering from the effects of the EMP. So long as they have toys to play with, games, and each other—and of course food and shelter, they seem happy as pie. They haven't been required to do much work yet, but I'm guessing that's gonna change. We've already talked about having them feed the chickens, gather eggs, and maybe even fill water troughs.

I led the kids downstairs to the basement. Mr. Martin had put the gun vaults into the safe room so now a large section of the basement is a playroom. As more families have joined us, we needed a place for the kids that was safe and wouldn't interfere with anyone's work.

On the way down I couldn't stop staring at the baby. At first I thought she looked different, but I couldn't place how, exactly. Then I realized it wasn't Lily who has changed—it's me. Now that I know she's my half-sister, I can't see her the same way I used to. I could tell already it won't change the way I feel about her—I'll always love her—but it sure has changed what I see when I look at her.

"Andrea, can we play in the safe room today?"

An instant chorus went up, of "Please, can we! Pleeeeeasse??"

We didn't use the safe room often because it was supposed to be kept ready for an emergency, such as an attack; but there are toys and games in there that the kids can ONLY use when they're in it. That's what they really wanted—access to those toys. I started to say no, but I thought of how much easier the kids are to watch when they're happily occupied. They'd leave me to my thoughts if they were busy. So I agreed. I wanted time to think about things—digest what I'd learned. I was feeling all mixed up.

"Yay, we get to play in the safe room!"

As they busied themselves looking through the toys, I sat by unhappily, obsessed with what my mother had told me. If I'd been alone, I'd have had a pity party, probably a good cry, too. I wasn't sure if I wanted to cry for myself, or for my father. Maybe for the whole family. I felt burdened.

I replayed scenes in my head where my dad was testy and difficult, wondering now if it was all because he knew Lily wasn't his. I recalled a particular day when he'd had to hold the baby for my mother. I remembered noticing it because he didn't usually hold her. And when he did on that day, he didn't look down at her or enjoy her like a normal dad. I thought then that he was such a loser of a father, but now I'm thinking he couldn't bear to enjoy the evidence of his wife's infidelity!

Lexie came in, looking at me appraisingly. "I have a few minutes," she said, coming and sitting beside me. "Tell me what's wrong."

"Lexie, wanna play with us?" Laura asked. Lexie shook her head.

"I need to talk to Andrea." I appreciated her so much right then. Making sure the kids weren't listening, I told her my conversation with my mother. She listened, frowning and nodding. Then, since I'd put Lily on the rug with a toy, she gave me a big hug.

This made the kids notice. Lainie shouted, "We forgot to let Andrea choose the game! Do you want to choose the game?" I'm sure she thought that choosing the game would bring instant satisfaction to whatever ailed me.

"No, it's okay, you go on playing," I said, forcing myself to smile. I turned back to Lexie, grateful for her support. She said she was sorry and she'd be upset too, if it were her mom. She said she'd pray for me, and I thanked her. Surprisingly, I did feel better. It was good not to bear that knowledge alone.

After Lexie went back to chores, I sat and reflected on things. I've never given a lot of thought to what constitutes moral behavior or not; but I am ashamed of my mother and saddened about it. In fact, now that

RESILIENCE

I think about my dad's anger, his always being on edge with my mom, I am sure he knew about Lily. I feel sad for him in a whole new way.

CHAPTER THIRTEEN

SARAH

Richard and I were strangely silent that night as we sat at Martha's kitchen table after dinner, our stomachs so full they ached. We were grateful beyond words for their kindness, these two, whose last name, we now had learned, was Steadman. To me they were like angels! They had asked us to wait while they spoke privately in the parlour.

They're deciding if we can stay," Richard said, tilting his head in their direction.

"How do you know?"

He shrugged. "What else?"

When the older couple returned, Martha's eyes were crinkled happily. "Well, if I can convince this old geezer to keep you two on, I guess I can convince anyone of anything."

Richard and I smiled. I bit my lip to be sure I wasn't dreaming. "You're going to keep us?" Richard asked.

"On a trial basis," Tom said. "Martha here thinks I need the help, what with chopping wood for the stoves and all. And you're a strong young man, by the looks of you."

"We'll get more weight on you," Martha added. "That'll help get your strength back." She looked at me. "And Sarah can help me with woman's work. God knows, there's plenty of it. We live like Pioneers, but if that's okay by you two, then you're welcome to join us."

Richard and I looked at each other. I think we were trying not to burst from relief. "I'd LOVE to live like a pioneer with you!" I blurted, unable to hold in my joy.

Martha smiled regally. "That's fine, then." She patted my hand. "We're going to get along just fine, you and I."

"C'mon," growled Tom, to Richard. "I'll show you how to spot the mines." His gruffness held no worry for me, now. Martha and Tom may have lined their yard with mines, and they had shotguns and knew how to use them, but they didn't frighten me anymore.

"Don't be too long," called Martha, to their retreating figures. "The one thing these two need now," and she turned her gaze upon me, scrutinizing me up and down, "is a BATH."

I almost couldn't breathe. The idea of a bath was so wonderful that I was afraid any sound I made might break this magic spell, make them change their minds, throw us out.

"Follow me," she said. We went back through the hallway, turning off to a living area that had a wood-stove. An old-fashioned porcelain tub was right beside the stove, off to one side. "This is where we take our baths, now," she explained. "The bathrooms are too cold."

I met her eyes. "What do you do for...."

She smiled. "A toilet? Oh, we have that covered, too." She said, "I'll show you later; unless you need to..."

"No. I'll take a bath, first!"

"We don't fill the tub—it takes too much water. You'll get just enough to sponge yourself off good. And one container to rinse with. Tom and I use the same water, except for rinse water. You and Richard will have to do that, too. But you can go first." She smiled again. "It's always ladies first, in this house." But then she stood, surveying me, a small frown forming on the delicately lined face.

"On second thought, you'll each need fresh water. Just this once. How long has it been?"

I tried to remember my last bath. It was at the library. We fully intended on bathing once things warmed up some, but even now in May, ponds and streams were far too cold.

"After the pulse there was a fire, and we had to live in the library with the rest of the people from our apartment building. I haven't had a bath since then."

Martha's eyes widened. "Oh, my! I'd better heat extra water up! Only Tom can lift the big hot pot if I fill it, but he'll be back to help."

She stopped, surveying me. "Are those the only clothes you have?"

"I have one change in my backpack. But they're not any cleaner than what I'm wearing."

"Oh, dear. You'll have to wear something of mine until we can get your clothes washed and dried. I'll show you how to wash them, and then you'll take the bath."

I followed her up a narrow staircase to her and Tom's bedroom, where she looked through her closet and found a housedress and robe for me. The housedress was something grandmas wear. Normally I wouldn't have put it on for anything. But I wanted a bath and I longed for clean clothes.

Martha didn't leave the room as I changed, and I didn't complain. We were still strangers, why should she trust me in her bedroom? But she tsk, tsked as I undressed, saying, "Why, you're nothing but skin and bones! We'll have to do something about that." I could only smile at her gratefully.

"And why's your hair so short? It's a boy cut."

I explained about the lice.

She showed me how to scrub my clothes on a washboard in that big metal sink in the kitchen. I could see why she had two kettles constantly going; the needs for hot water were many. I was pretty exhausted despite that hearty breakfast, and after I'd washed only one shirt, she took over for me. "I'll do it for you this time. Afterwards you'll do your own."

"Thank you." I was really grateful, too. It was hard work!

Richard and Tom returned, and Martha ordered Richard to hand over his dirty clothing, too. "Tom will find you something to wear in the meantime," she added, seeing his face.

I could understand Richard's hesitation. It felt vulnerable, taking off one's clothing, even if they provided others. They were offering us much, but we had to give up something to accept it. We had to abandon distrust. I'd give up just about anything to get in that tub with clean, hot water; but Richard seemed to find it difficult to relax. He said he could live with dirty clothes but Martha nipped that idea in the bud.

"Not under my roof, you can't." Richard left the room with Tom and came back in Tom's larger-sized clothes, which drooped on him. I didn't dare laugh, although I wanted to. Richard hadn't laughed at me in my housedress.

When I was finally soaking in the tub with sudsy water almost to my knees, I felt more than just dirt washing away from me. I was ready to welcome Martha and Tom into my heart like family. A little food, a little water—and they owned me! I guess it didn't have to be that way. But here's the thing: I wanted to be owned.

When Martha returned, I was already changing back into the housedress and robe. I'd noticed the two windows in the room were boarded up from the inside. Martha had placed curtains over the boards. She saw where I gazed and said, "Yes, I'm afraid we've had to board up

61

the house." Her expression was grim. "I don't think it will last for long, us having to live this way. Sooner or later there will be order."

"You think so?" I asked, hopefully.

"History proves it," she said, shrugging. "Order has always been restored, though it might be a brand new order."

"You mean a new government?"

She nodded. Brightening, she said, "Alright then, let's get the boys to empty out this tub." She peered into it. "Usually I use this water to wash the floors. But I think you've given it enough use." She smiled at me. "Doesn't that feel better, now?"

I smiled back at her. "You have no idea."

———————◆———————

For a few days Richard and I lived happily, almost in a dream, with Martha and Tom. We could have stayed with them forever. But it was not to be.

It was only the fourth evening with them. I was sitting in the little room off the foyer where we first saw Martha with her shot gun. I was resting, waiting for Tom and Martha and Richard to finish up whatever they were doing so we could sit in the kitchen together. The kitchen was the cheeriest room in the house so we gravitated to it. That's how we spent our evenings. Richard and Tom discovered they both liked chess, while Martha and I would work on a crossword on a card table, or continue kitchen stuff while we chatted, like soaking oats for the following day's breakfast. But as I sat there waiting for the others, the door opened, and I heard footsteps in the hallway. I assumed it was Tom or Richard, who were far more often outdoors than either Martha or I. Richard had already memorized where each and every mine was hidden, but I didn't dare go near the front yard. I figured I'd get about five feet and then blow myself to smithereens. Anyway, as I rested with my eyes closed, I suddenly felt something cold against my head and I jerked my eyes open, sitting up abruptly.

A strange man was staring at me, and he had a pistol pointed at my head.

"Who are you?" he asked. "And where are my parents?"

Chapter Fourteen

LEXIE

I want to do something for Andrea to cheer her up. I would be just as upset as she is if I found out Justin was my half-brother! The only thing I can think of is to organize a game night and make sure Jared comes. I'll sit him next to Andrea. She likes him, and she's always enjoyed having a guy's attention.

That large plume is still visible in the sky, though it's finally getting fainter. The council decided we need to keep as much water available as possible in case we're attacked with arson. So we've all been tasked with filling every container available with water. From our 55 gallon tanks in the barn and basement, to the smallest plastic containers, everyone has to keep them filled and ready.

Andrea and I spent about an hour filling everything we could find in the garages and the barn that would hold water. Then, I had to babysit Justin while Mom did the same for anything she could spare from the kitchen and dining room. We even emptied clothing bins from the attic and filled them with water. I will never forget after this that water is heavy! It was odd to see a line of people waiting for a turn at the well pump.

But will all this effort help? I guess we'll find out. A second precaution was to turn up the lawn in front of the house—grass will burn, but dirt won't, so we want dirt. Our oldest and only working tractor is small, but Dad had a man on it until it ran out of diesel. We can't use it again until a team goes and hunts out more fuel. But most of the front is already turned up. It looks just as if we were gonna plant it, only we're not. It's kind of sad and bare.

But there is one fat row of forsythia that the men transplanted across the front, even across the gravel driveway. Jared didn't like it, but he was outvoted. Forsythia is a tough bush. No one knew if it would survive being transplanted right now while it's in bloom; it's probably the worst time to pull up the roots for any bush. But dad said it would be a living roadblock, and we needed it as soon as possible. I think he really fears that we'll be attacked by these roving bands of military, whoever they are. They move in trucks, so the harder we make it for trucks to enter the property or get near the house, the better it will be for us.

So now we have a second line of defense against vehicles. It's closer to the house, and if they've got tanks, it won't stop them—but Dad hasn't heard reports of any tanks. (*Thank you, Lord!*) And the men are hauling more downed trees and other debris to put in front of the bushes, like they did near the street. My mother isn't thrilled about how unsightly the property has become—she likes things pretty. But she isn't complaining—it's safety first, these days.

What used to be our attic we now call the watchtower. There is no tower but it's more fun than just calling it an attic lookout. So we have two people positioned up there day and night, as well as on the hill, and we have two at our east border and sometimes two at the west. It's hard to get enough people for lookout duty because it's boring. You'd think that would be a good reason for Dad to let me do it! But he doesn't think so.

I've pointed out that good lookouts are hard to come by. Blake is often on duty with Mr. Prendergast, who falls asleep on the job! And two other lookouts were caught sleeping while on duty, too. "You need to let me go with Blake," I told my father. "I won't fall asleep, at least." But he still won't let me. Actually, I don't think he puts much stock into the lookouts keeping us safe. I've heard him say often that, "Our only hope is in God."

I know what he means. It's like this verse I have underlined in my Bible: *Unless the LORD builds the house, those who build it, labor in vain. Unless the LORD watches over the city, the watchman stays awake in vain.* I know that's true, but we still keep "watchmen" and I could be one. I could be a good one who wouldn't fall asleep.

———◆———

EVENING

I learned two things tonight! One is, I hate Andrea Patterson and I'm sorry my family ever helped hers and took them in! The second is, I hate Blake, too! I can't believe I wanted to marry him! Even as I write this I am reeling and feeling disgusted. I hate them both!

Here's what happened: I went through all the work of arranging a surprise for Andrea. I had to clear it with my folks because we seldom get a whole evening without chores. I brought a bunch of games upstairs, a card table and chairs. I put them in the kids' room, because it's bigger than mine. I wanted the kitchen but Mom and the women were doing a bunch of baking—they bake in large batches once or twice a week. I made special snacks. I got Jared to agree to come, though he'd smiled a little (in his creepy way, if you ask me), when I told him it was a surprise for Andrea. I didn't tell anyone what she was upset about and I didn't tell Andrea about the surprise; only that I'd arranged some free time for us and she was to meet me in the kids' room at 7pm.

So I was getting the snacks I'd prepared—buttery popcorn, packaged cookies from storage, and a cheesecake my mom made with homemade cheese. Lots of sweet stuff—I was going to say, "Sweets for the sweet" to Andrea, as I presented the tray of goodies, anticipating a huge grin from her.

But Justin got into the flour and was covered in white; Mom made me put down my tray and clean him up. Fortunately, he did not spill much flour because flour is precious. (All food is.) But I ended up having to give him a sponge bath, and then changed him into clean clothes. I was aggravated, but since we had the rest of the night off, I swept up the floor and cleaned up my brother and didn't complain.

I pictured Andrea upstairs with Blake and Jared, happily talking away, as they waited for me. Finally, I grabbed the tray and hurried to join them. I expected to find them sitting at the table, talking and joking.

I wish I had. When I got to the room, I hesitated at the door, grinning. I was going to enjoy Andrea's delight. When I pushed it open, I saw Jared hadn't arrived yet. Andrea and Blake were standing close together and, to my astonishment, I stood there and saw Andrea lean up and kiss my boyfriend. ON THE MOUTH. She kissed him! Right before my eyes!

As soon as she did, they both saw me. I said nothing, just turned and ran downstairs. It was all I could do not to drop the tray. I wanted to throw it at them. Instead, I dumped it heavily on the counter and my mother turned to me in surprise.

"Lex, for goodness' sake!"

I rushed past her, already crying, unable to even mumble an apology. Vaguely, I knew Andrea and Blake had followed me. I heard Blake's voice—"Lexie!"

I didn't answer, but headed for the door. I needed to be alone. The barn beckoned to me as the best place at that moment, so I hurried towards it. I'd have preferred to be in my bedroom but there was no way I was about to face Andrea or Blake. How could I ever talk to them again? How would I continue to share my room with Andrea? I wanted her out! If she wouldn't leave, I figured I could move to the barn. I'd use the loft. Or sleep with the kids in their room. But Andrea should be the one to leave since it is MY room.

Knowing Andrea, I should have seen this coming. She is nothing but a big flirt.

CHAPTER FIFTEEN

ANDREA

I ran after Lexie to apologize. I wanted to explain! But Mrs. Martin stopped me in the kitchen as I watched Lexie disappear out the back door.

"Whoa! Hold it right there, young lady. What is going on? What is Lexie upset about?" Blake sidled up behind us at that moment and Mrs. Martin looked at him. "What happened?"

I froze, trying to figure out what to say. Blake fumbled for words and then said, "It was a misunderstanding."

Mrs. Martin looked from Blake to me and then her eyebrows went up. "Really!" she said. "Oh."

"No, no, it isn't like that," Blake said. Then we both fell silent. Because, really, it was like that.

"Look—I don't need to know your business." Mrs. Martin dusted flour off her hands. "But whatever happened between you all, I'll tell you this. Lex seemed pretty upset. I don't know what happened—"

I opened my mouth to explain, but she held up one hand, stopping me. "And I don't want to know. I just think you both should realize my daughter is crying her eyes out right now."

I felt my shoulders slump. My whole being slumped. I knew it must have looked bad. The truth is I was just flirting with Blake. It's very difficult to even get near him, usually. I mean, in terms of him being aware of you. I know he's Lexie's, but it was a rare opportunity for me to feel like I could make myself more of a friend to Blake—and vice versa.

I was showing him how high I could get Moppet to jump. That cat is an amazing jumper. (Just having a pet is something to appreciate these days. We've heard stories of people eating dogs and yes, even cats to survive.) So anyway, Moppet can easily go up as high as five feet in the air when I throw her toy up. She catches it nearly every time. Blake enjoys the cats. His family doesn't have any indoor cats because his little sister and brother are allergic. So when he seemed interested and started throwing the toy up too, there came a moment when we were standing very close. I took his arm.

"Look," I said. "It works with anything—it doesn't have to be her toy." I withdrew my ponytail holder and threw it up. The cat went for it like it was raw fish. Blake chuckled. Looking at his profile at that moment as he stood very close to me, I felt intense admiration. Maybe I should say attraction. Without even thinking about it, I just leaned over, intending to kiss his cheek. Blake turned to me at that very second. The look in his gaze told me he was not comfortable with me being so close, but I ignored it—and planted my lips on his!

I don't know what came over me! I intended just to kiss him on the cheek, but when he turned his face, it felt like an invitation. So I took it! The moment my mouth touched his, I felt him freeze. And he didn't kiss me back. It was only for a second, I swear! I honestly don't know what is wrong with me, that I would do that. It's not like I planned it or anything. It just happened.

And then we heard a sound and there was Lexie staring at us. The look on her face made me hate myself. I couldn't believe it! Just my luck! Nothing really even happened between me and Blake. It was just me being an idiot! Blake immediately ran after Lexie.

I shouted, "I'm sorry! I didn't mean anything!" and then I tore after them. I know in my heart that if Blake hadn't been so shocked at what I did, he'd have pulled away. He's never given me the least reason to think he's even a tiny bit attracted to me. Not a hint! I wanted to explain that to Lexie. I wanted to make her understand it was 100% my fault!

And then Mrs. Martin stopped us. Blake went out the back door after Lexie. I hoped he'd realize she had probably run to the barn. When Lexie's upset she takes great comfort from her horse. She says Rhema is a calm creature, and very sympathetic. I sort of find that funny— thinking a horse can be sympathetic. Even though I love to ride, I'm not a horse person—I don't love the animals the way Lexie does. So maybe she's right. I hope it helps her feel better!

Anyway, Mrs. Martin told me to make myself useful. I picked up some dishes from the counter to wash and then suddenly we all heard it—a distant blast. Not gunfire--something bigger and louder, like an explosion! Right after that, the alarm blared. It's a new system that Blake set up which runs on car batteries. After a lookout sends an alert, whoever is nearest an alarm turns it on by connecting two wires. The sound is loud enough for us near the house to hear it but doesn't reach the road.

A tense silence fell over us as we waited. For a possible threat, we'd hear a bunch of intermittent whines. For an actual threat, the alarm was nonstop for a full minute or more. When the wailing didn't stop, I almost dropped the bowl in my hands. Another skirmish! So soon after the last one! And it was growing dark.

The atmosphere changed instantly. My arrival had already silenced the happy chatter of the women as they busied themselves, but now there was urgency in their voices.

"Leave everything, ladies!" said Mrs. Martin. "Jolene, you get the children to the safe room!" Jolene, who was Jared's mother, could not handle a firearm and refused to learn. She was good with kids, though. I was afraid I'd be ordered to help her round them up, but Mrs. Martin's gaze swept the room and she included me when she said, "Check your rifles, ladies. This sounds like trouble." Her walkie-talkie was already buzzing and I heard Mr. Martin's voice.

"Lookouts see vehicles on the road—possibly trucks. Get the lamps out quick! They haven't reached us, yet." It was standard procedure to douse all candles, oil lamps or battery-operated lights if an alarm sounded at night. The only exception was if the house had been broken into—we'd need light then, to see our enemy and not shoot each other. But there hadn't been many alarms at night. Marauders needed daylight as much as we did. So we went around putting out lights; then I hurried upstairs where I'd left my rifle.

I thought of Lexie and Blake. Everyone had instant protocol to follow when an alarm sounded. For those of us who lived in the house, we were supposed to return to it immediately if we were anywhere else, or get to the nearest refuge, such as one of the cabins. There were even some foxholes as well as the lookout posts, if worst came to worst. Had Lexie and Blake made it back to the house? Were they armed? I doubted it.

We often carried our firearms with us; but they were bulky and got in the way of chores, so more often than not Lexie and I would leave them on top of a tall dresser in her room. It was too high for any of the children to reach but easier to access than a gun vault. In the bedroom I grabbed Lexie's rifle along with mine, and rushed downstairs again hoping my friends had returned.

"Who's that?" It was Mrs. Martin's voice. The house was dark. I wouldn't have seen her as I reached the bottom of the stairs if she hadn't spoken. "It's me, Andrea. Did Lexie and Blake get back?"

"I don't know," she said. "Come with us." I followed her voice, barely making out the walls as we hurried towards the front rooms. In the living room we heard men's voices, and Mrs. Martin said, "Hon, are you in here?"

"I'm here."

"What's the plan? Where do you want us? I've got four women with me."

"Stay here for now. I've got lookouts on the line right now; those trucks are going by us."

"What was that explosion?" Someone asked.

After a moment Mr. Martin said, "We don't know, yet." Then the voice of one of the lookouts came over the crackling line: "Looks like they're all past us. Keep lights out for now."

"Roger that," said Mr. Martin. "Have a seat, folks. We're all gonna stay put for a little bit."

I went towards a window and got on my knees to look outside. There were muffled chuckles while the adults, making their way to the sofas, were apparently knocking into each other in the dark. I looked outside but saw nothing but the outline of the brush against the sky, far down by the front of the property. The walkie-talkie buzzed with chatter as some of the other families sought information or instructions. I wondered where Lexie and Blake were, and if they'd made up by now.

Remembering what had happened earlier, I felt shame creeping up my face like a stain. Lexie was going to hate me, for sure. I thought of Jared and hoped he wouldn't find out about it.

And then—I made a decision. It was time to get something going with Jared! If Lexie saw I was serious about Jared, she'd realize Blake meant nothing to me.

She'd have to—wouldn't she?

CHAPTER SIXTEEN

SARAH

I held very still. Tom and Martha's son was ready to shoot me on the spot.

"They're here!" I said, between clenched teeth. "Martha and Tom are here! They're fine!"

"Who are you?"

"I'm Sarah. My brother and I are staying with your folks. They—they took us in!"

He lowered his pistol and I let out the breath I'd been holding. Then I realized more people had come in behind him. I turned and saw a woman, recognizing her bedraggled appearance as that of a desperate survivor. She was the image of me as I'd been four days earlier—unkempt, exhausted, grubby. But she had a sleeping baby in her arms, and two more children clutching her clothing. They moved with her as she entered the room, shuffling past me to put the youngest child gently upon a settee against one wall. She must have heard what I said, because when she turned back to appraise me her eyes were kind

"We're family," she said. "These are Martha and Tom's grandkids." I nodded at them, two more children besides the baby, trying to look welcoming, but inside my heart was breaking. I felt instinctively that these new arrivals would not want us there. No one welcomed extra mouths to feed unless they needed something in return. We were extra mouths, and we'd been useful to Martha and Tom—but would they need us now? When new help had arrived? And family! We had no chance, I was sure.

I was right.

The next morning the Steadmans came to me and Richard and apologetically told us we'd have to move on. Their son did not want us there. The house was crowded now, the family needing every bed available. Tom's son, Mark, would take over the chores Richard had been doing. Their daughter-in-law, Charity, would help in the kitchen.

Though I'd seen it coming, I felt devastated. Martha and Tom's house was the safest place we'd been since the pulse. It was a place I could call home. And now we'd be homeless again, outcasts, on our own.

Martha filled my backpack with food and bottled water. She gave me a waterproof poncho—something I'd often wished for—and a new knit hat. Richard received food, a rope, a sharp new knife, and poncho. All items which the Steadmans could use themselves. They were being as kind as possible.

As we prepared to leave, Martha hugged me. "It was a blessing to us that you came," she said. "I wish we could keep you...."

"I know."

"We'll pray for you."

"Thanks. I'll pray for you, too. Thank you for everything. It was...wonderful."

Martha's eyes got teary and I turned away before I started bawling. I could feel it coming.

Richard and Tom said their goodbyes and Tom nodded at me with a stern expression. He patted my arm. I could tell he felt badly about our having to leave.

And so we left. It was the first time we'd traveled openly in daylight for weeks. Richard had used his topographical map to chart our direction. He and Tom had pored over it that morning after breakfast. Tom had many suggestions and tips—areas to avoid, population centers to go around, that sort of thing. What we didn't realize was Tom's son was afraid we'd come back; or maybe he was afraid we'd tell other people about the house, the provisions, I don't know.

All I know is, he came after us. With a loaded gun.

———————◆———————

Richard and I walked for miles without saying a word. We understood each other's misery for one thing, making conversation unnecessary. Since the pulse, we'd covered so much ground together that we were used to moving quietly, having only our thoughts to occupy us no matter the terrain. Sometimes we'd surprise a squirrel or rabbit we could shoot for our next meal. Today, we were depressed about being out on the road again, making us particularly quiet. And as always, we were attuned to any unusual noises around us. We'd gotten off the road as soon as possible and had been heading through a surprisingly long stretch of woods, so there were trees all around us. Birds chittered overhead in the branches, and a mild breeze whispered through the brush. And then we heard it: Something coming from behind us. Not a rabbit or squirrel, it sounded heavier.

"Get down!" Richard whispered. He shoved a folded knife at me. "Open it!"

I didn't hesitate, but accepted the knife, though I knew I'd never use it. I dodged behind the nearest tree. I had trouble opening it—stupid fold-up knives!—but finally I managed to get it opened. Richard had told me to, so I had. But even my terror couldn't induce me to use such a weapon. I'd explained this to Richard in the past—I just wasn't the kind of girl who could hurt someone with a knife, even in self-defense.

Richard had disappeared behind another tree, and we waited. The sounds grew closer. I knew that by now Richard would have his gun out, and my heart started thudding. I hoped we'd see an animal, maybe a wild dog that had survived without becoming some desperate soul's dinner. Maybe there was other wildlife that would appear. I took a deep breath and tried to be still.

And then I saw the source of the sounds, coming to a stop about three feet away. A man, bending down to examine the ground. It was Mark, Tom's son! I think he was looking for our tracks. I almost called out to him; only I happened to sense movement to my left, and saw Richard motioning for me to be silent, his finger over his lips. I frowned. What if Mark had come to take us back? What if the Steadmans had had a change of heart and decided we could stay? How could I let this chance pass us by?

I motioned back to him trying to convey that I wanted to speak, but Richard suddenly threw himself backwards in a move I found incomprehensible! But in the next moment my head rang from a gunshot to my right! Mark had shot my brother! But no, he'd missed, and there he was, going after Richard, who was trying to scramble to his feet. He hadn't seen me. He stood over Richard, his gun pointed menacingly at him.

"Where's your sister?"

Richard glared at him. "I left her to rest while I went on ahead, to check out our path."

73

"How far back?"

Richard shrugged. "Fifteen minutes."

The man took a breath. "Look, I'm sorry about this; but I know you'll come back to the house."

"We won't come back." Richard's voice was heavy, firm.

"I have to be sure." He took aim at my brother. And then, instead of shooting, he was howling, writhing, trying to grab a knife from out of his back. A knife which I had somehow just thrust into him!

I sobbed, horrified, but Richard scrambled to his feet. "C'mon!" He grabbed my hand and we took off, running. "He's still got a gun!" Richard said, "We gotta move!"

It was hard for me to run. I wanted to collapse and cry. I couldn't get the sight out of my mind—a knife sticking half in, half out, the blood spreading on his shirt! I'd stabbed someone! I, who was sure I could never do such a thing!

We ran on but I was not at full speed. Finally, Richard stopped for a moment. He saw me having trouble I guess, or else I was moving so slowly he figured it out.

"Look, Sarah." He stared hard at me. "You just saved my life." He was taking deep breaths, bending over, hands on his thighs. "You did what you had to do. He was gonna kill me."

I blinked, trying to accept his words. I knew he was right, and yet…and yet…

"You saved my life!" he said again. "Thank you."

We resumed running. I will probably never know if I killed Tom's son. I pray that I didn't! To think I might have killed someone so dear to Martha is too horrible a thought. And a father of young children!

I need Richard to survive, and of course we both want to stay alive; but I'm beginning to wonder who I am. If I have to be this new Sarah, this person who can mercilessly stab another human being in order to live—is it really worth it? Am I any better than Mark, who would have killed us?

CHAPTER SEVENTEEN

LEXIE

Blake found me in the barn near Rhema. I'd almost locked the door behind me but thought better of it. I wasn't ready to talk, but I was secretly pleased he'd come after me. But I was madder at him than pleased.

"Lex, I don't care about Andrea," he said, as I stood brushing my horse, my face still wet with tears. He came over and tried to take my arm. I shook off his attempt.

"You have a funny way of showing it!" I went around Rhema to her other side.

Speaking heavily, Blake said, "I didn't kiss Andrea, Lexie."

I narrowed my eyes at him. "Don't tell me you didn't kiss her. I SAW it!" My voice broke as I spoke, and I was embarrassed that Blake could see how much I cared. Even though I'd been fully prepared to marry him, he hadn't actually proposed, and suddenly I felt determined not to let him know I'd ever been that crazy about him. I'd envisioned our futures together, always seeing us working side by side, one day having our own homestead like mom and dad's. But the image of him and Andrea, mouths touching, was emblazoned in my mind, and it blew away my hopes of that future like a tsunami hitting a row boat.

"When Andrea kissed me, I was…too surprised to move! Trust me, I did not kiss her."

"Do you have any idea how LAME that sounds?" He'd come around towards me, and reached his hands out for mine. Again I shook him away. And then the alarm sounded and we froze listening, to see if it would be the warning short blasts, or the long frightening wail of an active threat. I hated the sound of the alarm. I hated the instant racing of my heart that accompanied it. When it held loud and steady, Blake whirled into action, grabbing my hand and moving us towards the doors.

"C'mon! We gotta get to the house. We'll talk later." I pulled my hand out of his and stopped.

"You go," I said, coming to a halt. "I'm staying here." I was too upset to even think about going to the house and possibly facing Andrea. I wanted time to cool off.

"You're not armed! That was an active threat alarm!" He paused. "You know the rules. We go to the house."

He was right. But I was in no mood to be accommodating. "You're wasting time. Go." I turned and headed back into the stall but I heard him behind me.

"If you're staying, so am I." When I looked back, he said, "At least I have this." He pulled a Glock 19 out of his pocket holster and checked the magazine to make sure it was full. "Get somewhere out of sight while I keep watch."

I went towards Rhema's stall while Blake retrieved the barn walkie-talkie, which we kept hidden under wraps near the rabbit cages, turned off, until it was needed. Why hadn't I thought of that, I wondered.

I didn't seem to be operating with all hands on deck, if you know what I mean. I was so angry I wasn't thinking clearly. Suddenly, the idea of marauders being on the property at night, which was rare, frightened the heck out of me. But we'd waited too long. If they were on the property, it could be fatal to go out there now. We had to stay put.

I clicked off the portable lamp so it wouldn't give us away. I shouldn't have been using up the batteries for it anyways, since I wasn't doing chores; and now I had put myself and Blake in danger by my stubbornness. I sat down against a wall of hay, my throat feeling tight.

"House lights are out," Blake reported. I could faintly hear the buzz of the walkie-talkie, as Blake listened. He did not speak or give our location, as it could be overheard by the wrong ears. I started worrying in earnest about not having gone to the house when we should have. What if my help was needed to turn away a frontal attack? What if Blake was needed inside? I'd been selfish and foolish not go to in when Blake said we ought to. And here I was, without a firearm.

I suddenly thought I'd ask Jared to get me an extra rifle I could hide in here somewhere. Just for moments like this, when we were caught out here defenseless. Except we hadn't actually been "caught"—I'd been too stubborn to return to the house. And now that I needed something, was it right I should ask Jared? When I distrusted his sources, believing his methods of acquisition might be shady?

Silence engulfed us. Minutes dragged by. We heard no shots, but I was afraid it simply meant no one had a clear target because of the dark. It wasn't necessarily a sign that we were safe.

I heard Blake coming towards me and dropped off my musings. "Lex? The lookouts said trucks went by; they didn't stop here or turn in; they probably didn't see us. I think we can go to the house now."

I was vastly relieved, of course, that we weren't facing enemies. I started to rise, but I was so relieved that my stubbornness returned in full force.

"You go. I'm staying here."

"Can I stay with you?" Blake's soft voice tugged at my heart. A part of me wanted him to stay; but why did he ask permission? Why didn't he just stay if he wanted to?

"No."

He was silent a moment and then he came towards me. "Take this."

I felt the cold, hard steel of his Glock and took it, mumbling, "Thanks." I would have been a lot more thankful if he'd stayed, if he'd continued to tell me he hadn't kissed Andrea and that he cared about me. But there was a lot of talk after an alarm or an attack and I figured he wanted to get the scoop. I did, too. But sometimes it's hard to give up being miserable. I stayed. I heard him leave. When he'd closed the barn door behind him, I took up right where I'd left off.

Crying.

CHAPTER EIGHTEEN

ANDREA

Wretched morning. Lexie never came to our bedroom last night. Or, if she did, I was already asleep. When I awoke her bed was empty, and I couldn't tell if she'd slept in it or not. I'm sure she's still angry so maybe it's just as well we didn't see each other. Hopefully she'll cool off before we do. But I'm on pins and needles—I want to have it out, tell her I'm sorry, and move on.

Last night we kept lights out for the next half hour after the alarm but no more trucks were spotted. When I saw Jared at breakfast, I asked, "What do you think caused that noise last night?" He had his rifle by his side; I placed mine against the chair and sat down beside him. "Do you think those trucks had anything to do with it?"

"We're not sure."

"But you have a theory, don't you?" I noticed Blake at the other end of the table but he looked away as soon as he saw me. I couldn't blame him.

"Well—" Jared said, "We'll be going to see what blew; that might help explain what happened."

"How do you know where to look?"

He raised his eyebrows. "You haven't looked outside this morning?"

I shook my head. It was Lexie's day for livestock chores, so I hadn't been out of the house yet. "Why?"

"Go look," he said. I stared at him a moment and then ran to the kitchen window overlooking the back pasture and barn. Most of our downstairs windows are boarded up—for security against intruders—and I couldn't see much through the slits, so I hurried to the door. Opening it, I drew in a sharp breath.

Just when that last ugly plume had been dissipating, the western sky now had a new dark blotch, massive and ugly and black. The smoke was bigger than anything we'd seen yet. It didn't look like a house fire—it had to be larger than that.

Jared joined me and we looked out. "What is it from?" I asked.

Washington was filling his plate at the counter and he interjected, "It's probably propane. There was a supplier over that way with a couple of thousand-gallon tanks. We tried to get fuel from those tanks, but couldn't get in. Looks like someone got mad and blew 'em up."

I refused to look at him, but turning to Jared I said, "That's stupid! What a waste of fuel!"

He nodded and then took my elbow, turning me away from the dismal sight. "C'mon, let's finish eating."

I was silently delighted that Jared had joined me at the door and then had me return to breakfast with him—as if we were a couple. I wanted to get to know him better and it looked like I might get my chance. I wanted to know for sure how old he is, for one thing; and whether he'd ever been married. I knew he was older than me. He'd already served in the military and was stationed in Hawaii until shortly before the pulse. I hoped sitting next to him would become an everyday thing, and that soon I'd find out lots more.

Back at the table, he said, "A few of us are gonna go investigate the area over there. Find out for sure what it is."

"Who's going?"

He gave me a look, slowly turning to a hint of a smile. "Not you."

"I know!" We girls never left the compound. It was disappointing, but I'd be nervous out on the road anyway. I noticed Jared was still looking at me; with an odd kind of look.

"What? What is it?"

"You and Lexie have a fight?"

I stared at him. "How'd you know?"

"Because she was in here and saw you and left." He smirked. "She looked mad."

"Just now?" I looked around hopefully—I was afraid to face Lexie, but I knew we needed to talk. There was no sign of her. I hesitated, wondering how much I wanted him to know. "I did something stupid, and she's mad at me." I bit my lip.

"What'd you do?"

I looked away. "She got the wrong idea. She thinks I'm after her boyfriend."

"Are you?"

"No!" When I looked back at him, he was smiling a little. He leaned towards me. "Why don't you come to my cabin later? After I get back to the compound."

"Your cabin? Is it finished?"

"Almost."

I felt alarmed by his suggestion but I was also intrigued. This was precisely what I wanted, wasn't it? To further my relationship with Jared? I wasn't sure what he had in mind but it was the first real interest in me I'd felt from him.

I picked up a spoon and stirred my oatmeal before I answered. "Okay."

CHAPTER NINETEEN

SARAH

We hurried through the woods for another fifteen minutes. I kept replaying the scene in my head as we went. I saw Mark with his weapon hovering in the air over Richard. Pure rage had overtaken me at the sight, as though I'd been white one second and in the next, bright red with fury. It took me over. I hardly remembered raising my arm or moving towards him but I could clearly recall the way I'd plunged that knife into his back! I'd used every ounce of my strength, more than I knew I had. I couldn't let him shoot my brother!

I couldn't lose Richard.

And then we ran off. I'd left the knife in Mark's back—I had no choice. Suddenly a realization hit me: I'd used the knife Tom had given Richard! If I hadn't fatally wounded him, Mark would return to his parents with that knife in his back; and they would know without a doubt who put it there. They would never suspect Mark of trying to kill us, I'm sure. He'd tell them he followed us to bring us back—and then show that knife as proof of our treachery.

We would be branded—literally—as backstabbers! It was enormously upsetting. "I have to rest!" I sat down heavily against a tree trunk but I turned myself to face the direction we'd come from. Just in case.

"We have to keep going. He could be tracking us again."

"If he can move, I think he'd go back home for help. He had a knife in his back!"

Richard sighed and plopped down next to me. "Okay, let's listen for a minute." So we did. We were good at that. And then, the strangest sound came wafting through the brush and trees towards us, not from the direction of the Steadmans' house, but from the north. We looked at each other, perplexed.

"That's a vehicle!" Richard got quickly to his feet and held out a hand to help me up. "We must be near a road! Let's take a peek. But stay behind me and be careful!" We moved hurriedly towards the sound.

"I thought all cars and trucks were down."

"I guess not. That sounds like a big engine—a truck."

As we hastened towards it, he added, "There's more than one!" The rumbling was loud now, and we suddenly got our first glimpse of the source through the trees, and stopped. An army truck lumbered past, followed quickly by another and then another.

"Stay out of sight!" Richard hissed.

I had no desire to be discovered so I stayed behind a tree, only peeking at the rear of the trucks as they passed. Afterwards we made our way to the road, which was now silent and empty.

"It must be true, what that guy told us last month."

I knew immediately what Richard referred to. Right after Jesse and then Mom died, we saw a farmhouse about a quarter mile back from the road. We'd been walking all day and needed water. We'd seen other wanderers as needy as we were but right now we were the only ones around. Richard said, "Let's try this place."

"For what?"

"For water. For anything. C'mon."

"No one's gonna help us," I said, but I followed Richard. I always followed Richard. He was the only thing keeping us alive, and I'd come to respect his decisions. So we made our weary way down the long drive.

"Maybe it's empty," I said.

Richard shook his head. "I doubt it. Even if the owners died, someone else would've moved in by now. It's got a pond, look."

And it did. Lots of homes had ponds, because here in Ohio the soil is heavy and full of clay. We followed the driveway past an empty field which normally should have been seeded by now with corn or soybeans. Instead, it lay unplanted, dotted only with clumps of weeds. As we got close to the house, a man suddenly stepped out from behind an old shed. He had a rifle.

"What do you want?"

Richard said, "We have money. We're looking to buy food, any food."

"Are you kidding? What would we do with money? And there's nothing here to sell. They picked us clean weeks ago."

They. *Who*, I wondered, were *they*?

"Refugees from the city?" Richard asked.

The man snorted. "Refugees? Heck no! It was government. Said they had the right to take any food they wanted. Said we was hoarding it!" He scowled. "We don't hoard food. Never have. We store what we need from each harvest to get us through to the next one. That's it."

"Can we buy something from that?" Richard asked. "What you stored?"

"Son, you're not hearing me," the man said, more gently this time. "They took it. They took it all! They even took our chickens and pigs. We have one cow left and we only have that on account of my young son and daughter. My wife begged them on her hands and knees for the sake of the children, to leave us something." He paused and gave us a pointed look. "I've had to shoot two people trying to steal her." His eyes narrowed. "So don't get any ideas."

I didn't realize it, but I'd started crying. The man looked at me and something in his face softened. "Look," he said. "Those men, the ones from the government, said they were taking the food to a public soup kitchen. So maybe you'll find that."

"Were they on foot? " Richard asked.

"They had a military truck," he said. "I asked them how come their truck still worked. They said it came from out of the country. Somewhere not affected by the pulse."

"If they could fly in a truck, they could fly in food," Richard said. "I don't get it."

"Tell me about it," he said, bitterly. "I don't like the government; but I never dreamed they'd be the ones to steal everything we've got in a crisis."

Richard eyed his gun. "Why didn't you fight?" he asked. "Why didn't you fight to keep your stuff?"

"Son, there was a truckload of them and only a few of us. Besides, they were yelling at us to come out peacefully or they'd burn our house down. Claire and I have seen lots of smoke these days...I believed them." He paused. "And I didn't know they were gonna rob us blind!"

He looked at me. "Try and find the soup kitchen. We'll be doing that ourselves one of these fine days, thanks to our good ol' USA government."

"Can we fill our water bottles from your pond?"

"What good'll that do ya? You can't drink that water."

"So can we?" Richard repeated. This time he wasn't volunteering the information that we could treat the water, which was just as well with me. Talking about it reminded me of how we got the iodide pills, and I still didn't like to think about that.

We were turning to leave when the man's wife came running out holding two bottles of clean water in her hand. "Here, she said. "Take these. They've been used, but they're washed and they've got good clean water in them."

The farmer turned to us with a smirk. "Those army fellas didn't recognize our water filter, or I guess they'd have taken that, too."

We never did see a soup kitchen, and we'd never seen any army trucks—until now.

"Maybe we should follow the trucks," I said. "Maybe the army will tell us where to find a soup kitchen."

Richard glanced over at me. "No. I doubt there are any."

"What? But that farmer guy told us—"

"He told us what he was told. But I don't think it's true. If these government troops were taking their food, it means they didn't have any. They weren't taking it for any soup kitchen. It was for themselves."

We were still on the road in the path of the trucks, so I said, "So what'll we do?"

Richard blew out a heavy breath. "Same as we've always done. Look for a place to hole up, and then keep walking."

"To Aunt Susan's?"

"I guess."

I figured Richard was having the same thoughts I was. That Aunt Susan was no better off than anyone else—if she was still alive. How could a woman who couldn't keep it together enough to take care of her own child following her divorce, have survived? She'd recovered enough to get a job and had kept the house and acreage...but she'd never sent for Jesse. We'd taken him in when he was just a baby...and he was three and half when the EMP happened. But Aunt Susan had come to see him only once, and had never hinted she wanted him back.

I think Richard and I both knew in our hearts Aunt Susan was just a pipedream. I think we both knew she was probably not alive.

But there was nowhere else to go. We walked on.

CHAPTER TWENTY

LEXIE

I woke up feeling peaceful, blinking away the fog of sleep. For a few seconds. Then it hit me like a punch in the gut—Blake and Andrea. They'd kissed! Aargh.

I'd crawled into a sleeping bag in the kids' room unbeknownst to the little ones, as they were long asleep by the time I got there. I got up quietly now, leaving them none the wiser they'd had an extra roommate. I hoped Andrea had noticed my absence and missed me. I have to admit I was planning on ways to punish her and Blake by not speaking to them. I knew the Bible said to forgive your enemies. Heck, we're supposed to love them. I didn't feel able to do either.

I hurried outside without stopping by my room to change clothes; I didn't want to risk seeing Andrea. Besides, I wanted to get Rhema out of her stall as early as possible. I hate that she has to stay locked in a stall every night but it's for the best. She isn't out there tempting looters to try and take her and make us fight them off. All the animals are brought in every night for that reason.

Anyways, when I got outside, deep in thought, I suddenly looked up and saw a strange darkness in the sky ahead of me. The sun had just risen. At first I was confused by what I saw but then I realized it had billowed out from one direction—it was smoke! I ran back in the house. Mom and Mrs. Patterson were starting breakfast in the kitchen.

"Mom! Did you see the smoke?"

She nodded at me sadly. "It's from that explosion last night. We'll find out what's burning today. Go get your chores done."

I led my horse out, fed the animals, and then fetched them water. But as I worked, I kept rehearsing the way I'd give Blake and Andrea the cold shoulder when I saw them. In fact, thinking about Blake, I got madder and madder. No wonder our romance hadn't progressed much! He didn't want it to! He liked Andrea! I closed the gate to the pasture, turned, and almost ran smack into him.

"Lex"

I tried walking around him but he stopped me, taking me by the arms. I was secretly pleased he cared enough to do that, but I was still more angry than pleased.

"I don't want to talk about it. Not now."

"I didn't kiss Andrea," he said. I stared at his pleading eyes and felt immeasurably sorry. But I saw clearly in my mind the image of him and Andrea, their mouths together!

"Liar! I saw you! Why don't you just admit it!" I shrugged off his hands and stalked back towards the barn. I turned only enough to say "Don't follow me!"

I still had to gather rabbit droppings for the garden and check on two mamas; plus see if all the kits were still alive. We preferred to keep their cages outdoors in warmer weather but they were safer in the barn. I made sounds to warn them I was coming. Rabbits don't like to be surprised—it spooks them. As I worked I blinked back tears. I knew Blake was guilty—and it hurt.

I needed to pray—but really all I wanted to pray for was that God would help me not to care about Blake or Andrea! I knew I'd have to forgive them sometime but right now I was stuck in angry mode. Partly because, even if I forgave Blake wholeheartedly, it wouldn't change the fact that we were through. We weren't on the "marriage track" as I'd imagined. Staying angry helped me hold off facing that. Maybe being stuck was exactly where I wanted to be.

I opened the door to the first cage, offering the mother rabbit a handful of clover I'd picked earlier. All I needed was to distract her while I checked the kits. I was just closing the door when I heard a sound and turned to see Jared coming towards me. He smiled, which was uncharacteristic of him, making me uneasy.

"Is everything okay?" I asked.

He nodded. "Yup. Your mom asked me to come and check on you."

This was decidedly unusual. I wasn't friends with Jared. I'd even tried to get Andrea to see he might not be trustworthy. Why would Mom send him, of all people? And she'd just sent me out there to do my chores.

"I'm almost done here. I'm fine."

He came and stood next to me and surveyed the rabbits. "They're kinda cute, aren't they?"

I glanced at him, surprised. "Yeah." I didn't think Jared would see future food on the table as cute. I tried never to think about how cute they were, knowing their fate. But they are pretty animals. Most all our rabbits are New Zealands except for two cages of Cinnamons. The New Zealands are snowy white and fluffy. We didn't used to tan the hides, but we're doing it, now.

"It's too bad, huh? That we gotta eat them."

I nodded.

"Good thing we haven't had to eat your horse!"

I stared at him in indignation. How could he even think such a thing!

He smiled and chuckled. "Just kidding."

He'd been joking? Jared, joking!

"Rhema's a pretty filly."

"She is, thanks." I was trying to figure out why in blazes he was talking to me, wondering how to ask him. Maybe the guy was just lonely or something. Wait a minute! He wasn't trying to get friendly, was he? I needed to end this, now.

"I gotta finish up. See ya later." This was meant to dismiss him but he took my hand as I went to open the cage in front of me and I turned to him in surprise.

"What—?"

And then, in a really quick and surprising move, Jared leaned in and caught me on the mouth with his mouth. To say I was surprised would be an understatement. He grabbed me around the middle and pressed down with his lips, but I came to life and started fighting. I think I kicked him in the shins and he let me go with an oath, and bent over, rubbing his leg.

I turned to run. I was going to run to the house and tell my dad to get rid of Jared! But as soon as I turned I saw Blake. I stopped in surprise.

He came to me, his eyes filled with soft sorrow. I felt confused. Why had Jared come to the barn and why did Blake happen to be here at the same time?

Blake came and gently put his hands upon my arms.

"What's going on?" I felt a sneaking suspicion, a tremor of distrust towards Blake, my Blake, whom I'd always trusted implicitly—before yesterday, anyways.

"You got yourself a wild cat there," said Jared, limping off. He turned to give me a rueful grin.

I looked accusingly at Blake. "What is going on?"

Blake took a breath. "Lex, when I got here, I saw you kissing Jared." My mouth opened in protest. But in a second, Blake's face descended towards mine and then he was kissing me. I was still angry about what I'd seen earlier, but it was so nice to have BLAKE kissing me rather than that awful Jared, and it was such a sure sign Blake cared, that I welcomed his kiss. It meant he hadn't misinterpreted what he saw—wait a minute! That was exactly what I'd done to him, I saw that now! I'd seen him kissing Andrea and assumed the worst, but I was now living proof that you COULD be so surprised you do nothing! At least for a few seconds, anyways.

After a good, long, kiss, we stared into each other's eyes.

"I'm sorry," I said.

"I don't want to lose you, Lex. I mean this with all my heart. Andrea doesn't mean anything to me."

I could have cried. Maybe I did.

Later Blake told me how Jared had found him looking all down and morose. When he'd explained the difficulty, Jared nodded knowingly. "Andrea said she did something stupid and Lexie was mad at her."

I was none too happy to learn I'd been set up. But Blake was so sweet and affectionate, telling me he'd do it again if it meant making me forgive him, that I couldn't stay angry about it. Already we're laughing over the whole thing. Except for Andrea's part in starting it all. That was no set-up. She intentionally kissed my boyfriend.

I'm still not talking to her.

———————◆———————

Outdoors, we stared at the ugly blackness spread across the sky. Other people around the compound were staring also. It was like a pall fell over us. The smoke is a reminder of how unstable the world is, of how precarious life is.

During lunch, Dad said, "If it's fuel burning it's a shameful waste of resources."

"If it's not fuel?" asked Mrs. Wasserman.

"Could be industrial buildings," my dad said, "but I can't remember there being any over that way."

Either way, if it was buildings or fuel, it was depressing. It meant more people might have died, and that arsonists were out there who might want to burn us down, too. And what if those foreign troops were responsible? So far, we'd had enough manpower to fight off marauders, but if an organized and armed enemy was taking over the land, what could we do to stop them? We had nothing that could withstand true military force.

Dad has said if we can get by for a year or two by careful rationing, then if the United States hasn't been taken over by a foreign power, we may get through to a new era of peace and prosperity. IF. There's a whole lotta 'if' in that scenario.

No sooner did we clear the lunch dishes than we heard it: Another alarm! When it didn't break up into short blasts after the first ten seconds, we all jumped into action. Here we go again, I thought. When would it end!

"Wait. Let's pray, folks," my Dad said.

My mother said, "I'm getting the children out of the yard. You all, please, pray." She disappeared out the door while the rest of us stopped and held hands, forming a little circle right there in the kitchen. A new compound member named Cecily prayed first—with great fervency. I admired her spirit. Then Dad prayed. When I thought afterwards of what could have gone wrong later, I knew the Lord had answered those prayers. He was watching over us. He had to be!

CHAPTER TWENTY-ONE

ANDREA

So I thought it was bad enough, having Lexie and Blake both mad at me. (I've tried to apologize, like, three times, but they're both being jerks.) But now I wish this was my only problem.

It was my day for child care. Knowing Lexie might be out in the barn, I took the kids outside. I knew the black sky might upset them, but they just pointed it out and then ignored it. I wanted to see Lexie and have it out. Get it over with.

So I took the kids to the playground, which is adjacent to the path that veers off to the barn. It's on the quiet side of the barn instead of on the side facing the cabins, where most activity is. But I cleared it with the lookouts and Mrs. Martin, and the kids were loving it.

I was daydreaming about what might happen between me and Jared, swinging Lily and Justin on infant swings, when all of a sudden we heard the alarm. I couldn't believe it—the third alarm in a week! And it wasn't a warning. I gathered the kids as fast as I could. Mrs. Martin appeared and helped herd the children towards the house.

As we got inside, Aiden started howling. "I need my Luke Skywalker!" Mrs. Martin was carrying the two babies but she stopped and sternly ordered Aiden to follow her. She was taking the kids to the safe room.

"We'll get it later," I assured him. But it was no use. Aiden was almost five, but still very capable of having a temper tantrum more fitting for a two year old. He cranked up his crying and clung to my legs.

"Aiden Patterson! You come here this minute!"

I gave Mrs. Martin an agonized look. "Find my mom! She'll get him to calm down."

"Your mother left the property with Mr. Washington about two hours ago," Mrs. Martin said.

"Where did they go?" I asked, annoyed. Of course she wouldn't be here when I needed her.

"I was going to ask you that," she said. "Carry your brother down. I don't care if he's screaming like a banshee."

I picked him up, but Aiden went into an all-out tantrum, kicking me and thrashing with all his might. "It's okay," I said to Mrs. Martin, who waited, holding Justin on one hip. "I know how to calm him. We'll be right there."

"I don't need him to be calm," she said as she turned away to lead the rest of the kids to safety. "He can come kicking and screaming, I just need him to come. Pick him up and get him along, Andrea."

I tried to pick up my little brother, but his screaming increased yet more and he threw himself down, grasping my leg like a drowning man does a life preserver.

"I nee--ee--eed my Luke Skywalker!"

I tried to pry off his arms but his hold on my leg redoubled.

I wanted to do what Mrs. Martin said; but something in Aiden's agonized cries pierced me to the heart. I guess that sounds pretty dramatic but that's how it felt. It was like his crying hit a soft spot inside me that I didn't know was soft; or maybe sore, is a better word.

"I ne-e-e-e-eed my Lu-u-u-u-u-ke Skywalker-er-er-er!"

As I hugged Aiden against my side, suddenly all the suffering we'd endured since the pulse—dad's death, the loss of our home and belongings, the disappearance of our old life—all of it, was in Aiden's cries. That toy was his security blanket. I couldn't let him lose that, too!

In the distance I heard shots. I knew no adult would ever give me permission to go outdoors for an action figure but as I stroked his head, listening to his sobs—and you'd think the world had ended, the way he cried—I got spitting mad about it, as Mrs. Martin would say. After all—the world had ended. Our world, anyway.

"Okay. Wait here," I said, bending down to look into his eyes. "I'll get your Luke Skywalker."

"You will?" Quentin's tone changed instantly into one of wondering hope. He sniffled and looked at me with great trust.

"I will."

People were scrambling into position at windows all around the house. I knew that outside, men were huddling behind partitions we'd put up around the borders of the building area. Most of them were lined with homemade sandbags—one of the less lovely chores we have is to make them using anything we can find. Plastic bags, doubled, and filled

91

with dirt and sand, did the trick.

Lexie came flying towards us with Blake right behind her. Both held rifles and were in a hurry but they skidded to a stop. They looked at me and then at each other. I sort of held my breath, wondering if they'd speak to me.

"What are you doing?" Lexie sounded annoyed.

"I have to get Aiden's Skywalker. He left it outside."

"You can't go out there," Blake said.

"Where's your rifle?" Lexie asked.

"I'm on childcare! I only have this," I motioned towards my holstered .380, which I wore clipped to a belt. "I'm going to the safe room with Aiden. I just have to get his Skywalker first."

"Where is Aiden?" Lexie asked, craning her head to look around me. Surprised, I realized he'd let go of my legs, but when I turned to reveal my brother, there was —nothing!

"Oh, great!" I said. "He's gone!"

A sudden volley of shots somewhere on the property ended our conversation. "We have to go!" Lexie said. "We'll be at an upstairs window! Find Aiden and get downstairs!"

"I will!" It was such a relief they'd spoken to me, I didn't even mind that Lexie hadn't been particularly nice. I still needed to retrieve Aiden's action figure though, and I'd have to hurry. But first I had to find out where Aiden had gone. Children weren't supposed to wander around during a skirmish and I certainly didn't want my little brother in harm's way.

I hurried around looking for him, growing increasingly worried. Where was he hiding? If I was to venture outdoors I had to do it quick! Every minute that passed meant whoever was approaching our borders might have crossed them by now. The longer I waited, the more dangerous it got.

And then I saw him, right where he was supposed to be in the first place. "Where'd you go?"

Ignoring my question, he smiled hopefully. "Did you get 'im? Did you get my Luke Skywalker, Andi?"

"Not yet. I need to get you downstairs, first."

He shook his head, and his mouth puckered up—he was gonna cry again! I knelt down to meet his eyes, taking him by the shoulders. I wanted him to listen really good.

"You have to go downstairs—" He started howling again so loudly I covered his mouth with my hands. "All right! Be quiet! I'll get Luke!" Immediately he fell silent, blinking back tears and staring at me with large, trusting eyes. "But only if you promise to stay inside. Do NOT come out, whatever you see. And if I don't come back in five minutes, you have to go to the safe room. I'll bring Luke Skywalker to you down there." He nodded solemnly.

"Okay."

"You promise?"

"Promise."

I got up and ran to the kitchen where the back door was. No one was there! Normally somebody would be guarding every entry but perhaps whoever was assigned hadn't arrived yet. Better for me. They would've prevented me from doing what I did next. I unlocked the door and peered out, looking in all directions—I saw no one. I took a deep breath and darted outside, praying silently. All I had to do was dash to the side of the house into the playground and grab the action figure. It had to be lying in plain sight on the ground near the slide where the boys had last been playing. I knew that hitting a moving target was difficult; only the most experienced shooters could do it, so I moved fast. Running, I skidded around the side of the house, darting split-second glances to all sides, making sure my path was clear.

I reached the playground and felt a euphoric sense of victory, but where was the toy?

"Andrea Patterson, get in the house!" It was Mr. Martin's voice. He must have been at a window.

But I couldn't leave yet! Not when I'd got this far. I hated to ignore Mr. Martin but I slowed down and let my eyes sweep the ground. No action figure. "Oh, Aiden!" I thought. "Where'd you put your toy?" I circled the playground. No action figure. The seconds were ticking by. I heard shots—they sounded closer. I hoped the fire was ours and would send any would-be looters running. That was always our hope—that they'd want an easy target and back off.

As I did my second round of the playground, I heard Mr. Martin again yelling at me to get inside. My heart pounded wildly and I'm not sure what made me keep looking for that stupid toy. I felt like I was going to be annihilated at any moment but somehow I needed to find it. For Aiden. Aiden needed it.

Beside the playground were two old oaks with tire swings hanging from them. The boys had played there earlier! I'd have to go around the chicken yard to reach the oaks—it didn't use to be that way, but the Martins had to move the chicken coop closer to the house because of thefts. So now it was between the playground and those oaks.

I ran. I was sure Aiden had left his toy there. The chickens squawked as I tore past. I prayed no one would start shooting over here thinking I was an intruder! I arrived, gasping for breath, and there! Inside the tire!

I grabbed the action figure with my left hand. I'd removed my .380 from its holster in case I needed it, and had it in my right hand. Then, just at the exact moment when I shoved the action figure into my pocket, I heard a noise behind me. It was no chicken.

I swung around into firing position, locking my arms with the pistol pointed out. Before me was a boy I knew from high school. I'd gone out with him once, to Home Coming! We'd briefly kissed good night. I hadn't wanted to see him again. He seemed miffed about it and we hadn't spoken to each other since.

I stared at him a moment, feeling suddenly confused. The juxtaposition of someone I knew when life was normal, against the reality of me standing there pointing a gun at him was too weird. But like somebody waking up, I realized skinny chicken feet were sticking out the bottom of his jacket—dripping blood—he'd killed a pullet! Maybe a hen! The next second I realized the red crown showing from the top of his jacket meant it was a rooster! We'd already lost two adult males recently in separate freak accidents.

"Drop it."

He was staring at me wide-eyed, looking from me to the gun and back.

He shook his head, no.

I remembered his name. "Drop it, Miles! That's not yours!"

"What do you care? You don't live here," he said, as if that meant anything.

"I do now. Drop it and get out of here or I'll have to shoot! Maybe you haven't heard but people who steal food get shot on sight, now. You just killed our last grown rooster."

"Don't break my heart," he jeered, staring at me, sizing up my threat. He looked around warily.

94

I realized he might be looking for a partner, someone who would come to his assistance. Frightened, I aimed at the ground by his feet and took a shot. I hoped to scare him into dropping the bird. He got scared all right—he jumped and started running—but he hadn't dropped the bird! My first instinct was to run after him but instead I let my firearm follow him, aiming just ahead of where he was, knowing I could probably slow him down—or worse.

But I didn't. I watched him go with a strange sense of helplessness. I should have stopped him, but I couldn't shoot a fellow high schooler. If he'd been a stranger, if he'd tried to shoot at me, perhaps it would have been different. But I hadn't seen a weapon on him, and knowing him from my school—from my old life—had thrown me out of whack.

I turned and hurried back towards the house, terrified every second of getting shot. From the upstairs windows, I heard them calling my name, telling me to hurry. A shot sounded somewhere nearby.

As I neared the door, it opened from the inside. Mrs. Buchanan, looking grim, waited to close it behind me. I pulled the action figure from my pocket, anticipating the happy smile of my little brother when he saw it.

"Look, Aiden!"

Only—he wasn't there. My brother was gone. Again.

While Mrs. Buchanan double-locked the door behind me, I asked if my brother had gone downstairs.

"All the children are down there," she said.

"But I left Aiden up here. He wanted his toy."

"You were downright foolish to go out there for that."

"I know, but I had to."

"You did not have to."

"I did." I despaired of explaining, so I asked, "Can you help me look for him?"

"Of course." We fanned out. I took a quick look in the nearest rooms but they were empty. Somebody must have taken him to the safe room, someone who wouldn't be swayed by his crying or histrionics, no matter how much he fussed. Perhaps Mrs. Martin had lost patience and come and fetched him herself. She would be angry with me for taking so long. She would be furious when she found out why I had done so. I took a breath and headed to the hallway leading to the basement.

On the way, I thought about Miles taking our rooster. It was frustrating, because we needed that bird for breeding. We'd continue getting eggs until a male pullet grew to adult size, but this would slow down meat production. But could I really blame him for taking the bird? Everyone needed food. He was probably desperate.

Then I got worried—would some people in the compound be furious if they knew I'd had a shot and not taken it? I determined right then not to say anything about the whole episode. It wouldn't be the first time an animal had disappeared with no explanation.

CHAPTER TWENTY-TWO

SARAH

"If we live through this," I told Richard as we ducked inside an old barn looking for shelter, "I'm going to write a book someday." We hadn't seen or heard more military trucks, and we'd crossed miles of land, straddling the edge of fields and tree lines, trying to put distance between us and them. This area of the state was more rural than Warren County, that was certain.

Richard wanted us to go back to our old method of traveling by darkness, so although it was still daylight, we were gonna lay low until sunset. We blinked, trying to adjust to the dusky inner light of the old structure. The door was old and wouldn't shut all the way, but that was fine. If it was in good shape, it could be a target for scavengers. The more broken down and neglected a place appeared, the more likely it would be passed by as having no value.

Richard hadn't replied to my mention of writing a book. Either he didn't think I was capable of doing it—I'd never been the brainy one in the family—or he didn't think we'd live through this. Maybe both.

A sudden scurrying sound caught our attention and a big, fat rat, dragging hay on its feet, scurried in and then back out of sight into a dark corner.

"I don't want to stay here."

"Are you kidding?" Richard said. "That's dinner."

I shook my head. "We have stuff in the backpack. I can't eat that." After all the good, normal food we'd had at the Steadmans I was sure I could not bring myself to swallow rat meat. Not until I was starving again.

He surveyed me. "O.K. But we need to stay here until dark."

———————◆———————

That night after crossing more fields, we entered woods. They were thick and full of ravines. Vines and downed logs tripped us up, and bugs landed on our faces, in our eyes, ears, anything open. The terrain was hilly and exhausting, forcing us to find a road. Luckily we were between towns, so it was as empty as we could wish.

We'd been on it for maybe half a mile when we came to an intersection with a huge sign. In the moonlight, the words were clear: REFUGEE CAMP. An arrow beneath the words pointed right, and writing, this by hand: FOOD! PROTECTION! MEDICAL!

"Refugee Camp—do you think that's the soup kitchen?"

Richard didn't answer. He was thinking.

"We should go there," I said. When he didn't answer, I added, "We both know that Aunt Susan—" I couldn't complete the sentence. I couldn't say she was probably not alive. But how could she be?

"You know we have nowhere else to go."

Still Richard said nothing.

"C'mon." I tugged on his arm, turning him to the right so we could find the camp. "It's a sign for refugees. That's what we are." We began walking but Richard was dragging.

"I don't trust it."

"I can't keep living this way," I said. "I'd rather die than keep living this way."

He gave me a reproving look but said nothing. I wanted to get a look at the refugee camp—we could decide after seeing it if it was a place we'd want to go. I think Richard was also weary of the way we'd been living, traveling by night, sleeping in old barns, homeless and lonely. Those four glorious days with the Steadmans—days that felt almost like life could be normal again—had ruined us for this life. Somehow, a taste of a home, a real home, made our hardened spirits shrivel up. We needed that hardness now, back out on the road, but it wasn't there anymore. Richard and I both—we longed to be cared for.

We lapsed into silence as we often did, when walking.

"I wonder if Dad is at a refugee camp," I said. "Hey! Maybe there've been camps like this all along, we just didn't know about them! We could have left the library sooner!" I continued to think about that. What if there had been places to go all along? All our suffering, hunger, danger—maybe we could have avoided it!

"Mom and Jesse might still be alive if we left the library sooner and went to a camp!" I was getting upset. Richard had been listening to me silently, his face grim as usual, but at these words he stopped and turned and gave me nothing short of a glare.

"Don't—" he said, and paused. "Nothing would have saved Mom or Jesse except if the pulse had never happened. Don't talk nonsense. I could barely make it to Wal-Mart and back in those freezing temperatures and Mom would never have been able to travel in that weather. Neither would Jesse."

We continued walking but I couldn't get the thought from my mind that my mother and little cousin might have died for nothing! They might have been saved if that sign was right and there really was food available at these camps. (I assumed instantly if there was one camp, there had to be more. They were probably all over the place. We'd missed them because we'd stuck to woods and fields!)

I felt madder and madder about it the longer we walked. We slowed as we approached a town, the outline of buildings against the moonlit sky giving us warning. Like most towns we'd seen since the pulse, this one looked like a band of drunken madmen had blundered through, destroying everything in their path. Even in the dim moonlight you could tell it was a mess. The acrid smell of burnt wood hit us. We scanned the buildings for lights, for signs of life. If there were people around, we'd have to hide. We heard nothing, saw no sign of occupancy. The houses, as we slowly walked down the sidewalk, were broken up, windows smashed, doors actually swinging on loose hinges. We came to a block where an entire row of small homes, all close together, were merely burnt remains.

We weren't surprised. Many towns we'd passed since leaving our own had looked like this. And we were used to seeing plumes of smoke in the distance, no matter where we were. Fires seemed commonplace.

"It's a ghost town," I whispered. But Richard shook his head at me, motioning me to be silent.

I wanted to talk. I wanted to say, "Why does this happen? Why do people have to be so savage?" But I already knew the answer. There were gangs of survivors who really were madmen; they didn't care about anything or anyone. We'd heard rumors they even ate people.

It was depressing. I stopped looking at the damaged homes with their weedy, overgrown lawns. As we neared the end of the street, I said, "I think we went the wrong way. I don't see any refugee camp."

Richard pointed. A sign, hung haphazardly across the wooden gate of an abandoned house, said, "Refugee Camp Ahead, ½ mile. Again the handwritten words were beneath the official words, Food! Protection! Medical! An arrow showed we were heading in the right direction. We continued on.

"What if the camp isn't being run by the government?" Richard said.

"Who else would run it?" He didn't answer right away and so I thought about it a minute. "A charity? You think it's being run by a charity?"

Richard stopped. "I don't think we should go to the camp."

I gaped at him. "Why not? They have FOOD!"

"We don't know that," he returned, looking up and down the street.

"The sign said so!" I was astounded by my brother. Didn't he want to eat a good square meal? Wasn't he as hungry and miserable as I was?

"Sarah, a sign saying so doesn't make it so."

I gasped in disbelief. "What possible reason would there be for anyone to lie?"

"To get people to come willingly!"

"But if they want us to come, they must have food and supplies! Why else would they—remember what that farmer told us? They took his family's food to bring to camps like this!"

"That's not what he said. He said they were setting up soup kitchens. A refugee camp is a thousand miles from a soup kitchen."

I started walking in the direction of the camp. "I don't care what they call it; soup kitchen, refugee camp, whatever—I just want a place to go!"

Richard caught up to me but he said, "Wait. Let's wait until morning to find the place. Then we'll watch it."

"Watch it?"

"I have binoculars, remember? I want to see what's going on. Once we get inside one of those places, we may not be able to leave."

"Why wouldn't we? And maybe we won't WANT to leave! If they have food and a bed, I'll be happy to stay!"

"Just humor me," Richard said. "If everything looks kosher, we'll go in. We still have provisions from Tom and Martha. You can wait another day."

I felt tears pop into my eyes. I hadn't realized how much hope that sign had given me until now, until Richard was taking it away. The idea of the government having food for us—even an unfair government that would take food from its rightful owners—still made me feel that the world hadn't ended. There was still a semblance of order, of help. Plus, I was tired of being scared and dirty and homeless. I wanted to go—even if I couldn't get out again.

"I'll go without you. Watch for me tomorrow and I'll wave something at you to let you know everything's okay."

Richard let out a heavy, exasperated breath. "No way. We stay together. And I'm not letting you in that place until we see it and watch."

"I'm tired, Richard." I met his gaze and could barely hold back tears.

"I'm sorry. I know."

He took my arm gently and turned me back toward the deserted street of broken-down homes. We headed back the way we'd come but he stopped in front of a house that had a little wooden gate. Most of the fence was smashed in, but the entry was intact.

"Wait here a sec," he said, and gently pushed, until it swung open silently.

"Where are you going?" I hissed. He motioned with a hand for me to stay put. I guessed he was seeing if it was fit to spend the rest of the night in. We'd stayed in lots of places that weren't exactly "fit," so even though the house looked eerie and empty, it was probably no worse than other shelters we'd slept in.

Richard had used the walkway and went right up to the front steps and then the door. He knocked! He looked back at me, holding up a hand, motioning me to wait, and then tried the front door. It was locked. I could stand it no longer and went to join him.

"I told you to stay there!'

"It's creepy standing out there alone! What if somebody comes and sees me alone?"

"Fine. C'mon." I followed him off the porch and around the side of the house. From the sides, the house and the neighboring one looked more normal. Dark, but not destroyed. Windows were intact. From the yard, we could see other backyards of the surrounding homes, and these homes looked untouched as well, except equally silent and empty. "Everyone's probably at the camp," he murmured.

"You see?" I cried, in a whisper. "They went to the camps for help!"

"Maybe they weren't given a choice," he said.

101

I felt disgusted with Richard. It was his pessimistic nature rearing its pessimistic head. I wanted to join everyone else and go to the camp.

At the back of the house Richard went up to a window and, pressing his face against it, peered inside.

"What are you doing?" I whispered. "It's too dark to see anything!" But he turned and looked back at me with a surprised expression.

"I can see enough! Things look normal in here!" He turned back and took another look, while I glanced around us anxiously.

"This place doesn't look looted like most houses!" he said.

This was a surprise. Back in Xenia, houses seemed universally broken into with shattered windows, smashed-in doors, and the contents strewn about. Many of the homes in this town looked that way, too—from the front. Why would this one be different on the inside? Richard took a knife from his pack and tried to jimmy up the window. In a few minutes he was able to raise it a couple inches and then high enough so he could climb in. I felt my heart thumping. He threw one leg over the sill and met my eyes.

"Wait here."

CHAPTER TWENTY-THREE

ANDREA

At the door to the safe room, I hesitated. During a skirmish, the only way anyone was supposed to open the door from the inside was if the person on the outside coded the word 'friend,' using tap code.

We were supposed to memorize the table, the whole alphabet, so we could theoretically knock code any message we wanted, but Lexie and I had both memorized 'friend' and then forgotten the rest. I knocked two taps, followed by one; that was 'f.' I gave four taps, followed by two—that was 'r;' I'd just tapped 'i' when I heard the bolt moving, and the door being unlocked. It swung open and there was Mrs. Martin.

I hoped she would say, "Yeah, he's here. I went up and got him because you took too long," that sort of thing. But she looked at me in surprise for a moment. "Where's your brother? Quentin's worried about him not being here."

"Oh, my gosh!" I felt like slumping to the ground. "I thought you brought him down!"

Mrs. Martin gave me a look of concern. "Where'd you leave him?"

I quickly explained to her what happened. I steeled myself for the disapproval that would follow–but hurriedly added, "I just don't understand why he'd take off when he knew I was getting his toy!" I held it up in frustration. "It doesn't make sense."

"All right, don't panic," she said. "Probably one of the other adults saw him and grabbed him so he'd be safe. They wouldn't want to leave a child alone during an attack." She hadn't meant it as a jab, but it cut deeply, because the unspoken reproof was that I had done precisely that. I'd left him alone while we had intruders on the property.

"I'm so sorry," I said.

Behind her I heard Quentin saying, "Is it Aiden? Did Andi bring Aiden?" His little face appeared beside Mrs. Martin. *Perfect! Just what I didn't need*!

"Where's Aiden?" he asked me, wide-eyed.

Mrs. Martin shooed him back into the room. She looked at me and said, "Go find out who's got him." But then she frowned. "No. Wait. You get in here and I'll go look for him."

But I felt guilty about letting Aiden go missing and I didn't want to stay safe and sheltered away. I wanted to look for him. Mrs. Martin had gone to the gun vault and she now slung her rifle across her shoulder and said, "I'll find your brother."

"Yeah, find him!" cried Quentin.

She started out, but I grabbed her arm. "Please, Mrs. Martin! I messed up and I want to find him!"

"It doesn't matter if you messed up," she replied. "You stay down here. Jolene and Mrs. Wasserman are here also." I felt deflated. She said, more gently, "It's always better to have several adults with the little ones."

I wasn't sure if she'd called me an adult on purpose; or if she was just trying to contrast my age with the children; but I felt she'd given me a compliment. Even though I'd messed up, Mrs. Martin considered me an adult! Nevertheless, I needed to find my brother. It was my fault he was out there.

"Mrs. Martin, please! I need to!" She stared at me a moment and then went back in the room and got me a rifle.

"OK. You check downstairs and I'll do the up. He's probably scared as all get-out—"

"Check under the beds!" I remembered how he and Quentin had stayed under our bunk bed last week during that attack. At the top of the stairs before we parted she stopped, meeting my eyes. "Andrea?"

I waited.

"Be careful."

"I will. You, too."

I double-checked my firearm to make sure it was loaded and cocked. Holding it carefully, I rounded corners like James Bond, reminding myself that this was no game, no joke, and not a drill. We did hold drills now and then; one of our families had a man who taught home defensive strategies. I'd learned how to enter a room that might be occupied; how to shoot in a dwelling to cause the least amount of collateral damage; how to use what I knew about the house against an intruder who would not be familiar with it. I put it all to use as I checked first one room and then another, lightly calling my brother's name.

"It's okay, you can come out," I crooned. "I have your Luke Skywalker!" Or, "Luke wants you! He's lonely!" Still no sign of my brother. As I passed other members of our compound watching at windows, I asked if they'd seen Aiden. No one had. I checked the small hallway where I'd left him again—just in case he'd returned. It was empty.

Then I heard him. "I want my Luuuuuuuuke!"

His voice was coming from outside! I rushed towards the back door—I had to go get him! But someone almost knocked me over, trying to get there first. It was Lexie.

"Don't open it!" she cried, throwing herself against the door. "They've got Aiden! We saw it from upstairs! They're using him as a hostage!"

"So let me out there! I can get him!"

"You can't! You can't, Andrea!"

I stared at Lexie unbelievingly. How could she act this way? I needed to help my brother!

"Wait for my dad!" she said. "We're not allowed to negotiate!"

"I don't want to negotiate!" I replied, gritting my teeth. "I want to kill those—"

"I know," she said. "But there's more than one. Just wait for my dad. See what he says to do."

I ran to the nearest window, frantically trying to lay my eyes on my brother. And then I saw him. He was kicking and thrashing, just like he'd done for me, but in the arms of a big man who was carefully keeping him right in front of him with one arm, holding a gun in his other. A second man was with them. Mrs. Martin and Blake had come down and joined Lexie near the door. I saw them from the corner of my eye, but my attention was glued to the scene in the yard.

"Like I said," the man called. "Bring us some food and nobody gets hurt!'

Aiden, crying, tried to struggle free and the man doubled his hold on him.

When no answer came from the house, the second man put a handgun to Aiden's little head. "We'll count to 50! Bring something out or say goodbye to this child."

A shiver of horror ran through me. I was literally seeing red. They were threatening to kill my brother! And it was my fault! And now, if we had to give them supplies, we were going to lose a whole lot more than a single chicken. All on account of me.

I stared at the door where Lexie stood guard. I wanted to know what exactly they wanted in exchange for my brother.

"You can't go out there," Mrs. Martin said.

"Let my dad and the others decide what to do," said Lexie, again.

"It's my fault he's out there!"

Blake, watching at a different window, said, "Lower your voices; they heard you."

I ran to Blake's window, and saw they'd come a bit closer to the back door.

"We know you're in there!" one hollered. "You want this boy alive? We want meat!"

"Okay! Hold on!" I shouted. Mr. Martin rounded the wall and came at us, his gaze filled with concern.

"Andrea. Are you negotiating with them? You signed an agreement, just like everyone who joins this compound, not to negotiate with marauders!"

"They've got my brother!" My voice broke.

He nodded. "I'm aware of that. And we are working on this. We will figure out how to handle this. But you don't have the right or the authority to promise those men anything."

"Figure out how to handle this? Mr. Martin! You don't know what to do, either! But you can't sacrifice my brother!"

He gave me a level stare. "I have no intention of doing that." He paused. "We have sharp-shooters getting into position as we speak."

I gasped. Why hadn't I thought of that?

"Let me shoot! You know I'm a good shot!'

He grimaced. "You are; but this is your brother's life at stake and it's going to feel different. Emotions have a way of tripping us up. Why do you think doctors don't operate on their own family? No, you'd better let the others handle this. I've got Marcus and Bryce upstairs right now." Marcus and Bryce were older men, brothers. They'd lived together before the pulse, before coming to the compound. Bryce, I knew, had issues--

"But if they miss—" I didn't finish the sentence. In a blink I knew what I had to do. I would run upstairs to a back window and take out

106

that man holding my brother! Mr. Martin read my mind and before I could dart past him, he stopped me and took my rifle. I gave him an agonized look, but there was no time to argue. I still had my .380. I turned and started running towards the main living area and the stairway.

"Andrea Patterson! You get right back here!" Mr. Martin could sound formidable when he was mad but I kept right on running. I figured if it was HIS baby brother, he wouldn't have stopped, either! I took the steps in twos. Those men had said they were gonna count to fifty. I prayed that hunger and desperation would be enough to make them wait longer.

I went into a guest bedroom, a room that overlooked the back of the house and found Bryce and Marcus, each at the side of a window, furtively peeking out.

Bryce had been a soldier in the Gulf War. Since his return, he'd had a tremendously hard time living with himself for accidentally killing two civilians during a skirmish. He hated having to shoot at people. I didn't trust him to do what it took to get my baby brother back.

I approached the windows. We had a clean view up here, unlike the boarded slits downstairs—which would give me a clean shot.

"What're you doing?" Marcus asked, as I knelt down to take a peek outside.

"No funny business!" one of the men below shouted.

I raised my gun, but Marcus put his hand on it, forcing it down.

"You're the kid who can shoot, huh? Well, so can we. Leave this to us."

"That's my baby brother out there!" Behind me I heard people entering the room.

"I'm sorry, gentleman—" It was Mr. Martin's voice; "I tried to stop her; It seems Miss Patterson is just filled with bad ideas, today."

I bit my lip. But it didn't matter. The man holding my brother was tall. I could hit him right in the forehead, I was sure of it—if I had a rifle.

"Look, Mr. Martin. If you give me my rifle, I can get the tall guy holding my brother. One of these guys can get the other one."

He shook his head in the negative.

"Let me do this, please!"

"Andrea, if you miss, if you hit your brother, or if one of them does,

107

you will have to live with that for the rest of your life! I can't let you put yourself in that position!"

"I'm already to blame! I already have to live with this! Let me make it right!"

"She's to blame?" Bryce murmured. "Did she bring 'em here?"

He stared at me differently, but I'd noticed he wasn't holding his gun tight; With a sudden thought, I grabbed his rifle—and, miraculously, he just let me!

No one seemed to expect me to successfully get the firearm because it was like slow motion: Mr. Martin's voice, calling, "Andrea! Don't you shoot!" as though from a great distance, another world. Ignoring him, I lifted the firearm, got my sight through the laser scope, fixing it right on the guy's head. Mr. Martin rushed forward, and just about reached me! But he saw it was too late and held back, not wanting to mess up my shot. If I missed and hit Aiden, it would be only my fault.

Bryce was far stronger than I was; I shouldn't have been able to take his gun. But I believe he didn't have a heart to shoot—for any reason.

I suffered from no such qualm.

I took my shot. The man holding Aiden fell backwards instantly, taking my brother with him.

CHAPTER TWENTY-FOUR

SARAH

I held my breath after Richard climbed in the window and disappeared into the dark recesses of the house. I listened with my whole being, expecting any second to hear a crash or a gunshot. I was already planning my escape route, which way I'd run from the yard. I would keep running too, until I reached that camp with food. But in a few minutes I heard Richard's voice from inside, coming towards me.

"It's okay. It's empty." In a moment I heard the back door being unlocked and then Richard was there looking at me brightly, holding the door open.

"Hurry up," he said. "Get in!" Once inside, he closed and locked the door behind me. He was almost smiling, now. "Do you believe this?" he asked.

The place looked like a normal house, like a house before the EMP made everyone go crazy and destroy everything. I found my flashlight and started looking around. Martha had given us two extra batteries—I could afford to use it.

"All the front rooms are a mess, as if looters had been here; but look at this kitchen! This and over here." He led me to a small sitting room which was neat and inviting. "Whoever lived here either cleaned up some of the rooms—or messed up some for appearances."

"The new 'keeping up with the Joneses'" I quipped. "How to make your house look ransacked!"

"Save the light," Richard said. "Your eyes will adjust in a minute."

I shut off the flashlight and we returned to the kitchen. I swept the light over the counters—and cringed. "They're dirty!"

"That's droppings! There are mice. Let me set our traps—we have bait from what Tom and Martha gave us."

Richard sounded excited but this news did not thrill me. On an impulse I opened a cabinet door, expecting to find nothing. Everyone used up their food after the pulse—they had to. But when I opened it, what I saw blew my mind.

"Richard, look!" He came over and we stared in disbelief. It was food. Real, honest to goodness food. Two boxes of cereal, sugar, flour, cookies, and lots of canned goods—Richard tore open a bag of cookies and gave me a handful.

"Maybe I won't set those traps." He paused. "Don't eat anything that isn't fully sealed." As we bit into the cookies, I stared at them as though they might disappear. The taste was unimaginably good. Chocolate chip. At Martha and Tom's we'd had oatmeal-raisin cookies and they'd tasted wonderful—all food tasted wonderful—but these tasted sublime.

Richard, his mouth full and working, began opening the rest of the cabinets. A few of them had more food. It was as if the people who lived here had never suffered the pulse. Only they had to have gone through it, just like the rest of us. How they still had all this normal food, we didn't know. And how we ended up here, when Richard might have tried to knock at a thousand similar doors, was an absolute miracle. I silently gave thanks to God. He was sustaining us, one way or another.

"Don't eat too much," Richard warned. I was taking handfuls of boxed granola and eating it as quickly as I could. I kept feeling like I had to prove it was real; as though it could be taken from me at any second. Just as I'd felt at the Steadmans' house, the sensation of chewing something so tasty and crunchy and processed—was heavenly.

"I can't stop!" I gasped.

Richard reached out and grabbed my arm. I thought he was trying to stop me in order to prevent me from getting sick, but he said, "Shh! Listen!"

We heard the sound of a vehicle approaching. We stared at each other.

"C'mon," he said. We moved to the front of the house, holding back from the windows enough not to be seen, but so we could see the street." He whispered. "Stay down!"

In the dim moonlight, approaching headlights cut swaths into the darkness, but as it lumbered past, we could make out the outlines of an army truck. The open bed in the back held cargo—or people—we couldn't be sure.

After it had gone by, I looked at my brother. "Was that people in the back?"

"Not sure. I think so."

"I bet they're rescuing people and taking them to the camp!"

"Rescuing—or rounding up." He looked around. "Whoever lived here didn't need to be rescued—not yet. But they're gone. And not looted. Why not?"

We returned to the kitchen but by this time my stomach was protesting the onslaught of food I'd given it. "I don't feel good."

"You ate too much. Go lie down."

I drank the last of the bottled water Martha had given me and went to lay on the sofa. I fell asleep almost instantly. I slept like Jesse used to after finishing a full bottle of formula.

When I woke up, the light in the room was different. For a moment I couldn't place where I was and I sat up, blinking, and looked around. Oh.

Richard was on a recliner, stretched out asleep, a blanket across him. I remembered we had food and I tiptoed to the kitchen, my heart soaring just because there was something to eat. A mouse scurried away. I watched it, feeling like a different person. Because the old Sarah would surely have shrieked to find a mouse in the kitchen. But I just watched it go, my only resentment being it might get into food we could otherwise eat.

I grabbed the granola but remembered my stomach and put it back. I started searching the cabinets for something that might be easier on my tummy.

I saw a lot of instant oatmeal. If only there was water...but it would have to be heated. "There's water in the lower cabinets," came Richard's voice.

"But we can't heat it, right?" I asked.

"No. If we light a fire it could be spotted. We need to stay beneath the radar." We settled upon the granola but I ate slowly, chewing each mouthful fully. It still tasted wonderful.

We discussed the mystery of why anyone would leave this house while there was still food. "It doesn't make sense," I said. "Everyone would have eaten up their supplies or been looted by now."

"I think these people went to the camp; I think the army or the government or whoever they are is patrolling this area heavily and they took everyone to the camp."

"But why would they go if they didn't have to?"

"Because if they didn't go along with it like everyone else, then people would know they still had food." He was chewing, and swallowed. "I think they figured they could come back. They went because they had to, but figured on coming back."

"So why didn't they?" As soon as the words left my mouth, I knew the answer: I knew it before Richard said it.

"Because they can't. The camps are prisons."

I didn't want to believe that but this house seemed to be proof. There was no other reason why anyone in their right mind would abandon so much food. We explored the rest of the house. The basement, like the front rooms, was a mess. There were two oblong windows, each with one board across them but with room to see inside. We now figured the mess was part of the facade, the front, to make people think everything valuable would be gone by now. They'd done a thorough job of that, with empty paint cans, rags, clothing, and all kinds of garbage strewn all over the floor.

There was a big pile of stuff against a small door in one corner; light stuff, dirty clothing and rags. Richard pushed it aside and tugged open the door. It seemed like some kind of dark closet, windowless. He shone our flashlight and we saw a metal shelving unit—stacked with white buckets. He drew in a sharp breath.

"These are food storage buckets! They're like ones we used when I worked at the bakery!" We walked in and saw the room had similar shelving on three sides—and all contained rows of similar white buckets or canned goods. "Eureka!" said Richard.

Smiling, I cried, "Look! They're labeled! This says, Rice, beans, tortilla chips and salsa! I can't believe it!" Richard and I looked at each other in amazement.

"I think I should have said, 'Open Sesame! I feel like Aladdin!'" Richard said. One unit held stacks of odd-shaped containers. "Water bricks," Richard said. "Amazing." Another unit was two-thirds empty, which we figured was the food they'd eaten before getting conscripted to the camp.

"This proves it," Richard said, turning to me. "Whoever lived here was ready for a long-term disaster. If they left, it was because they had to." We found books that added weight to this theory, because they were all about surviving disasters, storing food, preparing for Armageddon, and so on.

"But why wouldn't the government let people who can live on their own, do so? By taking them prisoner, they have to feed them."

"It's control, Sarah. In school, I was researching World War One for a history class. I found a newspaper article where two people were condemned to death—for hoarding food."

"Condemned to *death*?" I couldn't hide my shock. "What country did that happen in?"

Richard turned to me with a sardonic expression. "It was right here, in the USA."

"I can't believe that. America is a free country."

"There was a food shortage due to the war. Hoarding was declared illegal. But I agree with you—I couldn't believe they made that a crime." He paused, his eyes running over the round, white buckets of neatly labeled supplies. "What that farmer said is true. Government can be your worst enemy. They use a crisis to declare martial law and they decide that what's yours is theirs." He turned to me. "These people were not planning on leaving—at least, not on staying gone. They've got enough food down here...." He looked around, assessing the supplies. "Heck, we could probably live off this stuff for more than a year."

We continued moving around buckets, reading the wonderful labels: Dried Soup, Pinto Beans, Rice. Peanut Butter Powder, Dried Blueberries, Dried Peaches.

"They were here after the EMP in the winter," he said, thinking it through, walking around and fingering items on the shelves as he spoke. "So, in winter, you have to heat your house somehow." There were two fireplaces in the house upstairs, we'd noticed. "So, the smoke from the chimney gave them away!" He turned and looked at me, as though he'd figured out a mystery.

"Those soldiers probably came around real nice like and 'invited' them to the camp, promising food and an easier existence. So, in order to maintain their secret, they went." He shook his head. "And are probably still there."

I felt sad for them, whoever these people were. It must have taken a lot of work to put away all this food. And a whole lot of money. Hundreds of pounds of grains, pasta, rice, dried fruit and other dried stuff. They'd been so smart! And for what? So the government could come in with a monkey wrench and ruin it all! At that moment I hated our government. It seemed so unfair. If people were happy to stay at home and take their chances, why not let them?

Later that day, we felt like kings as we sat down to canned stew, peaches, tortilla chips and salsa. Richard said, "Thing is, we won't be able to stay hidden in the winter any more than the people who lived here could. In other words, if we try to heat the house, they'll find us."

"You could still be wrong about the camps," I said. Just then we heard the sound of a vehicle. Hurrying to catch a glimpse, we knelt out of sight as it approached. Another army truck. And in daylight we could now see without a doubt that the back of the truck held about a dozen people. People who looked like refugees—hungry, dirty, and tired. I recognized that look. You didn't live out on the road looking for food and shelter and expect to look like a million bucks. If we hadn't found this house, we'd be one of them.

As it passed, a soldier in the passenger seat searched the street, eyes sharp.

Richard jotted down the time they lumbered past. From then on, he did that, keeping track of their runs. He figures, being the military, they'll run on a schedule. He thinks we may be able to chance an occasional food fire if we time it right. He is so smart and resourceful. He found black plastic garbage bags, and, using two of them, dumped in some water and tied it up tight and put it in the yard in a sunny spot.

He looked like a secret agent, checking out the yard and looking around every which way to make sure no one was watching; then he darted out in the sun, propped the bags against a stone bench, and darted back. The heat of the sun will turn that water nice and warm. I had a bath at Tom and Martha's but I can't wait to feel warm water on my body again!

I don't know long we'll be able to stay here, but it's a reprieve. A blessed, welcome rest from the road.

CHAPTER TWENTY-FIVE

ANDREA

It all happened like slow motion and yet, in retrospect, at lightning speed.

I took my shot at the man holding Aiden and he fell backwards instantly, taking Aiden with him. The second intruder startled, turned and ran. Marcus shot at the running man, and more shots rang out from below us, but I wasn't waiting to see what happened. I had to get Aiden!

I found out later the second guy survived our first round of shells but he was confused about which way to escape and made the mistake of climbing the fence into the riding ring. That put him in an enclosed area. He made a beeline for the far side of the fence but we had men on the ground. More shots rang out and he fell, his legs sprawled out as if still trying to run.

Mrs. Martin was outside ahead of me and already held a frightened, wailing Aiden in her arms when I got there. The moment he saw me his wailing got louder and he cried, "I want my Luuuuke Skywalker-er-er-er-er!" Through tears, I pulled it from my pocket and held it out to him. He reached for it, but kept up his caterwauling; now holding his arms out to me. When I had him, I gave him a fierce hug and kissed his head effusively. He drew in a few shuddering, shaky breaths—and finally quieted. Then, ignoring me as I continued to kiss his face and head, he held up his toy.

"See his helmet?" he asked. (Shuddering breath) "I'm gonna get one like that. When I grow up," he assured me. "I'm gonna get a Luke Skywalker helmet." He met my eyes. "Right?"

"Right," I said, softly. Aiden threw himself against me then, his arms tightly clasped about my neck.

"Take him downstairs," Lexie's mother said. "Until we get the all clear." I noticed her eyes were troubled. I figured later on after the danger was past, I was going to get my head handed to me. Both Mr. and Mrs. Martin certainly had reason to be upset. I'd delayed getting

Aiden to the safe room. I'd gone outside to retrieve a toy after an alarm. I'd ignored clear directions and taken a shot at the man holding Aiden. They didn't even know yet, that I'd also allowed a young man to get away with a rooster! That alone was bound to have repercussions, because he'd come back to steal more. They always did. Hunger definitely brings out the worst in people.

Downstairs, Aiden sat on my lap while I filled in the other women about what had happened. But after watching the other kids playing with their toys, he climbed down to join them, getting on his knees beside Quentin, who was racing matchbox cars. He let Quentin look at Luke but snatched it away when he went to take it.

"It's mine! It's MY Luke!" Quentin shrugged and went back to his cars.

I sat watching, amazed at the resilience of kids. Aiden felt safe again and was picking up right where he'd left off playing. Maybe he had no idea of the danger he'd been in. Did he know he might have been killed?

I shut my eyes, sitting back and hoping to rest. The day's events kept playing in my mind like reruns. I was exhausted.

CHAPTER TWENTY-SIX

LEXIE

Andrea has no clue how lucky she is. She put Aiden in harm's way—during a skirmish—that happened while we were short on people! Jared, Mr. Wassermanm, and Mr. Buchanan were investigating the source of the smoke when those intruders came. After she shot that big guy who had her brother, lookouts reported seeing up to five more people escaping the property. It could have so easily gone the other way! The Lord had to be watching over us; that's all I can say.

At least she knows I'm still angry at her even though Blake and I spoke to her before. She keeps giving me sad looks but I can't forgive her yet. Even when my dad and mom called her aside after dinner—I knew she was in trouble for what happened with Aiden but I didn't feel one bit sorry for her. Later I asked my mom what her punishment was and all she would say is, "You'll have to ask Andrea if you want to know. It's between her and God, now."

This sounded mysterious enough to almost make me wish I was talking to Andrea. Almost. So I said, "Well, I'm not asking her because I'm still mad at her."

Mom looked at me, nodding. "Still? I see you and Blake have made up."

"I can't find it in my heart to forgive her. She was so—wrong!"

"You're looking in the wrong place, Lex."

"What do you mean?"

"You haven't found forgiveness in your heart because it's not there. If you want to forgive someone, you need to find that forgiveness in God. He's got it in abundance."

I frowned. "But how do I get it from him? I don't understand, Mom."

She looked at me evenly. "You pray. You ask God to show you how much YOU have sinned and offended a holy God. When you get a glimpse of your own sinfulness, the depth of it, the scope of it—how evil we are in our heart of hearts—and then you realize that God has forgiven us for all of it!—you'll be able to forgive Andrea. God has forgiven in us far more than we will ever be called upon to forgive in someone else."

This just made me feel ornery. I knew she was right in a technical sort of way. But emotionally, I wasn't there. "What if someone killed someone you love? That would be asking you to forgive a lot!"

"Not more than God has forgiven us for. We killed his Son. He forgave us."

"Well, I didn't kill him."

My mother gave me a searching look. "Oh, yes, you did, Lex. We all did. Jesus died for the sin of the world. Would you say you're a member of the world?"

"But I wouldn't have been in favor of killing him. If I was there, at the time, I would have been crying with Mary and John the Apostle, and whoever else was at the foot of the cross crying."

"Even Mary needed a Savior. Crying for his death doesn't take away your sin. Being sorry for it doesn't take away your sin. Only his shed blood on that cross, his dying, could. Even for Mary and the Apostle John, and the Pope, and anyone else who has ever lived!"

I felt defeated. I knew the only way I was ever going to forgive Andrea was by getting on my knees first. I guess I'd been avoiding doing that. I clung to my remaining objection. "I don't know if I could ever forgive someone who killed my son."

"That shows you the amazing grace of God, now, doesn't it? That he not only forgives us, but SENT his Son to die for us, to be a sacrifice for us, so we can enjoy peace with him now and heaven hereafter."

I was already familiar with the gospel—I'd been hearing it my whole life; but now and then I heard it as if for the first time. When I forgot the fullness of God's grace, as my mom pointed out; I also forgot how totally undeserving I was of salvation in Christ. I nodded my head, accepting this reminder, when we both looked up and saw Jared had entered the room. I wondered how long he'd been there, listening. He gave us a dark, unreadable look and walked away.

Mom met my eyes. "Now there's a young man to pray for."

I went up to my room and found—Andrea. Everything I had just heard about God's forgiveness and how much he has forgiven me for went flying out of my head. I felt a surge of anger instead—I was even angry she was in my room, though I had happily invited her to share it when she first arrived here.

"Lexie, can we talk?"

I could feel my heart harden. I turned and left the room.

Some Christian I am!

I saw my dad in the hallway. "The smoke's getting thicker; fires are moving this way. We're calling a prayer meeting."

"Did they find out what caused the explosion?"

He nodded darkly, and then shook his head. "Gas tanks. It's a crying shame."

CHAPTER TWENTY-SEVEN

SARAH

We've been here a full week and seen the trucks come through twice a day at roughly the same time. There's a morning run and an evening run. The first few times we saw the trucks we didn't notice the guns. Thanks to Richard's binoculars, we spotted them. Richard said they have AKs (whatever that is; machine guns, I guess.). But I try not to think about trucks or soldiers. Living here has been a dream. We've been reading their books and learning a lot about survival. The only downside is having to stay indoors most of the time.

Right after a truck passes, we feel safe enough to go outside, sit in the sun or the dusk and enjoy the spring air. We even feel safe from gangs here—the trucks are picking up anyone found in the area, so we don't worry much about marauders like we used to. As long as we don't let them know we're here, the trucks are the only thing to worry about.

Richard took the precaution of putting boards across the front door, on the inside, just in case anyone gets any ideas of coming in. The window already had broken boards when we got here; so we look like every other house. It was sort of harrowing to make so much noise with the boards, nailing and what not—I kept a sharp eye out to see if our noise attracted anyone; but he did it right after a truck went through—when it was safest.

Our plan, if you can call it that, is to stay here as long as possible. We have food and water. We feel unbelievably rich! It's only after you've had nothing for a long time that a broken down house with food and water feels like riches, I guess. But it does. When the cold returns, we'll have to move on because we don't want to get found out by heating the house. Richard says the soldiers can't be everywhere.

There's one other worry I have, but I haven't told it to my brother. What if the people who own this house escape from the camp? What if they come back?

Chapter Twenty-eight

LEXIE

So Dad called a prayer meeting even though we have scheduled meetings every Wednesday night. Thanks to a new woman in our compound who is a prayer warrior, Cecily Townsend, tonight's meeting was awesome!

Here's what happened. It was sorta fascinating. I always got antsy during prayer meetings and wasn't sure why, but now I think I know. Cecily raised the bar for us all. Compared to her idea of a prayer meeting, ours was tightly *controlled*. I'm not saying our usual prayer meeting was *wrong*—but now that I see how some people do it differently, I like the new way better. I feel like it's what I've wanted all along.

It started out like any other meeting as we sat in a circle on the sofas, side-chairs, and a few kitchen chairs which had been dragged into the room. Normally my dad would ask Blake to play his guitar and we'd sing a few songs. Then one of the adults would talk to us about something on their heart. Eventually, they'd announce it was prayer time, but then tell us what to pray for. (That's what I mean about tightly controlled.)

I always hoped we'd get to pray about *a lot* of things—not just what was mentioned. It made me feel ornery when it was prevented —so prayer meeting just brought out the worst in me. I complained once to my dad who said, "Even a little prayer is better than no prayer. But if you want to ask the Holy Spirit to lead our meetings differently, go right ahead. "

"I've read about praying really hard to get deep and reach the heart of God. But we need to spend more *time* at it," I said.

My dad nodded. "Go for it."

So when he handed around the sheet of songs as usual, saying we'd be singing the first two, Cecily took her sheet, looked it over and then looked puzzled. Maybe troubled is a better word. She's a pretty black woman, beautiful, really, about my mom's age. She wore a light, fringed shawl, and I noticed a gun clip on her belt before she sat down.

She said, "Excuse me, but is this meeting going to be for prayer?"

"Yes!" said my dad. "I thought we'd open with a few songs."

She eyed him for a moment. "We only have ninety minutes, right?"

"That's right."

"I'm sorry, but tonight I need to pray for ninety minutes." There was a pause. The room fell silent.

"I love singing to the Lord, don't get me wrong," she continued, "but, well, is this mini-church time or prayer time? I'd like to do what I'm called to do in a prayer meeting: PRAY."

Mr. Wasserman spoke up, frowning. "What, just jump into prayer?"

Cecily smiled. "Yes."

"You have an unorthodox idea of what a prayer meeting should be like, I think," said Mr. Wasserman, to which my dad nodded his agreement.

Cecily smiled again. "I suppose it's what you'd call a Pentecostal view," she agreed. "We Pentecostals like to get down to business!"

I sat there amazed. Cecily was new, yet daring to question the status quo. Even more, she spoke with no anger and yet was compelling. I wished I could learn to be like that. If I had spoken up it would have come out with sarcasm or resentment. (Like, "Hey! I have a bunch of things to pray for, too. Like my missing horse!") And I would have been embarrassed to pieces. But Cecily was cool, calm, and collected.

My father hesitated. "Well fine then, you can pray. While we sing."

But my mother had been listening with great interest on her face. "I think Cecily has a point," she said. "There's a lot we need to pray about and we're short on time."

"We'll still have time to pray," Mr. Wasserman interjected. "And we need to conduct this meeting in an orderly manner. Grant and I made a list of what we should pray for."

"No one is suggesting anarchy," Cecily said, gently. "The Holy Spirit knows what we need to pray about; and God will lead our prayers with or without a list." She held up a hand as though to silence objections and added, "I realize lists can be useful; but to guide us, not to *limit* us! Let's ask the Holy Spirit to guide this meeting."

Mr. Wasserman frowned. "What does that look like—er, Cecily? What does that look like?"

She took a breath and smiled at us—or should I say, *upon* us.

Cecily's smile is magnanimous. She has very white teeth—not as easy to achieve as when dentists were around.

"Here's what it looks like when a roomful of people decide to pray fervently. " Her tone was hushed. "You walk into the room. People are spread around, some circling the room as they pray while others are holding hands and praying together. You hear a low murmur from all the voices—including perhaps, someone praying unobtrusively in tongues. You stop to check a prayer request board. If you have a need on your heart you take a moment and add it to the other requests." As she spoke, her eyes smiled.

"You find a spot to pray and sit down or fall to your knees—whichever you choose. You start to pray, asking God to lead your prayers. Or you start with the needs on the board. When you're done, you add other needs the Lord brings to mind or that are on your heart. Maybe your knees hurt; so you get up and walk as you continue to pray. Or—" (here her voice swelled with emotion) "Maybe you get under conviction and fall on your face!"

"Maybe you get overwhelmed by a need the Lord drops on your heart and so you pray it through! You do spiritual warfare; you pray for the sad state of the country, or for that person you've lost touch with since the pulse. You pray," she said, with eyes full of conviction, "for whatever the Lord puts on your heart. If you feel the need to agree in prayer with someone, then you do that, ask them to join you for that need."

There was silence for a moment. My father and Mr. Wasserman looked doubtful. "You really think people can do that for an hour and a half?" my dad asked.

She eyed him steadily. "Oh, yes! People can do that for forty days and forty nights—(She met my eyes and winked.)—if God calls them to. Ninety minutes will seem like nothing when we ask God to fill our prayers! And I don't think anyone here would deny that we certainly have enough to pray for!"

"I like this idea!" said tall Mr. Prendergast. "Except that speaking in tongues part. I'm a Southern Baptist. We don't go for that stuff."

Cecily nodded. "I understand." She searched our faces. "If anyone here feels led to speak in tongues, please remember to do it in a low voice, or to yourself, or somewhere solitary. That is how the Apostle Paul says it should be done, unless there's to be an interpretation. I want to encourage you, if you do feel the need to pray aloud in a tongue, it may be someone else will interpret." She looked around. "Has anyone here experienced the gift of interpretation of tongues?"

A shy hand went up. It was Mr. Wasserman's wife! She had her sleeping baby on her lap. Her husband looked at her, his face blank, but slowly he nodded.

"Well, I like Cecily's idea too," my mom said. "If there are no other objections?" She was looking chiefly to my dad and Mr. Wasserman. When they said nothing, she got to her feet. "I'll get our home-school chalkboard. People can use it to write requests if they want." Before leaving she stopped and added, "I'd love to find you all in prayer when I get back."

Wow! What a difference after that. The room came alive with the sounds of murmured prayers, here or there getting loud and impassioned at times. I fell to my knees with every intention of praying through my stubbornness in not forgiving Andrea; but in a moment, Blake tapped my shoulder and said, "Wanna pray with me?" His question seemed shy and cute. I felt a surge of happy freedom.

I was glad to pray with Blake. We learn more about each other when we pray together. But I have to confess it's easier for me to lose myself in prayer when I'm praying by myself. I did ask for help in forgiving Andrea. I did not get a feeling of forgiveness for her. But it's coming. How do I know? Because I know God answers prayer that is according to his will. And he tells us to forgive others, so we know it's his will.

———————————◆———————————

One last note about our prayer meetings. My dad was fine with the format, but once I heard my mom say she wished it was more open so we could pray more. That was exactly how I felt. (It's not that I'm super holy and praying all the time, either! I'm definitely prone to skip praying all too often.)

In the end, I consider prayer like exercise. The more you do it, the better you get at it. Like, I'm getting better able to focus on God, not myself, and not those around me. And I've noticed that when Blake and I pray together, it brings us closer! It's like, while you pray with someone, God is there pouring glue between the two of you. It's weird, right? But it works!

I want to get to know Cecily. She's been taking lessons from Mrs. Philpot, our sole nurse, on first aid and medical care so I don't see much of her. Maybe I'll volunteer to learn first-aid too. But I still want to do lookout with Blake.

After the meeting it was time for lights out but I went and found my dad. He and Mr. Buchanan were cleaning firearms in the mudroom. They had folding tables set up and the windows open for ventilation.

"Dad, the marauders have moved on—can I do lookout with Blake tomorrow?"

"Lex, you know there'll be more. Unless we move to some inaccessible jungle in the middle of Africa, we will never be immune to roving marauders until there is rule of law again."

"Which means you need good lookouts." I pulled out my strongest argument: "Blake said Mr. Prendergast fell asleep up there again the other day." He and Mr. Buchanan paused to look at each other. I knew this was a concern.

Mr. Buchanan said, "We oughta replace him." But he looked at me and added, "With another adult."

I frowned. "Why not let me have a turn? I won't sleep on the job!"

Dad turned to face me, giving me a doubtful look. He lowered the glasses on his nose to see me clearly. "You may not fall asleep, but you and Blake are far too interested in each other to keep a good watch."

I think I blushed to the roots of my hair. "That's not true!"

Mr. Buchanan said, "No one ever thinks it's true when they're the ones involved."

My dad added, "Right. And I'm telling you as your father, I've seen the way you look at each other and I don't think it's a good idea to put you together on guard duty. Now that's final." The two men continued their work as if the conversation was over.

"So I'm being punished because Blake and I have feelings for each other?" Without turning to look at me, dad said, "You know better than that. Don't make this into something it's not."

"I'm just saying what it looks like to me, is all."

"Then you're not seeing the situation correctly. And if you went out and the two of you got distracted and someone down here got hurt, how would you feel about that?"

"That's not gonna happen."

"No, it's not, because you're not doing lookout. Now, isn't it time for curfew?" I hated being dismissed by my father and I hated that in my heart I saw he might have a point. At the same time, I was perfectly sure Blake and I would make a great team as lookouts. I had a good eye for movement on the field or in the brush—dad had said so himself, in the past. I was as good at hunting squirrel and raccoon as anyone on account of my sharp eyes. I guess it hurt my pride because the bottom line is this:

My father doesn't trust me.

CHAPTER TWENTY-NINE

SARAH

I awoke blinking. My eyes stung. *Smoke!* I scrambled out of bed, noticing the heavy, acrid air, grabbed my pack, and ran to wake Richard. "Richard, get up!"

He jumped out of bed as though he'd been stung by a scorpion. "What is it?"

"There's a fire somewhere!" We'd begun to relax so much lately that we slept in the upstairs bedrooms. Richard's room was across from mine and faced the street. Suddenly, I heard voices—on the street! Richard clamped his hand over my mouth as if I didn't have the brains to keep silent. I shot him a look and he took his hand away.

We crept to the window and peeked out.

"They don't sound American," Richard whispered.

I strained to hear but there wasn't a whole lot of talking. It came in snatches, carried on the wind—I couldn't tell.

A truck stood in the street, not the same as most of the ones we'd seen. The back was covered, for one thing; we couldn't tell if civilians were in there or not. Then we saw them: soldiers—carrying torches!— moving down the street, throwing the flaming brands into the houses! Others were going before them, dousing the homes with gasoline or some other fuel. The smoke wasn't just from outside—they'd set our house on fire, too!

"The food!" Richard said. "C'mon!" We crouched down long enough to be safely out of anyone's view and then ran to the steps. The living-room was on fire, one sofa and another small section of flames on a throw rug.

I followed Richard around to the door to the basement but I grabbed his arm. "What if we get trapped down there? We could suffocate or burn to death!"

"We'll hurry—but there are two windows! Don't worry!"

"Yeah, with a board across them!" I followed with a heavy heart.

While we were still on the stairs a loud crash told us a basement

127

window had just been broken. We saw a torch land on a pile of old paint cans and rags, and other of the debris, all of it flammable. A roar of flames followed quickly. I grabbed Richard's arm. "Richard! We can't! We'll die down here!"

He gave me an agonized look. "The food, Sarah! We have to save some of it!"

"No!" Our gazes locked in a contest of wills. I had always followed Richard; he was the reason we were still alive. He was older and smarter than me. But this time I knew I was right.

"I'll just grab one bucket," he said. "I'll be quick. You get the ones we brought upstairs. Wait for the truck to leave and get in the yard."

"No! I won't go without you!" I was already starting to choke from the smoke and heat. I just knew if my brother went to that storage room, I'd lose him.

"Then wait here," he said, and he turned. He stood looking, measuring the distance between us and the little door which led to the life-sustaining food. But the flames licked across the floor, feeding on anything and everything in their path—and there was all that debris to feed on. I could see if Richard hurried to the door he might make it.

But he wouldn't make it back.

"Don't go!"

He hesitated.

"Don't go, I need you, Richard!"

"The water bricks! I can use them to put out the flames!"

"No, you can't! The fire's too big!"

He gave me a deeply troubled look, then turned and surveyed the flames that were almost at our feet. I could see his mind working, the struggle going on inside. I could almost feel his body moving, wanting to leave the safety of the stairs so badly. I saw it on his face.

"Please," I said. "Please."

Finally he turned back, his face like granite. "Okay." We hurried upstairs. Richard grabbed two buckets we'd brought up the day before and I grabbed another. The fire had spread considerably! We both started to cough, and I'm sure Richard's eyes stung like mine. We had no choice but to exit the house or suffocate. We made it out the back door with our lungs bursting for air. The heat was awful. We ran off the porch.

"Get down! Hurry!"

Richard forced me low to the ground beside him, where the porch gave us cover. He had to drag me down because I had stopped in sheer amazement at what I saw around me. Flames. Flames everywhere!

The whole line of houses, of which ours was next to last, was burning. The houses to the rear of us, burning. The trees, which were just in bud, burning. Any minute the flames would leap into our yard and it would burn, too. I realized why we'd seen so many dark plumes of smoke since we'd been on the road. These soldiers, whoever they were, had done it! They were burning everything!

"We can't stay here," I said. "The flames are gonna take over this yard, like those." I nodded at the row of yards attached to our row, all raging flames.

"I know. Let's just wait and make sure they've gone."

We waited as long as we dared but we could feel the heat approaching.

Cautiously, we traversed the side of the house. Flames, smoke, and heat poured from the windows, so we kept to the far side of the drive, stopping when we came in sight of the street. The truck was gone.

Richard turned to me. "You were right. I wouldn't have made it."

I looked back at the burning house. It would never be livable again.

The shelter and sustenance we'd found there? Gone, too.

CHAPTER THIRTY

LEXIE

I am fit to be tied. When I went to the barn for morning chores, I found Rhema gone! I was concerned, but figured someone had put her in the pasture. But no, she wasn't there. It took me half an hour to find my dad—who checked with the lookouts—who saw Mrs. Patterson and Mr. Washington leaving the compound yesterday. On two horses! I am so mad I could spit! Now and then I let people borrow her—but they didn't ask permission! They just left and without even telling anyone here where they were off to!

I am almost sorry we ever saved their stupid lives. Besides the fact I dearly love my horse, we need every animal on this compound. Which reminded me—before the hostage situation with Aiden, Blake and I saw one of the looters running, holding his stomach—a high school kid! Blake said, "That's Miles Jernigan."

We couldn't tell if he was stealing something or was injured. Anyways, we sent out a warning shot. (I MUCH prefer sending out warning shots than having to shoot someone. And this was a kid! Even if he came to loot us, we couldn't bring ourselves to hurt a fellow teen.) Later when I found out we'd lost our only adult rooster, I realized Miles must have taken it.

I felt morose all morning. At lunch I wanted to see Blake, who was on the hill today. The lookouts don't get a lunch break—they either bring food with them or somebody carries it up. (I volunteered.) So guess what? Even before I got there, I heard snoring! Sure enough, Mr. Prendergast was leaning against a wall of the shed, eyes closed, not even lying down, and in dreamland! Being a lookout is a big deal. Our safety depends on good lookouts. Even some gangs go away when they realize we're guarded and ready to fight. They want an easy target. So if a lookout doesn't see them coming and they have an early victory, like, say, nabbing a chicken or two—they are much harder to fight off. People end up dead.

"He wakes up easily, watch this," Blake said, after we'd chatted a few minutes. He leaned towards the sleeping man. "Boo!"

Mr. Prendergast came awake with a vengeance, brandishing his rifle. "Wha-what! Who! Where!" He turned in frantic circles to locate the enemy.

"Whoa! It's just our lunch," Blake said, lowering the man's rifle with one hand.

Mr. Prendergast smiled sheepishly. "Sorry."

I handed out the food. Mr. Prendergast, perhaps because he'd been caught sleeping on the job, took his binoculars and did a reconnaissance of the property, going completely around, taking a full minute. Now and then it rather unnerved me, knowing the lookouts probably watched me heading to the barn and back, or giving Rhema her exercise. They could see a good deal of the back, the path to the barn, the riding pasture, and the back of a few cabins. More importantly, they could see the road and whether anyone turned onto our drive. Gone were the days of enjoying a beautiful sense of privacy on our own land.

But the hill was our best look point. It was from there we'd first seen Roy's gang approaching and it was the hill that gave more early warning alarms than the other two lookout posts. Thanks to Dad's ham radio, we were in touch with people from neighboring areas who gave us a heads up on things coming our way, but the hill told us when they'd arrived.

Here's the latest regarding the sightings of military: Bands of Islamic soldiers are out there setting fire to everything and killing anyone they come across who doesn't renounce Christianity (or any other belief) and embrace Allah; others said the U.S. military was around, and not just to fight terrorists—they threatened anyone who wouldn't join their FEMA camps. We aren't sure what to believe. But I envy dad and his ham radio. It's an astonishingly complicated piece of equipment—too much for me to understand! I wish I could use it, though, because I miss my stuff, I miss being in touch with the rest of the world, I miss movies and music and talking on my cell phone! When dad comes upstairs after being on his radio, he holds what Andrea and I call a "news brief." It's the closest thing to media we've got. Everyone scrambles to hear the scoop.

Anyways, after catching Mr. Prendergast asleep—again—I returned to the house determined to make my dad see reason and let me be a lookout with Blake for his next shift. I saw Andrea when I got back to the house and averted my gaze the moment she looked at me. I knew it was wrong but I can't believe that NOW she thinks I might talk to her—when her mother took my horse! I'm still working on forgiving her. Right now my feeling is, we'll never be close friends again because I can't trust her. She's jealous of me and Blake, and I don't need to hang out with someone who is jealous of me instead of happy for me.

I remembered she was raiding our storage buckets. As soon as I got the chance I went down to move the ones with special treats. All I was gonna do was hide them behind other buckets so access wouldn't be so easy. When I opened the door to the storage room where most—though not all—of our supplies are stashed, I stood there for a moment, blinking, trying to grasp what I saw.

Roughly half of the buckets were gone.

I knew we'd been steadily going through flour, sugar, rice and beans. Feeding this household takes a good deal of food. But it was *too* empty. All the buckets of "goodies" were gone, as well as an entire row which I'd seen only recently, and half of another row.

I ran to accuse Andrea.

"I didn't touch them!" she cried, her eyes wide with indignation.

"You've been into them before!" I returned.

"But I didn't move them! Ever! I don't know what happened to them!" I turned and ran to find my folks. I hoped they'd been the ones to move the stuff, but no such luck. After hurrying down to look for himself, my father called an immediate council meeting. Anyone not on lookout duty had to attend. But no one had any idea what happened to the missing buckets.

Afterward, I remembered about Mr. Prendergast and told my parents—and guess what! My dad reluctantly agreed that until he can find a substitute for Mr. Prendergast, I could do it! I can be a lookout! I'm psyched! When Blake got off duty, I found him. We celebrated with a kiss. Now, if only my horse would return with Andrea's mom, safe and sound, this would actually be a really good day.

So here I am with my journal remembering that kiss with a silly grin on my face, and looking forward to tomorrow—my first opportunity to join Blake on lookout! Sometimes before bed when I write in this journal I think about the old days and want to cry. I wish I could go to school and get bummed out over a math quiz, or worry about whether I'd finished all my homework for history class. Instead I have to worry about whether marauders are coming or a foreign invasion which would wipe us out.

I never appreciated, back then, how much of a privilege it was to live in the United States. We had it so easy! We just didn't know it. If this country ever recovers, I will never forget.

The other thing I worry about is whether Blake and I will ever get married. I don't mean I'm worried about whether he'll ask me to marry him. I know Blake—in good time, he will, I'm sure of it. But even if he does, how can we think about marriage and children when we're either fighting or training for war every day? When new members come and tell us horrific stories of things they've seen and witnessed before joining us? Stories of arson, rape, murder—you name it. It chills me to the heart.

Like David in the *Psalms*, I cry, How long, O Lord? How long will you forget your people?"

And then I remember we haven't been forgotten. We are in a time of judgment. Life is hard.

But we're still here. We are the remnant.

CHAPTER THIRTY-ONE

ANDREA

Mrs. Martin came to me while I was lugging in water to the kitchen from the pump. "Have you seen your mother today?"

"She's usually outside by the builders helping WASHINGTON." I was unable to keep the derision from my voice.

Mrs. Martin gave me a careful look. "Well, he's missing, too. Remember they went somewhere together yesterday? I didn't see when they got back; we got so caught up with what happened to your brother—" she stopped suddenly as if having a very bad thought.

"What is it?" A flash of worry went through me. "You do think they came back, right?"

She took a breath, measuring her words, it seemed to me. "I'm sure they did. I'll keep looking." She turned to go but stopped and looked back at me. "Did she say anything about wanting to go somewhere? If you remember anything, let us know."

As soon as she asked—did I remember anything—I did. "Actually, I have an idea. Mom has complained about not having more clothing. She wanted other stuff she had to leave at home when we came here, too. You don't think—they wouldn't have gone back to the house, right?"

Mrs. Martin's face dropped. "Oh, I hope not. I hope they would know better than to risk a long trek just for clothing. But they did take horses—including Rhema."

My heart sank. "They took Rhema?" Now I was really angry at my mother! Yesterday Lexie had accused me of stealing storage buckets, and just now I'd seen her leaving the house with Blake and tried to talk to her, but she wanted nothing to do with me. She must have known we Pattersons were responsible for taking her horse. No wonder she was still angry! My mom knew Lexie and I weren't speaking, so taking her horse was a supremely thoughtless thing to do!

"Lexie knows, doesn't she?"

"She visits that horse every day; she knows. She's doing lookout duty today—"

"I thought so. I saw her with Blake in camo and face paint. I'm so glad Mr. Martin let her! That's great! She's always wanted to do that!"

She gave me a sideways look, nodding. "It's just as well. It'll keep her mind off her horse." Then she frowned. "Clothing. Really? Why would your mother think it worth risking her safety—and that of our horses—to fetch clothing?"

"My mom was spoiled with stuff. She had a gigantic wardrobe. It was, like, her consolation prize for living with my dad. This has been hard for her," I said, surprised to find myself defending her.

"I know it. It's been hard for all of us."

"I'm not excusing her," I added quickly. "And maybe I'm wrong. I hope so. But we're both sick of wearing the same few things over and over."

Mrs. Martin frowned. "We could have rifled up some clothes from the other women who have joined our compound," she said, in her soft southern accent. "I could even have given her a few more things. I sure hope that is NOT what they are doing. But maybe we're getting all riled up for nothing; maybe they're back already."

In my mind I saw a picture of my mother's closet, stuffed with designer clothes; and her jewelry box, which was in a safe, still holding a healthy amount of expensive baubles (since we'd only begun to trade her jewels for food with Mr. Herman). She'd want that jewelry for future possible bartering, I was sure. And suddenly I was just as sure that she'd found a sympathetic ear in Mr. Washington, and that he'd taken her back to the house. She'd complained more than I had about all her stuff back there and how we could really use it.

Mrs. Martin turned to go.

"Mrs. Martin?" She looked back at me.

"I'm sorry."

She nodded but said, "You have nothing to apologize for."

"I do. I complained about all my great clothes back at the house and how I hated wearing the same few things over and over. She felt the same way. But I think my complaining egged her on. I'm really sorry."

Mrs. Martin was thoughtful a moment. "We should have Mrs. Schuman working on keeping us all in good clothes. There's plenty of fabric around—used fabric—but she's a whiz with that old-fashioned sewing machine she brought, and could probably be re-fashioning things we've salvaged into good, usable clothing for our people." She seemed struck by the thought. "We should have thought of this before now—using clothing from abandoned houses—before they're all burned down! I sure wish your mama would have told us her plans."

"I do, too."

All day I was restless, unable to relax. I lived with the constant worry that my mom was not coming back. And I dreaded the moment when Lexie would confront me about Rhema being gone. I felt so depressed. My best friend wasn't talking to me and now my mom was gone, probably in harm's way. My chores felt doubly difficult as grim possibilities assailed me.

What if they never made it back? What if those rumors were true and they'd run into extremist Muslims? Or what if they'd been forced into a FEMA camp—if there really were FEMA camps? What if they'd run into a ruthless gang? What if! What if!

Aiden had played contentedly after his fiasco with the looter, but at bedtime he'd wanted my mother. I'd assured him I would get her, but I could tell he was already on the verge of sleep, exhausted. So I never even tried. I didn't go looking for her because I was annoyed she'd gone off with Washington. Aiden fell asleep in a minute and I didn't give it another thought. As I searched the house now and didn't find her, I realized she'd never made it back.

Suddenly all the anger and resentment I'd been feeling towards my mother seemed like the most trivial, childish thing. What was wrong with me! So she'd had an affair—plenty of women did. I still didn't approve of it, but surely I'd overreacted. And what did I care if she needed a friend like Mr. Washington? Only, maybe it was his fault they'd left the compound and possibly run into foul play! I was almost in tears. I tried to get hold of myself. You don't know anything, yet. You're just imagining the worst! But a part of me felt dismally sure that after losing my dad, I had now lost my mother.

I'd gone through the whole house and then Washington's unfinished cabin when I saw Evangeline. She was heading towards the barn with the kids, who were being trained in rabbitry. I ran towards her. She was Washington's daughter. Maybe she'd know where her father went with my mom. I'd just about reached her when suddenly Mrs. Martin stepped into my path, stopping me.

"Don't go saying anything to frighten that girl. We don't know where they are. Don't jump to conclusions, and get her all worked up for nothing. Remember, she lost her mother after the pulse." I nodded. I felt worse than ever, sure something awful must have happened to them, but Mrs. Martin was right. Evangeline was only eleven. I didn't want to make her as messed up as I was about this.

"Mrs. Martin, can you ask the lookouts if they saw them leaving or coming back?"

She gave me an unreadable look. "I already have, sweetheart. They saw them leave, early yesterday, just after breakfast. No one saw them return."

I swallowed. She touched my arm. "It doesn't mean they didn't. Things do get by our lookouts, especially if they came back after dark." She paused, and stroked the side of my face. Mrs. Martin was very motherly to me and I'd always appreciated it, never more than at that moment. "They could also be perfectly fine, on their way back right this minute." She tried to give me a chin-up smile. "C'mon. Let's pray over it."

"If they are on their way back," I said, thinking it over, "maybe she brought some of my clothes, too!"

Mrs. Martin smiled. "There you go. Think positive!"

I immediately felt horrible. What kind of daughter was I, thinking about clothes when my mother's life could be in danger? But I couldn't help it; the thought crept back in. Wouldn't it be wonderful if they made it back with some of my stuff—especially underwear and jeans. Lexie gave me two pairs of new underwear when I first arrived, but I have to wash them by hand every night. I'm really sick of having no new things. In a way, I can understand why my mom went, despite the danger. We left a houseful of stuff when we came here. It would be like Christmas to get some of it back!

As we headed to the house to pray, I began to feel better. Maybe it wasn't so dangerous out there anymore. When we'd asked about getting some of our stuff in the past, Mr. Martin told us it was too risky to travel. But Blake used to come and go from the Buchanan's house to here and he never got hurt. Blake says after the EMP people left cities in droves, but they fan out, looking for resources to survive. As they go, they deplete the resources in their path, but then keep going. It's been almost five months now since the pulse, so shouldn't looters have moved on to new areas, for new resources?

We saw Jared in the house, and asked if he'd seen my mom or Mr.

Washington. He hadn't. I asked him if he thought it was getting safer out there as I hoped.

Jared shook his head. "Not likely."

"But haven't all the looters in the area passed through here by now?"

"From this area, maybe. But who knows where else they're coming from?" He frowned. "Even though some go through and keep going, others come, not knowing everything's already been depleted. And then we have those troops on the ground; and possible FEMA camps that aren't voluntary. No, I wouldn't say it's any safer out there." He must have seen my face drop, because he added, "The longer we survive, the smaller the marauding gangs will be. But the ones left will be the toughest—those strong enough and mean enough to get by at any cost."

"So even though there may be fewer marauders out there, the ones left are the most worrisome?"

"That's about the size of it," he said, nodding. I'd never had the chance to take him up on meeting at his cabin, and the way his eyes lingered upon me now brought his invitation to mind. I remembered it clearly. *Why don't you come by my cabin later?*

I still wasn't sure I wanted to, but life wasn't giving us much of a chance to get better acquainted anyway. We were always rushing from one disaster to the next, one attack to the next. Jared was not my ideal future husband, but I'd had to give up my ideals for just about everything.

I had found out from his mother that Jared was twenty-seven, divorced, and lived in Hawaii. He'd come to the states just to visit her—but then the pulse hit. She said he was bitter because he thinks Hawaii was probably unaffected by it.

"Isn't he glad to be here for your sake?" I'd asked.

She thought for a moment. "Oh, yes, I'm sure he is."

Somehow her answer didn't make me sure. I wanted to question Jared about it sometime. Lexie told me Jolene was a hoarder. Ironically, because of her hoarding they escaped having to defend themselves against marauders. When looters got to their front door, the mess, the mountains of junk inside made them figure the place was already looted. Then, twice, people had tried to set fire to their house, but Jared had been able to put out the flames with fire extinguishers. (His mother had a bunch of them, one of the few useful things she hoarded. The

Martins were glad of that. She brought about a dozen with her.)

She brought other things, too, even food. Because strange as it is, they had a lot to loot. Part of his mother's obsession was to save cereal boxes—full, never opened—because she hoped to sell them one day on E-bay as collector items. Some cereal boxes had apparently gotten valuable over time, so she saved them with a vengeance, wrapped tightly in layers and layers of plastic wrap. So she and Jared had been living on cereal and vegetable oil until they got here. Not the healthiest diet, but it kept them alive.

Anyway, Mrs. Martin had been listening to us, holding my arm protectively. She said, "Andrea and I are on our way to pray for her mother and Mr. Washington. Would you care to join us?"

He met her eyes for a moment. I actually thought he might agree, but then shook his head. "I got work to do." He headed towards the door but turned and looked back at me. "See you later."

I felt as though he'd just given a repeat invitation for me to visit his cabin some time. But as we fell to our knees in the living-room, I couldn't stop thinking about what he'd said about the dangers in our world. How things could be worse out there, not better! My mom's a goner! It's that idiot Washington's fault!

Mrs. Martin prayed. Her words were earnest and real, filled with concern. Then she praised the Lord; thanking him for many, many instances of help and protection and care. I started to feel better. I wished I could have the same kind of strong faith Mrs. Martin had. When she fell silent, it was my turn to pray. "God, I need your help!" Those were the only words that came to mind, and, it turned out, the only words I had time to utter.

The alarm sounded. My muscles tensed as we waited. I hoped to hear the short blasts of a warning. Mrs. Martin grabbed one of my hands and gave it a reassuring squeeze. "It's probably nothin'," she said.

But the loud siren wailed nonstop. We jumped to our feet.

"The little ones! Let's get them downstairs!" she cried, hurrying ahead of me. I soon passed her, my feet flying. No way was I gonna let my brothers or any of the kids face another hostage situation! I ran to the yard and looked frantically around.

The children were nowhere in sight.

CHAPTER THIRTY-TWO

SARAH

We needed a place to hide our buckets but behind us in a crackling, snapping fury, everything burned. I hadn't realized before how fire is loud. It was a beast at our heels, hurrying us forward, away from the area. My bucket probably weighed less than 15 pounds but I soon found it more than I could carry. There was no handle, for one thing. I had it in my arms—big, heavy, and klutzy. Richard had two—one stacked atop the other—and had to find his way looking around them. We'd only gone a short distance, leaving the street and crossing an adjacent, lumpy field, when I felt too weary to continue.

"I need to stop." Richard looked ready to protest but I plunked down my bucket and then sat on it. He grimaced, but ended up doing the same.

"You realize we're out in the open right now," he said, wiping his sleeve across his forehead and looking around. Since our house had been at the edge of town, we were now in the midst of what would have been farmland, soybeans, by the look of it. Ohio farmers planted two crops: soybeans or corn, and they took turns by seasons. If corn was planted one year, soy would go in the next and vice versa. This field was spiked with last year's corn stalk debris so they would have planted soybeans this year—if they'd been able to plant. But they hadn't, thanks to the pulse. It was now unplanted and weedy. It was astonishing how quickly the landscape went from small main streets to open fields. There was no in-between, no endless suburb like we'd known outside of L.A. Here in Ohio, we were either in a hilly wooded area, farmland, or the occasional small town, with small being the operative word.

"We need to keep going until we can hide somewhere."

Richard was right—but I was so discouraged! I felt weary of everything. Weary of life. I wanted my mom back! I wanted my dad and Jesse back! I wished I could go back to the way things were. I wanted to be watching a movie while lying on the sofa doing my nails. I tried not to think things like that anymore. It was just an invitation to a pity party, but right now my mind was open season for discouragement.

"This is never gonna stop," I said. "Why are we even trying? If we find anything good, it doesn't last. It *never lasts*."

"It won't go on like this forever," Richard said. "Look what you're sitting on! Food! We've got weeks of food here!"

"But no place to eat it! Nowhere to go! No home! This is a losing battle, Richard, admit it!" My voice broke. I didn't want to cry, didn't want to be the old Sarah, so easily broken down, but there were tears in my eyes. "If only the Steadmans could have kept us."

"Forget about them!" The sharpness in his tone surprised me. But he'd looked down the barrel of Mark Steadman's gun. He'd never talked about it afterward, but I guess it got to him. Well, things were getting to me too. In fact, I'd had enough.

"I want to go to the Refugee Camp."

Richard shook his head. "Aunt Susan is gonna need our help. If she's okay—"

"She isn't okay! You know that! You said as much!"

"Look, it's all we've got!" he cried. "I wish we'd gone from the beginning, to find dad. He might've been somewhere between Columbus and Xenia. We shouldn't have started for Indiana, but we did. We need to finish what we've started. Maybe dad headed there, too."

I felt the first inkling of hope at his words. "So you do think he might be alive? You said—"

"I know what I said." He paused. "I've thought a lot about it. Dad's no idiot. Unless he ran into foul play I think he'd still be alive. And I think our best chance of seeing him again is in Indiana. He'd think of Aunt Susan, too. He'd figure we'd head there."

Slowly I felt hope rising like a little wisp of sun entering a dark, dark night. Dad—alive? I attached myself to the thought like a second skin. I needed it to be true. I took a deep breath.

"Okay, let's move." I got up, and almost smiled at Richard's startled expression. But he said, "Wait." He slung off his pack. "Let's empty your bucket into our packs. It's too hard to carry." He took the bucket I'd been carrying which we'd opened the day before. That was fortunate, because they were sealed tight. We'd found a tool in the cupboard which was just for opening such lids but we hadn't thought to grab it on our frantic escape from the house. I watched as he transferred three pounds of pistachios, a six-cup bag of quick oats, one package of brownies (there'd been two, but we'd already eaten one); and a ten-cup bag of parboiled rice to his pack. I knew exactly how much of each item there was because it was all typed out on a label, which had been taped to the bucket.

We could eat the nuts and brownies while walking. Another of our buckets held crackers, tortilla chips, salsa, cough drops, instant oatmeal, raisins, and sunflower seeds. The contents had amused and delighted us. They didn't seem to be grouped in a logical order, but who cared? It was edible. Our last bucket held chopped dates, a pound of hazelnuts, a package of whole bean coffee, ground decaf coffee, black tea, peach tea, sugar packets, and powdered creamer. Not as much nutrition as the others held, but tea! I hadn't tasted tea since the Steadmans, and already it felt like ages ago.

So we started off. Richard carried the remaining two buckets while I shouldered both packs to lighten his load. We were heading to woodsy hills that lined the horizon to the west. Richard said, "Even if Aunt Susan didn't make it, we can live on her farm. I can chop wood. We can plant a garden. If dad joins us—or if he's already there—"

"You think?"

"He might be. And if he's there, we'll have a shot at this, at making it through next winter. By then the government should be reorganizing, sending help."

"Or—"

"Or God help us all." I turned sharply to see Richard's face. He never mentioned God, didn't believe in him, or so he said. I wondered if he was changing his mind or if it was just an expression. I couldn't bring myself to ask. I still had the small Bible I'd found in the library but hadn't had many good reading opportunities.

In the beginning when we first set out for Indiana, I'd thought of Aunt Susan's homestead as paradise. It would be a place where we could lay our weary heads, be loved, and not have to struggle to survive. I'd been thinking of it as if it hadn't been subject to the pulse. Somewhere inside I knew it was an illusion—that even if we made it there life would be a struggle. But I'd resisted knowing. My biggest worries had been about having to tell Aunt Susan her Jesse was gone; and my mom, her sister. But I no longer worried about that. I no longer believed there was an Aunt Susan to worry about. I also no longer believed in paradise—not on earth, anyway. It almost made me want to give up. But if Richard really believed Dad might be alive? That was something. That was hope.

———————◆———————

We came to a road before the start of the hills. It had recent truck tracks going both ways.

"This is an active road," Richard said. "They must lead to that camp. That sign was wrong; it said half a mile. We've walked more than that and I don't see it. C'mon. We need to get off the road before a truck comes." Richard headed into the brush lining the side, beyond which was an incline that looked challenging. The hillside seemed young as far as hillsides went because the trees were all saplings. The ground was sandy and the brush sparse. But it was steep.

"You won't be able to carry those buckets up that hill," I said.

He surveyed the ascent and sighed. "You're right. But there's nowhere to stop and empty them. Not safely, anyway. I'll take up one at a time. And then we'll get them opened and emptied out. They're slowing us down. We'll stuff both our packs, our pockets, everything we have so we can get rid of them." He turned to me. "Holler if you see anything coming. I'm gonna take a look over the hill."

I sat on one of the buckets while he scurried up the hill. In minutes, he came crashing and sliding back down.

"There's an old hunting blind up there! It looks intact. C'mon!" He took one bucket and started back up as I followed. We left the other on its side to reduce its profile, but the buckets are white plastic—not exactly camouflage on a spring day.

Richard took measured steps, digging his heels into the sandy loam for leverage. I tried to follow suit. I wasn't as fast as he was, even though I only had the backpacks. When we reached the top, there was better tree cover. Richard dumped his bucket behind one. He hurried past me to retrieve the other bucket—just as we both heard it: a truck!

"Get out of sight!" Richard cried. But instead of getting beside me or behind another tree, he went crashing back down the hill!

"Richard, don't!"

"We can't leave it there for them to find!" he yelled, as he disappeared over the ridge. I looked frantically down the road and spotted the vehicle. It was one of the army trucks alright, still pretty far, but probably not far enough to miss seeing Richard. I moved forward so I could keep an eye on my brother, who had grabbed the bucket and was heading back uphill, moving as quickly as possible. Among the young saplings on the hillside and the sandy soil, he looked like a big dark snake in the grass.

"You can't make it!" I shouted. "Stop and hide!" To my horror, I watched while Richard stumbled and went rolling, bucket and all, back down the hillside. I lost sight of him but I knew he must have landed near the road. The truck meanwhile was approaching, its sound loud and ominous. I had no choice but to fall to my stomach and hide.

I lay there on the scratchy ground, heart-stricken, waiting for the awful sound of those wheels slowing; of men grabbing my brother and taking off with him, leaving me all alone. I decided instantly that if they didn't automatically shoot him but took him with them, I'd show myself and go, too. No way was I gonna stay out there alone. I shut my eyes and thought of God. God was watching!

Help us, Lord! Hide Richard!

Lying there helplessly, I listened with growing dread as the vehicle reached our area. *Now-- it was here*! My throat tightened. And then, miraculously, it rumbled past! If anyone on that truck was watching the hill, even casually, surely they'd have seen Richard. He'd been a dark blotch against the sandy soil and thin saplings. But, after growling past us, the sounds grew fainter and finally all we heard was the sound of the wind in the trees. Richard called to me. "Stay there! I'll be up soon."

Five minutes or so ticked by and then Richard came over the top of the hill, bucket in his arms. He smiled. I was so happy to see him, I wanted to give him a hug—but I restrained myself.

"How did they not see you?"

He looked back towards the road. "When I slid down, I thought it was over. They'd find me. But I fell right into a ditch! It was deep, too! I landed right on top of this thing," he said, nodding towards the white bucket, "which is probably what saved my skin. That truck went right by!" He paused, and then added, "I didn't really notice the ditch before, did you?"

I shook my head. "No. But I prayed for you."

He met my gaze. "Thanks."

CHAPTER THIRTY-THREE

LEXIE

Blake has laser focus when he's absorbed in something. Nothing, not even I, can distract him. So yesterday when I told him I could do lookout duty, he apparently hadn't really been paying attention. (When he kissed me to celebrate, I figured that meant paying attention. Guess not!) Because he came to me this morning, frowning.

"I wasn't thinking, yesterday. About you coming up the hill with me. I think you're safer down here. I'll find someone else."

"I want to do this!" I stared at him in disbelief. "You don't want me along?"

His face softened. "Lex, lookout is one of the more dangerous jobs. We got a new guy yesterday. I'll tell your dad to put him up there with me. Why don't you give riding lessons today? I heard your mom say Evangeline needs to learn."

Bitterly, I replied, "If I had a horse, I might be able to do that!"

"Sorry—I forgot—Rhema's still missing?"

"And so are Mrs. Patterson and Mr. Washington."

"That's not good," he said, looking away.

"I don't want to give lessons, anyway. I want to be on lookout with you!"

"But the new guy..." he began.

"No!" I'd heard about our newest compound member. He'd come with a rifle and two pistols—nothing unusual there—except he had a guitar strapped to his back and a trumpet in another case slung over his shoulder. I'd been told we'd have a new alarm system once he got used to the drill: his trumpet! We needed something that didn't depend on battery power because batteries, even car batteries, run out. A trumpet fit the bill. But I was in no mood to think about our newcomer at the moment. I shook my head.

"My dad is finally letting me do this and now you won't?"

He stared at me, looking perplexed. "If it wasn't me—would you still want to do it?"

Inside, I wavered. I realized at that moment it was only because of Blake that I did want to! I hadn't realized it before. "Not as much."

He frowned again. "I don't want to be responsible for you getting hurt." He gave me a deep, earnest look. (I love Blake's deep, earnest looks.)

"You won't be. My parents okayed my going, not you. I'm in God's hands, same as you."

He nodded. "Hmmm. Yeah. I still don't like it."

"I'm sorry. It'll be okay!"

As I geared up to go with him, my dad came over and read us the riot act—all the rules, as though we'd never heard them, tips and reminders and finally—prayer. He prayed over us and the compound for safety and blessing. Meanwhile, I strapped my rifle around my shoulder, got extra ammo, and allowed Blake to put camouflage paint on my face, though I couldn't help but giggle as he did it. I then did his face. We both wore dark clothes, and Blake had a walkie-talkie and extra batteries for it. My dad had me test using it because I rarely got to touch one. I thought the whole thing was fun—it was like getting dressed up for Halloween. I should have known better.

I'd made us a thermos of tea, and my mom fetched us some snacks—beef jerky and homemade granola bars, which I shoved in my pack. I was raring to go. I could see what the daily grind of chores was doing to me—because here I was, excited to be going on lookout duty against violent thugs or worse! But it meant a day with Blake and a day when I wasn't babysitting, hand-washing clothes or hauling in water from the pump.

As we started down the hall towards the back of the house, I ran into Andrea. I automatically looked away and went to walk around her, but she touched my arm. I stopped, but didn't look at her.

Blake said, "I'll wait outside for you." I nodded.

"Lex, how long are you gonna stay mad at me?"

I didn't say anything because I didn't know. Every time I thought about what she did, and what we went through to get her and her family here, it still made me mad.

"C'mon, Lex! I told you how sorry I am. I was a jerk and I know it." I shot a glance at her face and she did look really sorry. But I was glad she was sorry.

"I gotta go," I said.

"Just give me an idea, okay? How long do you think you're gonna be mad at me? Because I hate it. I miss you."

"Maybe you should have thought of that before you came on to my boyfriend."

She sighed. "I know I should have. I wasn't thinking."

"I want you out of my room," I said. "You'll have to sleep with the twins."

"I'm not gonna share a room with boys!" She seemed really upset and I was secretly pleased. I'd actually meant she ought to sleep with my sisters, who, like her brothers, were also twins. She'd assumed I meant her siblings. "Fine. Sleep with my sisters, then. I don't want to share a room with you anymore. You—you betrayed me."

"Lex—!"

I walked away. It hurt to talk to Andrea. It hurt to stay mad at her too, but I have a stubborn streak and it was coming through loud and clear at the moment. ("That's not a stubborn streak," my mom had said once when we were discussing bad behavior on my part. "Call it what it really is—sin." Ouch.) But Andrea had gone too far.

I met Blake outside and we started up the hill.

"How'd that go?" he asked.

I was silent for a moment. "I'm still mad at her."

He took my hand and squeezed it. "You don't have to be. She's not a threat for you."

"She betrayed me," I said.

"Don't you think you ought to forgive her? As a Christian?"

I let out a big sigh. "Yeah, I know I ought to! I've prayed about it. It's just hard to do."

We didn't talk about it after that. As we climbed the hill, I sent up a silent prayer. *Lord, I need grace to see Andrea as you do—someone worthy of love. Forgive me for my stubbornness.* Conviction shot through me. I really was stubborn! Tears popped into my eyes as I felt it, the depth of my sinful heart. I hated seeing what a sinful thing I am, but you can't spend a lot of time before the Lord and not see it. Not if you're honest with him and yourself. *I know I should forgive her, but I can't seem to be able to do it. Please help!*

After that, I forced my mind away from Andrea. Instead, I imagined what a wonderful team Blake and I were gonna make as lookouts. I finally had the chance to prove to Dad he was wrong about us! In fact, I knew Blake well enough that I wasn't expecting a day of fun. He would not want me to be a distraction; he took lookout duty seriously. But I was glad just to be near him all day.

When we got up there, the lookouts we were relieving handed over their walkie-talkie and binoculars, and gave us their report. No unusual activity—*thank God*.

When we were settled in with our rifles, thermoses, packs of food, and other supplies, we did a reconnaissance of the perimeter of the property. Then we took turns watching different sides. The shed has a window on each wall so we don't have a blind side; but even so, we go outside now and then to get a better look around. I was keeping a special eye on the horse pasture, though being in the interior of the compound it didn't need special watching. But I was obsessed with my horse's absence. I kept looking through the herd, wishing she would turn up.

"I wish I would see Rhema."

Blake took a look at the pasture with the binoculars. "Don't worry about it right now. Keep your eyes on the perimeters."

I found it cozy in the small shed, but it wasn't actually much sturdier than a hunting blind. There were two camp chairs and a tiny table. In the winter we would put a kerosene heater up here. We were steadily collecting kerosene and any other fuel our people came across or brought with them, for next winter. Some people wanted to use fuel for outdoor grilling, but my dad and Mr. Buchanan, the default leaders even among the leadership team, say winter heating is more important than convenience in cooking. You can cook with wood, charcoal or anything that will burn.

I felt like a soldier up there in my camo and with a rifle at my side; and why not? We were all sort of holding our collective breath against the day we'd be fighting foreign soldiers. Slowly I let my eyes rove back and forth, out to the road and then the adjacent lands. I took furtive peeks at the horses while trying to concentrate as Blake said, on the perimeters. The binoculars were actually a hindrance for the most part; like a scope on a firearm, they super narrowed your focus. I did use them to take a careful look at each horse in turn, just in case Rhema was back.

She wasn't. I prayed silently for the safe return of Andrea's mom and my horse. Then Blake nudged me in the arm. "Look," he said, pointing out towards the main road. A line of trucks was snaking down the road, military trucks, heading our way.

My pulse picked up. "Is it our military?" I asked.

"Not sure," Blake said. He had already grabbed the two-way and was giving the alarm. "It's active!" he told my father, at the other end.

From below we heard the wail of the alarm. I imagined the mayhem it was causing in the house and cabins: Muster arms! Defensive positions! Move the children to the safe room!

Rifles at the ready, we crouched at the open windows. Somehow I hadn't expected anything but a pleasant day with Blake. We'd had so many alarms of late; it didn't seem possible that we'd be facing another threat so soon! But with any luck the trucks would go right by, continuing down the road to wherever they were heading. There were four of them, and we had no way of knowing how many men might be in the canvas-covered truck beds.

"The truck says FEMA!" Blake said, lowering his rifle.

"Then they're okay?" I asked. "Not a threat?"

Blake got back on the walkie-talkie but he shook his head. "Not sure." He gave the news, and then, as we watched, the trucks began ominously slowing down as they neared our driveway. We'd plastered the drive with debris precisely because we knew this day might come. But even as we watched, men poured out of the first truck and began moving the logs and everything else we'd planted there. My heart sank.

Why was this happening on my first day on the hill? Why had I demanded that my father let me do this? I wanted to be home with the family! Plainly I saw that, despite the obstacles we'd painstakingly built up down there, it was only a matter of time.

They were going to enter our compound.

CHAPTER THIRTY-FOUR

SARAH

When we reached the old hunting blind Richard had spotted, he cut the lid out of one bucket. We emptied it and our packs and then re-filled the packs more compactly. It was like dividing the loot—so much food! I felt like we'd just robbed a bank.

But we still had one bucket to carry. He cut it open and we ate from it. Then he removed a shirt from my pack and tied up the bottom, making a sort of hobo bag. We emptied the rest of the bucket into that and he tied the empty sleeves into a knot for easy carrying. Afterwards, we rested, waiting for dusk.

When I closed my eyes, I was back at the house. It had been so wonderful. Like the Steadmans, it still had toilet paper! It was the stupidest things I missed sometimes. The stupidest little things that now were luxuries.

We moved out before sunset so we could get a good look at the camp if we came across it. Fifteen minutes later, coming down the other side of the hill, we saw a fenced-in industrial complex. Sprinkled liberally on the grounds of the enclosure, as far as we could see, were white tents. Dozens and dozens, maybe a hundred!

"Here's your FEMA camp." Richard said. "Look at the fence."

"What about it?"

"It's topped by barbed wire. Why would a refugee camp be topped with barbed wire—unless you're not allowed out?"

"I want to see more." Staying at the edge of the woods, only a few feet from the fence line, we moved cautiously along until we neared the end of the building. I wanted to see the tent area, how people were faring. What we were doing felt as scary to me as anything we'd had to do to survive since the pulse. Anyway, now we could see a guardhouse at the main gate and soldiers around it.

"Whoa—we're not going here," Richard said. "This is no camp; it's a prison."

"You know, those soldiers might be there as protection. A camp's

no safer than anywhere else without it. The sign promised
PROTECTION, remember?"

Richard took in a breath. "Sarah, you can believe that if you want
to, but I can't." He stared at me, considering. "OK. Let's move back
around to the side. Maybe if we circle around we'll see people at the
other end, away from the guards." We again skirted the edge, going
back the way we came, staying behind brush cover. We worked our
way around, but in the back had to cross behind the large industrial
building. We kept low. The building itself had few windows and didn't
seem very risky to pass.

When we got close enough, we saw a few people going in or out of
the tents. A soldier was making rounds lighting torches that were stuck
in the ground—they weren't very bright. The civilians didn't look much
better than anyone on the road. But they must have been getting enough
to live on and they had company! That alone was worth something. We
had packs full of food, but eventually it would run out. And then
Richard and I would be alone again, and no better off than we were
before. We'd still be living like nomads, in a crazy, dangerous world.

"I'd rather go there and be fenced-in with other people, than out
here just the two of us."

"You're willing to sacrifice your freedom for maybe a little
security?" Richard frowned.

I swallowed. "I can't keep walking, and I'm sick to death of
sleeping in barns! I can't go back to that, Richard!"

Richard seemed to be thinking it over. He turned to me with a new
look on his face. "We'll wait until someone comes near and speak to
them. I'm not letting you go there until I know for sure you'll be okay."

"Aren't you gonna go with me? You said we stick together."

"You're the one who's breaking us up, okay? I want to stick
together, but I will not trust my life to the government—or whoever's
running this place." We laid our packs on the grass and sat against them
behind the building. It must have been a well-kept lawn in the past—it
was still fairly free of weeds. It was a nice change from the woods and
fields. Neither one of us meant to, but sitting there, waiting, we fell
asleep!

When I awoke, it was to a strange, repeated sound. A ball. Someone
was bouncing a ball! I sat up quickly. The sun was just peeking over the
horizon, and it seemed to me now we were in a really open spot.

151

Richard awoke and sat up. He took one look around and said, "We gotta move. This is too open." Somehow the darkness of night had given us the illusion of having cover. But I peeked around the building and saw a single little girl, the source of the noise. She was bouncing a ball which needed air and didn't have much bounce to it.

Behind her I saw an open tent with a cot. There was a pile of clothing and maybe a blanket on it. To the side of the camp stood a row of portable toilets. The little girl looked up at me. I instinctively drew back. She threw her ball hard at the fence. When it bounced off she walked over, picked it up and threw it at the fence again, each time coming closer.

"She knows I'm here," I said. "Stay back."

"Sarah, don't—!"

But it was too late. I darted out from behind the building, nodded at the girl and waved her towards me. She stood watching me with large eyes. As I drew up to the fence, I fell on my knees and peered at her.

"Hi," I said. "I'm Sarah. Who are you?"

"Madeline."

"Madeline, are you with your family here?"

"My father," she said, unsmilingly. "My mama's in heaven."

"I'm sorry! My mama's in heaven too."

She stepped closer.

"Do you like living in there?"

She stared at me. No answer.

"I'm thinking about living in there. Is it a good place to live?"

Her eyes widened, filling slowly with fear. "Run away!" she said, "Run away before they catch you!"

"But they're feeding you and taking care of you and your father, right?"

A tear erupted from one eye and was now making a tiny trail down her cheek. "Don't come here!" She turned around, looking to make sure we were alone and then turned back to me. The look on her face was one I won't soon forget; like she was haunted. "Run away or they'll catch you! HIDE!"

I hurried back behind the building. Richard was ready to go and held out my pack.

I looked at him to speak but he said, "I heard. C'mon."

My hopes were dashed. We hurried back to tree cover, moving into it until we felt safe. But the woods didn't last. Soon we were facing wide, empty fields and it was broad daylight.

"We'll follow the road," Richard decided. "At least it has some trees and brush on either side. If the trucks come, we'll hear them."

———————◆———————

A day later my feet were dragging and it wasn't because of hunger. For the first time we were on the road with plenty to eat. But my heart wasn't in it—the traveling, the hiding, the fear. The night before we'd had a close call with a large group of people who were coming from the opposite direction on the road. Fortunately their noise was enough to give us time to hide but we'd been forced to drop into dense brush, cramped and uncomfortable and I got bit up by mosquitoes.

Then I'd been walking with Richard all day. He said any time now we'd be entering Indiana. That gave me small comfort. I expected it to be no different than Ohio—only my dad might be there. It's what kept me moving

We started seeing a scattering of mailboxes along the road now; but the driveways went sharply uphill and veered off behind brush and trees. We wondered if there were houses that might be uninhabited up those drives but we were too tired to risk an encounter. We were too tired to stay off the road, too. It was too much darn work to walk through the woods all the time or even fields.

We came to an off-road trail wide enough for a small truck. The grass was growing high. "This is the right direction and it'll get us off the road," Richard said. Further down we saw a rusty sign hanging from an old, fence.

PRIVATE PROPERTY. KEEP OUT.

"It's just gonna lead to somebody's house. Let's turn around and find another route that's not private property," I said.

"Sarah, we've been traveling on private property since we left the roads."

"Yeah, but they don't usually have signs."

"It's old. Don't worry about it," he said. We continued walking. And came to another sign. PRIVATE PROPERTY. TURN BACK. AREA PATROLLED.

"Forget this!" I said. "It's hard enough avoiding people who don't announce their presence; these people are warning us!"

Richard was staring at the sign but he pulled out his compass. "This is due west. And that's where we're headed."

I sighed. I was used to Richard following his compass like a bloodhound after a varmint. He was adamant about following that compass. It was another little item we'd gotten shortly after leaving our hometown in an episode I wished I could forget. I don't think I ever will.

We'd come upon a small tent in a clearing. The fire had died out and there wasn't a sound to be heard. It took us some time to decide to approach. But we were so hungry and tired we were willing to risk danger to see if there was anything in the tent we could use. Richard approached it slowly and carefully, finally deciding it was probably empty. Only it wasn't empty. There was a dead guy in it! When Richard discovered he wasn't alive, it didn't even horrify me. That's how skewed this pulse has left me. Dead people were just, like, everywhere.

Anyway this guy was military—or he looked like it. Full camo, head to toe. And such gear! We couldn't believe no one else had taken his stuff already. We wondered why not—and then Richard noticed something eerie. He was checking the guy's pockets—not something I liked to see but he said "You never know," and found out the body wasn't stiff yet. He'd only just died!

Richard's gun came from that man; it was on the floor next to him as if he'd been holding it until the end. The thermal tee shirt I live in beneath my clothes came from him. And Richard's military issue pack, his boots, coat, watch, and compass, too. But the most important thing we got was iodide pills. We'd only been on the road for a week then, but we were out of clean water. Richard still talks about how good the compass is, how it isn't a cheap fake—but I think the iodide pills were the real catch.

Empty insulin containers on the ground told us why he'd died, poor guy. I like to think he's in heaven and glad we have his stuff. I feel no 'ugh' factor for using a dead man's things—we don't have the luxury of getting grossed out—but I do hate to remember the episode. It's sick how he died for no good reason!

So anyway, we followed the compass. Before long we came upon another sign. "KEEP GOING AT YOUR OWN RISK. INTRUDERS

WILL BE PROSECUTED."

Richard snorted. "Prosecuted, huh? By who, Superman?"

We kept going. I felt increasingly uneasy. We saw no further signs for fifteen minutes. But suddenly we came upon another and it looked newer. This one *really* scared me.

"PRIVATE PROPERTY. TRESPASSERS SHOT ON SIGHT."

"That does it! These people are serious! I don't want to get shot!"

"Look, we're in the middle of nowhere," Richard said. "There's no surveillance equipment right now, we're not hurting anything and we're just passing through. Besides, we're armed too."

"Richard, it says 'shot on sight.' With this moon they can see us the same way we can read their stupid signs!"

Richard sighed and suddenly looked behind me with interest.

"What is it?" I turned in a panic but he'd started walking over to a bush and was now picking away at it.

"Wild blackberries. I didn't know they could ripen this early but they're good. C'mon, eat."

"If we get caught eating their berries, they'll definitely kill us on sight," I said, but I was also intrigued at the thought of fresh berries. I tasted one. Soon we were picking away regardless of the scratches accumulating on our hands and faces. The berries tasted wonderful and fresh food was practically nonexistent.

We ate as many as we could. I took off the knit cap Martha had given me and filled it with more for later. I needed that cap at night; it got damp and cold even now, though it was June, according to Richard's military watch. But the berries were that good.

"We need to stop for the night. I'm too tired, Richard." At the house we'd grown used to sleeping at night again. I wasn't able to walk all night like I'd done for weeks.

"All right. I'm looking for a good spot." We walked on while Richard looked around for a place to camp. We'd seen nothing like an old barn or shed on this property. Meanwhile, I kept dreading the appearance of another sign or worse, a human being. We came to a wider opening of the trail. And another sign.

YOU'VE BEEN WARNED. YOU ARE NOW FAIR GAME.

I gasped. "I'm turning around! I'm not going any further!"

Richard grabbed my arm, his face creased in thought.

"I think we're okay," he said, finally. "I think whoever this is, it's a

155

bluff. If he was serious, he wouldn't bother with so many warnings. It's like, overkill."

"You're only guessing! You could be wrong!" I was hissing at him, trying to keep my voice down in case the psycho property owner was around.

"I have a gut feeling about these things, okay? Trust me."

He turned to move on. I had no choice but to go with him. We were heading towards a ravine. We'd found that staying as close to the water as possible was safer, more out of sight. Homes weren't built right on the water. And even though lots of people were now forced to get water from the nearest river, they were usually empty at night. Anyway, Richard was about a foot ahead of me when all of a sudden he cried "Ah!"—and disappeared!

"Richard!"

"Up here!"

I looked up. He was helplessly hanging by one leg, caught in a trap of some kind upside down, swinging slightly. Hanging there in the moonlight he reminded me of a sick Halloween decoration, like an effigy, only this was my brother!

"Don't move, Sarah!" he said. "There could be another trap."

"Great gut feeling," I muttered. He was struggling to grab hold of the rope that held him when suddenly his rifle fell to the ground, not far from where I stood.

"Good thing it wasn't cocked," Richard said. It took me a few seconds to get that he meant he might have just shot my head off. He let out an exclamation as his backpack landed with a thud on the ground.

I did not want to end up like Richard, hanging upside down. I was sure if I hung that way I'd burst a blood vessel—or maybe all my blood vessels. I wouldn't even do hand-stands in gym because I've always hated the sensation of being upside down that much.

I looked warily about me. "I don't see anything!" I called.

"Use your arms and feel around the area. If you don't feel a tug or a rope or anything, you're okay." I did as he said, swinging my arms around me as far as I could in every direction, turning to make sure I didn't miss a spot of my perimeter.

"I don't feel anything," I said.

"Hang on," Richard said. "I have a knife in my sock. If I can reach it"—I heard him grunting with the effort—"I'm gonna cut myself

156

loose."

"Don't! You'll fall on your head!"

"Put something under me. But be careful! Keep your arms out as you move. If you feel anything jump away immediately!"

"I could put our packs under you."

"Not mine! It's full of hard stuff!" It was true. Richard carried the single metal pot we sometimes cooked with, a small shovel, an axe, a handsaw, and other utensils and tools that came in handy. I hurriedly pulled off my own pack and placed it where I thought he'd fall. I carried our extra clothing, solar blankets and things like that but with all the food we'd stuffed it with, mine was about as solid and unyielding as his.

In the moonlight Richard's face looked swollen—he must have been very red though I couldn't make out his color. I felt awfully sorry for him.

I had no idea what else I could possibly find outdoors in the middle of nowhere for him to fall on but I saw a pile of leaves and headed towards them. I'd pile them over my pack to cushion his fall. Meanwhile, my heart was pounding. I expected any minute to be confronted by the crazed person who had warned us not to trespass on his property.

Deep woods like these sometimes housed old-timers, rednecks to the ultimate degree who wouldn't think twice about killing something on their property—human or otherwise. It made me crazy to think I was now alone and helpless with my brother suspended in the air. I hurried to the pile of leaves—and suddenly—Ah! I felt myself sliding!

"Ooooooooohh!" My voice rose as I kept sliding, and then I was falling. With an anguished cry, I hit the dirt hard. It was a deep pit!

"Sarah!"

"Sarah?" Richard's frantic shout reached me but I could hardly speak for a moment as I wiped dirt and wet leaves from my face.

"I'm here!"

"I saw what happened," he said, his voice tight. He was probably thinking what an idiot sister he had. When he needed help, all I could do was get myself into a helpless spot too. "Wait—I've just about cut through this rope."

I heard a big thump. Then silence.

"Richard?" No answer. "Richard!"

I was terrified that he'd cut himself down and was now dead on the ground! He'd probably broken his neck when he fell! Or at least knocked himself out. I had come to my feet but I fell to the ground, put my head on my knees and cried. The hole was far deeper than I was tall. I knew I couldn't get out and I was sure Richard was injured or dead.

I tried to cry but tears wouldn't come. Maybe I was too dehydrated, even though we'd drunk water back at the house. But I'd had it! I was ready to crawl up into a fetal position and just stay there until I died. Faintly I heard a dog barking and shuddered. What if that dog was barking because of us? How far could a dog hear, anyway?

But then I heard a low groan. Richard wasn't dead! I started calling him again.

"Quiet!" I could hear the pain in his voice. I made myself shut up. He'd get to me as soon as he could. In the meantime, I took out the little leather Bible I'd gotten from the library. Its home was the pocket of my coat. It was all I had with me since my pack was up there on the ground. I desperately wanted to read something comforting but despite the huge moon, I couldn't see the print well enough. I heard noises above me coming closer. I came to my feet. It sounded like something dragging. Suddenly Richard's head popped over the side of the ditch and he looked down at me. I could only see his outline against the moonlit sky but I knew it was him.

"It's deep," he said. "I don't know if it's gonna reach you, but—" and he disappeared for a moment and then passed down the fragment of rope he'd cut when getting himself down from the snare. It stopped, dangling, about a foot over my head. "Whoever dug this pit wasn't hoping for small game," he said. "We gotta get out of here."

"I told you!" I cried. Reaching for the rope I gasped, "I can't reach it!" I was on my feet, jumping as high as I could but my fingers weren't even grazing the end.

"Look, it's just dirt." Richard said. "Wait a minute." I heard him rummaging in his bag and then he reappeared above me. "Here." He threw a small trowel to the ground beside me. "Dig a foothold into the wall. Dig a couple; maybe that will get you high enough to grab the rope."

I got busy doing what he'd said. You wouldn't think it would be difficult, to carve out a few steps into a dirt wall. It was. I made two indentations and yet it was no good: without something to grab onto with my hands, the footholds weren't enough. Richard had been doing something while I dug; He now lowered the rope again and this time I could reach it!

"I twisted one of those huge garbage bags," he said, "and tied it to the rope. This should give you another two feet." It did. It was enough! Thank God for huge garbage bags!

I grabbed hold and when he was ready, I started climbing.

"You're not gonna drop me, are you?" I began to work my way up the side of the pit. It felt precarious to me. I knew Richard's strength alone might not be enough ballast for my weight. There was no answer but the rope held so I kept working my way up. My hands felt raw on the rope. As I neared the top I felt a great surge of hope but at the same time I felt myself slipping backwards a little.

"Richard!"

"Okay, okay, I gotcha!"

But I was stuck. I didn't have the muscle to pull myself to the top. I hung there, half supported by my feet against the wall of dirt, half suspended by Richard.

"I'm stuck!"

"Try, Sarah! You can do it," he said. He didn't sound good.

I gave a great effort and tried to lift myself with my feet hitting the wall but all I did was end up with my feet over my head. My feet went up but not the rest of me. I was now scrunched up but unable to go any higher.

I felt a slight tug from the rope. Richard was trying to get me up the last foot and over the edge! And then suddenly it was like he had superhuman strength because I felt myself being lifted easily and quickly and I was on my hands and knees on the ground! I gasped with relief and turned to thank my brother.

Only Richard was on the ground too, with a wolf standing on him with bared teeth at his neck! It let out a low, guttural snarl. Beside the animal stood my rescuer, a man with a rifle out, pointed at Richard.

When I looked up to see his face, it was like looking into the face of death. It must have been a man but he was hooded in a dark cape or coat, his face completely hidden from view. It reminded me of the *Ghost of Christmas Yet to Come*, the eerie being who takes Scrooge into the cemetery at the end of *A Christmas Carol*. If this was our angel of death, he certainly looked the part.

The wolf-dog growled again, now glaring at me. Even in the faint moonlight there was no mistaking the gleam of sharp teeth between curled lips. The growl grew louder.

"I'm sorry!" I cried. "We didn't mean to trespass! We're just passing through! We're going to my aunt's in Indiana!" But I was suddenly aware of a really sick feeling coming over me—oh no, was I going to faint? I knew this feeling…I'd fainted in the past.

The man slung his rifle over his shoulder and I drew in a breath of relief. Maybe he was reasonable. But then, in a single smooth motion he drew a sword from the folds of the dark cape. I guess I was weak from living on the road despite our recent bounty of food. I was definitely dehydrated. When I saw that sword emerge from the folds of his garment, I had a vision of him using it, passing it cleanly beneath my head. Doing the same to Richard, too.

He bent over Richard who was on the ground, hurt from his fall, and still beneath that dog's great jaws. He raised the sword.

And everything went black.

CHAPTER THIRTY-FIVE

ANDREA

As I searched outside for the little ones, Mrs. Wasserman came hurrying my way from the cabin grounds, holding her baby in her arms.

"Have you seen the children?" I asked.

"Jolene took them downstairs; I had to get my little one! She was napping. Come with me!" I'd wanted to peek inside Mr. Washington's cabin to see if he was back. I was very aware my mother was still missing and my constant hope was to see them return. But I hurried alongside Mrs. Wasserman towards the house where we met Mrs. Martin coming out.

"Jolene has the kids in the safe room," I told her. "I'm just gonna check that they're all down there."

"Good. You do that. Then c'mon up—we've got trucks entering the property. We're gonna need all the help we can get."

"That was my plan," I said.

Mrs. Wasserman had stopped to listen and now shook her head. "Trucks?" She sounded upset. "What kind of trucks?"

"Just get downstairs," Mrs. Martin said. "Get that baby safe! We'll fill everyone in later on the details, there's no time now."

I followed Mrs. Wasserman who, to my surprise, began to pray— right out loud—as we went. "Dear Lord, protect our compound! Protect each and every soul on this property! Put Your angel armies around us and grant us safety, I pray!"

Angel armies? I hadn't ever thought to ask God to put angel armies around us! Would he really do that? In the safe room, I saw my brothers and baby Lily and did a quick head count of the kids—we have fourteen altogether. I also stopped to give the baby a kiss on the head. She held out her little arms to me but I couldn't stay down there while we might be facing an attack.

Cecily had just taken a rifle from the vault and we hurried back upstairs together. I glanced at her. Cecily was a strong Christian.

"Do you believe in angel armies?" I asked.

She looked at me with interest. "Of course! Did you know when the Bible says the LORD of hosts, another translation is LORD of Heaven's Armies? And when it says LORD with all capitals, it means YAHWEH, Jehovah, All Powerful, Almighty! I know there's angel armies!"

I couldn't help smiling at her confidence. "I'm glad," I said, as we reached the top of the stairs and stopped, facing each other. "Because I think we're gonna need them."

Cecily smiled. "When I'm at my post, I've got my rifle, but I pray, too! I'll be praying for angel armies to cover this property!"

"Good! Me, too," I said.

We parted there and I hurried up the next flight to our bedroom. Lexie had told me she wanted me out but Mr. and Mrs. Martin gave me permission to stay, so I had. Lexie didn't like it, but I think the more we see each other, the more she'll realize she just has to forgive me!

Anyway, a man I didn't recognize was already crouched at Lexie's window. I'd heard someone new had joined the compound and figured this was him. My bipod was in position by the other window, so I got my rifle ready and carefully opened the pane—trying not to present a target for anyone out there. I glanced at the man, who turned and nodded at me—and I about did a double-take. This guy was beautiful! I mean it. It may sound funny to describe a guy that way but he was possibly the best looking guy I'd ever seen in my life. He had thick golden-brown curls that almost reached his shoulder; mesmerizing blue eyes, and a rough-shaven chin, with the beginnings of a beard. Most men these days had given up shaving without their electric razors, so beards are a common sight. This guy evidently continued to fight the growth.

He gave me an encouraging little smile but I was too astonished, taking in his good looks, to return it. So this was the new guy! I heard he was a musician. Then while he was filling a second magazine, he winked at me! I was probably gaping at him, I don't know, and now I looked away, embarrassed. I pulled on my eye protection and got busy with my rifle but that wink was so unexpected—so friendly—it made me feel confident about him. A guy who could wink at a girl during a skirmish had to be someone with self-assurance. We needed all the assurance we could get. I instantly liked him.

"Let's get 'em!" he said, and then shot a full grin at me. He was back at his scope before I could return the gesture—again I'd been too wowed to respond. What a smile! But I had to concentrate—I studied the scene before me. What I saw made my heart jump into my throat. Soldiers! And four trucks. It was true, then—there were foreign troops on our soil! At least I thought they were foreign. We'd been hearing rumors of guerrilla outfits and these guys looked the part.

"Don't shoot yet," I said.

He looked over at me. "I wasn't going to. I got the drill—we return fire, we don't start it."

I smiled. "Right." But my grin vanished. "Do you think they're foreign?"

He peered out front where soldiers were busily engaged in clearing their way onto our land. "It says FEMA on that truck. But I wouldn't be too sure about that."

"If it's our military, do we fight?" The idea frightened me.

"If they shoot first," he said.

Marcus came in and fell to his knees beside me. "Move over, sweetheart. I need this window."

I wasn't particularly fond of being called 'sweetheart' by this man. "It's my window!"

He stared at me and then nodded. "Oh, the little sure-shot. That's okay, we'll share!"

Reluctantly I made room for him but he was definitely gonna cramp my style. I was determined to stay, however; it was my room and my window and that beautiful stranger was there! Marcus dropped two boxes of bullets on the floor between us, and then the three of us waited, watching the steady progress of the soldiers as they removed our painstakingly placed roadblocks from the driveway.

For the first time I could remember, I had a really bad feeling about what was coming. I'd done my level best in many skirmishes, never feeling hopeless about our chances—but this was the military! I tried to swallow my fear. But frightful thoughts came at me unbidden: What if they wore body armor? They'd be doubly hard to take down. What if they just blew us off the map with some high-tech weapon? I remembered Mrs. Wasserman's prayer: *God, send us your angel armies!* I silently repeated it, trying to believe it could happen.

And we watched. And waited.

CHAPTER THIRTY-SIX

LEXIE

"What if it really is FEMA?" I asked Blake as we waited to see what would happen next. The trucks had come to a stop and the men on the ground seemed to be holding a little pow-wow. "Maybe they're just trying to offer help."

"It's not FEMA," Blake said. "This is a military outfit, no doubt about it." He paused. "I wish it was. It would mean we've got a working government."

There'd been plenty of speculation about whether the government was doing much to help the country. But all the sightings seemed to be of foreigners, guerrilla soldiers, not our own military. There was loads of talk about friendly nations who were shipping and flying in care packages, millions of dollars of care packages—only no one had ever laid eyes on any of it. It was all talk. People were claiming to have seen foreign soldiers, and FEMA trucks. Lots of FEMA trucks. Today we were getting our first look.

My dad's voice came crackling over the two-way. "Get out of the shack—you're a clear target. Take cover."

We shouldered our rifles and grabbed our bipods and backpacks. I followed Blake, keeping low and away from the ridge, to brush cover. We found a spot and fell to our stomachs. Looking through the binoculars, he said, "They're almost done. They got a lot of guys helping, maybe fifteen." I repeated everything to my father via the two-way, though he said they had a pretty good view of the front too. We listened while other men from our group, some who had scattered to various assigned locations at the alarm, spoke back and forth, now and then asking questions.

"Definitely says FEMA," Blake repeated to somebody on the two-way. Then suddenly down there by the soldiers, one man seemed to be motioning for the others to stop what they were doing. They'd almost finished opening a path wide enough for the trucks to get through, but even as we watched, the work halted. Minutes passed. The trucks on the road started moving—and went right by the drive. One by one they went past. Meanwhile the men who had been on the ground were returning to the first truck. In a matter of minutes, they'd all climbed up and then it backed off the entrance area and followed the others, moving on down the road past us. All was once again quiet.

Except on our radios. Voices buzzed back and forth. "Did you see that?"

"What on earth!"

"Why'd they leave?"

"We've been saved!"

Blake and I came to our feet whooping with joy. He took me in a great big hug and then we kissed. We could hear the sounds of other people rejoicing, their hollers crackling at us from the radio.

Our men immediately got busy putting all the roadblocks back into place. Every log, every fallen tree that the soldiers had moved. When they were done, they hauled more down there. We have no idea what made them stop when they had come so close to clean access but it didn't matter. We'd been saved.

At least for now.

CHAPTER THIRTY-SEVEN

SARAH

I came awake gasping, with a pounding headache. My eyes felt glued shut. When I forced them open, I felt terribly confused. *Wha— what was going on? Where was I?*

Suddenly I remembered—Richard! The man with the sword! I sat up and looked around. I was in an actual bed! In a strange room. Panic shot up my spine. How had I gotten here? Where was Richard? I swung my legs off the side wondering if that hooded man was going to confront me. Had he killed Richard? No, he couldn't have, I told myself or why would I still be here?

I surveyed the room with astonishment. It was a huge log-cabin, high-ceilinged, but cozy, with a black iron wood stove not six feet from me. I felt warmth radiating from it and moved closer; it was a cool morning for late May. There was an unfinished puzzle on a table near the bed. But wait, it wasn't a bed; it was a futon. The room was vast, but crowded with furniture, blankets, trunks, oil lamps, rugs, animal skins, quilts, and antlers on the walls. They weren't professionally mounted antlers, just one pair upon another, stacked like baseball caps. There were two bookshelves, stuffed with books and knick-knacks, and rattan baskets filled with yarn and knitting needles—knitting! A woman must live here! The thought gave me slight relief—but Richard was still missing. I couldn't let my guard down.

There was a corner devoted to exercise equipment—the sole nod to modernity that I saw. One end of the room served as the kitchen. I realized there was a wonderful smell coming from that direction. I felt myself pulled towards it like metal shards to a magnet. Something simmered on a big old iron pot on a big old iron stove—it smelled like beef stew! I felt a pang of nostalgia for Martha and Tom—this cabin reminded me of them, with its nineteenth century equipment and real food cooking. But where was Richard? I needed to look for him, but I couldn't resist running to the cast-iron covered pot. I had to get a taste of it, whatever it was. It smelled heavenly. All the food we'd found at the house was wonderful, but this was a meal. A *cooked* meal. To my delight, a loaf of homemade bread sat on the table with butter beside it. Bread and butter. It all looked so utterly normal. A human being or beings lived here. Not an angel of death! It was so unreal. How could this food be just sitting here? The world was full of roaming looters looking for anything to eat, and here was this surreal log cabin with food, and I was in it. I looked around and listened for the sound of anyone else but heard nothing.

I took a pot-holder from the table and gingerly went to open the covered pot. The lid was heavy. I peeked inside. I was right. Stew! The scent wafted over me. I inhaled deeply. It was almost intoxicating. But as I looked for a spoon to taste the bubbling brew, a sense of caution came over me. Maybe I was being taken in, lulled into complacency like Hansel and Gretel in the witch's lair--but too enthralled to get out while I could!

I spun around, ignoring my growling stomach, the soothing aroma of the stew, and the scrumptious-looking bread and butter. I saw my backpack on the floor near the futon—hooray! I had my stuff. I grabbed it and swung it on, adjusting the straps; then went and peeked out a front window—and nearly jumped out of my skin. The moment I got near the window, that large wolf-dog I'd seen last night jumped into wild, barking fury, throwing himself at the window, and snarling at me like a hound from hell. I was trapped. I sat down to think.

I looked out again, setting the animal into fresh fury. I was checking to see if it was leashed; but no such luck.

Oh, Richard, where are you? Please be okay! Please come and save me! What should I do?

I realized I was being an idiot—there might be a back door! Maybe that stupid wolf-dog wouldn't know if I sneaked out the back. Past the kitchen area was a narrow hallway—I hurried towards it. As I went by the tantalizing aroma of the bubbling stew, I felt stabbing hunger. A longing to eat. What would it hurt if I tried a little before going? I stopped and hurriedly banged open cabinets to find a bowl and spoon, and yet I was detached, as though my behavior wasn't my own—it was some other girl hurrying to steal someone's dinner. Who are you? I asked myself. That a bowl of stew is more important than escaping? But it was no use. I could not resist the aroma. If it was a trap meant to snare me, it was working, because I could hardly think straight as I finally found what I needed and quickly lifted the heavy lid again. Real, cooked, food!

I ladled in a large spoonful and sat down at the table, not removing my backpack. I had to sit—I had to savor these next few moments. The days at the Steadmans were like a dream to me now. This food was real, it was here. I was going to appreciate it. I took my first spoonful. It was wonderful; it was the best tasting food I'd ever eaten in my life. That was probably my hunger talking but I didn't stop to question it.

I grabbed a knife which lay beside the loaf of bread and cut a thick slice. I slathered butter over it and quickly ate it with the stew. Suddenly I felt like I had all the time in the world. After all, if anyone had been around, surely wolf-dog's barking would have brought them. I refilled my bowl and cut off another fat slice of bread, staring at it with appreciation. It was so wonderful to have bread!

I am the Bread of Life.

Wow. I wasn't sure where that thought came from. But I knew it was Jesus who said it in the Bible. *Thank you, Lord, for this bread!*

I was about to take a bite of it when I remembered my brother. I wished he was here enjoying this bounty, too. I saw then, in my mind's eye, last night's hooded figure drawing the sword. It occurred to me I could be eating while my brother lay dead somewhere in the woods. I had to get out of there! I jumped up. *Oh, God, please don't let Richard be dead! Please, God!*

I am the Bread of LIFE.

I halted, struck by the emphasis on the word, LIFE. It was strange. Words crossed my brain, but they didn't come from me. At the same time I felt warmed from the inside, like a burning that feels stirring but not painful. *It's the Lord! He's speaking to me!* I stopped and thanked God again. I realized that if God took the trouble to speak to me, then it had to be something important, something true. If he's the Bread of LIFE and he's telling me so right when I'm worrying about Richard, then I needed to believe my brother was alive.

Resuming my seat, I took a bite and held back a tear. I have days where I'm emotional and days where I like to think I'm normal. This was feeling like an emotional day. I can be a fool when it comes to emotions. I cry over the simplest things. In the old days, before the pulse, if I was premenstrual, I'd cry over certain commercials. Richard used to shake his head at me. He wouldn't do that now, I know it.

Richard! I know you're alive, but where are you?

I got up still chewing to look for a drink. My first thought was to find the fridge. I had to remind myself there could not be a working fridge. But there was in fact a small steel gray metal box, what they used to call, I think, an ice-box. I opened it, a wave of wonder coming over me. It held a pitcher of water, which I grabbed with zeal.

I found a cup and had just taken my first gulp when I heard something run up against the door of the house. It barked, and then lapsed into a low growl. That horrid wolf-dog.

I gulped down the rest of the cup and grabbed another slice of bread, not bothering with the luxury of butter. I ran over against the wall and tried to peek outside. I now saw there were two dogs, different breeds. The wolf-dog must have been some kind of husky; the other looked like a Shepherd. They were both big and menacing. The wolf-dog came and growled beneath my window, but at least it didn't bark as furiously as before. And then, with a sudden whimper, both dogs ran off until I couldn't see them.

Here was my chance to get away! I hurried to the door and grasped the handle, but I heard sounds. Voices! Pushing aside a curtain, I saw the dogs had run to two people who were approaching the cabin.

The hooded being was one of them, but the other was Richard! I felt such relief seeing him alive, I barely noticed his limp. They were conversing and my sense of alarm receded like a wave at low tide. I would have run outside to greet him except for those animals. As they got closer, the stranger bent over to tie up the dogs. I pushed open the door and ran to Richard. The dogs barked up a storm, tearing at their leashes. The hooded man astonished me by scolding them—because it wasn't a hooded man after all. It was a woman!

"Is everything okay?" I asked Richard.

"It's great," he said, nodding at the stranger.

I turned to meet the mysterious hooded person—a woman—who removed her hood to reveal a stocky blond with pretty green eyes. She smiled at me. "Hi, Sarah. You feelin' better?"

I nodded. "Thank you." I must have been gaping, because she grinned and said, "C'mon in, y'all. Let's have us some lunch!" I was still trying to comprehend that our angel of death wasn't a scary phantom, wasn't even a man. This was the darksome being who had scared the daylights out of me? The one I'd thought was going to

169

slaughter us with a sword? She threw off her cape and surveyed me for a moment, bright-eyed and friendly looking. She looked to be about my mom's age, maybe a little younger.

"My name's Angel," she said. For a ridiculous moment I almost laughed. I'd been thinking angel of death and her name was Angel? "Short for Angela. But my friends call me Angel so you can, too." She went towards the kitchen and I shared a look of incredulity with Richard, who smiled.

"It's cool," he said.

"Feeling better with some food in your stomach?" she asked, turning back to smile at me as she stirred the stew.

"I'm sorry; it smelled so good," I said.

She chuckled. "I understand. That's fine! Come and sit, you two, and we'll talk."

I looked at Richard wonderingly as we sat down. "Angel pulled you out of the pit last night." He smiled. "We used one of our plastic bags to carry your weight. We had to drag you back." Ruefully, he added, "You may be skinny, but it was still a job, getting you here."

Embarrassed, I said, "I'm sorry." I looked at Angel, who was carrying over the heavy iron pot. "Thank you for helping us. I'm sorry I passed out."

Angel turned and nodded at me. "That's okay. You're undernourished, and probably used to having terrible things happen." She paused, studying me. "You're safe here for now. Your brother and I reached an agreement. He'll explain it." She uncovered the pot and added, "After he helps me check our traps." She paused. "I'm gonna check on something in back. You two help yourselves."

Her words rang in my mind. *Help yourselves.* Despite the packaged food we had in our packs from the house, this was real food. Things you could eat hot. I felt like a kid in a candy store.

"So this is the scoop," Richard said. "It's like at the Steadmans'. I have to chop wood, check traps—Angel said she'll teach me how to set them, too—and do anything else around here that takes hard lifting." I nodded, but a sudden image appeared in my mind.

"She must be strong herself...I thought it was a man who pulled me out of that hole last night."

He nodded. "She's muscular. Did you see those?" And he nodded towards the weight bench and weights at the far end of the room. "I'll

170

bet she trains a lot." We were both digging into the stew by now. I was not truly hungry anymore, but I ate anyway.

"So she says we can stay here until her husband gets back; after that, it'll be up to him."

"Where's her husband?"

"He's out on a hunt, or trying to get in touch with someone—I didn't quite catch where he went. But as long as we help run the place, Angel says she'd rather have us with her." He hesitated. "Especially since I can shoot." He eyed me sideways. Richard was not a trained gunman. He'd only shot the rifle a few times, always when trying for game—and only once didn't miss. His pistol had been used once to scare off a small group of unsavory looking wanderers. But he was no sharp shooter.

"You told her you can shoot?"

He nodded, swallowing a spoonful of stew. "I can. I can shoot."

I stared at him, and he shrugged. "Look, I can shoot. I didn't say I was a good shot and she didn't ask, okay?" We fell into silence, eating. "You'll have to help, too. Cleaning and cooking, feeding the chickens, that sort of thing." He eyed me warily. He was probably waiting for me to object, call him a chauvinist or something, but right now those jobs sounded heavenly to me.

"I'd love to!" I said.

"You would?" he seemed pleased.

"Definitely! It beats living out there with nothing!"

He nodded at me, looking thoughtful. "You've changed."

I studied him for a moment, considering his words. "The world has changed."

◆

The wolf-dog's name is Kane, and Angel has two more, Kole and Kool. Kane is the leader of the pack, and the one most likely to attack a stranger, so Angel showed me how to make him my friend. She said I wouldn't be afraid of him once we're friends (but I think I'll always be a little afraid of him. He looks like a wolf and he's got a big wolf snout, and big wolf teeth!)

I tidied up while she and Richard went to check traps but there wasn't much to do beyond washing dishes. I searched the bookshelves and came across *Mere Christianity*, by C.S. Lewis. I started reading it. I've only read a few chapters but I now realize I knew nothing at all about Christianity! I thought I did, but I didn't.

So when they got back, with a big fat raccoon—Angel had Richard shoot it dead outdoors—she brought wolf-dog in on a leash. He immediately snarled at me something fierce. I noticed he wasn't snarling at Richard like that.

"I fed him," Richard explained. "That's what you're gonna do." Angel had already taken a container from somewhere in the kitchen and handed it to me. A foul odor emanated from it.

"What is it?" I asked.

"Entrails," she said. "Dogs love it." I blinked, trying to remember what entrails was, but Richard said, "Animal guts."

"Ugh." I hesitantly held out my hand, making Angel chuckle.

"OK, you see how Kane can smell it?" He was whining and pacing, as if he'd start climbing the walls if he didn't get it soon. I knew how he felt, having had my own brush with the tantalizing aroma of good food so recently. "Let him watch you put it in his bowl," she continued, holding tightly to his collar. I walked past fearfully, thinking the dog would've jumped me if he could!

In full sight of wolf-dog I emptied the innards into the bowl. He watched me, whimpering and salivating. When it was safely in the bowl, I moved away and Angel released him. I had to close my eyes as he bounded towards his bowl—and me—but he went right past me to the food, and devoured it in seconds. Angel made me wait for him to finish and then had me call his name. He regarded me more calmly than before, and slowly came, sniffing. He didn't growl or snarl!

"Go on, pet him," Angel encouraged.

I tentatively extended my hand, going for the area between his upright ears. Amazingly, he allowed me to nuzzle his head with my fingers.

"Now you'll be best friends," she said, smiling. "They say the way to a man's heart is through his stomach, but it's even more the way to a dog's heart."

It was true. That snarling menace who seemed to want my jugular was now docile, simply because I'd fed him. Angel told me later not all dogs would be like that, won over so easily, but it was wolf-dog's nature.

Having made peace with the dog was a big relief for me. Now we only had to worry about Angel's husband. I hoped he'd be gone for a long time, because, could we win him over too? Or would he send us back to the road?

I didn't think I could handle that again.

CHAPTER THIRTY-EIGHT

ANDREA

"It looks like they're leaving," Marcus said, in a tone of unbelief. We'd watched in silence while the frenetic activity of the soldiers suddenly ceased; there was excitement of some kind going on down there but we had no clue what it was about. Right before our eyes, they were abandoning the siege. The trucks in the street slowly started up and drove off, and the soldiers who had been moving debris headed back to the remaining truck.

"Why would they leave now?" the new guy asked. "They almost cleared a path." He gazed over at us.

Marcus shook his head. "I have no idea. They must be in touch with other units. Maybe they need backup somewhere else."

The last of the soldiers scurried into the truck, and then it backed out of the driveway and drove off. A sense of euphoria came over me and the new guy let out a whoop. "All right! This is awesome!"

Marcus and I smiled, enjoying his exuberance. Marcus stood. "Hey Roper, I'm gonna go see what the scoop is."

Roper! What kind of name was that?

"I want to find out if this outfit was really FEMA, too," Marcus continued. "Because I don't think they had a friendly visit in mind. Imagine our own government turning on us. Can you stay and watch? Just in case they have a change of heart," he said, wryly.

"It is the duty of the patriot to protect its country from its government," said Roper. "Thomas Paine."

Marcus said, "Huh?"

"Sure, I'll watch," Roper clarified, with a wry grin.

I stopped, amazed. One of our home-school subjects was to memorize sayings of the founding fathers. I couldn't believe he'd just quoted Thomas Paine like one of us! It's not like most people go around quoting early Americans.

Marcus left us. I wasn't ready to follow him and Roper was watching me. I said, "Rebellion to tyrants is obedience to God.

Benjamin Franklin." His eyes sparkled at me. He smiled. My heart skipped a beat. He assumed a mock serious expression.

"It is the first responsibility of every citizen to question authority. Also Benjamin Franklin." He eyed me with interest, waiting for my response.

I said, "If tyranny and oppression come to this land, it will be under the guise of fighting a foreign enemy. James Madison." He nodded approvingly. My heart was thudding, but not, for a change, due to fear. I hoped I could out-quote him; but whether I did or not, I was having fun! Lexie and I often practiced memorization together and held similar contests, so I felt I was on solid territory. Sometimes Mr. and Mrs. Martin joined in. I never liked having to memorize these quotes, but I was glad now that I had. I hoped I could hold my own with Roper.

"The means of defense against a foreign danger historically have become the instruments of tyranny at home," he cited. "James Madison." He raised a brow at me, as if to ask if I could top that one. I took a breath and gathered my thoughts.

"Experience hath shewn, that even under the best forms of government those entrusted with power have, by slow operations—"

"Have, *in time*, by slow operations." That gorgeous smile.

"Darn!—have, in time, by slow operations, perverted it into tyranny. Thomas Jefferson."

He nodded. "That's a good one." His blue-grey eyes surveyed me a moment. "I'm Roper." I told him my name, still drinking in the sight of this earthy, handsome guy. He wasn't high school age like me; I guessed in his early twenties.

"So what kind of name is Roper?" I asked. To my ears, it sounded like something you'd name your pet, not a person. I checked his left hand and felt a small thrill when I saw no wedding ring.

He gave me a funny look. "It's a last name."

"Oh!" I giggled. "Okay. Why do you go by your last name?"

He turned to scan the front; we were supposed to keep an eye out there in case our enemy returned, but he seemed to be thinking about his answer. "Because I prefer it to Jerry."

"So your name is Jerry Roper."

"No, not Jerry."

A mischievous grin lit his face, and his eyes searched mine, brightly. He has beautiful eyes, I have to say again. They're sort of blue but also sort of grey. It's hard to describe. All I know is, I love it when they're looking at me. "It's Jerusha."

"Oh!" I'd never heard the name, before. "I like it." It was better than Roper.

"Oh yeah? Well, I don't." But he gave me a little smile.

"Why not?"

He smirked. "In the Old Testament, it's a woman's name. My mother didn't know that, and she somehow heard the name and fell in love with it."

"Do you know what it means?"

He nodded. "Literally? 'Taken possession of,' like, in 'married.'"

That gave me a perfect reason to ask, since some men didn't wear wedding rings even if they were married. "So are you?"

He looked at me. "What? Married?"

"Yeah." I was smiling.

"No." He chuckled.

"When did your mom find out she'd given you a girl's name?"

He shook his head. "I don't know, I was little. So they started calling me Jerry. But I hate 'Jerry.'"

"So do I have to call you Roper? Or can I call you Jerusha?"

He smiled ahead, looking out the window. Softly, he said, "Call me whatever you like." Then, turning back to me, "Any other questions?" His eyes were merry.

I stared at him a moment, wondering if he was just making conversation—or was he inviting me to get to know him better?

"Okay. How old are you?"

He chuckled. "Twenty-four. How about you?"

"I'll be seventeen in September."

He nodded, looking thoughtful. "I took you for at least eighteen."

"I get that a lot." We both laughed. Outdoors we saw no movement except for our own guys who were now out there putting back all the logs and debris the soldiers had moved. Usually when I'm stuck watching after a skirmish for anything that may be there but never shows up, the minutes begin to drag pretty quickly. Today I was relishing the time because it meant I could chat with Roper.

We talked about our lives since the pulse—or I *should* say he got me talking about my life. How my family had hardly survived until the Martins brought us to the compound, which wasn't a compound then, but only their farmstead. I told him about my dad and that led to how my mom was missing. I explained how Mom and I weren't on the best of terms when she left and that led to how Lexie and I weren't speaking either. I never intended to tell him so much but he was the perfect listener. He seemed very interested and nodded or looked at me sympathetically whenever it was appropriate. I hadn't talked so much in ages, and I was enjoying every second of it.

"So what happened with you and Lexie?"

Uh-oh. This was one thing I did not want to explain. But I said, "Well, it was a misunderstanding."

He raised a brow, waiting I supposed, for a better explanation. I blushed. "She thinks I'm after her boyfriend." Now both brows were up.

"Are you?"

"Noooo!" I felt my face growing warm and suddenly I remembered I wanted to find out if my mom was back; and I wanted to hear the scoop too, if there was one, about why those trucks had left. "I'd better get moving," I said, getting to my feet. "So I guess I'll call you Roper?"

"Roper's good." He flicked those wonderful eyes at me.

"I'm sorry I talked so much."

"No problem."

"I didn't get to hear your story, how you got here."

He shrugged. "Nothing exciting, I assure you."

"I still want to hear it."

He nodded. "Sure, another time."

"Okay, so long."

"See you later, young lady." I grimaced, but he smiled—and winked again! It made my day. I got a lot of mileage out of that one small gesture. Somehow, it made me feel good on the inside. I needed that good feeling because downstairs Mr. Martin assured us those trucks would be back. And no one believed they were really from FEMA. Blake and Mr. Buchanan had binoculars and said they were armed with AKs, and did not look American.

There was still no sight of my mother or Mr. Washington, and I had little hopes of getting anything but the cold shoulder from Lexie. She'd be sorer than ever because of Rhema's loss. The only bright spot in my day, other than the sight of those trucks pulling away, was having met Roper. I hoped he didn't consider me too young to be of interest.

I found out he'd come to us by first approaching our lookouts on the east border. Apparently, he was alone after losing his friends, one by one, to sickness and starvation. He lived in California and had come east as part of a missions team from his church, visiting another church in Pennsylvania. His plan was to slowly make his way back, but it wasn't working very well. After all, he'd only gotten as far as western Ohio. I had to wonder if he planned on staying with us or if he would move on as soon as he got fed and rested.

"What made you let him stay?" I'd asked Mrs. Martin. Only people with a valuable skill or asset could be allowed to join us.

"He's going to be our new alarm system," she said. "He can blow that trumpet mighty good!"

"But anyone could probably do that," I answered, after thinking it over. She was stirring a big pot of oats on the woodstove. I realized it was going to be one of those nights—when oatmeal was dinner. Sometimes we had to make do with such fare because the women were as busy as anyone and didn't have time for more laborious meals.

Mrs. Martin smiled softly. "He was an intern for children's ministry and we've got a lot of children here. He can teach them the Bible better than the rest of us. I don't have time for lessons these days," she added.

"He's smart," I said. "He knows quotes like we do!"

She grinned. "Really! Founding father quotes?"

"Yeah!"

"Well, isn't that fun. Let's hope he knows his Bible as well."

I left then, to resume my usual chores. But I did hope Roper knew his Bible well. I wanted the compound to keep him!

CHAPTER THIRTY-NINE

LEXIE

The next few days passed in a flurry of activity. Between our usual chores everyone had to help carry garbage, broken logs and sticks, or whatever was available to the front of the property. We were building up our roadblock after seeing what quick work those soldiers had made of it the other day.

I was in charge of harnessing two horses to Dad's wooden cart and leading them with a full load of leftover wood and other building materials—as well as any debris we could find—to the front, where we all unloaded it and dumped it on the growing mound blocking our driveway from the street. When the mound was taller than I was, Dad called a stop to the work. No one complained, believe me.

It looks strange, the huge pile. Like a dam against a flood, only the flood we fear isn't made of water.

I've been feeling bad about Andrea and I'm almost ready to be friends again. Yes, her mother took my horse and I could spit nails over that, but that wasn't Andrea's fault. I'm missing a horse, but she's missing a mom! I just need to find a good time to talk to her. We've both been so exhausted at night we fall into bed without even talking. And forget about home-school. These days we're doing more practice drills, and making sandbags to pile in front of the cabins, and other chores I hate, like laundry. If there was one appliance we could have working again, my mother would choose the refrigerator. I would take a washing machine in a heartbeat.

CHAPTER FORTY

SARAH

Angel is teaching us much. I've started weight lifting, for one thing. (Skinny me!) She says it takes more food to feed muscle, but it takes more muscle to get food than it used to, and we need all the muscle we can get. I can see what she means.

Tex, her husband, left wood for the cook stove, but Angel keeps Richard chopping more every day to store up for next winter. I've been helping with the garden and learning a lot out there. But Angel's garden isn't like any other I've ever seen. She calls it a survival garden and its spread all over the place. "Survival garden" is more than just growing food to survive; it's growing *hidden* food to survive! Instead of a neat plot of rows fenced in or neatly bordered in any way, she has things planted where you'd least expect—or look, if you happen to be a wandering marauder.

There are peas beneath apple trees, between other trees, and grape vines too. Grapes, she says, grow wonderfully with apples and it does away with the need for staking them. There are blueberry bushes at the edge of a field to the left of us, wild strawberries on another side and all kinds of things planted in the weirdest places. I've gone foraging with her and actually eaten dandelions. She says the best, young leaves are gone already, but they're still edible; and she makes tea with the flowers. It's only late May and we've already gone foraging and come home with a big basketful of greens, and berries, and morels. (Morels are the only mushroom we can forage. Angel says the others all have poisonous look-alikes, but morels don't.)

She says it isn't enough to live on, foraging, but it's important to get the greens into your diet. "It's not like we can go to the nearest drug store and get some multi-vites," she said, bright-eyed, as we were bending down to harvest wild onions. I nodded. I pictured our town before the pulse. How easy it had been to run out and do exactly that— get whatever we needed right around the corner or down a few blocks where stores lined the streets. I also remembered how different it looked afterwards—how those streets looked like a war-torn district of the Middle East you'd see on the News, all broken glass and shattered doors and empty shelves. I would never have believed society would go completely crazy so quickly—but I saw it happen.

Angel never dwells on such things. She's an optimist if I ever met one, and it helps me feel better, too. Despite everything that's happened, she isn't depressed or gloomy. Even with her husband away she doesn't seem worried. I mean, he must be facing the same things we feared when we were on the road—people with no conscience. We did run into other normal folks struggling to get by in some honest way; but mostly we took to traveling at night because of the crazies; the people who feel life is cheap. They'd kill you just because they can, with no fear of law.

I wonder if the pulse gave license to people to act the way they already were, deep inside, or if it changed them into worse people. Even my brother surprised me more than once with how ruthless he could be.

Once we were passing a man curled up under an overpass. Richard drew close enough to determine if he was sleeping—or dead. It wouldn't have been the first time we'd come across a dead body. But then he motioned for me to be quiet. I thought it was uncommonly nice of him, to be concerned about not waking up the guy; but he started rifling through his backpack, which was on the ground sort of between the guy's legs. He pulled out a granola bar—it looked ancient, but Richard latched onto it like it was a hidden lode of gold, and then hurried me along to get away from there.

"You shouldn't have taken that," I said. Richard unwrapped it and took a bite, looking extremely gratified, chewing with great gusto.

"This is great!" was all he said, as he broke off a half and tried handing it to me. I wouldn't take it.

"Don't be noble, Sarah!" he chided. "This is not the time to develop a sense of honor," he continued, taking my hand, and pressing the food into it. But I felt upset.

"What if it was that guy's last meal? It looks so old—he's been saving it and now you've taken it away from him. Maybe he was saving it as his last meal before lying down to die!"

Richard was nonplussed. "If that was his plan, I'm not sorry I took it. That's a pathetic plan. Like I said, now is not the time to be noble."

"What is it the time for, then? What IS it the time for, Richard?

He looked at me with somber eyes and then stared ahead as we walked. "It's the time for survival."

I didn't say anything. I was grappling with the fact that we did need to survive but I did not want to become heartless to do it.

"Eat your half," he said.

"I don't want it," I insisted. When he tried to force it into my hand, I acted as though I would throw it away.

He grabbed my arm. "Don't be an idiot!"

"I'd rather be an idiot than someone who would take somebody's last meal!"

We glowered at each other. "Fine! I'll eat it. You're already malnourished and weak, and I'm trying to give you a chance to help yourself—at least a little—and you'd rather be an idiot than be smart. Fine." He took the half back and went to put it into his mouth in one huge bite, but thought better of it and broke the half into half.

"I can't be the only one with enough strength to keep walking. I need you to eat this."

When I just stared at it, he said, "Eat it, Sarah, or next time I'll shoot the guy first, so you won't have to worry about him needing what we take."

I stared at him, appalled at his words. "You don't mean that."

"I do."

I took the piece and bit it. Richard immediately looked placated, but I felt sick. I didn't know whether or not to believe him. Would my brother really be so cruel? I figured I'd play it safe and not find out. Because if he did mean it, if he was really capable of being like that, I did not want to be the one responsible. I ate the rest of my piece.

And Richard was right. It tasted great. I felt guilty for enjoying it.

Anyway, I was helping put melon seeds right into the ground with Angel when she asked me to tell her our story, how Richard and I came to be there. At first she took us for husband and wife, but Richard explained we're brother and sister. As I told her about our lives since January 11th, the day of the pulse, I had a hard time not bawling.

I told her about Dad, and how Richard thinks he might still be alive. I said, "We were hoping, if we ever made it to our Aunt Susan's in Indiana, we'd find him there."

"You know you are in Indiana, right?" she asked. And that's how I found out we're already six miles from the Ohio border! But I'm not sure I want to tell Richard. He might get ideas about going on to Aunt

Susan's—and I want to stay right here. My only misgiving is if my father did make it there, we might end up missing him. But deep down, I don't think he did.

I try not to wonder about him too much—whether he really is alive or not. But it bothers me that I can only picture him in the past, like Mom and Jesse. I see Dad at home watching TV, tinkering with his fishing gear (he liked to fish on weekends) and, inevitably, leaving for work. I can't even remember if I saw him on the last morning when he left for work but never returned. I told Angel this and she said, "I think your father is probably alive."

"What makes you say that?"

She shrugged. "Most men would be able to figure out a way to survive, I think."

I shook my head. "But how? He never made it back home—we have no idea if he lived through the winter."

She patted the earth firmly over the melon seeds and looked up. "Darlin', people have been surviving harsh winters ever since mankind got scattered across the face of the earth after the Tower of Babel. People find a way."

"But food," I said. "Dad worked in Columbus, and that whole city would need food."

She nodded but said, "Okay, but maybe he worked near the zoo. You know, the Columbus Zoo? That's one of the bigger zoos in this country. There's a whole lot of animal flesh in a zoo. Enough for a lot of people to live off, if they had to."

I didn't think he worked near the zoo. But I was struck by Angel's suggestion. I'd never thought about a zoo as a source of food. When people were starving, of course they would resort to zoo animals! Even Richard, pragmatic, practical Richard had never thought of such a thing. But Angel, with her unflagging optimism, had come up with it immediately after hearing about my dad's plight.

There was still no way of knowing whether he was alive but I liked that Angel thought so. I didn't think he'd stick around Columbus, zoo or not. He'd head for home if he could. But if he had waited, maybe to see if power would return, or if the government would offer help— he'd still have to fight for food, zoo or no zoo. Dad was only one person out of thousands who would've been desperate to get their hands on anything edible.

Still, it was a ray of hope. I wanted to believe it. After all, Richard and I were here, living in a place vastly better than anything we'd hoped for. Millions of people weren't so lucky. How could I of all people not believe in miracles? After the Steadmans', I never dreamed we'd find another place to call home. It was incredible that Angel took us in!

Our only worry now was Tex. Angel had not promised we'd be able to stay when he returned. Richard had been making the loft of the barn into a room for us just as if we'd be staying. He insulated the walls with hay and fur and other stuff Angel gave him. I think she wants us to stay but her husband sounds scary.

I hope Richard's work on the loft isn't in vain.

And he hasn't mentioned finding Dad again. If we stay here we obviously can't meet up with him at Aunt Susan's. I think Richard never really believed Dad was still alive. He just wanted me to have hope. Well, I do have hope, thanks to Angel's optimism. And it's a good thing, because if Tex turns us out we're gonna need every bit of hope we can muster.

CHAPTER FORTY-ONE

ANDREA

I was moving dishes from the drying rack into cabinets today when Jared came through from the dining room, saw me, and stopped.

"Hey, you never got a chance to see my cabin. Still interested?"

I continued putting dishes away, avoiding his eyes, while I thought how to answer. Roper popped into my mind—I was definitely interested in him but I didn't want to alienate Jared. He was my last hope as far as my mother was concerned. I figured if I stayed friendly I could ask him about going to look for her.

"Okay." I peeled off my apron and stuck it on a wall peg. All of us women wear aprons on kitchen days since things get very messy without blenders and food processors to neatly do our chopping. I followed Jared out the back door and fell into step beside him. I would never get a better time to ask him. But how to do it?

"So is your mom using the cabin now?" I hadn't seen Jolene that morning, so I was hoping she'd be in Jared's cabin. I didn't relish the idea of being alone with him in a private space. Either way, maybe I could turn the conversation from his mother to mine.

"She is," he said. "But I need to get back to our house and cart a mattress over here. She wants her mattress."

"Moms are like that," I said. It was a stupid comment, but my mind was busy trying to come up with how to ask him what I wanted. "My mom's still missing," I added.

He nodded. "I know. I guess that's tough, huh?"

I peered up at him—and took the plunge. "Do you think—would it be possible—for you to look for her?"

He seemed guarded, nodding his head, but then looked down at our feet, thinking it over.

"Where would you want me to look?"

My hopes soared. "Our house! I'm sure that's where they went. We had a great house. She wanted a lot of her stuff. You know, like your mom and her mattress? My mom wanted clothes and kitchen stuff."

"Where is that—your house?"

I gave him our address. "The Martins came and got us after the pulse. We were already out of food, and we'd have froze if we hadn't gone next door where they had a wood-stove." My voice dropped. "But my dad got killed coming back." I met his gaze. "I know it's dangerous."

He nodded again. "I heard something like that," he said, "about your dad. That's really tough."

I turned pleading eyes to him. "You see? That's why I need to know—about my mom. I need to know if—" I stopped, unable to continue without tears.

"Let me think it over," Jared said. "I'll help you if I can."

"Thank you!" And I meant it. I felt suddenly much better about Jared. Maybe he wasn't drop-dead gorgeous like Roper; and maybe he wasn't a barrel of fun, but he seemed, suddenly, like a good man. He was going to help me! He'd look for my mom!

We were among the cabins now, and I nodded at Mrs. Wasserman, sitting on a chair at the doorway to their little log dwelling, baby on her lap. She nodded at me thoughtfully.

We reached Jared's cabin. Like the others, it was a log cabin, pretty in its way but plain and small. The grass around it was beaten flat from all the work, turning to bare dirt in spots. But to Jared, it was home. He turned to me, expectantly. "Here we are. What do you think?"

I gazed at the new logs, uneven and rougher than modern log cabins; the one small window, still bare, and the starkly modern door— it stuck out like the proverbial sore thumb. Jared explained he had to get the window glass yet, which I understood would come from an abandoned home somewhere. And that he'd installed the door—it even had a lock—just yesterday. I already knew why there was only one window—the cabin was safer with fewer points of entry. All the cabins were built that way, except for a few with no windows at all. The compound looked like an old Civil War army fort if you asked me, with its small wooden buildings dotting the ground. All we needed was a guard tower and a high front fence to make the look complete.

"Well, you certainly did a lot of work," I said. "I like the smell." I inhaled deeply, relishing the scent of fresh wood, rich and earthy and spicy.

"It's even better inside," he said. "C'mon." He unlocked the door and we stepped inside. The lovely woodsy smell was even stronger. There was a table and two chairs, a small bedside table with an oil lamp on it, a box of bullets sitting open beside the lamp, and a few candles and boxed matches. One corner held a bed. "My mom sleeps here for now," he said. "But when I get her bed, it'll go over there—" he pointed at the far corner. "After I get a wall put up."

I nodded, staying just past the entrance. Jolene wasn't inside. "Very pretty."

Aside from the wall lined with boxes and plastic bins overflowing with clothing and supplies, it *was* pretty in a rustic way. It had the coziness of a small pioneer cabin—the kind I'd seen in reenactment villages, or on famous homestead museums—but they were old. This one was new and fresh.

Jared took my elbow. "Try the bed," he said, leading me towards it. "It's the only comfortable spot in here right now." He let me go and turned to put his rifle against the wall. I was frantically trying to think of an excuse to dart out, get away from him. Yeah, I felt better about him overall, but I did not want to get on that bed.

But as I stood there deliberating, I noticed the bed had no frame or headstand, no footboard. And it seemed to be an unusual height. "What's keeping the bed up?" I asked.

He looked over, one hand still on his gun. "Just some stuff. Works great, don't it?"

There was a sheet draped over the side, reaching the floor. I don't know what made me do it, but I bent down and lifted it up. Jared said, "Wait! Don't—"

But it was too late. I'd seen a row of white containers, standing neatly side-by-side, holding up the mattress upon which Jolene slept.

The missing food storage containers.

CHAPTER FORTY-TWO

LEXIE

"What to do about Jared." That could be the title for my journal entry tonight.

My dad called an emergency council meeting in his office to determine this. I wished I could've attended it. So did Blake, and I'm guessing Andrea, but only the leadership was allowed.

I don't know why there's any question about it—my dad said whoever took the stuff would be banished from the compound. Jared was caught with it red-handed so I think he ought to be banished.

Jolene is sitting in the living-room red-eyed, saying her son would no more steal our food than shoot himself in the foot. I didn't want to be the one to say it but I know what the rest of us were thinking. He took it! Period. There's no denying it. Jared is nowhere to be seen. Blake said he'd been told to stay in his cabin until a decision is made.

The storage containers have been moved back downstairs. One thing I wish I knew is how Jared got them all out of the house and into his cabin without anyone else knowing about it. He must have done it in the middle of the night. Even then, our lookouts should have noticed any activity—it doesn't make sense. Blake said if he chose a moonless night and didn't use a flashlight he could have done it without being seen, one bucket at a time. Especially because his cabin is between two others, not right out in the open.

Anyways, everyone was sitting around in the living room, chairs and floor covered in people, waiting for the council to get out and tell us their verdict. We were like a courtroom waiting for the jury.

Food is about our most valuable asset these days. So stealing it is like committing a felony, I guess.

Blake and I were playing Rummy on the floor. Andrea was sitting next to Roper in a corner, deep in conversation. They looked serious. I know she's frightened. As the person who blew the whistle on Jared, she's afraid of him now. Even though I don't trust Jared—and this episode proves I was right to feel this way—I don't think he'd stoop to hurting her. I hope not! I know my mom assured her she did the right thing, reporting the theft. To hear her tell it you'd think Jared was ready to silence her; only, he didn't actually do anything to stop her. He knew she'd seen the buckets; and all he said was, "It's not what you think."

"Yes it is," Andrea said. I could imagine her large eyes staring at Jared in horror. Andrea's eyes can look big! He shook his head, folded his arms and leaned back against the wall. Andrea took the opportunity to flee the cabin.

Suddenly we heard the door to my father's office open. Everyone came to attention and the room fell silent as we waited for the leadership team who filed in shortly. My dad and mom, the Buchanans, Mr. Wasserman, and Mr. Simmons, an ex-cop. Outside I dimly heard one of the dogs barking, and then Roper's whispered, "Ask not for whom the dog barks. It barks for thee." Andrea's little giggle. Blake and I shared a smile. I'd heard Roper was quick with one-line jokes. Leave it to him to joke at such a time!

"Okay, folks. Here's our decision. You all know Jared was found with the missing containers." My Dad was the spokesperson, as usual. "He says he never intended on using the food—he wanted to keep it safe."

Indignant sounds erupted among the adults. Mr. Prendergast snorted. "Likely story!"

"Safe from who? Everyone but him—and his mother," said Mr. Philpot.

"That's not true!" Jolene cried, her eyes wide with hurt. My mom went to her side and put an arm around her.

"Hold on, hold on!" Dad cried, raising his arms. "Hear me out. Jared pointed out—and I think it's a good point—that to keep all the food in one place could be a critical mistake. If anyone not from our compound found the storage, they'd find all of it. Jared says it's smarter for us to keep it in a few locations, and that two was better than one."

"Yours isn't the only food on the compound," said Mrs. Wasserman. "So it's not all in one place."

"We've got the most of it, though," said my dad. "Only the Buchanans have anything near it."

"But we have some, and I know a few other people still have a little," insisted Mrs. Wasserman.

"Well, Jared only knew about ours," my dad returned. "And he didn't think it was safe."

"Yeah, but why didn't he come forward about it? Why was he quiet when you asked who took it?"

My dad nodded. "I know, I know. We asked him about that. He said he was going to tell me—but he needed to make sure it would stay a secret," and he had to raise his voice here because objections went flying around the room, "TO KEEP IT SAFE."

When there was quiet, he added, looking around at all of us, "To keep it safe, people."

"I don't believe that!" said Mr. Prendergast. "How is it safer in a one-room cabin—that anyone could break into—than in your basement in a safe room?"

"That's not keeping it safe," Mr. Philpot added. "That's keeping it to himself. At our expense!"

My father held up a hand again. "Okay, but listen up. That food belongs only to my family. In the end, even if his intention was to steal it, he didn't steal anything from anyone but us."

"We've all been eating from your food storage," Mrs. Wasserman said. "That's everyone's food!" A murmur of agreement sped across the room.

"No, it isn't." My dad said. "We've been sharing it with you all," and he paused, looking around, "but that was our choice. It still belongs to us. And I have to tell you, I think Jared is an asset for this compound and we need to keep him."

Lots of raised voices after that! All of the adults were talking at once. Blake and I scooted against the wall near Andrea and Roper, so we could see the whole room.

Jolene was crying, wiping her eyes, or looking around despairingly. My mom was mostly silent, still keeping one arm around Jared's mother.

Finally my dad blew his whistle. Since whistles were how we first used to spread the alarm on the compound, (before Blake set up the current alarm system using car batteries) we were accustomed to stopping what we were doing at the sound of its shrill note. It worked like a charm now. Silence fell swiftly. My father's stern expression was nearly as commanding as his tone. "I'm sorry to disappoint anyone. But it was our food and we get to say what happens to Jared. He stays."

Some disgruntled comments were shared in low tones. Others shook

190

their heads. Andrea met my eyes. I saw fear in hers. We still hadn't exchanged a friendly word and I felt bad about it. I thought of saying, "If he gets to stay, there's nothing to be afraid of," but she looked away and I'd said nothing.

"Just how do you think he's an asset?" Mr. Philpot asked.

My father said, "Jared has lots of battle experience, and weapons know-how. He's building things we need, like pipe bombs, and smoke bombs, and I don't know what all. But I don't think anyone else here knows how to do that, do we?" He looked around. The room fell silent.

Mr. Clepps spoke up. "He's been a big help setting up the infirmary. Apparently he has experience with field wound dressing, too. He saw a lot of action over in Iraq." He paused. "I agree with Grant."

Grant—that's my dad. But I did not agree with him. I felt more distrustful of Jared than ever. Maybe because it was our food—stuff I'd seen Mom storing with painstaking steps. Every storage bucket had oxygen absorbers calculated to keep the contents fresh for up to 25 years, if necessary. Most of them had food that she'd packaged in Mylar with its own oxygen absorbers. I'd helped her seal each Mylar bag shut with a hot iron, racing to finish before the absorbers became useless. Once they were opened out of their packaging, they instantly started absorbing air, so you had to hurry and get them sealed in with the food before that happened.

Anyways, I felt protective of it all. And it didn't make sense to me that Jared really thought it was safer in his cabin than in our storage room in the basement.

But I guess my dad had the final say. I figured the council had already voted on it anyways. Jared would stay.

The talk shifted to the close call we'd had with the army trucks. My dad's demeanor became more serious yet. He'd heard on his radio that trucks similar to those we'd seen were sighted coming into the country from Canada in a long procession. A mile of trucks. An iron hand seemed to grip my heart. He went on to say they'd been sighted as far south as Kentucky.

"We already know they're in Ohio," he said.

"Where else have they been seen?" Mrs. Philpot asked, in a quiet voice. The room was so silent I thought I could hear myself breathing.

Dad sighed. "The latest sightings place them in Indiana, Wisconsin, Minnesota, Michigan, and Illinois. But here's the bad news: They are not American. They're not FEMA. They've been wreaking havoc wherever they go, killing people, destroying property, mutilating national symbols, buildings, artwork—you name it. They want to eradicate any vestiges that are left of this country's identity. It's a well-known tactic of guerrilla warfare, because they want to demoralize their enemy. They want to wipe out America."

"So who are they?" Blake asked.

My dad shook his head. "We think they're mercenaries."

"If they're mercenaries, who are they working for?" Blake persisted.

Dad took a deep breath. "That's still a mystery. Some say they're from Russia. Others say North Korea, China, or even Iran. Which means, no one knows."

Mr. Buchanan spoke up. "It doesn't really matter. The important thing is, we stay safe. We need to ramp up some outer defenses, like placing stop sticks all over the road, maybe for a mile in each direction."

"Do we have stop sticks?" Mrs. Buchanan asked.

Mr. Buchanan shrugged. "Maybe Jared does."

"Or we put other things in the way." Mr. Philpot said.

"The trees didn't stop them," Blake mentioned. I recalled how we'd watched in horror while a boatload of soldiers had quickly tackled the heavy fallen trees we'd painstakingly placed across the driveway. Our best efforts were merely delays against their numbers.

"We keep putting them down anyway," said a strong voice, from the doorway. It was Jared. Everyone fell silent. From the corner of my eye I saw Roper squeeze Andrea's hand.

Jared surveyed the room. "The driveway is blocked up real good. Now we put more roadblocks up the road, down the road, in every direction. And we can make stop sticks. They won't be as good as manufactured ones, and they'll only slow things down, but if we get slow moving trucks, we can hit them with pipe bombs."

"Is that the best you've got?" Mr. Prendergast asked. "Roadblocks?"

Jared returned his gaze, not warmly. "I've got other ideas, be sure of it."

"And you're making pipe bombs and smoke bombs?"

Jared nodded. "I've got dozens. We'll give them trouble, maybe more than they want to deal with right now." He paused. "If they bring in tanks, all we can do is run."

192

No one said another word about having Jared banned. He cleared his throat. "I've got the bombs, like I said, and I can build bigger ones, but there's a problem. I need supplies. And I need a volunteer to come with me to go find some." The men in the room turned to their wives, probably discussing whether they should go or not. I heard my mother say to my dad, "No, you can't! We need you here."

Andrea and Roper were talking, too. I think Roper was volunteering.

Mr. Prendergast said, "I think we need to find out if those mercenaries are still in our area before we let any able-bodied men go anywhere. We may not know who they are, but we do know they want to eradicate us, and could be back at any time. We need our manpower here."

"What good is manpower against RPGs?" Jared said. "Make no mistake, if they return, they will have big guns. We need them, too. We need bombs."

Jared's tone of authority must have been convincing because the talk changed to where they could go to find the things he needed to build the weapons.

Jared continued, "And they are not trying to eradicate us." His voice wasn't loud but commanded attention. "When a rogue government takes over," he continued, "they still need people to populate their country. They're trying to show their strength, instill fear into everyone. If they demoralize us enough, it paves the way for a government coup. We need to hold them off until our own military can reassert its strength." He looked around with his usual grim expression. "If our military doesn't get involved, this is guerrilla warfare and may go on for a long time and get even uglier than it is now."

I felt like Jared was drawing a black heavy curtain over the room, making us short on air or something. My chest felt heavy, listening to him talk.

"That may all be true," my dad said, "But here's the good news." He looked around, making sure he had everyone's attention. "I do not believe," and he paused significantly, "that America will go down easily. We will not go down without a fight!"

The room broke into cheers. Jared's expression barely altered, but Roper gave a whoop of approval, and cried "Angel armies, man! We call on God for angel armies!"

"Amen!" cried Cecily. "They saved us before! Remember Psalm 108:12! 'Oh, grant us help against the foe, for vain is the salvation of man!'"

"Amen and Amen!" Roper agreed, smiling, as they shared a high five. He then held his hand up to Andrea and we all slapped high fives. I have to say, Roper brings an element of fun with him wherever he goes on the compound. I saw Jared looking over at us like we were nuts, but that's okay. Not everyone understands why Christians take such confidence in God. Maybe someday we'd have a chance to talk to Jared about the gospel.

Anyways, breaking up on a high note helped my spirits immensely. The rest of the day felt almost cheery. Somehow though, by the time of curfew I was heavy-hearted. When Blake and I said goodnight, I said, "I guess it's good, Jared wasn't banished."

He nodded. "I think so." Then, a short grin. "But I guess if he'd taken *our* food buckets I might feel differently."

"My dad said it turned out well. Nothing is actually missing and it reminded him that we do need to spread out our hiding places. He's gonna dig a few holes and line them with tarps and put some of the buckets down there. With gravestones on top."

"That's a great idea," Blake agreed.

"Well. Goodnight." I stared into Blake's warm amber-brown eyes. Was he going to kiss me? He did. I gave him a good hug afterwards. I considered bringing up the future—like, would we ever get married? What were his thoughts about that? But we heard someone approaching and drew apart.

"Tomorrow's another lookout day," he reminded me.

"You think I'd forget that?" I smiled. "I'm looking forward to it."

And I was. When I was on the hill with him, hours flew past. My dad was wrong to have worried about us getting distracted, because I'd been right about Blake. He took the job seriously and wouldn't let me distract him. I'd gotten used to being up there and wasn't nervous about it any longer. But if I'd known how the next day was going to turn out? I would have been.

CHAPTER FORTY-THREE

SARAH

It's no accident Angel's house is optimal for wood heat, or that the stove runs on wood or coal; or that they've got a root cellar and ice house. They aren't preppers, she told me (to which I nodded as though I understood what she meant. Actually, I have no idea what a prepper is). Anyway, she said they bought 77 acres out here bordering Ohio in order to homestead. So when we lost electricity and felt like life was over, they barely even blinked. I mean, they had cable TV, and there was a water heater in the barn that was helpful in winter; but overall they were hardly affected.

They have a manual pump for the well; heat with wood, like I said; and have an outhouse, which is over a pit Tex dug by hand. (This is the worst part of not having electricity if you ask me. OK, one of the worst parts—there are so many.) But Angel and Tex built this house planning on using an outhouse! She explained that every year or two Tex has to dig a new pit and then they take up the outhouse and move it over the new hole. Angel keeps a supply of peat moss in the outhouse which you're supposed to throw in the hole after using it. She said it helps keep down the odor—but it also means the hole fills up faster, so they only use it if they really need it.

She keeps an emergency toilet in the house, but we try not to use it. However, if it's the middle of the night, I do. I won't go out, even with Kane beside me. I just make sure I'm the one to clean it out in the morning. Angel calls it their modernized chamber-pot (modernized because she lines it with plastic bags, which she stored for years and has a ton of; and it has a lid in the shape of a toilet seat on top.). Anyway, she says people have used chamber-pots for hundreds and hundreds of years. "If we weren't so spoiled in this country," she said one day, "we wouldn't be having such a hard time, now. People have survived on much less than we Americans have lived on since time began."

It does help to have her perspective. We've even made a game of finding passages in books we're reading that demonstrate this. It's an education in itself. We were a nation steeped in luxury! Even our poorest citizens had things much of the world has always lacked.

What else? Refrigeration—I asked how the ice box works. (She and Tex are kind of brilliant if you ask me!) In the winter they cut ice from the pond—they have to work together on it because ice is heavy—and, using a sled, cart it in sheets to the ice house, and then layer it on straw. The straw helps keep the ice from melting. She showed me the inside of the ice house the other day because we needed new ice, and there's still about four feet of it, including the layers of straw. The ice house is built right into the side of a hill, as is the root cellar which is beside it.

They had a cow, but lost it—she didn't say how, so I didn't ask—but this is one of Angel's rare sorrows. She misses fresh milk and butter and cheese. But she still has lots of powdered milk, and get this—powdered butter and powdered sour cream and powdered cream cheese! (Who ever heard of such things?) They also have a hen house with chickens INSIDE a fenced-in area for the dogs, who guard the fowl. On top of that, Tex hunts a lot and they fish in their pond. It's about an acre across, Angel says. Sometimes she goes hunting with Tex but this time he went alone because all the traps were set and someone has to check them daily. The eggs need to be gathered every day, too.

I'm sure glad Angel stayed home!

At dinner one night Richard and I told her how quickly people lost it after the pulse. On day two looting began in the stores, and by day three there was nothing available anywhere. I told her again about the fire and how we had to live in the library with all the other people from our building; then I told her about the man who was shot trying to get in to Wal-Mart. She nodded, clucking her tongue from time to time, and shaking her head.

"Haven't any people bothered you?" I asked. I was thinking of the numerous warning signs we'd seen along the way. There must have been intruders, for them to post so many signs.

"Well, living so far away from anyone else, we've always been wary of intruders," she said. "Usually our signs are enough to discourage people."

"Have you always had the sign out there about killing people on sight?" I asked.

She smiled sheepishly. "That one's new. We figured there's more desperation out there than we can handle." She gave me a sideways look. "If you saw that sign, how come you kept coming?"

I glanced at Richard. "We were heading for Indiana; Richard said we had to stay on course." I hesitated. "He also said he thought it was a bluff."

Angel's eyebrows shot up. "Well, you lucked out, didn't ya? If Tex had been here, I have to tell you, things might have ended differently!"

I'd seen a picture of Tex by now. Looking mean and grim, he was standing next to a sweetly smiling Angel. He reminded me of Hulk Hogan. I was not looking forward to meeting him. Angel was an angel, but it seemed to me that kind people often married their opposite, which meant that Hulk, er, Tex, was not going to look kindly upon us. To him, we'd just be two more mouths to feed.

"Have you had to shoot anyone?" Richard asked.

Angel shook her head. "No. But we will if it comes to that. If you'd been with a large group, I would have left Sarah in that pit, for one thing. But the two of you by yourselves didn't seem too threatening for me. After you passed out," she added, looking at me, "I about grilled your brother to death, finding out what you were up to and where you were going and whether or not there were more of you."

I suddenly had a vivid memory of her bending over Richard brandishing a sword.

"I fainted because I saw you take that sword out and you were holding it over Richard! Why did you? Was it to scare him?"

Richard seemed surprised. "That's why you fainted?"

Angel laughed. "I guess that did look scary now, didn't it? I was just cutting off the rest of the rope that was hanging on him from my trap."

I shook my head. I had to smile when the two of them broke up laughing. "I thought you were gonna cut his head off and then take mine, too."

Angel placed a hand on her heart, still chuckling. "Oh, my word!"

———————◆———————

We'd been at Angel's house for four glorious days and I was at the kitchen counter peeling carrots and potatoes. They came from the root cellar but Angel was fretting because the supplies of both are really low. "We need to pray that this year's crop is a good one," she'd said, handing me the vegetables.

"So these are from last year?" I asked. It seemed no less than magical to me, that fresh vegetables could last that long without rotting. I had no idea. I'm certainly learning a lot.

"They sure are," she said, explaining that in the coldest months they kept them in a dark place in the basement, and during the rest of the time they stayed in the root cellar, which is completely unheated. It stays cool enough in warmer months to extend the shelf-life of most vegetables and squash, but only warm enough until a deep freeze hits. If the veggies froze, that would ruin them; or, if they froze and then defrosted, they'd start to rot. So they worked out a system between the house and the root cellar to keep things from one harvest to last almost until the next. To me, it was a small miracle I was peeling vegetables from last year and they looked perfectly edible.

As I was thinking about this, I heard the door behind me open and shut, but I thought nothing of it. Richard, Angel and I came and went freely as we did our chores. Each morning at breakfast Angel would give us marching orders, our daily responsibilities. Richard was expected to chop ¼ of a cord of wood daily, so he didn't have to be told to do that. But Angel would assign us other things too, like clean the chicken coop, or collect eggs, or mop the floor. But in a minute I felt an eerie sensation— like when someone is looking at you even though they are way over across a room. I spun around with a gasp.

I expected to see Richard, because Angel was seldom silent as she came and went. I'd grown accustomed to her good-natured comments and enjoyed her companionship a lot. But when I turned, what I saw was HULK HOGAN. Tex was back! He had a hand-gun out, pointed right at me, his head tilted as he aimed with one eye.

I stared at him in horror, wondering why he was going to shoot me. No words came out of my mouth. I could think of nothing to say. After all, I didn't know this man. For all I knew, trying to reason with him could set him off even more, make him madder than he was. I stood there gaping.

"Who are you?" he snarled, in a voice deep with distrust. "And what have you done to my wife?"

CHAPTER FORTY-FOUR

LEXIE

It was a beautiful morning to be on the hill. The early sun shone prettily against the vibrant green grass, which itself was fresh and moist with the scent of dew. Birds flitted about the woods near our shed, while birdsong infused the day with life and hope.

Below us, even the cabin area with its scattered piles of timber, tools, and empty wheelbarrows looked picturesque, like a pioneer village. We happened to be 21st century pioneers, but there was no helping that.

Dunes of sand and small rocks sat heaped next to the playground— the sand was needed for our version of homemade mortar, and sandbags. The rocks also went into the mortar. As of yet the playground was empty—the children would be having their breakfast by now and wouldn't be out until later.

I'd passed Andrea coming from the barn as Blake and I left the house earlier but I didn't meet her eyes. Last night she'd asked me to forgive her, point blank. And, I can't explain why, but I suddenly felt all my indignation again for how she'd kissed Blake, and how her mother had stolen my horse—maybe I was just ornery from being so tired. We exchanged words, and I didn't feel good about it but I guess I'm kind of stuck. I never realized how stubborn I can be, 'til now.

Blake and I were enjoying coffee from our thermoses, and biscuits my mom had taken straight from a hot cast-iron skillet. We had butter thanks to Milcah, our cow, and jam from storage. Right now it didn't matter that we had no electricity or world wide web. Our little compound was coping well, in my opinion. We ate just fine—most of the time.

I'd just finished brushing the crumbs off my hands when Blake came to attention. He grabbed the binoculars that hung around his neck. "'We've got company," he said. "They're back!"

"What!" My heart sank. He passed the binoculars to me while he got on the two-way to sound the alarm. We were under attack. Again!

"Four, just like last time," Blake said to my father's question. Then, "Yeah, the same kind. They say FEMA."

It all went like a re-run movie, the way the trucks stopped on our road with one facing the driveway, and men in green fatigues pouring out like ants from an anthill to begin clearing our debris pile. It was about seven feet high now, much more substantial than what they'd had to clear last time. But they seemed to throw more men at the blockade than before, so it seemed they'd get through it without a greater delay. I checked that all our mags were full and tried to ready myself for combat.

Blake kept my dad updated. We could see the pile tumbling now and then, falling lower as the men worked it from the other side. I crouched at my window gripping my rifle, my heart beating hard and fast, my throat tight. I glanced up at the Scripture scrawled above the opening. *For the LORD your God is the one who goes with you to fight for you against your enemies to give you victory. Deuteronomy 20:4.*

We sure need that victory, Lord, I prayed. We need you to fight for us! But as soon as I prayed, I remembered another verse, Psalm 144:1, *Praise be to the LORD my Rock, who trains my hands for war, my fingers for battle.*

Were my hands trained for war? My fingers for battle? I hoped so, because just then Blake said into the two-way, "They've breached it. They're on the property."

"Get out of the shack," my dad said. As we had on the previous occasion when the trucks had come, Blake and I grabbed our stuff and headed to the side of the ridge, flopping onto our bellies.

We watched as the men on the ground made room for the trucks, which drove up in a slow line all the way to our second, weaker line of defense—the forsythia bushes, fronted with garbage and junk we'd put out there in another messy heap. The bushes had been a blazing row of yellow beauty two weeks ago, but were now spring green. They'd survived being transplanted. Their foliage struck an off note next to the dusty green camo trucks now lined up along the living fence.

Two men jumped out of the first truck and approached the house. No one from the compound came forward to speak to them which made sense since we'd had it drilled into our heads to stay out of sight in the event of military or anyone we didn't know coming onto the compound. Even if it had been U.S. military, many people didn't trust them at a time like this, including my dad. My parents even wore "Support your Military" stickers and donated to Veteran's causes during regular times. But dad says that historically when there is a breakdown in the structure of society, including law and order, "military powered efforts are often fueled by totalitarian mindsets." I could hear him saying it.

One of the men had a bull-horn and he lifted it and spoke. It was so effective we heard it all the way up there on the ridge.

"This is FEMA!" he called. "We're here to help. We have a safe place for you to live and you'll have food and protection!" The man had a decided accent. "We are not here to do you harm!"

"Sounds middle eastern," Blake said.

There was no response, no movement. I saw the man nod to someone behind him, and a few other soldiers leapt from the trucks.

"I repeat. We are the Fed-er-al Emer-gen-cy Manage-ment Assoc-i-a-tion!"

I looked at Blake. "Isn't it supposed to be 'Agency,' not Association?"

He nodded. "Yup. And he's having trouble pronouncing it, too. This is not FEMA."

"We are your friends. Come with us. We take you to a place of safety—with food!"

"Does he really think he sounds like an American?" Blake murmured.

"Medical care! Protection!"

"They sure try to make a good offer," I said.

"If it sounds too good to be true....." Blake said. He added, "Even if they mean well, a refugee camp is what he's talking about and the only reason to go to one of those is if you have to. We don't have to."

"We might need medical care at some point," I said.

"Yeah. And so will everyone else in the camp. Winter comes and there's an outbreak in the camp, everyone dies. There are never enough supplies to stop it or treat everyone. Even if they have supplies, they won't have enough. Unfortunately," he turned to me. "I don't think that's what we have to worry about right now."

Below us, more men were emerging from the canvas-covered back of the second and third trucks. "Now their true colors come out," Blake said. He was on the two-way instantly. "They've got A.Ks!" he told my dad. "They're coming out of the first two trucks."

201

No one exited the third truck.

"They're not FEMA!" my father said. "This is an attack! You know what to do. Do NOT come off the hill. I repeat, do not come down. We have some weapons that are gonna shake things up." We heard other people talking at once in the background and then my dad clicked off.

"What was he talking about?" I asked. "What kind of weapons could we have that will shake things up?"

Blake looked through the binoculars again, and said, "Jared fixed up some heavy-duty stuff. Don't know how he did it, or where he got his supplies, but we weren't asking questions, either."

My heart pounded. I broke into a cold sweat. Just like last time, I wished I wasn't up on the hill but in the house with the rest of my family. Encounters with marauders were bad enough, but at least we had a chance against other civilians. This was far worse. I was a sixteen-year-old farm girl, not a fighter. How ridiculous was it for us to even try our might against trained soldiers?

He trains my hands for war…my fingers for battle.

Blake sighted in the man with the bull-horn, who now stood in conference with a few of his men. "I could take him down," he said. "Maybe." We shared a smile. "I won't take the first shot, though. Maybe they'll decide to leave without a fight." He gave me another look. "Get someone sighted in, Lex! If shooting starts, it's gonna get hard to be effective from up here. We'll need to strike fast and hard."

The men who had emerged from the trucks seemed to be awaiting orders.

"C'mon, turn around," Blake intoned. "Go away!" His finger was still on the trigger, and I got sighted in on one of the guys in front. The soldiers had formed a line.

"They're gonna shoot!" I cried.

"Here we go!" Blake said.

I thought I was ready. I had on ear and eye protection, and my rifle was snug in a bipod. I had two extra mags—lookouts always got extra. I got ready to squeeze the trigger, letting my breath out first. I did not want to miss. But then, right before our eyes one of their trucks exploded, lifting off the ground with an enormous blast! Shrapnel flew in all directions, while soldiers scattered like pixie dust. I stared at the smoking truck, dumbfounded. Blake never lost his cool, and was taking shots as he got them.

"That was a grenade! Good ol' Jared," he cried. Men were pouring out of the other trucks, and everything broke into pandemonium. The guy with the bull-horn went down. As Blake sighted in someone else, or tried to since now everyone was a moving target, I finally began to aim and shoot. Men were running towards the house now, and spreading out towards the cabins. My heart hammered in my throat. You can do this, Lex, I told myself. *He trains my hands for war...*

Rapid gunfire filled the air. I saw soldiers fall but others were getting through! Worse, more of them were still piling out of the remaining trucks.

"Go for the ones closest to us!" Blake said. I was operating slowly, so afraid of what was happening that I didn't want to waste a single shot. But I felt almost drugged, like my mind was paralyzed. Even if I had a shot, I knew the odds of hitting someone from this distance were slim. Blake had been given more training with the AR-15, and had been able to pull it off. As I hesitated, he reloaded with a new magazine.

"Shoot, Lex," he said. "You can do this!" It was exactly what I'd been telling myself. But somehow inside, the real me wasn't convinced.

"I'm not a good shot at this distance."

"There's a lot of them! Just wait until they come into your scope." But he shoved the two-way towards me. "Check if the other lookouts are on their way. We need all our manpower up front now!" We had border patrols on the far ends of the property so I got busy trying to make contact.

Mr. Buchanan's voice came in saying, "We know. We're almost there. From your southwest; don't mistake us for the bad guys."

"We won't," I assured him. To my disgust, I noticed my hands shaking. It was happening again—I just wasn't cut out to be a fighter!

He trains my hands for war? If only I could believe it!

The noise from below continued. We did our best to defend the cabins. I suddenly noticed survivors straggling out of the truck which had been hit and, to my horror, I saw a few men pulling a large weapon of some kind from the back of another truck. *Oh, no! This was it—they had something huge and powerful and they were going to destroy us!* They'd probably demolish our house right in front of my eyes!

"What's that?" I said, nudging Blake and nodding in the direction of the emerging artillery. "We can't let them use whatever that thing is."

"It's an RPG!" Blake said. He grabbed the two-way. "Jared, you on here? You got another of those grenades? They're unloading an RPG—truck number three!" We heard my dad talking, but not Jared.

"Jared? Jared—" Blake looked worried. "Now would be a good time to use one if you got any more of those grenades." He shoved the two-way back at me. "I gotta take a shot at those guys."

I had no idea what an RPG was but his words sent a wave of fear through me anyways. It sounded bad. Later he explained that an RPG is a rocket propelled grenade launcher. Ugh. If they had discovered our whereabouts, they could have sent a grenade right at us!

Meanwhile, I saw some soldiers moving among the cabins! We had families in some of those cabins, people who weren't ready to fight. Mrs. Wasserman and her baby! The Wassermans were preppers like us but didn't believe in violence. They had no guns! Suddenly, my sluggishness vanished. I didn't like shooting at anyone, but these guys were going after innocent civilians! I felt a surge of anger—and it was directed at those crawling insects called soldiers.

He trains my hands for war!

Finally I got shooting as busily as Blake. It was like I'd transformed in one instant to a new woman. My protective feelings put me into mama bear mode, I suppose. Two men came directly in our range, and I sighted in. I took my shot. And got one.

Blake stopped to reload while I took aim at the man I hadn't hit, who was running. He went down from somebody else's bullet. It was good to remember we weren't alone in the battle.

"C'mon, C'mon," Blake muttered. He'd been targeting any man who tried to get behind the RPG, and suddenly—finally!—a second grenade hit! The truck with the RPG rocked and again shrapnel went flying—but the vehicle stayed upright.

"Did we get it?" I asked. "Did we take out that RPG?" Just as I asked, a third explosion hit the truck. It burst into a pyre of flames.

"Yeah, Jared!" Blake cried. We shared a happy smile. It felt like a miracle! We'd had grenades thanks to Jared, and had taken down two military trucks! But then the real miracle happened. They were retreating! I saw them swarming towards the two remaining trucks!

"They're leaving!" Blake confirmed. "They didn't expect grenades. Let's keep at 'em, Lex!" Normally I shrank from shooting at anyone from behind but soldiers did not evoke the same regret in me. They'd already come back once. Their retreat did not mean we were safe.

Mr. Buchanan and two other men joined us, falling to the ground beside us. Below, others kept up the defense too, as shooting continued. One of the trucks revved its engine and started moving. Then another grenade hit the back of the bed and blew up! Amazingly, the truck kept going. I was glad it kept going. I wanted them all to go.

We noticed projectiles being thrown from the last truck. Projectiles that hit the ground with a flash and burst into flame. Fires broke out in the trees and brush lining the road front.

"That's Molotovs they're throwing," Blake said, his voice grim. "There goes our brush cover."

"At least they're leaving," I said.

"Yeah. C'mon!" Blake jumped to his feet, grabbing his equipment. "Let's get back to the shack. It's got a better view of the road."

"We'll fan out," Mr. Buchanan said, as he and the other men went further downhill, staying among the trees.

"We need to make sure they don't get out to the road and regroup. They got to keep going. I want to see it to know for sure."

From the shed, we watched until they drove out of sight. I threw my arms around Blake as soon as we'd lost view of the last truck. He circled his arms around me and gave me a sweet, warm, kiss.

"Good job," he said.

"Better job by you."

"Good enough job by you."

"He trains my hands for war," I said, with a smile.

"Amen!" Blake agreed, softly. We kissed again.

Afterwards he said, "You realize this changes everything. It's not about getting by without electricity anymore, or fighting off marauders, or not having a government. It's about surviving a hostile takeover. We're at war, Lex."

CHAPTER FORTY-FIVE

ANDREA

Once again I was at my bedroom window looking out at the grim sight of four army trucks trying to access the compound. This time Marcus was at the adjacent window and Roper was beside me. I hadn't seen Cecily that morning, but I hoped she was praying. I'd seen her at target practice—she was good; but I happened to think she'd be more useful to us by remaining closeted in prayer during a skirmish. Maybe before and after one, too.

I quickly got my ear buds in place and had only taken a single shot when I almost fell over from a loud explosion out front. One of the trucks blew up right before our eyes!

My handsome companion let out a cheer. "All *right*! That's what I'm talkin' about!" He met my eyes. Another heart-stopping smile. Roper was the sort of guy who should be in Hollywood making movies only there probably wasn't a Hollywood that made movies anymore.

"Let's keep at 'em," he said. So we did. We had to keep as many of those uniformed men away from the house, the cabins and animals, as possible. My magazine held thirty rounds, which I emptied quickly. Stopping to reload, I jumped involuntarily when another blast occurred.

"Yes!" Roper cried. "Man, I didn't think we had any big guns," he said, shaking his head with a little smile. "This is awesome!"

I was equally surprised, as was Marcus who said, "I didn't know, either." Then he cried, "Look out! Here come theirs! That's an RPG!" But before we could see them use it, a barrage of bullets struck our window, shattering the glass and sending it flying into the room in a million little pieces. We threw ourselves to the side, but glass fell over me and all around us. I felt like a swarm of bees had stung my face— thank goodness I'd put on eye protection.

Marcus said, "C'mon, don't let up! Get back at it!" I glanced at Roper, who was sending a concerned look in my direction. He nodded solemnly when he saw I could still shoot.

We kept fighting. I realized during this battle that the countless hours I'd spent playing shoot-em-up video games with my little brothers had actually inured me to fighting. I'd never believed what they said, that such games could make people less sensitive to killing; but now it seemed true. Lexie found it far more difficult to shoot at the bad guys—even though they were ready to shoot her. She didn't have the hours of war-play behind her as I did. She'd played fashion and shopping games with her sisters and found these skirmishes nerve shattering.

I felt less frazzled by them. Especially when fighting guys in uniform. The fatigues definitely switched on my video game mentality. They were the bad guys and we needed to take them down. I even felt in my element while doing it.

I don't mean I enjoyed killing anyone. It was seeing them fall, like game pieces. It didn't feel real. The thought of death was not on my mind, as though a solid wall had crashed down between this game-play and reality. Maybe I needed to do this, to keep it that way. All I thought about was every fallen man out there meant a small victory for us. As they fell, it was victory upon victory. If we got enough of them, we'd come through this.

The RPG was frighteningly real, though. We couldn't take down men fast enough to keep it unattended. When the third blast hit it, making the whole truck explode into a beautiful plume of fire and smoke, we cheered.

"They're takin' off!" Marcus cried. We continued to barrage the soldiers with as much fire power as we could. We had to send the message that we weren't an easy target. Mr. Martin had drilled it into our heads at council meetings that, just like common thugs, organized thugs wanted easy targets, too. If we were aggressive enough, they'd probably go elsewhere. If we held out long enough, the U.S. could send military support. We had to hope for that!

After the last truck left, I sat staring out at the burning brush in front and the smoking truck which they'd had to leave behind. Men were on the ground, bleeding out or dead. The video-game sense of play suddenly left me and I found myself blinking back tears. Roper gently touched my arm.

"Hey," he said. "You're bleeding. Come here."

I started brushing off shards of glass, noticing the pain on my face.

"Keep watch," Marcus said. "I'll see if we've got an all-clear, yet."

Roper, meanwhile, dug in his pockets for something and pulled out an old, worn, but still unopened sanitary wipe. He handed it to me. It looked like something he'd been carrying a long time.

"Your face is cut."

I got up and went to the mirror and saw little scratches all over my cheeks, nose, and forehead. I wiped at them gingerly, making sure not to press in the glass fragments. There was one long cut on my forehead which was seeping blood.

I did not present a pretty picture. But Roper joined me. He took the wipe and turned me to face him and began gently going over my cuts, talking in a soothing tone. His own face was remarkably unscathed. I drew a piece of glass off his jacket.

He said, "Can you see outside? We're supposed to be watching."

I turned and looked out. "I see our guys," I said.

"Checking for survivors?" he asked.

"Yeah. Or stragglers." But something was odd. "Why are they wearing gas masks?" I asked.

Roper peered out at them. "Maybe the Molotovs included poison gases. They have to be careful."

Checking for injured survivors was the worst possible job, in my opinion. Besides the fact it could be dangerous, if you found someone badly injured you were supposed to put them out of their misery. If they were only superficially injured you had to take them prisoner so they could be questioned. Jared, being ex-military, usually led the reconnaissance after a skirmish, giving the all-clear only after the grounds had been searched. He and a few other men were the only ones who had the stomach to do the job the way it was supposed to be done, like picking guns and other things from the bodies.

Thankfully, we young people weren't expected to do these after-battle "clean ups." I hoped I never would.

"You got one bad cut," he said, wiping my forehead. "Go get it bandaged."

Our eyes met. His were blue-grey beautiful. I wished I was older. I felt Roper liked me but was holding back. I almost wanted to reach up and kiss him softly on the lips. I might have, too, except for what happened with Blake. I had vowed never to be so forward with a guy again.

"Okay," I said. "Thanks for helping remove the glass."

His expression changed. "Did you hear about the optician? Two glasses and he made a spectacle of himself." He smiled, and I caught the joke. Roper had been sprinkling our conversations with silly one-liners every chance he got. I loved it.

"Ha ha," I said. "Not one of your best."

"Oh!" His face scrunched in thought. He enjoyed a challenge, I saw.

"Ok, what's an outpatient?"

I shrugged, trying not smile.

"A person who fainted."

I rolled my eyes.

"Wa—wait, I have a better one." He rubbed his chin. "What were the sleeping soldiers wearing?" He waited a beat and continued, "Fatigues—tired army clothes." I groaned. He chuckled, which made me smile.

"I gotta go."

"One of these days I'll surprise you with something that's actually funny."

"Don't worry, I love your jokes."

"You do?" His eyes sparkled at me. But they strayed to the cut on my forehead and his expression turned to a frown. "Go get a bandage."

He winked at me before I left, and I felt instantly lighter. I can't explain what it is about Roper when he winks at me, but I eat it up.

The gash on my forehead was beginning to throb. When I got downstairs I put off going for a bandage because I wanted to find out what people were saying about the attack. Instead, I grabbed a rag and pressed it against the gash.

I found out two of our cabins had taken heavy gunfire, and three people were badly injured. Miraculously, we suffered no casualties! The soldiers, on the other hand, had lost twenty men, and maybe more—we wouldn't know for sure until the fires burned out and we could check the two trucks.

All I wanted now was to see my mom return to us in one piece and to patch things up with Lexie. If both those things would happen, even though we knew these troops might come back—I would consider it a banner day. I'd had time with Roper—I had a really good feeling about him—and I'd have my two most important relationships back.

Lexie was especially on my mind. I needed our fight to be over. She needed to forgive me! The night before, I'd asked her one more time,

209

Look, can we just make up? When she said nothing, I added, *I'm sorry! I really am! I wish I could take back what I did; only I can't!* But she was like a rock—I never knew Lexie could be like that. I figured if I apologized really well, she'd never stay mad at me. But she did. I miss the old Lexie. If she'd just get over this, we could go back to the way we were. I'd said, *C'mon, Lex! You've punished me enough. Whatever happened to 'Vengeance is mine; I will repay, says the Lord?'*

For the first time she softened a little. *I'm working on it*, she said.

What do you mean?

I'm working on giving it to the Lord. She met my eyes. *But I'm not ready to trust you yet.* I felt my temper rising. I was trying to mend things but she was being as obstinate as a mule. The compound has a mule, named Callie. So I said, *You're as obstinate as Callie!*

I may be obstinate, but there's only one ass here, and it isn't me!

At first I was shocked to hear her say something that was almost a cuss. Lexie had never cussed in my hearing, not even once. My second urge was to burst into laughter that she'd been goaded to it now. In the past we'd have both burst into laughter at such an absurd exchange, but she was still mad and didn't laugh, and this made me madder.

I dropped the subject. She wasn't ready to trust me? Fine! But that was last night. Today, I wanted to try one more time to regain her trust. Only I had no idea how to do it.

I found the first-aid kit and stuck two band-aids across the gash on my forehead. My other cuts were still seeping little red spots of blood so that I looked like I had the measles. But I wasn't about to plaster band-aids all over my face.

As I went towards the back door with the idea of visiting her up on the hill, I was planning on what to say. I'd remind her that Jesus said we had to forgive others if we wanted to be forgiven ourselves. As an added measure I said a quick prayer: *God, I put this relationship into your hands. Please help me and Lexie to be friends again!*

210

L.R. Burkard

CHAPTER FORTY-SIX

LEXIE

After the trucks left, Blake and I waited and watched on the hill for the next hour. We saw our own men searching the grounds, going through the smoking debris and checking the cabins for stragglers. Our shift wasn't over but I was itching to check in at the house. We had heard reports of some damage and three badly injured—including our sole nurse. I guess I also wanted to know I wasn't the only person feeling shaken up by the appearance of foreign soldiers.

I wanted to hear the theories about who we thought they were and whether they'd be back—and then, what we were gonna do about them. I wondered if Jared had more grenades, or maybe other weapons that would mean something against their firepower.

But honestly? Most of all, I wanted a good hug from my mom. What can I say—I'm not even seventeen yet! I like to think I'm pretty grown up. I'll be seventeen in July. But now and then a girl needs a mom's hug.

Blake took out his thermos and he nodded towards my backpack.

"Have a cup of tea or whatever you've got in there."

"I think I need a brandy." We both understood I was totally joking.

He gave me a piercing look. "Why don't you call your dad and see if you can go to the house? We beat those guys pretty soundly. They may come back, but not today."

I loved how he understood me. "You think they'll be back, though?"

He took a sip of his coffee and looked towards the road, which was now empty. He glanced over the two trucks that were out of commission, still spewing smoke into the air. He nodded. "They'll be back, all right. With bigger guns."

I got on the two-way and asked for permission to go to the house— "Just for a few minutes, Dad."

He said, "Well, we've seen no sign of stragglers; it's been about an hour. I guess it'll be okay. Leave the two-way with Blake. And stay armed—just in case."

211

CHAPTER FORTY-SEVEN

SARAH

I felt paralyzed as I stared down the barrel of Tex's gun.

It had to be Tex, because he looked like Hulk Hogan, all right. My heart was beating loudly in my ears but I couldn't find my voice.

"WHAT did you do to my wife!" he repeated, coming a step closer. He kept both hands on his pistol which pointed at me.

Suddenly I was able to talk. "Nothing! Angel's here! I think she's checking her traps! She said we could stay here until you got back!"

The door opened. My heart sang for a second as I anticipated Angel coming in and setting her husband straight. It felt like someone's snarling dog was after me and I was waiting for the owner to take responsibility and order it away. Hulk, er, Tex, really looked the part of the snarling dog.

But it was Richard. He took one look at us, sized up the situation and held up his arms. "Hey, we're here on friendly terms. Your wife needed our help."

Richard was brilliant in that moment. He pointed out that we were there to help, when he could have said, "Your wife gave us shelter; or, your wife saved our lives," but he cut to the quick with what would be most disarming for Tex. That WE were the good guys, helping Angel! Though it was true (we were helping) it was equally true we needed Angel and her home a lot more than she needed us.

"How, exactly, are you helping?" he asked Richard, moving at the same time behind me and grabbing me by the arm so I couldn't bolt. "And where is Angel?"

Richard shrugged. "I don't know where she is at the moment. I've been chopping wood. And that's how I'm helping mostly, but Angel gives us lots of chores. I think you'll find we've been an asset for your household and can continue to be."

Richard was supremely calm. I was proud of my brother. He could have been upset Tex had me at gunpoint. I felt the cold steel against my neck. Maybe he'd anticipated such a thing happening, Tex returning at an off moment while Angel wasn't in the house. He acted like he'd rehearsed for this.

My heart still pounded but I was calming down. Here I was, the girl who before the pulse could barely leave her house without having a panic attack. And yet I was enduring this—a gun at my neck, and being stuck at the mercy of an angry man! As I thought about it, I realized that I'd been without the anti-depressant I used to take daily for months now. And I was actually feeling more stable than I had in years.

Richard, still holding up his hands in the classic show of surrender, moved forward a step. "I'm Richard, and this is Sarah, my sister."

"Stay right where you are!" Tex barked.

Richard halted immediately.

"We're gonna wait right here for my wife to return. I'll give you one hour. If she's not back by then, I'm gonna use this thing." He waved the gun slightly and then nestled it once again against my neck.

"Look, I can go find your wife while you wait here with Sarah."

Tex seemed to think about it a moment, but said, "For all I know, you're gonna go and bring back more of your friends. Or go get some weapons. No, I think you'll stay here, too. We'll just wait together, nice and cozy like."

He motioned for Richard to take a seat at the kitchen table. Keeping an arm about me, he led me to an adjacent seat. Then, with his pistol at the ready, he moved a chair away from the table where he could keep his eye on both of us.

Richard and I looked at each other. Our lives at that moment depended on Angel coming back within an hour. I tried searching my mind, to remember how long Angel usually kept busy outdoors. She might be extending her survival garden with a new planting or checking a faraway trap for a catch; she might be out in the barn, though most barn chores now fell to either Richard or me. There was nothing we could do except sit there and wait.

And pray.

CHAPTER FORTY-EIGHT

ANDREA

Before I left the house to confront Lexie, I saw Mr. Martin in the kitchen on the two-way. I recognized Lexie's voice on the other end. Since I was on my way to speak to her, I stopped to listen, hoping to hear an update about the invaders.

But she only asked to come to the house. Mr. Martin told her it would be okay, but to leave Blake the two-way and to stay armed. I continued heading outside, determined to try and reason one last time with her. I wanted to catch her before she reached the house, though. I wasn't sure if she would relent; and if we argued I wanted it just between us.

Mrs. Martin saw me in the hallway and stopped. "Don't forget to bring your rifle for cleaning later. We want to keep our firearms ready for the next time." She studied me.

"Are you okay?"

Somehow I knew she wasn't asking about the skirmish, or even about the cuts on my face. I rarely needed comfort after an encounter; I guess it was that video game mentality, I don't know. So I knew she was referring to my mother still missing. I'd been telling myself Mom and Washington had likely holed up at the house for awhile. Now that things had warmed up, I understood why she'd want to revisit our old life. I would too, if I got the chance. And she'd be forced to think about my dad at the house—I liked that idea. I liked that Washington would see how good my mom had it with my dad.

I never pictured our home as having been ransacked or worse, burned down—even though I knew many homes had been. I kept it in my mind like a sanctuary—a place we could return to one day.

Mrs. Martin was waiting for an answer. "I'm okay."

"You get that pretty face looked at by Mr. Clepps."

I certainly wasn't feeling pretty, so I appreciated her kindness.

"We're still praying for your mom and Mr. Washington to get back safely. Don't lose hope!" She squeezed my hand.

I felt suddenly bereft of my mom and as though I might cry. I didn't want to, so I said, "Thanks," and rushed off. Lexie should have been getting near the house by now, anyway. When I reached the back door, I saw her just starting to descend the hill.

The hill has a line of trees about thirty feet across on one side but it's wide open in the middle. At the top, there's more tree cover and brush, which is why the shed is up there. I darted past the chicken coop and riding ring, into the trees. The all-clear sounded as I started up, keeping Lexie in view above me. She was heading down the open middle. Her way was the fastest going down or up, but I didn't want her to see me yet. I was afraid if she saw me coming, she'd harden her heart against me again! I needed to get a word in before that happened. When we reached the halfway mark, I figured I'd cross over and meet her on the hillside.

I concentrated on what was in front of me, moving quickly, but taking note of Lexie's progress along the way. Suddenly I heard her— she sounded surprised. It was a quick, muffled sound. Had she fallen down? I hurried forward. When I came to the opening, I stopped.

Lexie, below me already, had her hands above her head and was being prodded forward by the barrel of a rifle! A soldier! He'd been left behind! Our scouts had missed him, and now he had a gun against her back!

I started down after them, about twenty feet behind, as quietly as I could.

I can't describe the feeling that came over me as I watched that man with a gun at Lexie's back. I was petrified for her! He was keeping her close, too—his human bodyguard. I figured Blake was still in the shack and had to be seeing this, but he wouldn't risk hurting Lexie. If he shot the guy, his bullet could keep right on going and kill Lexie too. Down below, no one had a clean shot, either. The soldier kept her too close. I suddenly realized it was going to be up to me to take him down!

As I followed stealthily, I wondered, what would I do if something happened to Lex? What if I didn't get a good shot, and he killed her? I was no more able to shoot his back than Blake. Our bullets had found their way through tree trunks a foot and a half wide. That's solid wood, and we'd found exit holes on them. What if Lexie became 'collateral damage?'

I fought against the notion of losing somebody else I loved, blinking away tears that threatened. I hastened my steps, still intent on keeping quiet, but I had my rifle on my shoulder so I stopped and tried to sight it on the man's head. If only he'd stay still! Since he was moving, I had to move with him. Much as I would have loved to come to Lexie's rescue, it didn't seem possible. Not while they were moving. If I shot and missed, he might shoot her!

I had hit moving targets in the past during practice—and even a few times during skirmishes. I'd shot Roy, saving Mr. Martin when all I had was moonlight and shooting was brand new to me. And I'd taken down the guy who had Aiden. *You can do this, Andi.* Every member of my family would tell me I could. Mr. and Mrs. Martin would say I could. Even Lexie would say I could! With renewed determination I lifted my rifle and scoped the guy. He was keeping her firmly in front of him, his human bullet-proof vest.

We were almost at the riding ring, after which came the barn, chicken coop, playground, then the house. The man stopped, looking around, trying to decide where to go with his hostage. I wished I could take a shot then but it was still too risky.

He moved them on, more slowly now. Mr. Martin came out of the house holding up his hands to show he was unarmed. The soldier stopped; I inched a few feet closer—thank God for soft grass, hiding the sound of my footsteps! If this had happened in the fall with dry leaves on the ground, I'd never have been able to be so quiet.

I got close enough to hear Lexie. She said, "That's my father. What do you want? He'll give it to you if you let me go." She didn't sound desperate or frightened—I felt so proud of her! I was just about to shoot—and then everything happened quickly. Lexie turned to face the guy as she finished her question—and saw me. Something in her eyes made him turn in alarm, and for a second I saw the barrel of his gun pointed in my direction. Lexie dove into the grass—and there was my clean shot! In the background Mr. Martin shouted, "Don't shoot!" But that barrel was pointed at me and I knew Lexie was no longer in my line of fire.

When my finger pulled the trigger, the last thing I saw was that man's face, filled with rage. I'd heard two shots, actually, and only later did I realize one of them had come from his gun.

And hit me.

CHAPTER FORTY-NINE

SARAH

Forty-five minutes passed as Richard and I sat silently at the table under Tex's watchful eyes. Every minute I hoped Angel would appear.

"You know, I could be peeling vegetables for dinner. Angel's gonna be mad you stopped me."

Tex stared at me sullenly. "Angel's gotta show up first before she can be anything. And if she don't show up soon, you and your brother are gonna be stew meat."

"Stew meat?" I asked, angrily. For some reason, I took him literally; for all I knew, he meant it literally. We'd heard of people becoming cannibals. "Like, as in, stew meat for your dinner one night?" My voice was filled with derision.

Tex stared at me for a moment. His mouth twisted. "No; but I would happily feed your no-good stinkin' bodies to my dogs if you did anything to my wife."

"We didn't do anything to Angel!" Richard cried. "She saved our lives! I was caught on a rope trap and Sarah fell into the pit. I cut myself down but I took a good fall on the head. I was too sore to pull Sarah up by myself. Angel came and pulled her up; Sarah got so frightened she passed out—"

"I was weak from not eating!" Why did Richard have to embarrass me?

Richard continued. "We had to pull her here using a black garbage bag as a sled, and on the way Angel grilled me and learned all about us and decided we could help her here—at least until you returned. We wouldn't do anything to hurt her!"

"We think she's great!" I added. "She's taught me a lot and we've only been here a few days."

Tex's eyes were softening—I think. I wondered if he was really soft-hearted like his wife. But he stood up to remove his jacket, carefully watching us, revealing brawny, tattooed arms. The side of his neck was tattooed as well. It didn't make him look less formidable, that's for sure. I glanced at Richard. He met my eyes and shrugged. He didn't seem very worried! Either that or he was beyond caring. I felt sort of beyond caring myself. I'd had Martha point a gun at me and she turned out to be nice. Her son had pointed a gun at me and he turned out not to be nice. It remained to be seen whether Tex would be more like Martha or her son. Either way, he might still send us back to the road. The idea now seemed worse than death.

I would not go back to living like that. I still bore marks all over my body from fleas and other insects. If we didn't get bitten up while crossing through wooded areas, we got bitten up in the old barns we slept in. My skin felt coarse; as if it was never really clean, despite Angel's homemade soap. I despised the lack of hygiene, the lack of a toilet, the absence of any small comforts—life with Angel, as brief as it had been, was far better. And I'd already grown fond of her. I could see myself living with her a long, long time. Tex was going to ruin it! Once again, just when life got comfortable! Why did something always have to happen to ruin it? Even if Angel came home right now, Tex would send us packing!

I started squirming in my seat, uncomfortable at the thought of what was ahead.

"Please—don't—make us leave!" I said. My head sank, my eyes falling to my lap. "I can't live like that again." When I looked back up, Tex was scrutinizing me.

He took a deep breath. "Well," he said. "I'd like to believe you two. Sounds like my wife, being too soft-hearted for her own good." He paused. "But until I see her, I can't take your word for it, that she's okay. And you've got--" He glanced at his watch. It was an old wind-up model. "Twelve minutes left."

CHAPTER FIFTY

ANDREA

A terrific pain shot through my left arm and the next thing I knew I lay flat on my back on the ground. Dazed, at first I thought I'd been kicked by a horse. I grabbed my arm and felt warm blood running over my hand. *Blood!* It ran through my fingers and down my arm. Had I been shot? The next moment Lexie fell to the ground beside me.

"Andrea?" Her voice was frantic. "Oh, my gosh, Andrea!" She yanked off her jacket and proceeded to take off her tee shirt. I gazed at her, still feeling hazy, but I was conscious enough to know Lexie was beside herself. Right before my eyes, she'd stripped to her bra. She wrapped my arm with her tee shirt. I groaned as she pulled it tightly around the wound. What began as a hard thwack was now a burning, stinging hornet's nest in my arm. I couldn't keep from moaning.

With large, sorrowful eyes, Lexie cried, "I'm sorry! I'm so, so sorry! For everything! Please be okay!"

She sounded agonized. I figured I must be dying. To someone else she cried, "There's a lot of blood!" Blake came into view, gently placing Lexie's discarded jacket over her shoulders. She wriggled her arms into it but kept her gaze on me. Tears ran down her face.

Vaguely I heard a lot of noise in the background as more people joined the scene. Then my eyes grew heavy, so heavy I couldn't keep them open. I felt terribly, terribly tired. With great effort, I forced my lids apart.

"Did I get him?" I asked.

Lexie sobbed. "Yes! But he got you, too!"

"I know." The enormous, throbbing burning in my arm engulfed me.

"You saved me, Andrea! You did it again! You are so important to us, to all of us!"

"I know," I said again, but I was hardly aware of her words or mine. I felt as though my entire body was in pain.

Someone said, "Here. Take a sip of this." It was Roper! I could hardly keep my lids open but then I heard Mrs. Martin's voice. "Don't give her anything." I felt her tuck a blanket around me. "Get her feet raised. C'mon, you guys, let's get her to the house." In a lower voice, she said, "Before she goes into shock."

I felt someone dabbing my face gently and then heard Roper's voice beside me, "Her face got cut upstairs—the window took a hit. Where's that nurse? You said you had a nurse, right?"

"Our nurse is wounded too," Mrs. Martin said. "But we have a D.O.. Let's hope he can handle this, otherwise we'll be following the book on this one. Hurry, now! Be gentle!"

Someone held my right hand. Hard. Lexie said, "Her hand's so cold!"

I thought I heard Jared. "Was there an exit wound?"

Lexie cried, "I don't know! I just saw a lot of blood!"

"Okay." Jared spoke to me then in the voice of the soldier he'd been, the one with field experience with men down. "You're gonna be okay. It's a flesh wound, went right through you most likely. I've seen a lot worse. We'll have to sew you up—but you'll be okay, Andrea. And you got that guy right in the head. Good shot!"

Normally I would have beamed from his praise but I was unable to respond at all.

I felt myself being lifted onto something.

And then the world went black.

CHAPTER FIFTY-ONE

LEXIE

When I saw Andrea fall, I can't express the pain and remorse that hit me. I realized in a split-second how stupid and stubborn and wrong I'd been to stay mad at her. She saved my life—and got shot for her trouble! After I'd been treating her so terribly! I ran blindly past the soldier she'd shot to reach her, frantic with worry.

Why did it take something so dire for me to learn the error of my ways? Why couldn't I have forgiven her earlier?

When they moved her, I insisted on going too, though my mom told me to report to my father and see what needed my help. She was trying to distract me. But I followed along miserably while the men carried her on a sheet which they pulled taut, four of them, one at each corner. My mom kept at them to keep Andrea's feet higher than her heart.

In the house, Mom said, "Take her to the women's bedroom. We'll make that our new infirmary." The infirmary tent had been targeted and took a lot of bullets (which is how Mrs.Philpot, our nurse, got injured).

I heard Jared saying you never, ever, ever, identify the infirmary tent from the outside. Same for medics on the field. They shouldn't wear a red cross or any other symbol that identifies them as medical personnel. They're targeted by the enemy because they save lives. The enemy doesn't want lives to be saved.

Mom looked at me. "Lex, run to the infirmary tent and get all the equipment you think we'll need—especially the I.V. stuff." I hurried to the door but she said, "No, wait; I'd better go." I was glad she did. In my state of mind, I wouldn't have known what to grab, anyways.

Mrs. Philpot was asleep on the bed adjacent to Andrea's, drugged, (I found out later) after sustaining a bullet wound to her left calf. Like Andrea's, hers was a flesh wound. She'd been bandaged up by the D.O., and now it was Andrea's turn. My mother returned and dumped a basket load of instruments and packaged gauze and gloves and wipes and other things out on a clean white pillowcase, which she had me open and spread out at the bottom of the bed.

Mr. Clepps had been checking Andrea's vitals and readied her good arm for the I.V. He began grabbing things from the stash. He said, "We need to get her hydrated." Afterwards he carefully unwound the tee-shirt dressing I'd wrapped around the wound, telling Jared to don gloves and "get the Celox A" ready. As he took a pair of sharp scissors and began cutting away the bloodied fabric of Andrea's shirt, he asked my mother, "How'd you get this stuff? This is a perfect wound kit here." Then, "Quick, Jared! Now. Inject the Celox right here."

I watched, surprised. Jared seemed perfectly at ease helping Mr. Clepps, as though he'd done it a thousand times. Maybe he had.

My mother took a deep breath. Seeing Andrea's open wound was harder for her than me; she didn't even hang around to watch most births on our farm.

"We've been buying stuff little by little for years," she said, answering the question. "And Mrs. Philpot brought great stuff with her." She glanced at Jared. "You did, too, didn't you, Jared?" He nodded silently, keeping his eyes on Mr. Clepps's progress. Mom added, with a little smile, "You brought us all kinds of surprising things."

He glanced at her then quickly and almost smiled himself. "You mean the grenades?"

"Yes. I think you saved the day, today!"

He nodded. "They were homemade. A little trick I picked up in Iraq—from the bad guys." I gaped at him a minute. I felt suddenly that maybe Jared wasn't so bad after all. He'd just been through a lot. Stuff that I probably couldn't even imagine. Returning my attention to Andrea, I changed that thought. I probably could imagine, now.

I sat by with my arms crossed, engrossed in my own misery. I'm not squeamish—I've seen our farm stock give birth and I've seen animals injured and bleeding—even torn up sometimes from coyotes or a broken fence. I've watched while a vet stitched them up. So I was able to watch what Mr. Clepps did to Andrea but I was consumed by guilt.

Mr. Clepps suddenly raised his head, smiling. "No reason to cry, Lexie! She's gonna be all right. If this shot went to her abdomen or chest, it could be a different story; but look here, the bullet missed the major artery!"

"Thank God!" my mother said.

He turned to Jared, clearly pleased. "It didn't mushroom; that's

222

something to give thanks for—went clean through."

Jared nodded, knowingly. He saw my face and added, "Some bullets are hollow points—made to mushroom on impact, spreading out to inflict greater damage. Some are made to splinter apart—they're even worse. Andrea's lucky this outfit wasn't using either of those."

"We're blessed, not lucky," my mom said. She turned to me. "We had protection from above."

I nodded but I was still unhappy. It would have been better protection if Andrea hadn't been hurt at all, it seemed to me. Yet I knew my mother was right. We'd come up against an organized band of fighters—either an actual army or a guerrilla outfit—and they'd retreated. That had to be a miracle!

Jared continued to watch everything Mr. Clepps did, jumping to assist if necessary. In fact, he presided over it like the Chief of Surgery at a hospital watching an underling. I knew Andrea would be gratified to hear about this later.

Roper popped his head inside the door. He met my eyes. Everyone else kept their attention on the patient. "How's she doing?"

"Good."

"She's not in shock?"

"No. It was close. They gave her something." I went on to tell him how the bullet went clean through and didn't mushroom or anything.

He smiled. "I know that." And he held up a tiny shiny object. "Here's a souvenir. I cleaned it off. I think it's her bullet."

"Wow, thanks!" I said, receiving it from him. I was genuinely pleased. I figured Andrea would keep it as a trophy. She'd sacrificed her safety for me, and I wanted to make sure she was proud of it. I was certainly proud of her.

Jared glanced over at me. "Let's see it," he said. I handed the bullet to him.

My mother said, "Lex, you've been here long enough. Andrea's gonna be okay. Go see if anyone needs your help in the kitchen or anywhere else."

I hesitated. "My shift with Blake isn't actually over yet. We were supposed to be on until 6pm."

"So why were you near the house?" she asked, softly. I knew what she meant. If I had stayed on the hill with Blake, that soldier wouldn't have grabbed me. "I—I—was coming in to look for you. Dad said it was okay. I was gonna go back up."

She stared at me. I looked away, feeling teary again. I wished sometimes I would just grow up and stop being sensitive. I didn't use to be so sensitive. What was wrong with me, anyhow? But my mom came towards me. I thought she might scold me for leaving the hill; instead, she enveloped me in a hug. Normally I'd be embarrassed to let my mother hug me in front of other people. I was almost seventeen, for crying out loud. But I didn't care.

"This was upsetting today. But God protected us." I drank in her soothing tone and the comfort of her arms.

"Thanks, Mom."

Roper went past us. "Anything I can do here?"

I looked over in time to see Jared turn icy eyes on him. "No. There's nothing you can do here. There's nothing you can do for Andrea." Even my mother raised her head to look at the two men.

Roper held up his hands and backed away a step. "Just trying to be helpful," he said.

"She don't need your help."

I didn't like the look on Jared's face. Just like that, he was once again his former scary self. My newfound trust in him vanished. I had no idea if anything had started between Andrea and Roper but Jared certainly made it clear he didn't want there to be anything between them. Wowzers. I knew Andrea used to like Jared—but did she still? And what about Roper? Of the two men, I immediately sided with Roper. He was super good-looking but more importantly he was a believer and had kinder eyes. He also joked around a lot. I hoped Andrea would like him better than Jared.

But if she did, would Jared be trouble? He wasn't the kind of guy you wanted to cross. He looked at me then, with dark, forbidding eyes.

I got the distinct feeling we had trouble brewing.

CHAPTER FIFTY-TWO

SARAH

Hulk came abruptly to his feet. "Time's up. Outside. Let's go," he ordered. My hope—that he'd extend our waiting period—vanished.

"Angel could be doing plenty of things that take longer than an hour," I said.

Tex pointed his pistol at me. "Move." He motioned at the door.

"What're you gonna do?" Richard asked, his voice heavy. "We didn't do anything to Angel!"

"Outside," he repeated.

We walked to the door and went out. I was praying Angel would appear. Maybe we'd see her coming towards the house or near the barn or chicken yard. I looked around in every direction but saw nothing.

Richard turned to Tex. "Look," he said, I don't think you're a killer. And you don't want to do anything you'll regret."

"Keep walking," Tex said. He was leading us towards the barn, which was actually a relief. He could've headed us to the area where Angel slaughtered the occasional chicken!

"If Angel comes back and we're hurt, she will not be happy," Richard said. "And you don't WANT to do this, I can tell. Besides, she is coming back!"

"Yeah. You keep saying that but I don't see her," Tex said, gruffly.

"Just give us more time," Richard said.

"She could have caught something big in a trap," I suggested. "That could take her longer to get back."

"Traps are for small game," Tex grumbled. "Nothing that would take her long to manage."

"What if a deer got its leg caught?" Richard asked. "That could happen."

Tex snorted. "A deer would run off and take the trap with it."

"Maybe Angel tracked it!" I cried. He didn't reply but I thought I'd seen a change in his face. He thought it was a possibility, too!

"She would go after it," I added, with more assurance. "Angel is not

225

afraid to go after what she wants."

Tex stopped. He looked as if he could almost crack a smile. But instead he unlocked the barn door and motioned us inside. My heart sank. It occurred to me that Angel had said they did use the barn for slaughtering sometimes, like in winter. Especially for small game like rabbits. Were we going to be slaughtered like pieces of meat? Was he really going to feed us to the dogs?

"God," I prayed, silently. "You didn't bring us this far just to let us die like animals!"

Tex had rope now and he motioned for us to sit down against a wooden support beam. Richard fell heavily on his bottom, drawing his feet up—the next thing I knew there was a scuffle and then Tex came up holding a second pistol.

"Nice try," he said, sardonically. I'd completely forgotten about Richard's gun in its ankle holster. My brother had tried to draw it quickly but he was unpracticed and wasn't fast enough. Tex glared at me saying, "Don't you move, or your brother's toast." I watched helplessly as Tex tied him securely to the beam, first with rope and then duct tape. But I realized this meant he wasn't going to kill us! At least, not yet. If he was, then why bother tying us up? I felt calmer.

"Please don't cover my mouth," I said, when he got to me.

"Did I cover your brother's mouth?" he asked, in his gruff voice.

"No. But in movies they always do that. I don't want you to do that."

"This ain't a movie," he said. "But you'd better pray for a happy ending, sister; cuz' if I don't get my wife back soon, the two of you are gonna have starring roles in a tragedy."

He left us tied up and staring at each other.

"At least we can talk," I said.

Richard nodded. I waited for him to start spewing anger. He was usually only a few degrees from bitter, even before the EMP. He'd fly off the handle when people did things he didn't like or couldn't understand. Here we were, tied up and uncomfortable, thirsty and hungry; for all we knew he might still kill us. But Richard was calm.

"Aren't you mad?"

He looked at me. "About what?"

"About being tied up! When we're telling the truth! Aren't you mad that Hulk isn't believing us?"

"Hulk?" He almost smiled. "You mean, Tex?"

"Yeah, Hulk Hogan. Anyway, how come you're not fuming mad by now?"

He fell silent. "I guess because I can't blame him. He doesn't know us. He doesn't know whether he can believe us. And Angel isn't here— I sure wish I knew what she was doing or where she went but I guess I'd feel the same way he does if I was in his place."

I nodded. "But he might still KILL us!"

"I know. But we've had a few lucky breaks before now so maybe she'll be back soon and we'll get another. What do you think is keeping her?"

"Lucky breaks? It hasn't been luck."

He looked at me, questioning.

"It's God. He's watching out for us."

Richard grimaced. "Like he watched out for the millions of people who died after the EMP?"

"We don't know why that happened," I said. "But he HAS been looking after us! Ever since that day when he—when that guy showed me how to find water at the library—I've known God is watching out for us."

"How can you say that? Mom died, Sarah! Jesse died! Dad is lost and probably dead too! I don't call that watching out for us!"

I swallowed. I was still upset when I thought of Mom and Jesse or Dad. "They're in a better place," I said. "They can't be hurt anymore."

"That is the lamest thing I've ever heard! That is the sorry excuse for reality religious people use to make everything okay when really nothing is okay. It's a fantasy, Sarah."

"To you, maybe. Because you don't believe it. But if you knew it was true—if you KNEW—wouldn't you feel better? Wouldn't you be glad for them?"

He shook his head. "Can we just change the subject? Heaven's a fantasy for the weak."

"Maybe those who can't believe are the weak. Maybe heaven is a reward for the strong—in faith." I was no Bible scholar, but I spoke from what I knew. I'd been reading my little Bible whenever I got the chance since we'd left the library. Whenever I had a few minutes and enough light, that is, which wasn't actually very often. But what I did read felt stirring to me, powerful. I felt like, reading the gospels, I was

227

getting to know Jesus. "Jesus said heaven is real. So unless you want to believe he lied, you have to believe it's real."

He hardly blinked. "I don't have to believe anything."

"No, you don't, Richard. But I have a Bible that says heaven is real. And that's good enough for me."

He nodded. "Uh huh. That's what I thought. You have no proof."

"The Bible is proof."

"It's just a book, Sarah!" He paused. "Look, you've come really far since this started, you're not having anxiety attacks anymore and maybe believing in this stuff is helping you. But I don't have to believe it too, okay?"

Just then the door slammed open. Our heads swiveled sharply at the sound. I hoped to see Angel but it was Hulk. He held a satchel in one hand and had a rifle slung across one shoulder. He looked fierce. My heart started pounding. I hoped I would not faint. Then I changed my mind and wished I would. For the first time in my life, I actually wished I would pass out—I did not want to be around to witness what was going to happen next. If Tex's face hadn't looked so dreadful I might have thought Angel had returned and he was here to set us free. But his face was hard, his eyes steely.

I gaped at him as he came forward, glowering with that hardened look, clutching that bag. I did not want to know what it held…instruments of torture? I could only guess, but one thing seemed certain: We were dead meat. I was sure of it.

CHAPTER FIFTY-THREE

ANDREA

When I came to, blinking, I was in my mother's room. Well, the women's room we called it because women slept here. Jolene, my mother, and any of the wives who were waiting for their cabins to be finished. *Why was I here?* A terrific pain in my left arm answered that question. It came flooding back. Lexie walked in, looking sad. Her eyes brightened when she saw I was awake.

"Hey! How are you feeling?"

I swallowed. "Like my arm is on fire. A blazing, raging fire."

She frowned and sat beside me on the bed, shaking her head sorrowfully. "I'm so sorry, An. I—"

"Did I kill him?" I couldn't seem to remember.

She searched my face. "Oh, yeah! Instantly! He got a shot at you right before you got him, unfortunately."

"I'm sorry," I said, wincing from pain.

"Sorry for what?"

"For not keeping him alive." It was always good to keep a guy alive so we could get information.

"Don't be sorry," Lexie said. "You saved my life! I don't know what would've happened if you hadn't—"

"So you're not mad at me anymore?"

Her eyes grew large, haunted. "I'm so sorry I stayed mad at you! I wasn't thinking! I—I love you, Andrea. You're like my sister." She leaned down and kissed my cheek.

I felt so good at this that I got teary. "You're like my sister, too." Lexie had taken my right hand, my uninjured side, but even that hand was sore from the I.V. needle stuck in it.

"Your skin feels better, now," she said. "You were cold and clammy yesterday."

"Oh—I don't know why."

"Shock. Mr. Clepps explained it to me. He said the body needs all its energy for life-sustaining functions. Everything else, including temperature regulation, gets put to the wayside."

"I went into shock?"

"Not really; but you would have, if they didn't get you warm and pump some fluids into you."

I shifted slightly on the bed and an onslaught of pain made me want to cry. But having Lexie there made me be brave. "Lex—can you ask Mr. Clepps if I could have something for pain?"

Her eyes widened. "Absolutely! I'll be right back!"

Lying there, I kept replaying yesterday's events. I'd seen that guy's face before pulling the trigger. His eyes were filled with rage. I wondered if he was furious that he was facing a bullet, or that he was facing one at the hands of a young woman. I felt no joy, no sense of victory, for having ended his life. My only comfort was I'd saved Lexie. But I wanted to know: Why were these foreigners attacking us?

———— ◆ ————

So I've been getting a steady stream of visitors. I'm not great company because the pain in my arm is consuming, like a fire that won't go out. Jared came by and gave me a step-by-step account of what they'd done to patch me up. He seemed extra attentive, for Jared. I got the feeling he wanted to say more to me than just chat. Finally, he sat down next to me.

"I'm glad you're okay." He was eying me steadily. I blushed. He reached over and touched one of the marks on my face from when the window shattered in front of me. He gently thumbed over my cheek. "Nothing here's gonna scar, I don't think."

"That's good!"

He smirked—Jared's usual smile. "We wouldn't want to ruin that pretty face."

Just then Roper popped his head in. When Jared saw him, his face hardened. He leaned in and deliberately, slowly, kissed me on the mouth! I think Roper saw how surprised I was. He smiled.

"Just checking on the patient. How're you feeling, young lady?"

I smiled, recognizing his jab. I liked that we had a little joke between us.

"Not great."

The smile vanished. He nodded. "I'm praying for you."

"You are? Thank you."

That beautiful smile. "Of course." He paused and gave me a funny look. He ignored Jared, who looked almost comically annoyed.

"I saw a great headline once." He ran a hand through the air, as if reading an imaginary line of print. "Typhoon Rips Through Cemetery; 100s Dead."

It took me a second or two to get that it was a joke, after which I giggled. Jared frowned but I saw his lips almost turning up at the ends.

Roper continued. "Man Struck by Lightning Faces Battery Charge." I tittered appreciatively. Roper's eyes sparkled at me and he said, "A dentist and a manicurist fought tooth and nail."

He kept up a steady stream of one-liners, keeping me giggling in delight.

"What happens if you get scared half to death—twice?"

"I was married by a judge; I should have asked for a jury."

"Support bacteria. They're the only culture some people have."

"Okay, so what's the speed of dark?"

I was laughing by now, but I winced in pain. "Ow! You're making me laugh too hard." But even Jared's hard-lined face had softened somewhat.

"Laughter is good medicine," Roper said, gently. "Proverbs 17:22. I'll come by again later to give you another dose."

"Please do," I said, smiling. "Wait, give me one more!"

He gazed at me, thinking, and then stifled a smile. "Do Roman paramedics refer to I.V.s as '4s'?" That one took me a few seconds but I snickered when I got it.

"That was a good one."

A brief smile. "Why do they lock gas station bathrooms? Are they afraid someone will get in and clean them?" Even Jared had to smirk at that one.

"See ya later," Roper said. "Gotta get back to work. We're fixing the infirmary tent." His eyes flicked at Jared for the merest second, and then returned to me. "Feel better."

When he'd gone, Jared said, "Got work to do, too. See you later."

"Thanks for coming by." He nodded. I was relieved he hadn't kissed me again. Before, I'd been thinking of Jared as a real possibility, romantically speaking.

Roper was making me wonder why I had.

———————— ◆ ————————

When Lexie stopped in later, I asked if my mother was back. Her face fell when I asked so I knew right away she wasn't. Later, I realized it meant Rhema wasn't back either. This must be so hard for Lexie. And she didn't even say anything about my mom thoughtlessly taking her horse! All she said was, "We have to pray and trust. Have faith."

I'm trying not to worry about Mom and Washington—but it's hard. Mrs. Martin stopped in to check on me and I asked her if she had any news about my mom. She didn't.

But she said, "We don't know they're hurt. We don't know anything for sure. This is what faith is all about; believing in the face of darkness."

The Martins are a big comfort to me. And I am sooo happy Lexie and I are friends again! Saving her life was a God-given privilege and an opportunity for us to heal. Getting shot was a painful way to heal but heck, I guess I deserved it. I was totally wrong to get anywhere near Blake. I'm ashamed of it now. And a good thing coming out of this is Lexie and I both realize that, no matter our differences, we're on the same team; we've got each other's back.

But I wish my mother was here. I want her to feel badly for me, to say nice things because I've been hurt. I also want to know she's okay.

I'm not mad at her anymore.

CHAPTER FIFTY-FOUR

LEXIE

I've got all of Andrea's chores as well as my own now which keeps my hands busy but my mind buzzes with one thought: My father is unfair! He's decided I can't be a lookout! I wasn't doing a bad job—Even Blake hadn't seen there was a straggler on the property! Blake says he saw the guy only when he darted out of the trees and grabbed me. It was a scary moment. He forced my rifle out of my hands and then kept me in front of him. He spoke to me in a foreign language. I didn't need to understand it to know he was angry.

Blake radioed my dad and then went after us, keeping further back than Andrea but wanting to be around if she needed backup. My father told him to stay put but he didn't. Blake is the kind of guy who will do what he's told but he said he couldn't this time; he couldn't just sit up there when I was the hostage. My dad was tempted to take Blake off lookout duty also, but really he can't. We barely have enough people for border surveillance as it is.

I'm glad Blake didn't get penalized because of me. I feel badly enough about Andrea. But Dad should let me be a lookout. I'd stay up there next time until our shift ended, I know I would. As for Andrea, thank God we had antibiotics! Mr. Clepps says she was fortunate he did. All medicines are like gold, now. Some people have traded food for aspirin or other medicines, but to get real stuff like antibiotics, you have to have a lot to trade—or have a nurse and a D.O. with precious supplies join your compound, like we did.

So that soldier Andrea shot—he had no personal I.D. None of the casualties did. Save for a dog tag with a number. The trucks we took down are Russian trucks but they've been out of commission for two decades—so says Jared. They were probably sold to whoever attacked us. The council met last night and the general consensus was, these guys are mercenaries—but hired by whom? We don't know.

Dad reported how he'd spent hours on the ham radio to find out whether these attacks are widespread or if anyone knows who is behind them. Some foreign stations were buzzing with word that the U.S. is putting citizens into FEMA camps for safety and sustenance; and that some allies are sending aid. But he also heard a disturbing rumor—we hope it's just a rumor—that Russia is in talks with the President about a possible deal in which half of the United States would be given to them. HALF OF THE COUNTRY! They would get the western half, from California to the Mississippi. In return, they'd bring food and supplies and even restore electrical power. They would help us survive—in return for merely being Russian citizens! Can you imagine? Even so, we're east of the Mississippi—and we still got attacked by a foreign outfit.

No one here thinks the agreement will fly with the American people. Despite the fact we have been sheltered, spoiled and lulled into complacency by our affluence and (until now) peace on our shores—we are still America. Some of us at least, still hold freedom to be an inalienable right. My father says if we accept these terms we'll never be a sovereign nation again. The United States will be like Rome—gone, gone, gone.

Oh, something's up with Jolene, Jared's mother. We know she's got issues—her hoarding and tendency to be sloppy. But at the meeting she grew agitated, fidgeting around in her seat until it became so noticeable my mom went over to her.

"Jolene, are you okay? Do you want to leave the meeting? Because you can. No one has to be here except the leadership." Jolene looked ready to cry. She shook her head yes, she wanted to leave, and hurried from the room.

I looked at Jared to see how he reacted to this—after all, he'd received high praise for his homemade grenades or "fireworks" as Mr. Buchanan called them. His help during the skirmish was invaluable and everyone was grateful. You'd think Jolene would enjoy seeing her son getting acknowledgment; and that Jared would want her to see it. But his face was blank—as it often is.

I don't play poker, but if I did, I wouldn't play against Jared!

Blake sat next to me as usual. But even though he held my hand, I felt like he was distant, not with me at all. And today I felt as though he was avoiding me! Twice we could have had a few minutes together but he hurried off both times, mumbling something about a task he had to do. Tonight we had no chance to speak alone. I know he cares about me—for him to disobey my dad's orders by coming down the hill to help me is proof right there. But he's been different ever since. Does he blame me for Andrea's injury? Is he having second thoughts about us? I don't want to believe that. I am gonna find out.

As for Andrea—if she had died, I'd be living with guilt and regret. I thank God we both lived through this. But I am ashamed of myself for not forgiving her sooner.

CHAPTER FIFTY-FIVE

SARAH

Tex strode in and stopped. He looked back and forth at us, then plopped to the ground closer to Richard than me. He began rummaging in his satchel. My heart went into my throat. I closed my eyes, praying silently. If he was going to slaughter my brother I didn't want to see it. But I couldn't stand the suspense.

"Do me first!" I cried, opening my eyes.

"Huh?" Tex raised an eyebrow. "What do you mean?"

"Are you—are you going to kill us?" My voice was tight. Before the pulse I'd have been in an absolute panic by now. But Richard was right, I hadn't panicked in a long time. Yet if there's anything to feel anxious about, it's facing the man you know is about to kill you.

Tex didn't answer me, but frowned. Then leaning towards me, he grasped the ropes on my hands, making me gasp. Even though I'd told him to kill me first, I wasn't what you'd call *ready*. I held my breath while he took my tied hands in one of his. He removed a mean-looking sharp-edged, 12-inch knife from his boot.

I gasped again but he looked at me reprovingly—and proceeded to hover the knife over the ropes around my wrists. *Was he going to cut me loose?*

"You believe in the Bible?" he asked, in his slow, heavy voice. I gaped at him, trying to understand why he'd ask me that. Then with another frowning look, he replaced the knife, tucking it gingerly inside his boot. It didn't allay my fears. Then he began to untie me, undoing the knots manually!

"No sense in wasting good rope," he muttered. Stunned, I was silent. He continued until I was completely free and then he sat back and peered at me. Still afraid of what he might do, I could hardly comprehend the question he'd asked.

"So you believe?" he asked again. It seemed like an extraordinary question because Richard and I had just been discussing that very thing!

"I do." I looked at him, daring him to ridicule me the way Richard had. Was he going to kill me on account of being a believer? Jihadists—radical Muslims, do that. Communists hate Christians, too. Was Tex a Christian-hater also?

"So do I," he said, finally. He moved the loose rope to the side and turned to Richard. "You'll have to stay put until I see my wife. But if she's a believer," he motioned with his head towards me, "I'm willing to take my chances with her." He gave me a sideways glance. "Besides, if she tries anything, she's dead."

"I won't!" I assured him.

Richard was looking around and up, at the rafters. "So you have a bug in here? How do you power it?"

Tex almost smiled. "Not a bug. Just this." He stood up and went to a stack of hay which was no more than a foot from where we sat. After rustling his hands into it for a moment, he pulled out a two-way radio. "I turned it on before I left. Runs on batteries. We still have a few."

He surveyed the gadget in his hands. "These have a two-mile range in good weather. Angel is supposed to carry one with her if she goes off galavantin'." He looked at Richard. "That's another thing I don't like— if she went off willingly, why didn't she take this?"

Richard shrugged. "I have no idea. We didn't know about the walkie-talkies."

"That's precisely my point," said Tex. "Angel knew."

I wondered why Angel hadn't told us. They'd be useful anytime we were separated on the property.

Tex motioned for me to sit in front of Richard, and he sat beside me so we both faced my brother.

"I came out just now," he said, speaking slowly and heavily. "To set you straight about something important."

Richard waited. I was waiting too. I had no clue what he wanted to set Richard straight about.

"The Bible," he said, and reached into his satchel. He pulled out a worn, leather Bible. "IS the Word of God. This ain't no regular book," he said, as if anyone should know it. I stared at that old Bible as if it were a dove pulled from the hat of a magician. A Bible! It was possibly the last thing I would have ever expected Tex to have in that satchel!

"How do you know?" Richard asked.

Tex looked downright solemn. "There are lots of reasons. But before we get into that, have you ever read it for yourself?"

237

Richard stared at the tome in Tex's hands. "I think so."

"You THINK so?" Tex sounded scandalized. "Oh, you ain't never read it, man," he said. "If you read this book you wouldn't just THINK so. You would KNOW so. You would be different!"

He glanced at me and I nodded vigorously in agreement. "Yeah!"

Richard listened, unconvinced. "Well, maybe I just read parts of it," he said.

"Like what parts?" asked Tex.

Richard thought about it. "The New Testament, I guess."

"Well, you're going to hear it again," Tex said. "I'm gonna read you stuff from this book until my wife returns or I have to kill ya!"

"That wouldn't be very Christian," Richard said.

"How would you know? You haven't read the book."

"Everybody knows that."

Tex gave him a hard stare. "It is my Christian duty to protect my wife. And if she's already dead, killing you would be a whole lot more Christian than leaving you alive to go kill someone else's wife."

"I didn't do anything!" Richard cried. "To Angel or anyone else!"

Tex sniffed. "You better hope that's the truth. Now shut up and listen." He was thumbing through pages in the New Testament, searching for what he wanted to share when we all heard the dogs barking.

I met Richard's eyes. "I bet it's Angel!"

"If she's with 'em, why are they barkin'?" Tex said, darkly. "They don't bark at Angel." He put down the book and got to his feet, motioning for me to go ahead of him.

"Don't put Sarah in front!" Richard cried.

"I need to keep an eye on her," he said, "so she don't let you free."

He stopped me when we got to the door of the barn though, and gently pushed me behind him. He'd already pulled his gun and was holding it up, ready to shoot. He opened the door a crack and peered out. With one foot, he opened it wider. The dogs continued barking wildly as they approached the barn, which I could tell by the growing noise.

Suddenly, Tex opened the barn door wide, grinning from ear to ear. He tucked his gun into a holster at his waist.

"Hey, darlin'," he said, welcoming a smiling Angel into his arms. The dogs were jumping like crazy all over him but he enveloped his wife in a great big hug and kiss. Those ferocious dogs whined for his attention like little cry-babies. I couldn't believe they were the same animals that behaved like vicious wolves to strangers. The two broke apart and Tex turned his attention to the dogs who licked his face and arms and anything they could reach.

Angel meanwhile, turned to me. "I wondered where y'all were at," she said, giving me a smile.

"We wondered where you were at!" I said, wide-eyed.

"I'll tell you all about that later." Then her eyes fell upon Richard all tied up and her smile disappeared.

"What's going on?" She turned to Tex who was still on one knee petting the dogs.

"I only tied him up," Tex shrugged, suddenly sounding like a sheepish little boy. The Hulk-Hogan demeanor vanished.

"What for? What'd he do?"

"I didn't do anything!" Richard cried. "He was worried about you and thought I hurt you!"

"Well, my word! Let's untie him!" Angel cried, and the two of us descended upon Richard at once. Angel was clucking her tongue and apologizing to my brother all at once. "What were you thinking, honey?" she said to Tex.

"I didn't know what to think, darlin'," he said. "I got home and found strangers in my house and no sight of you."

Angel sighed. "I was tracking a deer, I think, only I never found it. I did find our trap," she added, cheerfully. "But there's a wounded animal out there and the coyotes are gonna get it if we don't." She stopped and looked up at Tex and stroked the side of his face. "But you were worried about me. I'm sorry I followed that rascally animal for so long! I wanted our trap back and I thought I could finish off whatever was dragging it and bring home meat." She let him swoop her into his arms.

"I understand," Tex said. He kissed the side of her head. I smiled at Richard. There was only one word that came to my mind to describe this tender couple: cute. Both of them had scared the daylights out of me on separate occasions and now both of them, it turned out, were softies at heart.

"I'm starving," Angel said, breaking apart from her husband's embrace. She turned to me. "Did you get that stew going, Sarah?"

"Uh-oh." From Tex.

"What'd you do? Did you stop her?" She turned to me and I nodded.

"Now what're we gonna do for dinner?" she asked.

Tex just shook his head.

She looked at me. "Did you take the meat out of the ice house?"

"I didn't get to that yet. I wanted to have the vegetables ready first."

"Okay then, Tex will grill up some meat and we can boil the vegetables up quick. It'll have to do."

Richard came over to where the three of us stood near the barn door, rubbing his arms where the ropes had been tightest. He and Tex met eyes.

"I'm sorry I tied you up," Tex said, in his slow, heavy voice.

"I understand," Richard said. "It's a crazy world right now."

As we left the barn Angel said, "It's always been a crazy world, darlin', since the Fall of Mankind. But the United States is sure crazier now than ever; I think our country has taken its own fall now, just like Rome did."

Hulk added, "This country fell when it took God out of the classroom and the public square. When I was in school, we had truancy and paper fights and cafeteria food fights. You kids have had to live with school shootings. You tell me which is better."

Angel took up the torch. "And we've been murdering our own babies—I read once that we killed more Americans by abortion than any war in history. Yup, this country has raised a stink to heaven! Because God values life—every life."

Richard was frowning. Angel caught it.

"You don't agree, Richard?"

He sniffed. "If he values every life, why did he let the EMP happen? Millions have died, you know that, right? More than however many were killed by abortion."

"Well, now you're talkin' about judgment," Tex said. "When nations fall, it's judgment." He stared at my brother. "God has always judged nations sooner or later. We just got ours. People die when there's judgment, and heck, even that ain't nothin' next to what happens after death."

As we entered the house he added, "I mean, Richard, if you think this is hell, it ain't. Life ain't pretty; it ain't fun, but wait'll people get to the real hell. It'll make life, even what it is today, look like a walk in the park. That's why Jesus always told people to repent while there is time."

"Does judgment mean we're out of time?" I asked.

"Darlin,' as long as you're still breathin', there's still time," Angel said, whizzing by us to the kitchen. "C'mon now, help me finish up over here."

When I walked over she said, "This EMP is a call to repentance. For individuals and for our nation." She shook her head. "All I can say is, worse is yet to come if we fail to do it."

Richard had been listening and he said, "It still seems to me, life is cheap to God."

"Oh, Richard!" Angel gasped. "God values life so much he sent his own Son to die for us! But he is a God of justice. This world is in rebellion to its creator. Don't ever forget that. Whatever happened, we've had it coming. God sent warnings, time after time. He always does. Our country did not heed those warnings and it did not repent."

"I didn't see any warning."

Angel and Tex looked at each other. Angel said, "Maybe you weren't watching."

We all got busy with chores then but I heard Tex say to Angel, "I was just gettin' ready to give Richard the gospel." He looked over at me. "Sarah—I think she's okay."

"I want the gospel too!" I said. I wasn't sure what he meant by giving us the gospel, but if it had to do with God, I was interested.

Angel beamed at me. "Bless the Lord! We'll have a Bible study tonight."

As I set the table and cleaned up the kitchen I had to marvel at Angel and Tex. They were rough-edged, hippie-types. If they'd told me they belonged to a motorcycle gang, it wouldn't have come as a surprise. But I hadn't expected them to live by the Bible. And yet they weren't anybody's doormat. They believed in God *and* guns. I'd always thought Christians were against any use of force. Some are, I know it. But I guess I have a lot to learn about what it means to be a Christian.

CHAPTER FIFTY-SIX

ANDREA

Lexie's been visiting me every chance she gets. I love our time together. Mr. Clepps checks on me, but Mrs. Philpot is now hobbling around with homemade crutches and a fat left ankle wrapped in gauze. She's taking care of me, too. She's supposed to stay off her leg as much as possible, but I can see she isn't the resting type.

Happily, she and Mr. Clepps agree I can go off the I.V. tomorrow, as long as I stay hydrated. I'm still in pain, but I'm bored. Lexie says that means I'm getting better. She gives me the latest news. When I asked why I wasn't hearing any construction sounds—unusual because someone or other is always working on a log cabin around here—she said building has stopped because of the extra manpower needed for surveillance, especially guarding the perimeters. We've even sent guys out a mile or so in two directions with flares. They're posted in spots with a good view, our "early warning system." If you consider a mile an early warning.

Roper is in one of the teams. Lexie said he volunteered. I wished he hadn't—I think it's dangerous. And I miss his jokes and his smile. Jared has come around every day, sometimes twice a day. I don't know how to discourage him! I came up with an idea, though. It may be a little underhanded, so I'm gonna bounce it off Lexie. My idea is to ask him to go look for my mom and Mr. Washington. If he says no, I have a good reason to turn a cold shoulder to him. If he agrees, well, that's two birds with one stone. He'll either find out they're alive—which would be great. Or maybe he'll not return, either! You see why my idea is underhanded? (Sometimes I think I'm hopelessly wicked at heart.)

I am clinging to the idea that my mother and Mr. Washington are still alive. But every day that passes makes that hope seem foolish.

Chapter Fifty-Seven

LEXIE

I caught Blake this morning right after breakfast and told him I needed to speak with him. He was already in full camo, face smeared with greenish-brown goo and all. He looked at me, brightly. "Shoot!"

My little sisters were watching us, giggling. They love it when they see me and Blake together, even if we're not holding hands. To them, there is nothing funnier than when we show affection for each other. Somehow they'd learned that age-old chant, "Lexie and Bla-ake up a tree, K-I-S-S-I-N-G."

Kids will be kids. So anyways, before they got started I said, "Let's go outside."

"I'm on the hill today. Wanna walk up with me?"

"Sure." I didn't really need the reminder that he was still a lookout while I had been banned but at least we'd get to talk.

Outside, the spring morning was warm. It was gonna be a hot day. We walked in silence for a few minutes, passing the spot on the grass where Andrea had bled out some. I felt a pang in my heart at the sight. Meanwhile, Blake waited for me to start. He was not a big conversation starter.

"Okay, so here's the thing," I said, glancing over at him. He nodded, waiting. Blake has big, serious eyes, and I still feel a small thrill when they're directed at me.

"I feel like you've been avoiding me."

He stopped walking. Stared at me. "How come?"

I shook my head. We were facing each other now. "I don't know, you just seem distant. Ever since Andrea got hurt!" My tone was accusing, though I hadn't planned on it being so. I suddenly felt like I was about to cry. I wished I wasn't so darn emotional!

Blake was still studying me in his intense fashion.

I got hold of myself and continued, "Do you feel like it's my fault? That she got hurt?"

He let out an exasperated breath. "No!" He stared at me with

243

puzzlement. There was an awkward, painful silence. I wished he'd speak!

Finally, after looking around as if he'd find the words in the air somewhere he said, "If I'm—distant—it has nothing to do with Andrea. It wasn't her getting hurt; it was you—almost getting killed!" He took my hands in his. "Lex, you gave me a real scare. I'm just trying…." He fell off for a moment and looked around, groping again for words. Blake is a brilliant guy in many ways but verbal ease is not his forte. "I'm just trying to come to terms with how I feel about you."

I waited. I wanted him to be more specific. How *did* he feel about me? Was he trying to determine his feelings? To see if he cared or not? I needed reassurance. When I just stared at him, I guess he realized his answer hadn't satisfied me.

He added, "It's hard…to love someone."

Better; but oh, Blake! That's not good enough! "What do you mean?"

He stared deeply into my eyes. "I—I love you, Lex."

Those words were like honey to my soul. I threw myself into him and we almost fell back, but he chuckled. "Whoa! I've got a lot of weight on my back!" Besides his rifle on a strap, he had his backpack with food and coffee and other gear for his day on the hill.

When he regained equilibrium for both of us, we were still in an embrace. Vaguely, I wondered if now would be the time. Was he going to propose? While we looked into each other's eyes for a moment, my question changed to, "When is he going to kiss me!" We were both aware that we were in full view of anyone looking, certainly in view of the lookouts above us and the house below, not to mention a number of the cabins. I didn't care—but did Blake?

"Everyone can see us," he said.

"I know. I don't care."

That was enough reassurance for him because he finally leaned in and gave me a warm, wet kiss. I tightened my arms around him. "I love you, too!" I whispered afterwards.

"I know," he said, nodding, with his usual serious demeanor. I had to grin at that. He was cute, being confident that way.

"I'll try not to be—distant."

"Good."

"But you—stay safe."

"I want to be up on the hill with you again."

He frowned. "That's not my call. I think you did fine. But I don't mind you staying down here. It's safer."

"Maybe. Not unless I'm in the safe room, really."

"I got to go," he said. We looked up and realized Mr. Wasserman, whom Blake was replacing, was already on his way down the hill.

He gave me another quick kiss. Mr. Wasserman whistled at us. I thought, *Puh-leeze! A grown man, acting just like my little sisters!*

Back at the house I started kitchen clean-up, but the twins popped in. Lainie said, "We saw you kissing Bla-ake!"

I shrugged. "So?" I felt my cheeks growing hot, even though I told myself I didn't care who saw us.

Then they started: "Lexie and Bla-ake up a tre-e-e…"

"Go away," I said.

Mrs. Wasserman rescued me. "Lainie and Laura! You get over here this instant!" To my relief they went running from the room.

I stayed with my chores, doing dishes, washing off the table, and checking the daily list for food preparation, which hung by a magnet on the defunct fridge. We used the refrigerator for holding firearms, now. The days of keeping it running with our generator were long gone. I dreamed of us having enough fuel some time to power it up again. To have cold food! That would be a joy.

Blake was studying in his spare time how to generate electricity using hydropower. We have a year-round running stream which could work if it ran stronger, but it's often a sluggish flow. After a storm we get a much deeper and faster flow but it doesn't last.

Blake said we need to figure out a way to get more water down the stream. We all had high hopes of Blake in that regard—there was no one on the compound smarter. I was proud of him. And of course I had high hopes of his proposing, too. If he did, we could get married. We had no reason not to. There was no big wedding to plan, no expensive photographer to hire or flowers to buy. It would be simple and homey because that was our life.

I just needed to know one thing: When was he going to do it? Propose?

CHAPTER FIFTY-EIGHT

SARAH

At dinner that first night after Tex got back and Angel finally appeared, talk turned to the traps and how Angel had tracked a wounded animal without luck. She told us she always felt trepidation when checking traps because twice she'd found people at them, helping themselves to the game she'd caught. She put one hand to her heart as she spoke.

"I hate it when I find nice people at the traps," she said. "It about breaks my heart to tell them they can't have the game. But we learned we can't let them have it," she continued emphatically, shaking her head and speaking to Richard and me. "They keep coming back for more."

Tex added, "We gave away as many traps as we could; so people could catch their own meat," he said, "but we can't do that anymore. We need what we've got."

To my mind, Tex had said he and Angel didn't have enough food to take in me and Richard. How much longer, I wondered, would we be able to stay? Angel had always said, "Until Tex gets back." Now he was back. I didn't raise the subject; I didn't want to remind them we were like those other people, without food and dependent on their mercy. We were on borrowed time.

Angel said, "Let's clear up the dishes and have that Bible Study."

Richard frowned. I knew he'd prefer to do most anything other than study the Bible. But he was just as aware as I was of our dependence on Tex and Angel. He said nothing. Later with the cleaning done, Tex motioned us all back to the table. Angel handed a soft-cover, dog-eared New Testament to me and gave one to Richard.

"First things first," said Tex. "Don't let's beat around the bush. If you died tonight, do you know where you'd be going?"

Richard said, "Huh? If we died?" I listened uneasily, because no one had ever posed such a question to me. It sounded faintly threatening. When Richard spoke, I knew he felt it, too.

"Why would we die tonight?" he asked. "Was that our last meal?"

Tex frowned at him. "No! This is just—theoretical. I'm not saying you're gonna die tonight, but we all die sometime. So IF you died right now, where would you go, Richard?"

Tex glanced at my face then, and chuckled. "Did you also think I was threatening you? I am not. I'm just askin' a question you need to answer—while you're still on earth. So, I'll ask you differently—if you were to die tonight, would you go to heaven? Or hell?"

After a moment's reflection, I said with some confidence, "I'd go to heaven." I wasn't one hundred percent sure, but who could be, right? I wasn't a bad person. I certainly wasn't bad enough to deserve hell!

"What about you, Richard?"

Richard took a deep breath. "I'm not sure I believe in heaven or hell."

Tex raised an eyebrow. "So what do you believe?"

Richard shrugged. "I don't know. I guess I believe this is all there is."

"And that makes sense to you?" Angel asked.

Richard glanced at her. "Nothing makes sense to me. Life doesn't make sense. So why should anything make sense?"

Tex cleared his throat. "Actually, Richard, the whole universe makes a whole lotta sense. You ask any scientist whether things make sense and they'll tell you about the laws of nature, the laws of gravity, the order in the observable universe. It does make sense. God didn't create no senseless universe. Everything that happens in nature follows laws of nature—outside of special miracles, like when the sun stood still so Israel could fight a battle, or when Jesus walked on water or fed the five thousand with a handful of food. God alone has the power to supersede his own laws—but that's why we call it a miracle; it ain't natural. It's supernatural. But you want to see order, just study the universe."

Richard shook his head. "That's not what I mean. How does the EMP make sense? How do you explain why God would let this happen?"

"We talked about that. Our country is under judgment. It may not seem fair to you, but I want you to forget for a moment about the EMP. I want you to think about you only, Richard. It's you and God, right now. And I'll ask you one more time, if you died tonight, would you go to heaven or hell?"

"I can't just forget about everything else. We lost our parents and our cousin!"

He nodded. "I heard something about that when you two were talking in the barn. I'm sorry about your mom and dad and your cousin." He looked genuinely sorry. But he continued, "Your real concern is not about what makes sense or not; it's not even about who died, or what's happened to this country. Your real concern should be your own destiny, and what's gonna happen to you."

Again Richard shrugged. "Look, what ever's gonna happen, is gonna happen. There's nothing I can do about it."

"That's not true," Tex said. "The Bible says there is a way to know where you're going after you die, and there is something you can do about it. "

"What?" Richard asked. "What can I do about it?"

Tex said, "You can put your faith and trust in Jesus Christ, God the Son. Let me tell you why." Suddenly Tex spoke faster, quoting Scripture verses and showing Richard that Jesus Christ claimed to be God.

"I already know what he claimed," Richard said.

"Did you also know that he claimed you could go to heaven—if you turn from your sin and trust him to save you?"

Richard looked as though he'd raised a wall around himself. His face was hard. But I was fascinated. I was eating up every word Tex spoke. I'd been reading my little Bible, but I loved hearing someone else talk about it. I'd read mostly the Psalms up to this point. I noticed they echoed my own thoughts and feelings. But this was about heaven and hell! If there was a way to know for sure where I'd end up, I wanted to know it.

"What difference does it make, what I believe?" Richard said. "God's gonna do what God's gonna do. I can't change that."

"Actually, God's gonna do what he says he's gonna do. And he says, if you believe in the Name of Jesus, you will be saved," Tex answered. His voice had an edge of authority—surprising for a motorcycle gang-type person, anyway. His hair, now that I saw him without the leather jacket, was held back by a bandana; he was the last person I would expect to be hearing a sermon from, frankly.

"See," Tex said, flaring out his hands, "it's like this. Jesus affirmed the Bible is God's word. And he gave more warnings about hell than he did promises about heaven. He didn't want us to doubt for a single second that hell is real and waits for those who are heading there. He wanted us to take warning and to prepare—so once again, I'll ask you, are you prepared? If you died today or tonight, do you know where you'd end up, heaven or hell?"

Richard shrugged. "I have no idea. I'm not convinced they exist just because Jesus said they did."

"That's why you've got to decide if Jesus is who he claimed to be," Tex explained. "If he is, as he claimed, the Son of God, sent to die on your behalf so you could escape hell-fire, then you'd better pay attention to his message, don't you think?" He paused. "If Jesus is God the Son, then only a fool would ignore him. If he isn't, then he's a liar or a madman."

Angel said, "Richard, Jesus didn't leave any room for neutrality on this issue—either you believe in him as God or you must accept he was a lunatic and a liar, because he *claimed* to be God. Everyone in his day understood his claim—that's why the Jews wanted to kill him. They considered it blasphemy. And if you prefer to think of him as a lunatic, then how do you explain his miracles? He healed the sick. He raised the dead. He turned water into wine. He walked on water." She paused. "There have been plenty of lunatics who claimed to be the Messiah. But they didn't give sight to the blind, or heal anyone of anything. They didn't feed five thousand people from a few loaves and fish—and they definitely did not rise from the dead."

"You don't know those things really happened," said Richard.

Tex jumped back in. "No one of his time even tried to deny his miracles—they couldn't. There were too many eyewitnesses. The only thing they did deny him was a fair trial—and that, it turns out, was God's plan for salvation. Jesus had to die for us so we could be forgiven. But he could have refused. He didn't, because he loves us. He loves *you*, Richard. He died for you, for your sins, so they could be forgiven."

"Even that doesn't make sense to me," Richard said. "Why couldn't God just choose to forgive us?"

Tex didn't blink. "The Bible explains that. It tells us, 'without the shedding of blood there can be no forgiveness of sin.' Something has always had to die for atonement to be given. They used to sacrifice animal after animal in the Temple for the forgiveness of sins. That's why Jesus is called the Lamb of God. Our sacrificial Lamb. Except his sacrifice was perfect, it don't have to be repeated, and it can never be repeated. There is no other sacrifice that can be given or accepted for sin." Tex shook his head.

"Look, let's keep it simple. There is one way to be saved, according to God. And you're goin' to hell unless you take that road. You need to accept that you deserve punishment, but he died for you, as Romans 6:23 says: 'For the wages of sin is death; but the gift of God is eternal life through Jesus Christ our Lord.'" He paused, studying Richard with penetrating eyes. "So here's your dilemma, Richard. If you don't receive what Jesus did for you, you'll remain in your sins. You will end up in hell. It's like—choosing to stay dirty and grimy when he's offering you a clean white robe!"

Richard was silent. Tex said, "Will you pray with me right now? You can tell God you're sorry and ask him to forgive you—and he will! It ain't rocket science, man. He does what he says he will do and he promised to forgive us if we ask him."

Richard still said nothing.

"I'll pray with you," I said. I hadn't actually said a formal prayer asking for forgiveness before. I'd done penance as a Catholic—I'd have to find out if that meant anything. Angel took my hand, smiling, while Tex murmured, "That's good, that's good, Sarah. Let me just read a couple more verses to back up what I've told you."

Opening his Bible, he read things like, "God so loved the world that He gave his one and only Son, that whoever believes in him shall not perish but have eternal life." He looked up. "You hear that word, 'perish'? It means die the second death. That's what the Bible calls it when you are cast into hell. It's the second death. It's the death God referred to when he told Adam, 'The day you eat the fruit, you will surely die.' It doesn't just mean physical death. It's perishing, in the final and ultimate and most terrifying sense of the word." He studied Richard, who was staring hard at the floor.

"Anything that happens down here on earth, no matter how awful it seems at the time is a drop in the bucket next to the suffering that will take place in hell. Because it never ends. It's unending agony—"

"But Adam didn't die physically, did he?" I asked. "I mean, not the day he ate the fruit." I remembered that much from catechism classes at

250

our old church.

"He did," Tex said. "That is, he started to. He was made in perfection—to last forever—so he still lived hundreds of years before his body actually died. But death began its work on that day. And he also died spiritually. And he would never have had to face death at all if he hadn't sinned. And neither would we. Think about that."

He looked back to Richard. "If you perish, Richard, you'll be eternally separated from God and all that is good. There's no salvation available for those in hell. It's too late, then." He paused, waiting to see if Richard would respond. When he didn't, Tex continued, "Jesus said for those who go to hell, 'there will be weeping and gnashing of teeth.' That is a picture of misery. Sheer misery."

"Yeah, well, I think if 'God so loved the world,' there wouldn't be a hell!" Richard stood up, and took a deep breath. "I've had enough of this for tonight, if you don't mind."

Tex stood up too and he took a breath, folding his arms. "I do mind, actually. Listen here, Richard, if you expect to live beneath our roof—"

"We're staying in the barn, Tex," he intoned, as if it made a big difference.

"That's still my property," he returned. "I'd like to let you stay here. But I won't keep someone unwilling to examine the Scriptures with me. That's like contributing to your death. I see you as heading for a great big cliff. You tell me, Richard, should I just let you keep going towards that cliff at breakneck speed, knowing what's coming for you? Huh? I can't do that."

"What if there is no cliff?"

Tex cleared his throat. "Search your heart and ask yourself what happens when you reach the end of this road we call life. Just ask yourself. The Bible says God has put it in the heart of man to know He exists. All creation shouts, there is a God. And if there's a God then he knows what's coming and HE SAYS THERE'S A CLIFF!"

"Now, if you think you know better than God, then I guess there's nothing more I can say to you. But take this—" he picked up the dog-eared copy of the New Testament and handed it to Richard. "And read it. Read the words of Jesus. Read it and pray that if it's the truth, God will speak to your heart and let you know it."

Angel was looking on. She did not look happy. Richard took the Bible from Tex but said nothing. He strode off, letting the door bang behind him.

Angel said, "You were a little hard on him, hon, don'tcha think?" She went to him, stretched out her arms and circled his neck. He lifted her off the ground to get her face even with his. "You can't strong-arm someone into faith," she said softly, looking into his eyes. "You have to let the Holy Spirit speak to his heart."

"I know that," he said, gruffly. "But we are called to snatch the lost out of the fire. I'm just snatchin' is all." She rubbed her nose back and forth against his.

I figured they were about to make out—maybe they'd forgotten I was there. I stood up to follow Richard but Tex called, "You wait just a minute, young 'un. We're not finished with you." Tex's voice was deep and ominous but he didn't fool me any longer. The only thing scary about him was that he could turn us out. Smiling, I said, "You mean, we're gonna pray?"

"Right." He tried to sound ornery. When I only smiled he said, "Uh-oh."

"She's got your number, hon," Angel said. "Sit back down here," she added. "We're gonna pray for you. And then we need to do something to celebrate!"

"Cool!" I said. In a minute, I'd said a prayer at Angel's leading, word for word, after her. I told God how sorry I was for all my sins. I asked him to forgive me because of what Jesus did on the cross. And I told him I wanted to follow him for the rest of my life. We talked and laughed at the table and played a game of cards. Angel made a big stockpot of popcorn, and we had water flavored with lemon powder and sugar. It was so fun.

I was happy, floating on air. My worries about being kicked out had vanished, and Tex and Angel were just too neat for words. I felt like I'd just joined a church, like I was a member now, formally. I now felt sure—I was going to heaven when I died! I felt a new love for the Lord. One day I might even tell Angel and Tex about my encounter at the library when Jesus had given us water.

When I reached the loft, I was hoping Richard might be sleeping. He wasn't. In fact, he wasn't there at all. His things were gone, too. I found only a note:

Finding Dad. I'll be back.

CHAPTER FIFTY-NINE

ANDREA

I. AM. IN. LOVE.

I can't stop thinking about Roper! He is a beautiful guy. And he's sweet. And funny. And nice and just…perfect!

Lexie and I were here in bed in our PJs when there was a knock at the door. Well, it was him! He popped his head in and eyed me gingerly. "Sorry to bother you girls; I just wanted to leave Andrea with a parting thought for the night."

I said, "Oh, really?"

He said, "I figured you might need something to feed sweet dreams." His gaze strayed to Lexie. "Maybe you do, too." I wasn't thrilled that he'd included her, but only because I want his attention all to myself! Nevertheless I smiled, guessing he had a silly joke in store. Roper always had silly jokes in that handsome head of his. I didn't know how he did it. But his look turned serious and he gazed at me.

"I was reading the Bible and thought I'd share what spoke to my heart." He came a few steps into the room, holding a small candle-sconce over the open Bible in his other hand. He cleared his throat.

"With God we will gain the victory; and he will trample down our enemies. Psalm. 60:12." He flipped to another page. *"The LORD is a warrior; the LORD is his name. Exodus 15:3."*

"I have one," said Lexie. A stab of remorse filled me because I hadn't done much Bible memorization, and I envied Lexie at that moment. *"The horse is made ready for the day of battle, but victory rests with the LORD. Proverbs 21:31,"* she said.

Roper nodded. "Good one." He glanced at me. I was covered by a sheet and light blanket but had sat up. Was he waiting to see if I had a good one too?

To hide my sad lack of Bible knowledge, I said, "Got any more?" with a smile.

He continued, *"I called to the LORD, who is worthy of praise, and I have been saved from my enemies. Psalm 18:3."* He added, "Here's a really good one from Leviticus. '*I will grant peace in the land, and you will lie down, and no one shall make you afraid.*" He glanced at us. "Good stuff, huh?"

"Yeah!" We agreed heartily. I was so touched that he'd come up to lift our spirits. The room, with only candlelight, held a soft glow that seemed to wrap Roper in a halo. It was perfect.

He continued, "*You will pursue your enemies, and they will fall by the sword before you.* Leviticus 26:7." Lexie and I whooped appreciatively. Smiling, Roper continued, "*Five of you will chase a hundred, and a hundred of you will chase ten thousand, and your enemies will fall by the sword before you.* That's 26:8."

More whoops. We were having fun.

He read on, "*I will look on you with favor and make you fruitful and increase your numbers and I will keep my covenant with you.* 26:9." I didn't whoop at this one because it embarrassed me, words of being "fruitful" and "increasing." But Lexie cried, "Yeah! Read that one to Blake!" and then we burst into laughter.

Roper gave us a moment to contain ourselves, and then, still smiling, said, "Wait; I've got more. Check this out, it's the next verse! '*You will still be eating last year's harvest, when you will have to move it out to make room for the new.*" He looked up, "Another version says, 'you will eat old store long kept.' Is that cool, or what?"

We whooped appreciatively, and would have kept it up except Mr. Martin's head appeared in the doorway.

"What in heck—" he started. He stopped in surprise, seeing Roper, and then the Bible in his hands. He stepped in frowning, and shut the door behind him. He turned to us. "What all are you doing?"

Roper grinned. "I was just reading the Word to the girls. Words of encouragement."

"It certainly sounded like it," Lexie's dad said. "The whole house can hear how encouraged you are."

"Sorry," Roper said. Lexie and I apologized also.

"Okay then, wrap it up and get to sleep. Tomorrow we're doing drills." His eye lingered on me. "You'll have to stick with a .22—on a bipod—until that arm gets stronger, but you need to keep up with practice."

After he'd gone, we thanked Roper for reading to us. He shut his Bible and said, "My pleasure, ladies. And now I'll leave you with a different kind of thought." He rubbed his chin, thinking. "Ok. This one's for Andrea." Straight-faced he said, "A man told his doctor, I've hurt my arm in several places. The doctor said, Well, don't go there anymore." It sometimes took me a few seconds, but I always got Roper's jokes and I giggled. Suppressing a smile, he went on, "I used to be indecisive. Now I'm not sure."

After we said our good-nights and he'd gone from the room, Lexie's head came into view as she hung over the side from the top bunk to see me. In the dark, I could only make out her outline. She'd almost scared me.

"What?" I asked.

"He likes you."

I smiled in the dark. "How do you know?"

"Oh, c'mon. His coming in here. It wasn't for me."

"I like him too."

"I know. I'm glad you don't like Jared anymore."

"Well—Jared's okay, but when I was in his cabin, I didn't want to be alone with him. I don't feel that way with Roper. You know what I mean? I like Roper more."

"Jared'll get over it," she said.

"I hope so. I don't want to hurt his feelings." An even bigger regret was now he'd probably never take the risk of looking for my mother and Washington.

My mother! I didn't want to think about her. Baby Lily had cried a lot the first few days but she was better now. What if Mom never returned? Lily would forget her entirely. I forced myself to stop thinking about it. There was nothing I could do.

CHAPTER SIXTY

SARAH

I was stunned by Richard's note. I couldn't believe he'd abandoned me! And the thought of him being out there alone terrified me. I'd saved his life, hadn't I? Without me, who would watch his back? I got angry. How could he leave me without even saying goodbye? I'm his sister!

But after the initial shock wore off, I remembered a conversation we'd had. Richard had overheard me and Angel talking about the Bible. I found him afterwards in the loft, lying down with his hands beneath his head, staring at the barn ceiling. He didn't look at me as I rounded the top of the ladder, but said, "So is religious instruction over?"

I sat down near him. "For now, yeah."

He grimaced. "I was thinking. I'm gonna find out if Aunt Susan is still alive."

I opened my mouth to object but he hurriedly continued, "I'll leave you here. You're safer here. If I find out that we can live on the ranch over there—and maybe see if Dad ever showed up—I'll come back for you."

"What if you find out we can't? What if Aunt Susan's dead, which she probably is? And what if you get yourself killed going off alone?"

He rolled over to face me. "You mean, alone without you? Have you been keeping me alive? Are you saying I need you to survive?"

I stared at him. "You don't need to get mean about it. I think we need each other to survive. We are all the family we have."

His brown eyes were serious. "I said I'll be back."

I frowned. "Tex and Angel are letting us stay here! They have everything we need and I—I care about them. Why can't we just stay here?"

"They could change their mind at any time. Maybe they have a grown son who's gonna come back and put a gun to my head, too. Or maybe it'll be a nephew. Who knows? We're not their family, Sarah. They don't owe us anything, and I don't want to get kicked out in the middle of winter."

I was feeling upset but I tried to stay calm. I had to think like Richard, use an argument he'd appreciate. "They realize the more hands they have around, the easier the work for all of us."

Richard was staring at the ceiling again. "The more hands to work, the more mouths to feed. I think we're on borrowed time and one day we're gonna wake up and they'll tell us to be off."

"They wouldn't do that, Richard! They aren't like that!"

"You don't know what they'd do. We really don't know them."

"Well, tomorrow I'll ask them. I'll ask what they think about us staying; and whether they might want us to leave when the winter comes and it's harder to get food."

"What makes you think they'll be honest with you?"

"Richard, you don't get it because you're an unbeliever. They are Christians, and I'll ask them to tell me the truth before God."

"Oh, that's gonna make a big difference," he said, sarcastically. "Don't kid yourself, Sarah. Just like everyone else, they will do whatever it takes to survive, and if that means getting rid of us they'll do it. Tex had us tied up at gunpoint, remember."

"He thought we killed his wife! I'd say that's cause to be suspicious of us and tie us up!"

Richard took a deep breath. "Well, if you want to talk to them, fine, go ahead. But I'll probably be getting out of here tomorrow morning."

"If you're so sure they're not trustworthy, then why are you willing to leave me here?"

He cleared his throat. "I trust them with you. I just don't trust them with me."

"That doesn't make sense." I turned and went to my little bed. Angel had found two sleeping bags and mattress pads which we put beneath the bags. It was comfortable, as we had built up about a foot of straw to go beneath them. I would never have dreamed I'd enjoy sleeping in a barn, but this one didn't bother me. When we first started sleeping in barns, even ones without animals, the smell of what used to live there still seemed pungent and overpowering. At times it made me gag. I guess I'd gotten used to it because we were now sharing our barn with a mule, and I could handle it just fine.

I was angry Richard wanted to leave. But then days went by and nothing happened, so I thought he'd abandoned the idea. I forgot all about it. I knew he didn't enjoy the Bible discussions or questions, but I still found it hard to comprehend that he preferred to take his life in his hands than submit to that.

I feel sure Aunt Susan's house will be bare even if it's still standing. And who knows, because she owned a wooden ranch and nowadays anything made of wood is fair game to get torched by those horrible soldiers. Even Tex and Angel's house is mostly wood. I like it here and I'm growing fonder of the McAllisters by the day. (That's their name, Tex and Angel McAllister.) I chuckle that I ever called Tex Hulk Hogan. He laughs about it, too.

What bothers me is, when we had that discussion where Richard told me he might leave, I'd asked him not to go without telling Tex and Angel.

"Don't just take off," I'd said. "They might think you have evil plans, like to come back with a gang."

"If we had a gang we wouldn't have come here on our own," he said.

"Still—just let them know what you want to do before you do it, okay?"

"Fine."

But he hadn't. He'd taken off without even telling me.

———————◆———————

I feel guilty about Richard's leaving as if I had something to do with it. No one is blaming me, but I can't believe Richard would actually leave me here without him. What if the McAllisters decide I can't stay? Richard has left me on my own!

I sat down and started to have a good cry about it up here in the barn after I spoke to Tex and Angel. Then, in my heart, I felt a gentle tugging, as if a part of me was saying, "Why are you crying? It will be okay." At first I tried to ignore that voice. I fought against it, actually, because I *wanted* to cry! Richard had abandoned me and I'd already lost the rest of my family! I was alone and scared. But the feeling grew stronger.

You aren't alone. Don't worry about Richard.

It made no sense to me why I would have these thoughts when I believed the opposite— I *was* alone and I had to worry about Richard. He was in danger out there. And then it hit me.

That wasn't me—it wasn't my voice! It was the Holy Spirit!

Those thoughts hadn't come from me. My tears stopped. I was amazed and grateful. I didn't know what to do or how to react, so I quietly thanked God, sitting there on my bed. The least I could do was thank him, right? And then, as I was thanking him, I got the urge to sing to him. Maybe that's why Christians are always singing. Did you ever go in a church and NOT see a hymn book? I remembered how the Powells used to sing at night in the library, a song that went, "I Surrender All." I remembered the chorus, so I sang it over and over.

I surrender all, I surrender all,
All to Thee, my precious Savior,
I surrender all.

I will try to describe how I felt while I was singing. (I don't want to forget it and I don't know if it will ever happen again.) I felt like Jesus was really close to me. I was almost ashamed that I wanted to worry about Richard. God told me not to. So I surrendered that worry. And then I felt something really light and free and beautiful. *Joy!* Just joy. All my cares seemed small and God seemed really big! It was the most religious experience of my life—except maybe when Jesus came to me in the library.

Why have I been blessed with such experiences? I have no idea.

I want Richard back—but I know my life is in God's hands and I know this, too: He cares.

Richard would scoff at me if I told him about this, but I was so energized, singing on the inside, that I ran to the house to tell Angel.

"There you are," she said. Her eyes were searching mine, kindly. She and Tex knew I'd been upset Richard had left.

"You okay?" she asked.

"Angel!" I said, and she must have seen the glow in my eyes. Her eyes widened as she stopped what she was doing in the kitchen to listen.

I opened my mouth and then I realized I didn't know what to say; how to describe my experience.

"What is it, hon?" she asked. She could tell I had something different to tell, I guess.

"The Holy Spirit spoke to me!" I finally blurted out.

Angel's face crumpled into smiles and she came towards me, her arms outstretched. I say, 'crumpled,' because when Angel smiles, her eyes smile most of all. They crunch up into happy little slits. So she came towards me and when I saw her arms outstretched, something inside me broke and I rushed into her embrace like a little child who's been lost in the supermarket and then found its mother.

I would have been embarrassed if Richard had seen me. But no one was there—and it felt wonderful. Angel cared.

"Tell me what happened," she said afterwards, holding me by the arms and looking deeply into my eyes. "C'mon, we'll take a tea break."

My heart took a little leap. Angel's "tea breaks" were a reward for labor well done. She'd pull out treats from a storage source I didn't know the location of. It was like a small visit to the past, to when grocery stores existed. She called her treats "absolute junk food," which meant they would be bad for you but taste great.

So today we had packaged ®Twinkies with our tea. They tasted wonderful. Angel joked that everybody should have kept ®Twinkies because they wouldn't go bad for anything—they were so full of preservatives and chemicals you could probably keep them forever.

Then we talked about my experience and for the first time I told her about Jesus giving us water in the library.

She looked at me soberly. "Sarah, don't get the wrong idea about what I'm doing here. Usually we have a tea break as a reward, you know that." I nodded, wondering where the conversation was headed.

"I want you to know this is not a reward. You haven't done anything to EARN it. I wanted a tea break because I'm celebrating with you. We're celebrating your Christian walk. God rewards those who seek Him, Hebrews 11 tells us that. I just want to rejoice with you. For now on, when you pray, you'll learn to always listen to that still, small voice. I did that when I first saw you and Richard on the property."

"What do you mean?" I asked. "What did you do?"

"Well, I was scared!" she said, her eyes wide. "Tex was gone hunting and I saw there were two of you, and at first I was ready to high-tail it back home. But I prayed for help. I prayed for wisdom. I asked God to protect me and show me what to do. I got there just when Richard cut himself down and that scared me; then I saw he was hurt, and I felt a little safer. Then I heard him call your name. No offense, but when I realized it was a woman and not a second man I was dealing with, I felt relieved." She paused and took a sip of her tea.

"So I was still praying and I heard you saying you couldn't make it out of the pit. I said, *God what should I do?* Her little eyes were huge in her face. "And all I heard was *Go!* But see, in my heart I was planning it out, how I would come to your aid. So when I heard *Go*, it didn't even occur to me that he might have been saying Go away, or Go home. It was Go help them, to me. So that's what I did. If God had wanted me to leave you there, I would have known it. You see, that's how the Holy Spirit works. He knows us inside out and he knows what we need to hear when we need to hear it. But you will NOT hear the voice of the Holy Spirit if you are not regularly on your knees seeking God. *Draw near to me,* He says, *and I will draw near to you.* That's in the book of Hebrews."

"I understand," I said.

"And listen here, Sarah. Don't go thinkin' that you're gonna hear the voice of the Holy Spirit every time you pray. It doesn't work like that."

I nodded. "Okay."

"It's a lot more common not to hear God's voice than it is to hear it," she added. "Remember, we walk by faith. If God spoke to us every time we spoke to him we wouldn't need much faith to believe, now would we?"

Smiling, I nodded and took another bite. Here I was, after the apocalypse without any family or familiar friends, sleeping in a barn— and I felt joy. I was crazy about Angel and fascinated by God. Angel talked to me about him like no one else I'd ever met. I used to wonder if God was real and how a person could know it for sure. I don't wonder, anymore.

I'll never be happy we've had the pulse, or that my mom and Jesse and Dad are gone; but I almost feel like I needed it to get where I am today. I trust that Richard will return.

Life doesn't feel so bad right now.

I'm happy.

CHAPTER SIXTY-ONE

ANDREA

I could have been up and around three days ago—that's how much better I feel— but everyone's treating me like I'm fragile. I still have pain—Mrs. Philpot says there's no way around it, bullets cause pain. But it will heal. And she says my wound looks good. She says I'm lucky it isn't infected. I guess I am, because we certainly don't have a lot of antibiotics and apparently they already gave me some when I got sewed up by Mr. Clepps.

It really hurt to use my injured arm, so Mrs. Philpot had to help me change my clothes—majorly embarrassing—but at least I was excused from my usual chores. Downstairs, though, I felt useless. Everyone else had something to do—except me. So with one arm, I found I could help with meal cleanup, clearing tables, fetching utensils and that sort of thing. I told Mrs. Martin I could do childcare too, but she said, "Not today." Still, it felt good to be out of bed and doing something.

I rested for awhile but went back down to help with lunch. The children were curious about my arm but I couldn't let them touch it. Even a slight touch sends fire through the wound. I held Lily on my lap with my good arm to give the ladies on childcare a rest, but my baby sister makes me sad now. She reminds me about my mom. I guess I fell into a blue funk. I mean, I'll probably never see Mom again. How could she still be alive? If she and Washington were okay, they would have come back.

Jared came looking for me just as lunchtime was ending. He said, "So—do you still want me to check out your old house? See if your mother and Washington are there?"

I was surprised he would still do this—considering. I thought he might be angry after I blew the whistle on his having the food buckets, but he never once behaved as though he was. I looked up at him. "Sure! You would do that?"

He slid onto the seat next to mine. "Yes. If you want me to." He handed me a pen and paper. "You're right-handed, right?"

I smiled. "Yup."

"Write your address."

I wrote the address, suddenly aware of how long it had been since I'd done that. There was no writing anymore except in my journal, no forms to fill, no paperwork. When I wrote out the address, it felt like writing somebody else's information.

"Thanks," I said, as he took the paper and tucked it in his pocket.

"Good to see you on your feet," he answered. "How is it feeling?" He nodded toward my bandaged arm.

"It hurts."

He nodded. "Bullet wounds are like that. They go right through ya." He smirked, and I gave a belated little laugh, realizing Jared was joking! He joked differently than Roper, and with such a poker face that I'd almost missed it.

"Do you have a key?" he asked.

"A key?"

"To your house."

"Oh, of course. I think I do. It must be upstairs in my purse." Purses were also things of the past. Since we never left the compound there was little need for one. I'd brought mine with me when we came but I hadn't touched it in months.

He stood up. "I'll come by later to get it."

I looked up at him gratefully. "I don't know what to say. I really appreciate your going."

He nodded. "We leave tomorrow."

"Who's going with you?"

He took a deep breath and then stretched his neck as though it was stiff before he answered. "Roper."

After he'd gone I ran around the house looking for Roper or Mr. Martin. I couldn't let this happen! I couldn't let Roper go with Jared. Lexie had told me how Jared treated him when I was getting sewed up. And here I'd thought he was being so nice! When all along he may have been simply planning a way to get rid of Roper! And the stupid thing is, nothing was happening between me and Roper. I liked him a lot—no doubt about it, but we had no understanding and nothing had happened between us. We hadn't even kissed.

I finally found Mr. Martin out by the cabins and asked to speak with him alone. I explained the situation and said, "Please, Mr. Martin. Don't let Roper go with Jared! Let anyone else go, but not Roper!"

"Well, Andrea, there's two things about this situation I don't think you understand."

"Like what?"

"Well, first off; Jared is going on a supply mission. He needs certain ingredients to mix us up more of those grenades he makes. So, if he's planning on stopping off at your home that's news to me. Second thing is this: Roper volunteered to go. He's a grown man. It's out of my hands."

Chapter Sixty-Two

LEXIE

Andrea and I tried to talk Roper out of leaving the compound with Jared. We brought him up to our room so we could be alone with him and sat in a small circle on the floor.

"We need you here," I said. "You're our alarm, now!"

He grinned. "You still have your old system. I won't be gone long."

Andrea said, "You don't know Jared like we do. He's not trustworthy."

"Why not?"

"Well, he took the food buckets," I said.

"He had a reason to," Roper replied. "It made sense to me."

"He gives us the creeps," Andrea said, wide-eyed.

Roper grinned. "Is that all?"

"He's sneaky! He's always got something up his sleeve, and you never know what it will be." But nothing we said made a difference to Roper.

Finally, Andrea said, "OK. I'm just going to tell you the truth. I don't like to do this, but you're forcing me. You're forcing my hand."

Roper grinned again. "You don't like to do this. You don't like to tell the truth?"

Andrea gave his hand a little slap. "That's not what I meant."

He waited, trying not to smile. "Jared is jealous of you," Andrea said. I met her eyes and for some reason we both broke up into helpless laughter.

Roper grinned, but he clearly didn't get it. "Jealous of what?"

We stopped laughing. Andrea looked at me, but it had been her idea to come clean. The ball was in her court. I said nothing.

"He's jealous because he knows I think you're funny, and you're a lot more handsome than he is (Roper let out a breath of disbelief) and because...he knows...I like you."

He didn't smile this time. "Are you and Jared?..."

"No! We're not."

He kept looking at her, with his brows raised.

"OK, I flirted with him. Once! That's it!"

"I think Jared likes Andrea," I said. When he just looked at me blankly, I added, "He got angry when you came in just to ask how she was doing, remember?"

Roper nodded. "I remember. He's known her a lot longer. I figured he cared about her. He didn't know me from Adam. I didn't blame him for that."

"He told Andrea he was leaving tomorrow to go look for her mother! He didn't say a word about having to get any supplies! He's not honest."

"He wanted me to think he was going out just for me!" Andrea added.

"Well, he mentioned what he thought you'd be interested in," said Roper. "I don't have a problem with that."

Andrea and I were taken aback. Roper was a sweet guy. So sweet, he couldn't conceive that Jared was not.

"I think you're being foolish," I said.

He met my eyes. "Would you rather Blake went along with him?"

"No, of course not!"

"Well, I volunteered to go because I don't have a girlfriend." He didn't look at Andrea. "I volunteered to go because Blake does."

I stared at him. "Are you telling me Blake volunteered? To go with Jared?"

He nodded. "That's right."

"And you volunteered so he wouldn't have to?"

He nodded again. I stood up and paced the room. I couldn't keep still. Finally I said, "I don't think either one of you should go! You know who should go? Mr. Prendergast should go! He's got no family here and no girlfriend, and no one will care if he goes."

Roper looked thoughtful. "I think that's sad."

"What's sad," I said, coming back and resuming my seat on the floor, "is that you are insisting upon doing this when Andrea will have to worry about you nonstop." He looked at Andrea, who blushed. "And if something happens to you, and she doesn't get her mother back, then who does she have?"

Roper looked like he was trying to be patient. "Girls, girls," he said, getting to his feet. "I appreciate your concern. But I have to do this. I volunteered. And we may bring back stuff that will save this entire compound if we're attacked again. And you know we are likely to be attacked again."

I felt frustrated. By the look on Andrea's face, she did, too. Again I got to my feet. "Well, I think you two should at least say goodbye." I left the room.

I went to see Blake who confirmed that he'd volunteered, much to my consternation. I told him about Roper and our misgivings, but he was almost as thick-headed as Roper had been. They just didn't see it.

Blake asked me to go for a walk with him. It seemed like a revolutionary idea because we go nowhere these days. He only meant to walk on our land, but part of our 126 acres is a good strip of woodland. Dad used to hunt it during deer season and took down a number of good-sized bucks in it. Nowadays lots of our men hunt but we haven't found much big game.

Anyway, it felt like a visit to our old life—just walking hand in hand and wandering the woods. We didn't feel a sense of peril such as we'd get out on the road. Maybe that's because we knew there were lookouts around the property. But we also knew they couldn't possibly watch the whole perimeter. We could easily get intruders coming through the woods; it was often their point of entry to the compound. But somehow we didn't worry about it. That's why it felt so wonderful, I guess. Other than just being with Blake.

We stopped in a grassy glade and kissed a few times. I love Blake. I said, "Do you think things will ever change? When we can get on with life without having to worry about defending ourselves all the time?"

He bit his lip, thinking. "I hope so."

I was, of course, hoping he'd say more. I wanted him to talk about the future—our future.

"Do you think we have a future—together?" It was hard for me to say that but Blake is the kind of guy who needs a little nudge now and then. So I gave it to him.

He seemed startled; then gazed at me. "Yeah. I hope so."

That wasn't what I wanted to hear. "We may not have a lot of time, to do things the usual way, you know?"

"What do you mean?"

I looked away. Staring at the trees ahead, I said, "I mean, like, waiting to finish college before marriage; or waiting to get married and have kids. We may be on borrowed time, already!" I was upset, now.

He turned my face towards his. "Lex. You're not even eighteen yet. I wouldn't think about proposing—marriage—until you're at least eighteen. Your parents would never let us—MY parents wouldn't, either."

I took a deep breath. He was right, of course. "But maybe the rules need to change," I said. "Because the world has changed."

He leaned over and kissed my forehead. Softly, he said, "If we got married and—well—if you got pregnant—do you really think that would be a good thing right now? Considering the danger we're in—we don't even know for sure yet, what we're up against when it comes to hostiles. We don't know if those mercenaries were just the beginning— or when our country is going to get its act together; IF it's going to."

I felt very mixed up and wanted to cry.

"Let's go back," I said, starting to rise. But he grabbed me and then pulled me up against him in a warm hug. Speaking softly in my ear, he said, "Look, I love you. I know it's hard, waiting. But we need to do that. If we were older and already married, that would be one thing; but we can't plan on bringing babies into this dark world."

I pulled away to stare at him. "You mean, ever? Even after I'm eighteen?"

"I mean, now."

◆

So this morning, Andrea and I watched from our windows while Roper and Jared left by horseback, their packs fat with supplies. She continued to stare out the window as she spoke in a subdued voice.

"After you left yesterday, I was so angry at Roper I could have spit nails."

I almost laughed. That was a saying of my mother's but it seemed like all of us on the compound had adopted it. But Andrea's voice was serious and she wasn't joking, so I stifled my amusement and listened.

"He was so stubborn!" She turned to give me an exasperated look. "So I said, 'Help me up,' because with my one arm I couldn't get up. When he did, he kept his hands around my waist, and I stared up at him." Her voice got even lower. "You know how beautiful he is...Well;

I stretched myself up and kissed him!"

She darted her eyes at me to see if I was shocked I guess, or if I'd disapprove of her having kissed him. I smiled.

"He didn't stop me," she added, quickly. "Unlike Blake." Her face took on a rosy hue, because we both knew this was precarious ground to be on, discussing her 'indiscretion' with Blake. Anyway, she smiled. "He kissed me right back!"

"Wow, that's great!" I said. "I knew he liked you."

She looked at me sideways. "It about killed my bad arm when he held me but I wouldn't have complained for the world. I actually started crying, it hurt so bad! He thought I was crying about him leaving."

We had a good laugh about that, but then she said, gasping, "But I *was* crying because he was leaving, too!"

"So what else happened?" I asked.

"He said, 'Don't worry, I'll be back.' He said it so nice. And he said, 'If your mom is at your house we'll get her and bring her back too.'"

"Is that all?"

She smiled to herself, remembering. "Well, he asked me why I kissed him."

"And?"

"I said, 'I told you why! I like you, you big goof.'" She wiped her eyes. "And then he said, 'I like you, too. Young lady.' That's a joke between us," she explained. "And then he kissed me again." Fresh tears rolled down her face.

"So why are you crying? I think this is great!"

Andrea pointed out the window. "Because he just went out into that crazy dark world—with Jared, who may be crazy too, I don't know— and I don't know if I'll ever see him again! If Jared comes back without him, I swear, I'll shoot him!"

I don't think Andrea really meant that but I do worry about Roper. And even Jared. We need him to make more of his bombs.

We are left with so many questions! Will they make it back? Will Jared find the supplies he needs? Will Mrs. Patterson—and my horse!— ever be returned to us?

Honestly. I wish I knew.

Now Available!

DEFIANCE: Book Three in **The PULSE EFFEX Series**

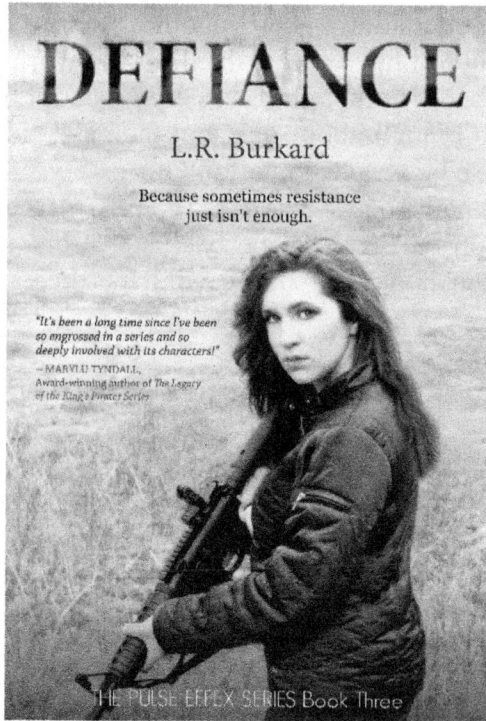

DOWNLOAD FREE CHAPTERS OF
DEFIANCE:

http://www.LinoreBurkard.com/Excerpt_DEFIANCE.pdf

(Enter the address into the browser for best results)

Did you catch the first book in The PULSE EFFEX Series?

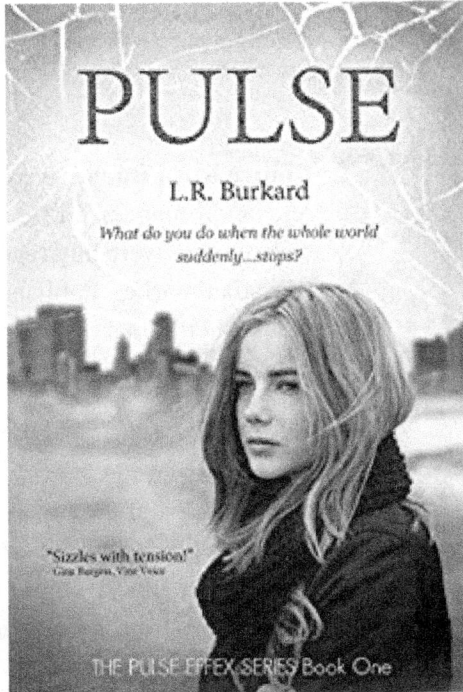

BEFORE YOU GO:

Did you enjoy this book? The best way to thank an author is by sharing your thoughts with other readers.

What did you enjoy about *RESILIENCE?* Please tell others on places such as **Amazon.com** or **Goodreads.com.** *Thank you!*

Linore Rose Burkard wrote a trilogy of regency romances for the Christian market before there were any regencies for the Christian market. Published with Harvest House, her books opened the genre for the CBA. Linore also writes YA/Suspense as L.R. Burkard.

Linore grew up in NYC, graduated *magna cum laude* from City University, and now lives in Ohio with her husband and five children. A long-time homeschooling mom, Linore enjoys teaching workshops for writers and is developing a coaching program for newer writers who are as yet unpublished. She is a co-host of the upcoming podcast "The Thriving Writer," and she writes a monthly e-newsletter for "writers, readers, poets and dreamers." Filled with links, articles and entertainment, get it free by joining her list at http://www.LinoreBurkard.com, or at the Pulse Effex Companion Website: http://www.LRBurkard.com

MORE BY THIS AUTHOR

Read L.R.Burkard's popular Regency romances written as Linore Rose Burkard.

Other Titles

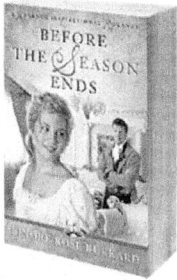

Before the Season Ends – The first installment of the Regency Trilogy sparkles with heartwarming and humorous regency romance in the vein of Georgette Heyer. *Reader favorite!*

The House in Grosvenor Square -- Mystery, perils and adventure—as well as romance—beset Miss Ariana Forsythe, our lovable heroine from *Before the Season Ends,* in this continuing delight of a story.

The Country House Courtship—The third installment of the Regency Trilogy finds Beatrice Forsythe, younger sister of Ariana, ready for her own romance. A country house courtship like no other!

CPSIA information can be obtained
at www.ICGtesting.com
Printed in the USA
LVOW03s2346060318

568947LV00001B/139/P